Broken Bombs

*A Second Amendment victory of the people,
by the people, and for the people*

**By
Ron Lee Jones**

Other books from Ron Lee Jones

Emancipation Expedition

(Already on Amazon)
Where can you hide when the bad guys with guns
are also with the FBI?

Tom Sanders witnesses a murder and is forced to shoot his way to safety. The murderers are corrupt agents of the FBI working in combination with a drug cartel, and Tom and his wife know he will never receive a fair trial—if he even lives that long. They decide their only hope is to escape from the control of the federal government by disappearing into America's heartland. They become separated and their love for each other, their faith in God, and their determination to survive keep them going as they face intense personal hardship in their struggle to remain alive and free and be together again. They must rely on sharp wits, quick tactics, and help from God and others, but will all of that be enough to escape from the power of the federal government and from the ruthless members of the drug cartel who seek revenge?

Still to come:
(Titles to be announced later)

Shattered Schemes (intro chapter at the end of Broken Bombs)
The sequel to Emancipation Expedition
Wolves in Wyoming
Cavemen with modern weapons
Cavemen sequel
Captain Moroni
Defending yourself after a shooting
A disaffected park ranger
Collection of Second Amendment short stories

Front cover by SelfPubBookCovers.com/RLSather

To Ellen
My Big Sister

Forward

Life, Liberty, and the Pursuit of Happiness.

Nobody ever said it better than the founders of our country. However, since Cain killed Abel we have had to deal with bullies who want to take from us our life, our liberty, and our pursuit of happiness, which includes the property that we acquire as we pursue happiness.

Weapons have been used throughout history for people to protect themselves from bullies. Weapons used either individually or on the grand scale are a critical part of our individual and national security. Unfortunately, bullies use weapons too.

I wrote this book to not only provide entertaining stories that appeal to conservatives, both women and men, but also to show the many ways weapons can be carried and used to protect us from bullies. Contrary to the mindset of liberals, leftists, and progressives (you pick the term, but they're all in the same category), carrying weapons is normal, sane, rational, and safe.

A tool is a tool. How you use the tool determines what you will accomplish with the tool. You can pound stakes in your garden with your neighbor's four-foot level and the stakes will go into the soil quite nicely but your neighbor will not be too happy. If you don't handle a razor knife carefully someone will get cut. If you don't handle a nail gun carefully someone will get a nail shot into their hand or their foot. If you carry and handle your gun carefully nobody gets hurt or killed except for the bully who is trying to deprive you of life, liberty, or your pursuit of happiness. If the bully would have left you alone he or she would not have been hurt or killed and you wouldn't even have had to use the tool in the first place, which was your preference.

The founders of our country knew that the Second Amendment was critical for our security against bullies, both for our country and for the individuals in our country. Those situations occur either on a one-by-one, face-to-face basis or on the grand scale when power-hungry leaders turn the government into their own tool that attempts to deprive the people as a whole of Life, Liberty, and the Pursuit of Happiness.

It's critical to be prepared and have the tool ready *where* it's needed and in the split second *when* it's needed. If your weapon is at home locked in your gun safe or still in your car you can't protect yourself from a bully on public transportation, in a restaurant, at the movies, at work, at the ballpark, at the mall, or anywhere else that you are pursuing happiness.

This book was written as my contribution in the critical fight against gun control and in support of Second Amendment rights. If conservatives lose that fight the results will be catastrophic to our society, to our country, and to the whole world.

I hope you enjoy and learn from *Broken Bombs*. I hope to get all the other books that are in my head put into print for you to enjoy and as my part in the fight for Life, Liberty, the Pursuit of Happiness, and the Second Amendment.

Ron Lee Jones, October 2019

SUNDAY

1   Picnic

It looked like a simple picnic on a warm Sunday afternoon but in reality it was the last planning session before a cell of Islamic terrorists would attack Phoenix, Arizona. In the coming week their goal was to spread death and destruction in the sixth-largest city in America, slaughtering thousands of people.

The park on that Sunday afternoon in February was busy because the weather was beautiful. Puffy clouds floated high in the blue sky, some of the trees had no leaves, but others carried bright green foliage through the entire winter. The Bermuda grass was brown due to the cool evenings but where the landscapers had planted ryegrass it was lush and beautifully green. You could lie back in the green grass in your T-shirt and be perfectly comfortable while you enjoyed the sunshine and the pleasant day.

One of the groups of people in the park consisted of ten different families, some related by blood or marriage, and some unrelated. The concept of "friends" didn't necessarily apply here. These weren't friends as much as they were fellow soldiers; warriors with a mission of jihad. They were fulfilling their interpretation of the call to rid the world of infidels whether they were men, women, or children.

Some of the women and older girls, covered in traditional Muslim clothing, were cleaning up after the meal. Since many of the children were anxious to go play, other women and older children were taking them across the grass toward the playground equipment. Most of the women knew what was going on and all the men certainly knew what was going on but the children were innocent of what was happening.

The men pulled off toward the furthest table but were still under the peaked, metal awning. On hot days the awning provided shade. On rainy days it provided shelter from the rain. Today it provided protection from satellite surveillance. The men had worked very hard to make sure they remained undetected and were trying to not even trigger curiosity. Despite the serious nature of their meeting they had discussed the need to occasionally break into laughter in case any other picnicking family took notice. They wanted to appear as close to normal as possible. However, they knew that within days they might kill some of those who were passing by on the street or throwing a Frisbee across the nearby grass.

Their leader was an Iraqi named Mansoor Fatik Al-Musawi. He was well over six feet tall and at 240 pounds he was not huge but he was big, muscular and fit. He had been in the U.S. for four years. He had been trained in Iraq in holy war techniques and strategies, and had come to America as a "refugee," portraying himself as a Kurd. He was focused, ready, and anxious to kill infidels. Others in the group had come as he had. Still others had walked across the porous southern border of Arizona, New Mexico, and Texas.

Al-Musawi thought: *The Americans are so stupid! In their quest for inclusion of all people and all groups they invite us into their country— men and women who want nothing more than to destroy them. It is as if the Americans stand with open arms to welcome in the very people who are out to destroy their way of life.* He smiled and shook his head incredulously as he turned his attention back to the "picnic."

There were other men, many of them, who were a part of Al-Musawi's terrorist cell but who were not at the picnic. These at the picnic were the leaders. The entire terrorist cell was comprised of nearly one-hundred and fifty men. They worked out of a corner of a warehouse in the industrial district of south Phoenix which was well-hidden and very secure. However, it was just as easy to gather for a picnic on a bright, pleasant Sunday as it was in the warehouse. In addition, Al-Musawi was taking great pride in being able to pull off a planning session for a week of jihad right out here in the open. He was proving to himself that he was superior to the U.S. intelligence agencies and he reveled in the thought that he had outsmarted them today and would outsmart them many times in the coming week.

Al-Musawi was so intent on his mission, he had tattooed, in Arabic, words that inspired him in his cause. The tattoos were not on the backs of his hands and knuckles like some people had. Instead, they were tattooed on the inside of his fingers and in his palms so that when he wanted to, he could place his hands palm down or simply close his fists to hide them. But when desired he could show them to himself or to his fellow jihadists. In Arabic, they included words like Jihad, Allahu Akbar, and the flag adopted by ISIS showing black and white letters on a black background. Translated into English the tattoos said messages like Holy War, For Allah, and other words that inspired Al-Musawi in his cause. Some Islamists thought Al-Musawi was overzealous and even crazy but to Al-Musawi, the messages inspired him to be the best jihadist he could be.

Al-Musawi had been looking forward to this day, actually the day after today, for a long time. Today was the final planning session and tomorrow all America would see the superiority of Islamic jihadists. By the end of the week many Americans would be dead and America as a whole would be on its collective knees wondering what happened and how to stop it from happening again. At the end of the week many of Al-Musawi's team would have slipped away back into secret lives of apparent simplicity and mediocrity.

As the men gathered, they quickly reviewed their list of targets for the coming week: the Tempe light rail train, a hotel in downtown Phoenix, an office for the Motor Vehicles Department, an elementary school, a busy shopping mall, and several other sites. All the attacks were designed to cause destruction, fear, and confusion around Arizona and especially death to infidels.

Al-Musawi had worked very hard in the last few months to stay off the radar of local law enforcement. He had connections that helped him know some of the workings of the FBI and he had planned so well that he had been able to stay below their triggers as well. As he met with his men he quickly discussed their assignments and reiterated his prior instructions: No emails, no texts, no cell phone calls, nothing that looked suspicious or could be picked up by the NSA or any other surveillance organization. They only allowed one set of phone calls for the last attack and those would be in code so they would sound plain and ordinary to the American way of life. Al-Musawi did not tell his men the location of the final attack. That was a secret from even these men. They asked, but Al-Musawi dismissed their question abruptly and let them know that it was not to be discussed.

Having reviewed all their gruesome assignments the men filtered back in among the women and children and back to their families. Some had to leave. Others remained. It looked like a completely innocent picnic but as Al-Musawi watched the picnic disband he couldn't help but get excited for what tomorrow would bring. He smiled in anticipation at how completely off-guard U.S. law enforcement would be.

It would be a blood bath—guaranteed to bring terror to the hearts of the Americans and make them question their weak, pathetic dream of freedom.

They will look like fools!

2   Hunch

Alan Clevenger had a hunch that something bad was about to happen. The problem was, he didn't have any evidence; quite the contrary actually because the hunch was caused by the very lack of evidence.

Alan was a Special Agent with the FBI in the Phoenix field office and he supervised the counter-terrorism division. He kept his ear to the ground using information gained from social media, informants, and surveillance that had been authorized by search warrants regarding known terrorists.

Alan didn't know it but there was even some surveillance done by one unit of their office that was slightly beyond the fringe of legality, but those in that department kept that part of their operation as low key as possible, justifying to themselves that they were fighting terrorism. They knew that some people still believed in the Constitution, which they thought was foolish and had old-fashioned ideas.

Alan was of average size and build at five feet eleven and 190 pounds. He had to stay fit as an FBI Special Agent so he worked out regularly and he was strong and muscular. He had dark hair, a very fair complexion, and an almost boyish face. However, he was smart, thoughtful, and intelligent so no one who knew him perceived him as young or inexperienced. He had been with the Bureau for eleven years and had risen quickly in the ranks due to his skill and hard work and the ability to make good decisions.

Alan worked closely with the Department of Homeland Security, with local law enforcement agencies, and even at times with the CIA. Despite statements in the media and from politicians that America's greatest challenge was climate change Alan knew the greatest challenge was security from encroachment by foreign enemies and home-grown domestic enemies.

The permeable southern border of the U.S. was the greatest threat in Arizona and there were frequent crossings from terrorists and members of various drug cartels. However, much of that activity was kept quiet because of the need to track the crimes and launch raids at the right time. Much of it was also kept quiet to advance the political agenda of certain people who were in control. Even when known terrorists came across the border Alan's team did not always tell the media. Sometimes it was because of a direct order from someone higher up. Other times it was politically undesirable for various reasons and still other times it was because they didn't have enough evidence to give a complete story. Also, if they released a statement and then couldn't follow up with some arrests they ended up looking bad even though they were doing all they could do.

Through all the monitoring they did and through all the efforts Alan exerted, he was constantly getting little bits of information here and there. One time it would be a snippet of a text message from surveillance or another time it would be a tip from an informant or a comment on a social media site. It all served to keep a constant trickle of information coming to him. Usually, it was not enough to trigger arrests or a news conference. They kept looking for the right set of circumstances which would allow them to successfully strike and shut down some clandestine operation somewhere, but that took a certain amount of evidence.

Then suddenly in mid-January the trickle of tips and information just stopped. Others didn't notice but Alan did. He worried about it for a few days and then explained it to Victor Pilchick, the Agent in Charge and his supervisor. Alan also talked to some of the other special agents but Victor and the others dismissed it. No evidence or tips about something happening means nothing is happening, right?

He didn't have anything that could persuade them but he was convinced. However, with nothing more to go on than a change in patterns it was still just a hunch and that was all the credit they gave it.

He kept searching for the information that had been there earlier. He reached out to his informants. He either couldn't reach them or they didn't have any comments. He redoubled his efforts to find something on social media but found nothing. He continued to check in with their surveillance personnel. Nothing. *What was going on?!*

Over the past year Alan had picked up a developing body of information that he believed showed that there was a specific cell of Islamic terrorists in the Phoenix area. From his best efforts and analysis he determined that there were around thirty or forty members of the cell and that their leader was an Iraqi named Mansoor Fatik Al-Musawi. Alan had photos of many of them and while the individual make-up of the group changed from time to time Al-Musawi seemed to remain the leader. Alan even had photos of Al-Musawi's tattoos showing various words and symbols on his palms and fingers. He didn't have photos of every tattoo on Al-Musawi but he had enough to know he was an eccentric terrorist, doing things that even other fanatical terrorists didn't do.

Alan had watched their activity and he was gathering evidence and learning behavior patterns. His team had a plan to conduct a raid and make multiple arrests in March. The chatter of information on the activity of the Arizona cell was part of what Alan received and analyzed on a daily basis.

Then in January he was baffled when it just stopped. Even the informants that he could count on for one or two new gems of information each week suddenly seemed to grow deathly quiet. At first he thought the Arizona cell had left the state. Maybe they went to help another cell somewhere or were off gathering resources or training. He couldn't figure it out. Then one day right at the end of January he got one bit of information from the surveillance team that indicated that Al-Musawi was still in the Phoenix area. However, there was nothing else. *How did they go so quiet?*

He was very troubled by the silence.

His wife, Cindy, noticed the change in Alan. One Sunday night she rolled over in bed and put her arm around him and said, "What's wrong Alan? You have become very somber these last few days."

Cindy and Alan had married six years earlier when they were both in their late twenties and Alan had already been with the FBI for a few years. She knew she was marrying a man in law enforcement and it brought a lot of anxiety to her at times but she trusted in God and trusted in her husband . . . and prayed fervently for him.

6

Cindy was five feet four and had naturally blond hair. She was of average size but had to work hard to not gain weight. She was not obsessed with beauty but she did lots of walking around the neighborhood with her friends to stay trim. She had a warm smile and a fun laugh and she made friends easily. It was that smile and laugh that won Alan's heart when they started dating.

Alan and Cindy Clevenger were very devout Christians. They prayed together and they went to church every Sunday together unless Alan was on assignment somewhere, and at those times Cindy went without him. They studied their scriptures together. They also prayed and studied individually. They tried to be good parents to their two little boys, Curtis, age four, and Carlton, who was eighteen months. They prayed as a family and spent Monday night together as a family, making an extra effort to be a faithful Christian family.

On that Sunday night as Cindy lay next to Alan in bed with her arm around him she said, "Alan, I've noticed you spending more time in prayer these last few days. I even noticed that you have been fasting every Sunday for the past few weeks instead of just today on the first Sunday of the month when we normally fast. Something serious?"

He was hesitant to say anything at first and then it all came out, or at least as much as he could say. "Yes. Something serious. I can't talk about it much, as usual, but I get the feeling something bad is about to happen. It's just a hunch based on a change in the patterns of intelligence we usually get. I can't convince anyone else that something's wrong but it just keeps eating at me."

She hugged him tighter and didn't say anything for a long time. She didn't exactly know what to say and she felt like he needed her comfort and support more than he needed instructions.

She quietly asked, "Will people die, Alan?"

"Yes, Cindy. In my industry when bad people do bad things people always die. The question is whether good people die or bad people die . . . and how many of each?"

"Will you be able to stop them before they do the bad things?"

"I hope so."

"What would stop them before anything bad happened?"

"We'd either have to get enough evidence so that we could arrest some of them in advance of an incident or we'd need a tip of some kind; where or when, so we could be there. Another thing would be for the right people to be in the right place at the right time—people with

7

weapons. As Wayne LaPierre from the NRA said, "The only thing that stops a bad guy with a gun is a good guy with a gun." He's right, and it's been that way since the beginning of history . . . well, with weapons at least since guns didn't come along until later.

"Actually, I guess I might correct Mr. LaPierre to say that God can also stop a bad guy with a gun and that has undoubtedly happened at times but I think for the most part God expects us to work out the details of our lives more often than Him having to step in.

"The hard part, Cindy, is that until we know that something is in fact happening and until we know what or where, we are helpless to stop it. And then we only get there after the fact. That's why we are called First Responders. In reality we are *only* responders. We usually aren't participants. We respond after the participants take action. I feel ineffective when all I can do is analyze a situation instead of preventing it.

Cindy shuddered and said, "Meanwhile someone has to clean up the gruesome mess and heartbroken families have to mourn and the news media gets something salacious to talk about."

"Yup."

"Can I change the subject?"

"Please do. Do you want to tell me how proud you are to have a husband who is so smart and handsome?"

She giggled, "Now let's not go overboard, but it is about how much I love you. Next Friday is our anniversary and I thought we could get a babysitter for the weekend. I've always wanted to go to Rustler's Rooste Steakhouse. It's a Phoenix landmark and the legend says the location was an actual hideout for cattle rustlers in the early days of Arizona. We could put on our jeans and boots and have a real western evening. Then we could spend the night at one of the hotels over there near the Restaurant. We could spend Saturday hiking on South mountain and then spend another night and go to church over on that side of town and come home Sunday afternoon. My parents would love to watch the boys for a weekend. What do you think?"

"Sounds wonderful. Maybe I can get off a little early on Friday. Victor is pretty good at supporting family things since we all deal with such long, stressful hours. In fact, if my hunch is wrong as Victor says it is, then it will be another quiet week and he won't have any problem letting me leave early on Friday."

She put both arms around him and kissed him tenderly. Alan held his wife in his strong arms as they fell asleep.

MONDAY

3 Anticipation

Mansoor Fatik Al-Musawi stood on the old Tempe Bridge on a chilly Monday morning in February, acting like a photographer. He had a camera with a telephoto lens slung around his neck and he carried a black camera bag in one hand and a tripod in the other hand. He had been walking slowly along the bridge looking in all directions, stopping occasionally to raise the camera and take pictures from different angles. He shot pictures of the old bridge he was on, he shot pictures of the nearby bridges, he shot pictures of "A Mountain" bearing the symbol of Arizona State University, he shot pictures of the surrounding buildings, he shot pictures of anything that a real photographer might shoot. But he wasn't a real photographer.

Al-Musawi was wearing cargo pants and an ASU sweatshirt. He was trying to blend in and look like an ASU photography student, but in fact he was waiting for the detonation of two bombs on the Tempe Light Rail Train and the slaughter of many people.

This was the first attack that would begin a week of jihad on the people in the Phoenix Metropolitan area. The plan was for his men to board the train with two powerful bombs. Then they would have the engineer drive the train to the middle of the bridge that crosses the Salt River at Tempe Town Lake. Then right at 8:00 a.m. they would detonate the bombs, killing many people, destroying the bridge, and possibly damaging the Southern Pacific Railroad bridge which sat about 20 yards west of the light rail bridge.

By detonating both bombs on the train right at 8:00 they would be in sync with the detonation of a bomb in a hotel in downtown Phoenix and also in sync with an attack on a restaurant on the west side of the Phoenix Metro area. They wanted all three attacks synchronized so that the whole nation would know it was orchestrated by the same group. They also wanted to send the message that they had the sophistication to attack when and where they desired. Their goal was not just violence but to send the message that *they* were in charge.

Al-Musawi had been on the walkway of the old bridge for about 30 minutes, giddy with excitement and anticipation. It was all he could do to maintain his composure and look normal as the light morning traffic continued southbound beside him. The occasional bike rider or jogger would think nothing of his presence on the bridge. Rush-hour traffic was on the newer Tempe bridge to the east of him and on the light rail bridge to the west.

This vantage point would give him the best view as the bombs exploded and parts of the train, people, and bridge fell into the water. He intended to stay and watch the situation unfold the entire day as rescuers, law enforcement, and engineers came to deal with the situation. It would take hours. He would relish every minute of it.

He planned to do what any photographer would do who ended up in the right place at the right time. He would take lots of sensational photos and post them on social media. However, he would do it in a way that could not be traced back to him or any of his group. Part of his goal was not to just wage jihad but to do it in such a way as to rub it in America's collective face that the terrorists had succeeded and America had failed miserably.

Al-Musawi checked his watch. It was time for the Tempe Light Rail train to make its stop at Mill and Third Street just before it crossed Tempe Town Lake. He glanced at the tattoos on his hands and smiled with satisfaction. The tattoos inspired him to be a loyal jihadist in the fight against infidels.

The train approached and Al-Musawi watched as it crossed Mill Avenue. He was about 200 yards north of the train and the bridge angled west as the road crossed Rio Salado Parkway and rose up over the water. Al-Musawi couldn't see anything more than the top of the train as it passed one spot on the track just east of Mill Avenue.

However, Al-Musawi didn't need to see the detail. They had planned this very well and he was intricately familiar with the details of the plan.

The train would stop. Their van would be the first car at the curb waiting for the train at the Mill Avenue stop. His men would get out of the van with their concealed arsenal and board the train. The rest would happen just as they planned.

Al-Musawi smiled to himself.

It was a beautiful day for jihad.

4   Broken Bombs

Jared Anderson was just another passenger on the Metro Light Rail headed to work on a chilly morning. He left his car at the "Park and Ride" in Mesa and boarded the train to head to work in downtown Phoenix. It was the first Monday of February and this train was due to arrive in Phoenix in time for most people to walk from the train and reach their office by 8:00 a.m.

This morning the car was comfortably full but not packed. The light rail usually ran with two cars coupled together, each car consisting of two sections with somewhat of a hinge in the middle to allow for turns in the track. Jared was seated in the front half of the first car on a bench seat facing the aisle. By the time the train had made a few stops there were a few people standing but many passengers on this end of the train would get off at one of the two stops at the Arizona State University campus, freeing up a number of seats.

Jared glanced at the other people on the train from time to time as he read an e-book on his phone. He had a large-screen phone and the big screen made it easy for reading and Jared loved to read. He preferred fiction, either suspense, sci-fi, fantasy, or western. He also liked a good historical or political book now and then. He didn't care for horror or romance.

Jared had ridden this train for a couple of years now and was familiar with some of the other "regulars," although they never talked much. He heard once of some commuters who became such good friends on a bus that they had potlucks and parties to celebrate the different life events of each other. If someone was going to have a baby they had a potluck on the bus and gave gifts. If someone got another job and was going to move they had a farewell party on the bus. That was fine and sounded fun but this train didn't get into that practice. People mainly kept to themselves and it was a quiet ride.

The outside temperature was around forty degrees Fahrenheit, balmy for some parts of the U.S. in February but chilly for the Phoenix metropolitan area. At the two ASU stops many people got off the train, heading for class or work on campus. The train was about half full to make the last stop in Tempe before heading to Phoenix.

Around Jared were other commuters, some with backpacks or professional-looking bags or briefcases. To Jared's immediate right was a mom with two kids, a toddler and a child about four years old. To Jared's left was a man in a business suit who appeared to be of Middle Eastern descent. Across from Jared sat a young man in a black coat with a black bag under his seat and a young couple, obviously in a relationship, but both texting instead of focusing on each other. Jared shook his head slightly, his brow furrowed. *This younger generation!* But who was he to say? His mom probably had the exact same thoughts about things he did when he was young.

The car contained several other people of various ages and walks of life. The second car was filled to about the same capacity and a couple of people were in the bicycle section in the middle of the cars; sitting by their bikes which were hanging by the front wheel on hooks suspended from the ceiling of the car. There was little or no talking, everyone just kept to themselves.

As the train stopped at the Mill Avenue and Third Street Station it sat there for a minute or two while some people got off and a few others got on.

That stop was near to "A" Mountain, which was officially known as Hayden Butte. The butte was named after Charles Hayden who settled on the south bank of the Salt River and started a ferry there at the base of the small mountain in the late 1800s. The settlement of Hayden's Ferry was renamed Tempe in 1879 because it was reminiscent of the Vale of Tempe near Mount Olympus in Greece. Locals pronounced the name Tem-pee with both syllables having the same accent. It would rhyme with the way you would say "ten peas" if you were doing a story problem in math: "If you had ten peas on your plate and you fed six of the peas to your dog when your mother wasn't watching, how many peas would you have left to eat before you could leave the table?"

Tempe, Arizona eventually became the home of Arizona State University and a large "A" was painted on the side of the mountain right by what became the location of the football stadium. Over the years, ASU's rivals had painted the A many different colors as meaningful football contests loomed, but the ASU students always changed it back to either white or the preferred goldenrod, one of ASU's colors. Jared had looked at the A and at A Mountain many times as the light rail train passed by, but on that morning he was more focused on his book.

As Jared was reading, there at Mill and 3rd Street, he suddenly realized the train had stayed motionless for longer than normal and that there was a slight, cool breeze in the car. He looked up to see what was causing the delay. He noticed that the young man who had been across from him was now standing in the doorway of the first door on the north side of the car, his black bag still under his empty seat. The young man was straddling the three-inch gap between the train and the platform with his left foot on the platform and his right foot in the car. He was facing east, looking toward the second car or maybe looking toward something to the side or end of the train.

A female voice, apparently the conductor, came over the intercom, "Please step out of the doorway so the train may proceed." The young man continued to stand there stoically, making no motion either in or out.

After another twenty or thirty seconds and another more firm announcement over the intercom, Jared's curiosity got the best of him and he stepped up to the second door of the car, also on the north-facing side of the train. As he got to the door he didn't want to straddle the doorway and risk being accused of delaying the train so he put his left hand on the inside wall of the train, his phone in his right hand, and he leaned out a bit to see what could be attracting the young man's attention.

As he looked toward the back of the train, he noticed a black minivan sitting on Mill Avenue close to the rear of the train. It was in the street, stopped close to the train tracks. There were some bushes and decorative metalwork as part of the train platform so Jared couldn't see all of what was going on with the minivan but it appeared that there were some people standing about. A second commuter had positioned himself in another door of the train, one foot in the train and one foot on the platform. The young man who was standing in Jared's car yelled something toward the back of the train in a foreign language.

Finally, Jared noticed a man walking very quickly from the area near the minivan toward the front of the train. He wore a bulky black coat and looked like he was huddled against the cold.

Suddenly there was a deafening blast and a ball of fire erupted from the minivan. The concussion tore the minivan apart, sending large chunks of glass, metal, and plastic flying in all directions. Car alarms when off up and down Mill Avenue, set off by the concussion from the explosion. The force of the blast rocked the entire train and blew off the front of the building next to the train stop. At that corner of the seven-story building was The Zany Lady Bar and Grill on the ground floor and the blast completely destroyed more than half of the restaurant and severely damaged the remainder. Anyone inside was likely dead.

The powerful explosion also went upward, consuming the modern building which was made of glass and steel, and ripping off a large portion of it, damaging nearly every floor. Chunks of concrete, glass, rebar, and finished metal hung over the rubble below. Hundreds of pieces of paper of all sizes fluttered in the air and started drifting downward to settle on the street and parked cars. Office equipment hung out of the hole or fell to the sidewalk, which was now covered with debris. People in the building were screaming and one man had fallen partially out of the hole. He was hanging upside down from some of the jagged pieces of the building, his chest and neck covered with blood. He hung motionless.

When the blast occurred it jolted the train, tipping the rear car up and rocking it sideways, causing the front car, Jared's car, to lurch. Jared grabbed the door with his left hand to keep from falling and nearly dropped his phone. He quickly holstered it and stepped slightly out of the car. The back half of the second train car was missing or crushed as if it had been stepped on by a giant. Where the crumpled part of the car met the intact part of the car there was a gaping hole with twisted wreckage emerging, similar to the nearby building. Glass and metal stuck out everywhere and pieces of the train car hung loosely from the electrical wires that ran through the train to make all the parts work. The chunks threatened to fall on whatever was below.

The light rail was powered by overhead electrical wires and sparks started popping and arcing around the back of the train. Jared figured that the blast had damaged the cables that powered the train from above, about eighteen to twenty feet in the air. Perhaps the pole tipped over or maybe a portion of the minivan or other wreckage had been hurled through the wires.

People were screaming and some started to run. Some looked like they were dazed and didn't know where they should go. Others were just so shocked they didn't know what to do. Jared leaned out and did a quick visual inspection of the train and realized that the front car which he was in didn't seem to have suffered any serious damage. However, this train was going nowhere. This run-of-the-mill commute had quickly and unexpectedly turned into what looked like a war zone at the Mill Avenue stop in Tempe.

Jared started to step further out of his door to see what he could do for the injured people in the second car but just at that moment the young man standing in the doorway yelled again. Jared realized that the man in the black coat had been knocked down by the blast from the minivan but he struggled to his feet and ran toward the train. As he got to the door where Jared was standing he shoved Jared back inside and yelled at Jared in English, "Get out of the way, infidel!"

The young man who had been standing in the doorway yelled something to the second man. Both men drew what appeared to be automatic weapons out of their coats and pointed them at the passengers. Some people gasped and others swore as they realized this situation had just gone from bad to worse. One of the two men yelled, "Everybody to sit down!"

As Jared sat down he noticed another man whom he had not noticed earlier standing in the second half of the train car. He had also pulled a weapon out from under his coat and was aiming it at the passengers in that half of the car. He yelled, "No one is try to escape!"

The man who had just gotten on the train reached with his left hand into a pocket on the inside of his long coat and pulled out something that he held in his hand. It had wires that trailed toward his body and in his fist he gripped a cylindrical contraption about the size of a small cell phone. With his thumb, he flipped a black cover to one side and then he pressed down on a red button. He yelled, "I have bomb. If anyone is try to stop me, I let go of red button . . . Boom! All die."

The man nearest to the front of the train stepped up to the conductor's door, pounded on it and yelled, "Open door or I shoot!"

The conductor's door slid open to reveal a woman. Her eyes reflected the terror she obviously felt but she was doing her best to keep the rest of her face neutral and in control. Jared appreciated her efforts. The man pointed his gun at her and yelled, "Close all doors!" The conductor half turned toward the control panel and the doors slid closed.

15

Apparently there was enough power for that. Then the man said to the conductor, "Lock all doors," and the conductor flipped another switch on the control panel.

The man turned back to everyone in the car and yelled, "No one leaves! Everyone turn off cell phone! Anyone who try anything will die," and he held up his snub-nosed gun, perhaps some kind of Uzi. Everyone stared with a shocked expression as if they couldn't believe this was happening. The woman who had been seated next to Jared pulled her frightened children closer to her.

The man looked at everyone near him in the front of the car and said, "All of you go to back of car. Not pass bicycles." He motioned with his gun toward the area just past Jared. Some people started getting up but others just sat there.

"MOVE NOW!" he yelled and slapped one of the women in the face with the back of his left hand.

The people jumped, got up, and started moving. They were joined by the conductor. They all moved to the back half of Jared's car, passing the man with the bomb who was pointing his gun at them and still holding his left thumb on the red button. Some of them were able to sit but some remained standing in the back half of the car. A woman comforted the one who had been struck.

After the few passengers passed him the man with the bomb walked to the front of the train and sat in a seat near the conductor's door. Now there was no one within about fifteen feet of him. There would not be enough time for anyone to rush him and stop him from releasing the red button.

The man with the gun pulled out his cell phone and Jared watched his thumb move as the man pressed three numbers. After waiting for a few moments he said, "Hello. This is Hamza. I am one of the jihadists on Tempe Light Rail. We have a bomb. No one is try to come onto train or everyone dies. Tell police and FBI to stay back. We will not negotiate." Hamza disconnected the call.

Hamza walked over to the black bag under the seat across from Jared and, using the toe of his shoe, he dragged the bag out from under the bench. He reached down with his left hand, picked up the bag, and placed it on the seat. With a few tugs he pulled open a zipper on the bag. He reached in and pulled out a can of spray paint with a gray cap. He shook it as he stepped near the door, the little metallic ball inside making a clacking rattle. He struggled to get the cap off with one hand and

16

finally he looked up at the man with the bomb. Their eyes met and the man with the bomb raised his gun and pointed it toward the passengers. Relieved of that duty, Hamza let go of his machine gun to use both hands on the spray can, leaving the gun hanging from a strap over his shoulder. He tugged at the cap and pushed it to the side, snapping it off the can. Hamza gripped the gun again with his right hand and then, using his left hand, started spraying the nearest window, coating it with gray paint so you could no longer see through the glass.

Hamza turned to the man in the nearest seat, who happened to be the middle-eastern man in the gray suit. Hamza said, "Paint all windows." He reached in the bag and pulled out another can. He handed it to the young woman who had been texting earlier and pointed at the windows. She started shaking the can but had to get help from her boyfriend to get the cap off. She started painting. Hamza let go of his gun again and reached into the bag with both hands, pulling out two cans of paint which he handed to Jared. Hamza pointed to the rear of the train and said, "All windows. Give other can to someone."

Jared walked toward the back of the train, pushing through the people and passing through the bike rack area. The gunmen were watching and as he walked he shook the cans, the metallic and rapid clack, clack, clack of the ball inside each can breaking the stillness as everyone watched. Jared handed a can of paint to the first man he came to in the second car. No one said a word as the two started painting windows.

As paint fumes started filling the enclosed space several people began to cough and groan. One woman passed out in her seat and the man next to her held her so she wouldn't fall to the floor. One man in the back half of the car coughed and coughed until Hamza walked back and yelled, "Stop cough!" The man rasped, "Can't stop. Asthma." Hamza said nothing in reply but raised his gun and shot the man at point-blank range in the chest with a short burst of automatic gunfire. Everyone jumped and some people cried out in surprise. The man crumpled in his seat. The woman next to him let out a loud moan, shut her eyes, and started gasping for breath. Hamza yelled, "All quiet!" The woman whimpered and struggled to breathe but she managed to control the noise for the most part, although she kept her eyes closed and her entire body was shaking. Blood started dripping from the seat below the man onto the floor, leaving glistening spatters of red on the light-colored surface. There were still a few coughs from various passengers and Jared saw many of them lift their shirts to filter the polluted air through the fabric. The woman with the children was holding them close to her and fanning the air in front of them with what looked like a clean diaper.

Stunned by the sudden and brutal violence, everyone had become still. Hamza snapped, "Keep paint!" Those with cans raised them to the windows again. As Hamza walked back to the front of the car a man quietly traded places with the crying woman so she wouldn't have to continue sitting by the dead man. The terrorist didn't seem to mind.

As Jared painted he started planning. He carried a concealed weapon. He had started carrying a few years ago after he heard several distressing reports on the news: a disgruntled employee walked into a business and started shooting, an angry man walked through a mall killing people, a vicious dog tore up a child while helpless neighbors looked on. Jared had read many news articles about people who saved lives because they carried a concealed weapon and were able to stop an attacker before more people were killed. It was very sad that the mainstream news media chose to report on the tragedies from weapons instead of the people whose lives were saved because a law-abiding citizen had a gun.

Jared had watched the video on You-Tube of a young woman who was in a Luby's restaurant in Texas years ago during a mass shooting. The video showed her testifying later to Congress about how she likely could have saved many lives, including those of her elderly parents, if she had been carrying her concealed weapon in her purse. However, she had taken it out of her purse a few days earlier because carrying it in that manner was against the law at that time. She spoke of her regret for taking it out of her purse because as the situation unfolded she likely could have shot the gunman and saved many people. Jared had thought about her story often and was determined to never be a helpless victim. He carried a concealed weapon and hoped he never had to use it but he had decided that he would be prepared to do so if needed. He realized it could mean sacrificing his own life to try to save the lives of other innocent people but he knew he could make that sacrifice if needed.

He had suggested a few times to his wife, Vicky, that she get a concealed weapon but she had not been very interested and Jared didn't feel that he should pressure her.

Jared carried a Ruger LCP 380, a small semi-automatic pistol intended to fit in a pocket. The weapon was designed with a long trigger pull, which made it very safe to carry with a live round in the chamber. Jared heard on the news once of a young child who reached into his mother's purse and unknowingly pulled the trigger on a pistol there, causing the gun to fire. That was next to impossible for a gun such as the Ruger LCP because it required an adult amount of strength to pull the trigger far enough for the gun to fire. The firing pin was not close to the chambered round and therefore no safety was required. The gun was not "cocked." That also meant that dropping the pistol would not cause it to misfire, which could sometimes happen with other handguns.

The LCP model Jared bought included a laser sight for greater shooting accuracy. Jared had practiced many times in the desert and at local shooting ranges and was proficient with the weapon, although he wouldn't call himself a master.

Jared normally loaded his Ruger with hollow point bullets which were designed to be more effective at stopping an assailant and less dangerous to innocent bystanders. If a solid point slug were to strike someone in the leg or even in the torso, it could and often would, go out the back of the body part relatively intact and still traveling at a high rate of speed. An innocent person behind an assailant could be struck and even killed by the slug after it passed through the first person. Hollow point bullets were designed to come apart more quickly on impact and spread out in the assailant's body rather than pass through it, thereby minimizing the chance of striking someone else. Granted, it did more damage to the assailant but the whole purpose of shooting an attacker was to stop the threat of a dangerous situation and if the dangerous person is the one who is killed then innocent people are saved. Jared was in full support of that concept.

Jared always carried his weapon. Well, almost always. He didn't have it with him in bed or in the shower, but due to its small size it fit in the front pocket of his business slacks or his jeans so he had it every time he went out. He even carried it around his house and to church, although that felt kind of funny to him at first. After a shooting in a church, which ended up all over the news, he changed his mind. He didn't need a fanny pack or a vest or jacket to hide the Ruger LCP, as was often needed for larger concealed weapons.

The .380 caliber, while not as big and powerful as some pistols, could still pack a punch. A .380 slug would come out of the muzzle at about 900 feet per second, or about 600 miles per hour.

As Jared started painting windows he was trying to figure out what he might be able to do to stop the terrorists, but since there were three of them and one had a bomb that would detonate if the man let go of the button, Jared knew he needed help. He had thought about shooting the terrorist as he first pulled the detonator out of his coat pocket but it happened so fast that he didn't have time to even try to draw the Ruger. Besides, with the other guy standing there with an Uzi, if that's what it was, Jared probably wouldn't have accomplished anything. Doing the wrong thing in haste could be worse than doing the right thing later after some careful planning.

As Jared moved from window to window with his spray can he started glancing at the passengers. Near the very back of the train he noticed a young man, probably in his thirties, with a little bit of a beard. He was wearing jeans and work boots and also a camouflage jacket and a hat with the Browning logo, the stylish profile of a mule deer buck.

Jared looked to see where the terrorist was in this end of the train and saw that he was about mid-car. "Mr. Browning" was further back. Jared arranged his painting efforts to draw near to the man and when he got close enough he leaned slightly down and quietly whispered "CCW."

CCW stands for "Carry Concealed Weapon" and was the early acronym for the concealed weapons permit law when it was first passed in Arizona. That law officially recognized the right of Arizonans to carry a concealed weapon. It was not the perfect acronym—CWP for Concealed Weapons Permit would make more sense—but many people who carried a concealed weapon still used the original term, CCW.

The man sat calmly, but as Jared got to the other side of the car and started painting another window Jared turned and made eye contact. Jared had his back to the terrorist and, facing the Browning hat guy, Jared made a gun shape with his left hand in front of his stomach, even as he continued painting. Then Jared pointed to himself. The man with the Browning hat nodded and very subtly pointed to himself too.

Jared noticed that a woman one seat behind "Mr. Browning" mouthed the words, "Thank you" and she held her hands together as if in the manner of prayer. He understood that her silent prayers were with him and she appeared to be grateful that he was armed.

Jared was reminded of an instance at work where one of their female staff had been threatened by her violent ex-boyfriend over the phone. They had called the police, but when Jared quietly told the young woman that he had a gun and he would arrange to stay close by throughout the day she was very relieved and expressed her gratitude to him. Despite some people being anti-gun, when their lives were at stake they realized the comfort that came from knowing a law-abiding friend was armed and prepared to defend them.

The man and woman in the front car finished painting the windows just before Jared and the other man finished the second car. All windows, including the conductor's, were covered with gray paint. In places the painters had sprayed too much and the paint dripped down leaving wobbly gray streaks on the glass or below the windows. With painted windows the cars took on a subdued look although there was still enough light to see.

Outside they could hear people yelling and screaming and sirens coming from a distance, apparently to help the victims of the bomb blast. However, they could only see what was going on inside their own car.

*   *   *

Hamza walked up to the man with the bomb and they talked quietly for a few moments as they looked at their watches, always with one or both guns aimed at the passengers. Hamza's cell phone rang and he carried on a brief conversation in a foreign language. Then he turned back to the other man and they talked some more, frequently checking the time.

Jared guessed they were waiting for some designated moment to do something. With no way to effectively attack them now he sat and thought and waited to see if anything would change. He thought of that part in the movie *National Treasure* where one character talked about the status quo. Jared understood. Right now, the three terrorists, one with a bomb ready to explode, had complete control. Two hostages with pistols would be ineffective at stopping that bomb. They had to wait for some change in the status quo, if it came.

As they all sat, and as Jared tried to come up with some strategy to stop the terrorists, he started thinking of his family. When your life is on the line you think of those you love. *What would become of my family if I died today?*

Jared Anderson had grown up in Tempe in the 1950s. His dad worked for the public schools and his mom was a stay-at-home housewife. Jared had an older sister named Patty and a younger brother named Mahonri Moriancumer, which was a whole other story. Jared's brother chose to go by the nickname MM.

After high school Jared volunteered as a missionary for his church and was assigned to Colombia, South America. He learned Spanish and saw what life was like outside the U.S. It made him grateful for the wonderful blessing of being raised in the comfortable lifestyle of the United States but he also gained a great love for the Colombian people.

During college, he met his wife, Vicky. She had also volunteered as a missionary before they met; she had been assigned to England. After they married they worked their way together through Jared's undergraduate degree in chemical engineering from ASU and had two children. The oldest was a son named Michael and the youngest was a daughter named Kristi.

Right out of college Jared got a job with a company called *Trippple P Labs*, serving the petroleum, plastic, and propane industries. The employer Jared started with became his career employer and now Jared was one year away from retirement. Even though he had only worked for Trippple P it wasn't a boring career in any sense of the word. Jared and his family lived in Texas for twelve years, then Louisiana for five years, then Wyoming for seventeen years and several other states as well.

Jared had been moved back to Arizona by Trippple P just a year earlier and he was just about ready to retire. Michael was an attorney in Texas and he and his wife, Jean, had four children. Kristi and her husband, Wade, lived in New Jersey where he worked in the financial district in New York. They had two children.

Jared was six foot one and slightly overweight at 230 pounds. At age sixty-three that was somewhat expected but he knew he should do better at watching what he ate and spending more time exercising. He still had most of his hair although he had lost some at the temples. His hair was light-brown mixed with about half gray. He had plenty of wrinkles, though not too many, and years of joy and laughter caused his wrinkles to show that he loved life and he had a pleasant demeanor. Even if you didn't know him you would deduce from his face and his smile that he was a nice guy.

Life was pleasant, semi-relaxed, and after a long career Jared was content to be a husband, a grandpa, and a senior member in his company without too much stress or authority. He had pulled his load well and had done much for his company and he was at that point in his career where he didn't have to struggle with management challenges each day as some of his co-workers had to do and as he had done in the past. He tried to be a good employee so as not to increase their burden. He was the choir director in his church and that was both fulfilling and relaxing all at the same time. Life was good and fairly routine and he was happy with that. However, today on this train life had become very non-routine.

Jared thought of Vicky. *Would he see his Vicky again? Would he get out of this situation alive?* They had had many good years together and he loved her with all his heart. They had gone through some tough times too and had stayed together, which deepened their love and commitment. Jared realized that if he didn't get out of this alive she would be well-off financially. Jared had a good 401(k) and substantial life insurance. Those things did matter to a husband who realized his wife might suddenly be alone. She had two sisters who lived in the Phoenix area and a brother down in Tucson. She had lots of support from extended family and from others at church.

Still, it worried him that she would end up alone earlier than she should. If they were in their late seventies or early eighties it might be different. Jared had decided years before that if something happened to him and she remarried, that was OK. He didn't want her to be alone.

That thought brought him to a passage of scripture. In a battle in 74 BC one general inspired his warriors with a reminder that they were fighting for their wives and their children and their freedom and religion. Jared would fight for his wife and for their freedom and that was indeed inspiring to him. It was ironic to Jared that Hamza and the other terrorist were also fighting for their religion and were no doubt inspired by that as well.

Jared knew that many times in history people stood for or fought for a cause that they believed was just and in harmony with God's will and yet it was not. It was possible to have false beliefs. That thought always made Jared question and re-confirm his own beliefs. Jared believed God's cause was not that of the radical Islamists but instead was the cause of freedom and of innocent, law-abiding people being allowed to live their lives and to believe what they wanted to believe. Jared was inspired by thoughts not only of his own wife, Vicky, and their children and grandchildren but also by the thoughts of the other people on the train and their loved ones—the couple across from him, the young mother with her two children, the man at his left. He suddenly felt a protective urge in his heart and mind that motivated him to want to do something to keep these people, and himself, safe.

Jared suddenly remembered Vicky's prayer that morning. Each morning he knelt by his bed and prayed silently to God. Then before he left the house he and Vicky prayed together. They also both prayed individually and together at the end of each day. This morning as they prayed together it was her turn. As she said the usual, "And please keep us safe from evil and harm today," she also added, "and help us to know what to do in the events that this day brings and then help us to do it well." Thinking about it now, Jared was impressed by Vicky's prayer. Was she inspired to say that? He decided she probably was because he did need to know what to do in this situation and he surely needed to do it well.

He loved her with all his heart and he realized he may never see her again. At the same time he had an overwhelming feeling of gratitude to her for the power of her prayer. He prayed in his heart now that her prayer would be answered and he would know what to do and then do it well.

Jared was determined to do his best. He had been praying silently since the ordeal began and his prayers continued, asking God for guidance and for wisdom and strength.

He also asked God for help. If he had to use his gun he asked God to help him shoot fast and straight.

5   Broken Silence

As Alan Clevenger was driving to work just after 7:00 a.m. on Monday morning the aggravating silence in his department's intelligence and surveillance was suddenly broken—shattered in fact. He was on the I-10 freeway at a point where Tempe borders Phoenix and as he was crawling along in the bumper to bumper traffic listening to the radio he heard a muffled boom. He heard the boom even through his rolled-up windows and with talk radio going.

Alan quickly started looking around in all directions, searching for some sign of an explosion. He almost hit the car ahead of him but avoided a collision by jamming on his brakes at the last second. He kept looking and then saw a mushroom of smoke floating into the air to his right, somewhere in the vicinity of downtown Tempe.

24

He was law enforcement but he had no official right to ignore traffic laws in his private vehicle. He had just passed the Broadway Road exit but that was where he needed to get off. He squeezed his car through the traffic and then started backing down the right-hand shoulder of the freeway. If he met a highway patrol officer he had his FBI badge and he hoped that would talk a pretty big talk.

He got a text from a dispatcher in the Phoenix office: "Huge explosion on Tempe light rail. Downtown Tempe."

He stopped his car only long enough to thumb in a reply: "Near Tempe. On my way there."

Alan finally got far enough back down the freeway that he could turn through the edge of the off-ramp and the dirt at the shoulder of the freeway and start up the Broadway exit. Traffic was stopped and he had to roll with two wheels out at the edge of the pavement. He ignored the shouts and finger signals from several cars as he went past.

He got to the end of the off-ramp and worked his way through Tempe, watching the smoke as he drove. There wasn't a lot of smoke but he didn't really know what that meant. He kept listening to the radio but all they said was that there was an explosion. There hadn't been time yet to figure anything out. He got as close to the light rail as he could and found a place to park. He ran toward the tracks and came out west of where the smoke was originating.

His phone rang and Victor Pilchick's voice said, "I guess you were right, Alan. The police scanners are indicating an explosion that took out part of the light rail train in downtown Tempe, and there's a hostage situation in another part of the train. How soon can you be there?"

"I'm actually here now but I just got here. I'll find out where a command center is and see what I can do."

He talked to several police officers, and with the help of his FBI badge he always got at least some information. By radio they found out that a command center had been set up north of the tracks. He worked his way far around the west end of the train and headed toward that area.

As Alan walked he thought about the police officers he had just talked to and the others he was passing who were securing the area around the train. He also thought of the firefighters whom he had seen waiting by their trucks, anticipating the possible need for their services in addition to the police.

Alan wasn't really a first responder. They were. He had great admiration and respect for them. Most of the time he sat behind a desk.

On the contrary, the men and women in a police uniform put on a badge each morning or night and went out into the city, prepared for anything to come their way. They were called on to deal with crime, domestic violence, simple arguments, reports that had been called in about some kind of issue, and countless other situations. They risked death and personal trauma every day in an effort to help keep the peace and enforce the law. They were underpaid and had great demands placed on them and their families. Alan was one of their greatest fans.

Yes, there were some who crossed the line or didn't do what they had been trained to do. They were human just like anyone and susceptible of making mistakes and succumbing to the lure of too much power. That was not an excuse; it was just the reality of the situation. However, Alan had found that the vast majority were very good, decent people who wanted to do their best, wanted to go home safely at the end of their shift, and wanted to maintain order and the well-being of the citizens they served. Sometimes their demeanor could appear over-controlling and less than friendly, but Alan knew that many times that was what it took to maintain an attitude of being in command. That "take charge" approach helped them maintain control of a situation and helped others see them as being the authority figure they needed to be in order for them to keep the peace and stay alive.

Alan's thoughts continued as he thought about the current situation. When an incident was occurring, the police had to think quickly and make split-second decisions that were very difficult to make. They trained and trained and then trained some more, trying to make as many appropriate reactions as they could, often enough so that the appropriate reactions would become automatic. There were often times when they went into situations that were very dangerous, not because they really wanted to but because that's what society asked of them. He also knew that many of them did enjoy the rush of adrenalin which helped them deal with difficult situations. It was similar to the way athletes enjoy the rush of adrenalin in an athletic competition, but in the case of the police, the "game" was often deadly and they were trying to keep people alive, especially those who were willing to follow the law.

Alan also thought of the families of the first responders. They had to accept the fact that their loved one risked his or her life each day, and the families had their own stress to deal with because of that. Spouses and children and the parents and siblings of police officers prayed for their family member constantly, hoping they would be safe and do what is right. They also lived with the reality that at any moment they could get that phone call that they hoped would never come, informing them that their loved one was injured or killed in the line of duty. Alan realized their families were also heroes, and it made him think of Cindy. He couldn't call her right then but he wanted to. He wondered how often police officers and firefighters wanted to stop and call their loved ones at times, just to remind them how much they loved them and to thank them for their quiet sacrifice as the first responder put themselves in harm's way on a daily basis.

When Alan arrived at the command center north of the train he found some of the senior law enforcement personnel whom he had worked with before and considered friends. As he walked up to Graham Fenton, the Tempe Chief of Police, Alan said, "Hi, Graham. What do we know so far?"

"Hi, Alan. Looks like a bomb went off in a van on Mill. Any terrorists at the site were obliterated. The bomb damaged the train as you can see and we just got a call from a guy calling himself Hamza. He says they have another bomb in the undamaged cars and if we try to do anything they will set it off. They already spray painted the windows so we can't see in. It's a waiting game right now. We have the power turned off to the train so the electrical risk is minimized but there's still a bomb on that train."

Alan wished he had his file on the Arizona terrorist cell so he could see if he could find someone named Hamza. He thought he recognized the name but he wasn't sure. He called into his office to have them send someone down with his Arizona Cell file as soon as possible. He and that file would be very close companions all day today, he was sure.

This was his chance to find out more about his hunch and the dead silence in their intelligence. Perhaps if he could identify the terrorists involved he could start figuring out if it was Al-Musawi. That is, if the terrorists got out of this with body parts big enough to identify. Alan hated the way bombs destroyed much-needed evidence.

As it turned out, there wasn't much that law enforcement could do regarding the terrorists and hostages on the train. The terrorists weren't willing to negotiate so the police, FBI, and the Department of Homeland Security personnel just sat there waiting for something to change. Emergency personnel were working on rescue and recovery in the back half of the train, knowing they were taking a risk in case the second bomb was detonated.

At one point the first responders heard a short burst of what sounded like machine-gun fire from inside the train but nothing else happened. They continued to wait as the long minutes ticked by. These were the times Alan felt the most helpless. They were fighting to save lives and all they could do was sit and wait.

*   *   *

The phone rang and Vicky Anderson paused in her reading. The house was quiet and she stared at her book without focus, saving her place but not reading the words, waiting for the caller ID to identify who was calling. The mechanical voice said, "Call from Kristi Jorgenson" pronouncing Kristi Jorgensen in a funny way, as it always did. Vicky leaned over and picked up the phone, "Hi Kristi. How are you today?"

"Mom!" Kristi yelled with a shaky voice. "Turn on the TV. The light rail in Tempe was bombed. Is that the train Dad rides to work?"

Vicky jumped up in a panic, dropping the phone and sending both the phone and the TV remote clattering across the floor. With quivering hands she picked up the remote and turned on the news. The pictures were taken from Mill Avenue showing the back end of the light rail train torn and shattered and tilted as the young female reporter explained what they knew so far. In the background were flashing lights from emergency vehicles but it was clear that no one was getting near to the train except right at the back end. Vicky looked at the clock. That was probably Jared's train. She stared at the TV for some time trying to absorb what was happening.

Vicky suddenly remembered that Kristi was on the phone. She grabbed the phone off the floor. "Kristi! Are you still there?"

Kristi's voice was calm and forgiving but it had an edge of fear. "Yes. I figured you were glued to the TV and I knew you'd finally remember we were talking. Do you think that's Dad's train?"

Vicky quietly said, "Probably."

Vicky leaned over and picked up her cell phone. She pressed the spot on her home screen that said, "Jared Cell." It went straight to voice mail. Jared's phone was off.

"Dad's phone is off," Vicky said.

Kristi replied, "I know, I already tried it."

She heard Kristi start crying. That made Vicky start to cry.

With a quivering voice Vicky asked, "Have you called Michael?"

28

"Not yet," Kristi said.

Vicky made a quick decision. "I'm going to Tempe. Call Michael. I'll be on my cell phone."

Vicky had exercised that morning but had not yet showered. Her morning routine of exercise followed by some quiet reading while she cooled down had now been disrupted. She wanted to shower but didn't want to waste the time it would take. Finally she decided that if she ended up on the news she didn't want to look gross. She quickly jumped in the shower. Half-way through her shower, perhaps caused by the hot water, the initial shock finally wore off. She slumped to the bottom of the shower and sobbed and prayed. She knew that was an odd time and place to pray but she was suddenly overcome with grief and fear. She knelt there in a ball on the floor of the shower for a few minutes, the hot water spraying on her back. She finally forced herself to get up.

She finished and dressed and quickly threw on some makeup. One advantage of being older and having some curl to your hair was that if you kept it short it would look OK when it dried. At least now that she had showered she didn't feel and look gross.

She got into her car and drove as quickly as she could to Tempe. It normally took about forty minutes but she made it in thirty. She hoped she wouldn't get pulled over but planned to explain that her husband was on the bombed train and maybe that would help her avoid a ticket. She hoped the red eyes from crying for the last forty-five minutes would also help.

When she reached Tempe she found a place to park and walked quickly toward the train stop. Of course there were crowds and police tape and news vehicles with their booms high in the air. She walked up to the police tape and got the attention of an officer that was standing about ten feet away. Vicky called above all the noise, "My husband is on that train. Or was." The realization hit her and she started crying again.

The officer stepped over and lifted the police tape. He pointed to an area over by a building a safe distance away from the train but still near enough to be involved. She walked over and saw that there were some other people milling around, and a man and a woman with badges. There were also some people with jackets on that looked like they were from the American Red Cross. She walked over and as she approached, a woman said, "Do you have a close friend or relative on the train?"

Vicky said, "My husb. . . ." and the sobbing started again. The woman reached out to her and held Vicky in her arms while she cried.

6 Hostages

The people on the train talked quietly among themselves as they sat waiting. The terrorists continued to check their watches but did little else. Apparently they didn't mind the talking because they didn't tell anyone to stop.

The Middle-Eastern man sitting next to Jared leaned over and quietly said to him, "These are not my people."

Jared was surprised by the comment. He said, also quietly, "What did you say?"

"These aren't my people," was the reply. "My name is Yawar. I'm from Yemen. I came to America nine years ago with my wife and children. I'm Muslim but these guys are not. They would say they are, and that they are fighting a holy war in the name of Allah but Allah does not condone this behavior."

Jared noted that Yawar was very eloquent and spoke fluent English. Jared prepared to ask a question, and he believed he knew the answer Yawar would give but he wanted to hear the reply anyway. He said, "These guys are Muslim or Islamist so why are they not representative of all Muslims or Islamists?"

Yawar's method of answering the question surprised Jared. Yawar said, "You're Mormon, aren't you?"

Jared was caught off guard. "Yes," he said.

Yawar smiled. "I saw the CTR ring on your finger."

CTR stood for *Choose the Right* which was a common slogan of members of the Church of Jesus Christ of Latter-Day Saints, commonly called Mormons. Some members of the church wore such a ring to remind them to choose the right and to be faithful throughout the day.

Yawar continued. "I have worked with Mormons for eight years. We have had many discussions about Islam and Christianity. I know that Mormons are Christians. Our faiths actually have much in common."

Yawar then asked, "The people in Colorado City are Mormons so why are they not representative of all Mormons?"

"Actually," Jared said, "the people in Colorado City are members of the Fundamentalist Church of Jesus Christ of Latter-Day Saints. Their doctrine and practices are an off-shoot of the original Church of Jesus Christ of Latter-Day Saints. To faithful members of the Church of Jesus Christ of Latter-Day Saints, the polygamists in Colorado City are so far removed from our practices and doctrine that they should not be connected with our faith in any way. They are something else but they are definitely not Mormons!" Jared's emphasis caused him to speak a little too loudly and he shrank down a bit and got a hushed look on his face. A few others looked at him.

Yawar said, "*You* know they are not Mormons and *I* know they are not Mormons but many people in the U.S. don't know that when they listen to the news. They think the Colorado City Mormons are part of the other Mormons, just like the average American thinks that these three jihadists are part of the other Muslims. I disagree with them just as much as you disagree with the people in Colorado City for their doctrine and practices. I believe the concept of jihad is an internal, personal struggle to follow the principles of Islam but it does not mean to kill innocent non-Muslims."

Jared grew quiet. He had had discussions similar to this before but had never had someone use a parallel that hit him so close to home. It was a powerful reminder that stereotypes among religious groups could be very wrong. Jared was also encouraged by this opportunity to meet a Muslim who passionately disagreed with the Islamist extremists.

Jared said, "It seems that part of the war against Muslim extremists should be to make sure that terrorists don't get rewarded for doing things like this. I've heard that some terrorists in Syrian prisons are paid a salary while in prison because they succeeded in killing people and that the U.S. government payments to Syria help fund those salaries. I also heard on the news that terrorists are promised 72 virgins in the afterlife as their reward."

Yawar said, "I have also heard about the salaries for terrorists in prison, and sadly, I believe it is true. And, yes, they are promised 72 virgins. However, as I said earlier about these men distorting our beliefs, I don't agree that Allah or the Prophet Mohammed taught or condone that. It is another of their distortions to support their extremist ideology."

Jared said, "I heard somewhere about a strategy used with terrorists who were stopped while committing an act of terror and were killed, or maybe later executed. The idea was to bury their remains with pigs so the

31

pig carcasses would defile the remains of the terrorists and they wouldn't receive the reward of 72 virgins. Is that true?"

Yawar got a pained look on his face and he said, "Yes, that is true. It would be very offensive to the terrorists and it would be somewhat of a deterrent to those who are weak and unsure of their cause. It is offensive to all Muslims but those of us who disagree with the Jihadists would probably understand. It is said that Israel already does that, and that angers many Muslims who already hate Israel. I personally don't like it but I would understand if the U.S. decided to do that."

"So how can we stop these guys? Can you speak to them and reason with them?

Yawar just shook his head and said, "I'm afraid their thinking and logic are beyond the point of being able to see any reason but their own."

Jared felt like Yawar was sincere and Jared quietly said, "I have a gun and I'm going to try to stop them but I don't know what I'm going to do yet."

After a silent and thoughtful pause, Yawar said, "Allah be with you."

Jared said, "Thank you."

A phone rang in the other car. Everyone looked at the terrorist in that car, and then realized it was not his phone. All eyes in the train focused on a young woman whose cell phone was lying on her skirt in her lap, continuing to ring loudly. She had obviously not turned it off when the order to do so came. She had a look of horror on her face. The terrorist stepped over to her and started yelling at her in his foreign language. The phone kept ringing. The young woman didn't understand what he was saying but his yelling was very loud. She was too scared to touch her phone. The terrorist pointed his machine gun at her face just inches away from her nose and yelled at her again. The phone rang one last time and was silent.

Of course the young woman didn't know what the terrorist had said. She just sat there staring wild-eyed at him. She started whimpering and crying. The terrorist shifted his machine gun to his left hand and with his right hand he struck the young woman on the side of the face with his open palm. The blow was powerful enough to knock her sideways and she cried out and fell partially out of her chair and onto the lap of the woman next to her. The young woman's long, blonde hair was tousled and hanging sideways over her head.

The terrorist started laughing at her and turned away. Suddenly, he stopped and wheeled back toward the young woman, who was still frightened in the lap of the other woman. He glared at the woman and then looked around at all the passengers and yelled, "Next time anyone cell phone ring I will not so nice. If any phone ring, you die!"

The cars grew quiet and subdued again and many people pulled out their cell phones to make sure they were off. This time all talking stopped.

Hamza and the terrorist with the bomb checked their watches again and then talked briefly. Then Hamza looked at all the passengers in the front half of the car and spoke. "All of you go to back of car. Move now!" He said the last statement without added volume but with much emphasis and this time everyone quickly got out of their seats and moved to the back of the car, passing the bike racks as they did so.

As they moved Jared looked at the man next to him and Jared gently touched his own wrist. The man turned his arm so Jared could glance at his watch and he saw that it was 7:50 a.m.

Jared was still looking and hoping and praying for something that would change the status quo in the situation to give him or the guy in the Browning hat an opportunity to start shooting.

As Jared got into the other car he looked at the Browning hat guy. Their eyes met and Jared shrugged slightly. He hoped Mr. Browning would figure that meant Jared didn't have a plan yet. Mr. Browning nodded slightly.

Jared tried to arrange it so that he would end up standing near the front of the passengers. As they got to the other half of the car the terrorists made some other people get up and move back. They ended up with all the passengers crowded together about a third of the way back from the mid-section of the car a few feet past the bicycle area. It appeared to Jared that they were leaving a space for the terrorist with the bomb to still be a few steps away from the passengers.

Hamza was standing a few feet from the place where the crowd of passengers began. The third terrorist was at the back of the car near one of the doors, close to Mr. Browning. The terrorist told the people near him, "Stay back. Too close to me and I shoot." As the people made as much room around the man as the crowded car would allow, Mr. Browning strategically shifted to where he could have an open shot. Mr. Browning looked up and caught Jared's eye. Jared nodded.

Jared tried to position himself so that he could be partially behind another passenger but still have a clear shot. He hoped to draw his gun while he was partially hidden and then step to where he had a full field of fire ahead of him. He didn't dare try to sneak the Ruger out of his pocket earlier for fear Hamza would see the movement. He also worried about someone seeing his gun and either trying to stop him out of fear or saying or doing something that would draw attention and cause Hamza to also see his gun.

With the people pushed away from the front of the car the terrorist with the bomb came from the other car and through the bicycle area and stepped into the open space at the front of the car. With everyone this close the bomb would surely kill them all. Jared still couldn't figure out how to get to the terrorist with the bomb so Jared could keep the red button pushed down.

By now they had been on the train for a long time. People were stressed. Some were silent but had tears streaming down their faces. Some had their eyes closed and their lips were moving, apparently in the act of prayer. They were terrified. The young mother was doing all she could do to keep her two children quiet and content. On occasion the baby had cried and Hamza or the other terrorist had glared at her.

What was only a few minutes seemed to take hours.

Suddenly a chime sounded as a cell phone booted up. The woman with the two children was standing across from Jared and the little boy had evidently found his mom's phone in the diaper bag and had somehow turned it on. The terrorist with the bomb was intent on staying at the front of the car and was carefully watching the time. He merely glanced up but Hamza yelled in rage and quickly turned toward the little boy, raising his machine gun and roaring, "You die!"

The mother's voice cut in with great firmness, "Over my dead body!"

Hamza was completely caught off guard as the young mother started firing at him with a semi-automatic pistol. She was only a few feet away and Hamza was so focused on the little boy that she caught him completely by surprise.

She was shooting a Glock 28, which was a small gun but still slightly larger than Jared's Ruger. The Glock 28, also a .380 caliber, was easily carried as a concealed weapon. The Glock 28 was supposed to be strictly for law enforcement and military but apparently this young woman had connections to that market or maybe she had bought it when the government released used weapons for sale to the general public.

The young mother fired three times and Hamza didn't even get off one shot. He was turned toward the woman and her son and every one of her shots hit him in the middle of the chest. The woman was obviously well-practiced because she was skilled enough to correct her aim after the recoil of each shot. She put each succeeding shot right next to the previous one. The whole thing took little more than one second. *Man, that woman could shoot!*

A law-abiding woman with a gun just changed the status quo.

Within an instant there were shots and commotion at two other places in the cramped train car at the same time.

Jared turned to look at the terrorist with the bomb while he was drawing his Ruger. He had hoped to grab the detonator to keep the red button from being released and at the same time shoot the terrorist. It was a risky scenario with a low probability of success at best but he quickly realized he would be way too late. As he lunged toward the terrorist he saw the man lift his thumb off the red button. The man yelled loudly, "Allahu Akbar!"

But nothing happened. The bomb didn't explode! The terrorist was completely confused.

By then Jared had reached the man and was trying to get his hand over the detonator. The terrorist swung his arm to the side to avoid Jared's reach and flipped the black lever back and forth with his thumb and then jammed the red button and released it again and again. Still nothing. The detonator must have been damaged when the man fell to the ground from the first bomb blast. The terrorists' second bomb was also broken.

Jared shoved the terrorist into the wall of the train with his body and with his left hand kept trying to reach the detonator to gain control of it. At the same time he brought the Ruger up to a shooting position and placed it against the terrorist's throat, pointing slightly upward. Jared was face to face with the terrorist—just inches away. Jared's eyes were intent and focused but the terrorist's eyes grew wide with fear. Jared fired one shot and the man went limp and slid down the wall.

While all of that was happening Jared heard several shots at the other end of the car—semi-automatic shots. Apparently, Mr. Browning was also engaging the third terrorist.

The sound from Jared's shot and the shots from the Browning hat guy died out about the same time and Jared suddenly heard the sound of children crying. He had been so focused on his task that he hadn't realized that the woman's kids had been frightened by the noise and were wailing loudly. Everyone else was holding their breath, waiting to see if it would get worse or if it was over.

The passengers realized that all three terrorists were down and the bomb had failed to go off. They burst into applause and cheers and called out praises to God, some crossing themselves and looking heavenward. People started grabbing and kicking at the windows and doors trying to activate the emergency exit mechanisms. The doors and windows were forced open and people began climbing out and running from the train car in all directions. Many of the passengers stepped over the terrorists as they began rushing from the train.

Jared looked to where the young mother was. She still had her gun in her right hand, aimed at the ceiling, and with her left hand she had pulled her children back away from the door to let the passengers out. The children continued to cry but the mom was focused on making sure the threat was completely gone before she reholstered her weapon.

As the passengers got outside they saw that there was no one near the train. Many armed law enforcement officers were standing in defensive positions at a distance on both the north and south sides of the tracks.

A distant blast, possibly from another bomb, sounded from somewhere across the city. Jared wondered whose lives were shattered and broken in that event.

As it became clear that the threat was over and with the passengers pouring from the train, the law enforcement personnel started running toward them. The first responders began motioning and pointing with their arms and hands to guide the running people into one area so the people could be checked and secured.

The train was now mostly empty and Jared turned to the young woman who had shot Hamza. With a huge grin he said to her, "Nice shootin'!" She smiled up at him from her crouched position as she soothed her scared children, her Glock 28 already nowhere to be seen. Yes, she carried *concealed*!

Jared looked up and Mr. Browning had just arrived from the other end of the car. He was just getting ready to holster his handgun, a Browning of course. Jared finally pocketed his Ruger and reached out to shake the hand of his battle buddy. Then he picked up the older child while the mother picked up the younger one and Mr. Browning reached out to pull them all into a group hug, the two little children happily and gently squished in the middle.

Jared said, "Well done, you two" and they returned the compliment. Jared and Vicky's prayers had been answered.

7   Arizona Hospitality

At 3:00 a.m. on a chilly Monday in February, Lance Parmentier was ready to go hunting. He had the day off and he was excited to go with his buddy, Marcus Bautista, out in the desert near Four Peaks. They were taking their AR-15s out to do some varmint calling or maybe just go shooting. They had been planning this trip for weeks. They'd love to get a coyote or two, or even better, a bobcat. A mountain lion would be a dream but that was a long shot. In spite of the odds one of them always bought a mountain lion tag each year, just in case. If their varmint calling wasn't successful they'd just do some shooting—ARs were a lot of fun.

Lance had gotten up very early to get everything packed—jerky, granola bars, Gatorade, some of those little donuts with the chocolate coating that is waxy and smooth when they are about room temperature, some cans of fruit cocktail and peaches, bottled water.

Lance was supposed to meet Marcus at 4:00, but at 3:30 Lance's wife, Misty, got a call telling her she had to go to work even though she was supposed to be off that day. The other supervisor had come down with the flu. Misty reminded Lance that their little Mazda had died and he would have to take her to work. Lance was going to take the Mazda to a mechanic on Tuesday when Marcus had to work but that left Misty without a car. Lance had no other choice than to take Misty to work. She promised she could get someone to give her a ride home or she could call her mom, but getting her to downtown Phoenix before 8:00 a.m. was too much to ask someone else when Lance was able to do it.

Lance texted Marcus and told him he couldn't leave until after 8:00. They decided that would still be OK and Lance went back to bed for an hour, although he didn't sleep well because he was so excited to get out in the desert with his AR-15. Lance had grown up in the Phoenix area and he hated the desert in the summer. It was too blasted hot to enjoy it! However, in the winter it was gorgeous. The days were warm and the mornings were crisp and very cool. Winters in Phoenix kept Lance from leaving Arizona when the heat was so miserable in the summer.

At 6:00 they were up again and Misty got ready for work. She was one of the supervisors of the cleaning crew at the Grand Legacy Hotel near downtown Phoenix. She had been employed there since she was in high school and had worked her way up to her present position.

Lance was still basically ready so they were out the door at 7:10. Lance drove a Ford F150 with the extended cab and four full doors. He loved his truck. The back seat was roomy and both parts of the bench seat flipped up so he could put a lot of stuff in there on the flat floor. His AR and all his shooting gear were right behind him.

The Parmentiers lived in Chandler, so downtown Phoenix was about twenty-five miles to the northwest. With two of them in the truck they qualified as a High Occupancy Vehicle and could take the HOV lane. As they drove they listened to some music on a CD and talked. At one point they heard a loud boom, like a big explosion, but couldn't see anything unusual. Despite the heavy Monday morning traffic, they arrived at the Grand Legacy at about 7:40. That put them there early enough to talk a little before Misty needed to be inside.

The back of the hotel was an L shape with the service and employee entrance tucked into the inside corner of the L. A sidewalk ran the whole length of the L so that a service vehicle could approach from either side and easily roll a hand truck to the back door. A parking lot surrounded the whole area.

Rather than drive into the parking lot at the back of the hotel Lance stayed on the street and pulled up to the north curb but far enough back that the hotel itself blocked their view of the back door. This meant that he and Misty could spend a few more minutes together without a co-worker seeing them. As they talked he pulled out his two ten-round magazines and started feeding .223 shells into them. He also had a couple of thirty-round mags but he preferred to hunt with the tens. The larger clips got in the way while hunting, but when just shooting at targets the banana clips were more fun. He didn't mind calling them "clips" instead of "magazines" but he knew some people hated that term. The big clips were expensive though; burning through thirty rounds in fifteen seconds cost about $25. At $100 a minute he couldn't stomach too much of that.

With Misty helping him Lance soon had all four magazines loaded; eighty rounds ready to go, even though he wouldn't need them for a couple of hours. *Some guys got very excited about hunting!*

Finally Misty needed to go in. She promised she'd get a safe ride home and would text him the details. She thanked him for postponing his outing for her and gave Lance a lingering kiss before jumping out of the truck. Lance inwardly smiled as he put the magazines back behind the seat; Misty's kiss was well worth the few hours he'd lost with Marcus. He repositioned his water bottle so it wouldn't tip over, and grabbed a granola bar. He opened it with his teeth as he started the truck.

As he slowly rolled forward he cleared the corner of the building and looked over to see if Misty had already gone in. He almost choked on a mouthful of granola bar as he jammed on the brakes. A whole group of people were by the back door underneath the overhang that protected that area from rain and sun. Some were standing and some were sitting and a couple of them had what looked like AK-47s. The funky barrel that seemed like it was bent and the curved banana magazine were tell-tale signs.

These guys looked like they were from the Middle East and, judging by the guns, Lance would say that they were terrorists. It was kind of funny, and almost pathetic really, that so many in his government and in the main-stream news media could rarely bring themselves to call terrorists "terrorists."

The two guys with AKs were standing by the cleaning crew, one against the wall and the other one facing Misty. Lance's heart skipped a beat when he saw her defiant expression. Leave it to his Misty to be sassy in the face of an obvious threat. Lance was one part proud and three parts terrified. Her co-workers, some of whom Lance knew, were almost all Hispanic, a reminder of the flood of immigrants crossing into Arizona from Mexico daily. They spoke mostly Spanish, which Misty had learned from her years of working with them.

There was a black minivan parked by the east curb out of sight from where Lance had first stopped. There was a terrorist in the driver's seat and another one standing by the opened side door. There was one more guy kneeling inside fiddling with something on the floor. Lance had a fleeting thought that the van could get a ticket by being parked facing the wrong direction.

The guy in front of Misty seemed to be saying something to her and she was answering back. As they spoke she reached for her purse which dangled from a narrow strap at about her upper thigh. Lance knew what she was doing. Misty carried a concealed weapon. They had done their research and found a design that allowed her to put her hand into her purse and either draw the weapon out of it or shoot right through the side of it. She had practiced and knew how to use it effectively. Lance was grateful that the terrorist didn't seem to realize what Misty was doing.

Lance and Misty had been married for four years and he had learned that she could have a fiery temper. She was very protective of her nieces and nephews and although they didn't have any kids of their own yet, Lance knew she would be even more defensive of their children when that time came. Lance was not the least bit surprised that Misty was protective of her co-workers, all of whom she cared about.

When they had gone to buy Misty a gun she had chosen a Taurus Judge revolver. It was kind of big for a concealed weapon but it fit into her purse just fine and she liked the feeling of power that the big pistol gave her. They had looked at various models and decided on the double action which had a short stubby hammer—and was an ideal option for keeping in a purse. It could be drawn from the purse without the hammer getting caught on anything. And without the moving slide of a semi-automatic pistol the revolving cylinder could turn inside a purse when fired, without encountering interference or needing a second hand to cock it.

The Judge shot 410 shotgun shells or .45 caliber bullets depending on how you had it loaded. The 410 shells could be loaded with slugs, buckshot, or even disks. The disks sat in a stack inside the shell, like a roll of pennies, only smaller. They didn't always fly straight but at close range that didn't matter; they were heavy enough to do quite a bit of damage. They had the effect of a shotgun but with the weight and penetration of slugs. Misty liked the disks.

In the few seconds it took for Lance to take in the situation he had reached back and grabbed his Bushmaster .223 AR-15 and the two thirty-round magazines. He wasn't going to let Misty face a gang of terrorists all on her own. The thought of her facing terrorists at all had his anger flaring dangerously high.

Without taking his eyes off his wife Lance inserted a magazine in the bottom of the AR and pounded it in with the palm and heel of his hand. He stuck the other magazine into the back of his belt. He noticed that Misty had finally got her hand inside her purse. Lance pulled the slide back on the rifle and released it to lever in a round. He thumbed the safety to "Fire."

As Misty stood there defiantly in front of the terrorist the man finally got angry. He had been holding his rifle across his chest with the stock down by his right hip and the barrel pointing upward near his left shoulder. He yelled at Misty and started swinging the gun around to point the muzzle at her. Before he could bring it to bear she lifted her purse about waist high and Lance heard two shots. The ladies behind Misty screamed and the terrorist fell back, dropping his gun. Lance knew the multiple disks from two feet away through the side of a purse had done their job.

Misty quickly turned to shoot at the terrorist who was standing by the wall fifteen feet from her. If she was shooting slugs she may have missed, but with the disks her aim didn't have to be perfect. She fired two shots and that man screamed in pain, dropped his AK, and grabbed his face with both hands.

By that time the terrorist standing by the open door of the van was swinging his gun toward Misty. Lance had jumped out of his truck, leaving the door open, and stepped in front of it enough for a clear shot. The commotion at the back door of the hotel had masked Lance's movement; as yet no one had realized he was even there. Lance started firing the AR-15 as fast as he could pull the trigger, firing as many shots as he could. So much for all the people who say an average citizen doesn't need a thirty-round magazine.

With his first shots he took out the guy standing by the van. That man crumpled against the back panel of the van and slid to the ground. Three terrorists were down.

A man in the passenger side of the van sat in the open window, hanging out so he could shoot at Lance. Lance heard a couple of shots smack into his truck but he didn't have time to worry about that. Lance fired back but because of the angle of where the man was sitting in respect to the windshield Lance's shots weren't effective. However, the terrorist did retreat back inside the van.

Lance's first magazine was empty and he used the small reprieve to reload. He quickly dropped out the first magazine and jammed in a second mag and levered in a round. He hoped that the terrorist wouldn't turn his fire on Misty and the others. He knew he needed to keep the pressure on.

When he looked up he saw that the van had started up and had begun to accelerate forward, the sliding door remaining open. The terrorist riding shotgun came out the window again and resumed firing his AK at Lance. The movement of the van probably saved Lance's life as the terrorist couldn't hold his weapon steady. Lance kept shooting as the van approached the corner. After it rounded that corner it was going to be coming right at him.

Suddenly there was a massive explosion and the van blew apart in a ball of orange flame. Apparently, there was a bomb inside the van and either one of Lance's shots hit something or another one of the terrorists detonated it. Again the hotel workers screamed in terror as they held their ears and cowered away from the blast. Lance vaguely saw Misty crouch and turn away. He felt the heat from the flame, felt his ears respond to the pressure, and saw pieces of the van go flying. They landed all around the parking lot. One piece about the size of a garbage can lid landed on the hood of his pickup and then crashed into the windshield, shattering it. A tire had been blown away from the van and it rolled through the empty parking lot and continued past his truck before it toppled over. Shrapnel from the destroyed vehicle, including the whole engine, hit the other cars in the parking lot denting hoods and breaking windows. The concussion set off car alarms in the cars around the parking lot and nearby.

A few cries from the back door of the hotel told Lance that the debris had blown into that area as well. One piece of something hit high on the wall of the hotel and fell onto the workers, hitting a woman in the shoulder and knocking her to the ground. He hoped no one was seriously injured.

The terrorist near the wall, who Misty had shot before, was now on his knees and had taken up his AK. He was trying to point it toward Misty but it looked like he couldn't see well, either from injury to his eyes or blood in them. He was moving sluggishly; it was obvious he was badly hurt. He was still armed and therefore was a threat. His efforts reminded Misty of his presence and Lance knew she had one shot left. She quickly rose and pulled the Judge from her tattered purse. She purposefully squeezed off the last shot at the terrorist. This time she was able to aim and her shot caught the man with full force. He fell back and didn't move again. Lance wondered if the terrorist would get any punishment in the afterlife if he was killed by a woman infidel.

It was over that fast. Misty turned to her crew, most of them in tears, and said something in Spanish. They all nodded and hugged each other, grateful to be alive and relieved that the terror was over.

Misty moved toward Lance as he walked toward the group, his AR in his right hand pointed up to the sky. She came to him and threw her arms around his neck and said into his ear, "I hoped you hadn't left yet. Thanks for being my protector!"

Lance held her close with his left arm, not sure who was trembling more, him or her. He tried to hold his voice steady as he said, "It didn't look like you needed a protector. You done good girl!" Then with her still in the crook of his arm he turned his head to face the women of the cleaning crew and said so they all could hear, "Misty es muy brava! (Misty is very fierce!)" They all burst into laughter amid their tears.

By then the commotion had triggered lots of excitement and they heard sirens. The back door of the hotel burst open and several employees came running out. In a few moments police cars and SWAT vehicles came screaming into the parking lot. Lance still had the AR in his hand, now with the safety on and pointed skyward, and Misty still held the Judge. The police jumped out, aimed their guns at Lance and Misty, and yelled at them to get down.

Lance and Misty had talked about this often. After a shooting, the police had to make sure no one could still be a threat so it was expected that the good guys (or gals) would be treated like suspects at first. Lance and Misty slowly laid their guns on the ground and lowered themselves to the sidewalk, spread eagle, faces toward each other while the police handcuffed them and secured their weapons. They were completely cooperative.

At the same time Lance noticed when the adrenaline rush suddenly left his wife. She looked tired and scared. It didn't take long for the police to get the facts and Lance and Misty were soon uncuffed and back on their feet. Lance kept his arm protectively around her as Misty deliberately avoided looking at any of the bodies or wreckage that littered the area. As bravely as she had acted, Lance knew that this incident would deeply affect her. He silently vowed to be very understanding and supportive of his amazing wife.

Lance asked permission to put his AR in its case in the truck while the police did their investigation but was told that their weapons were now part of the evidence of a crime scene and they probably wouldn't get them back for a while. Lance looked at Misty and then said to the nearest police officer, "Then can I at least call my buddy and tell him I have already done my varmint hunting today and I won't be meeting him to go to Four Peaks? Besides, my truck is trashed."

Everyone laughed at that, including Misty, and Lance turned to the hotel personnel. He spoke in English, knowing some of them wouldn't understand but others would, "I'm sorry that my wife didn't demonstrate very good Arizona hospitality. Do you think she can still keep her job at the hotel?"

8   Pair of Colts

As the waitress handed him his receipt she said what she was trained to say and what she had probably said hundreds of times: "Thanks for visiting Baigs & Beggs this morning; we hope you'll come back soon." However, while her mouth was saying one thing her eyes were saying, "I'm really looking forward to seeing you again."

As the customer looked at the receipt, sure enough there at the bottom he saw she had written her phone number. From the conversation he had just had with the waitress as he ate he already knew they would spend more time in the coming days getting to know each other. Today she was just going through the formalities.

He told her he would come back tomorrow and he meant it, but just then gunfire outside the restaurant interrupted their conversation.

The customer and the waitress both jumped at the sound. They stepped toward the window, but not too close, and looked out. Standing on the front sidewalk they saw four gunmen with AK-47s, dressed in black, looking like stereotypical radical Islamists. Lying before them, obviously shot to death, was an older couple who had just left the restaurant. Next to the woman was a to-go box that had contained the portion of her meal that she couldn't finish. The lid was open, the box was upside down, and the contents were scattered across the sidewalk. What would have been a meal later in the day was now evidence at a crime scene.

Inside the restaurant the customer reached toward the back of his waistband under his sports jacket and the waitress simultaneously reached into a pocket deep in the black waiter's apron she wore. Both drew out their own weapon and started walking quickly toward the front door.

Outside the restaurant the terrorists turned and walked toward the front entrance then stopped and talked as if coordinating their tactics.

That moment had come that almost all good people who carry a concealed weapon hope will never come. They carry a lethal weapon hoping to never need to use it but also hoping in the back of their mind that if that time ever does come, they will have the courage and the cool head to use their weapon safely and wisely to successfully defend innocent lives. They especially hope, in that suddenly critical moment, that they will shoot quick and straight and true.

The customer was Colt Terry. His great grandfather, Armond Terry, was a cowboy back in the late 1800s and early 1900s. He owned a matching pair of Colt .45 revolvers which he had won in a poker game from a spoiled, rich young man in Abilene, Texas. After the poker game Armond quickly left town, worrying that the rich kid's arrogant father would come looking for him. Armond Terry had used his pair of Colts in the early 1900s as he settled a ranch in northwestern Colorado near the tiny town of Meeker. He named it the Bar 90 Ranch, which stood for two times 45—a pair of Colts.

The Colt .45 revolver was affectionately dubbed "The gun that won the West." Whatever impact Armond's Colts had on the West, he for sure knew that they had won his heart. They never left his sight even when he went to church. When he met his wife and they married she won his heart only slightly more than his guns. He wore them during the wedding ceremony, one on each hip, as always. His friends even jovially wondered if he wore them on his wedding night.

Armond's son, Elijah Terry, inherited the Colts and the Bar 90 Ranch when Armond passed away. Elijah, in turn, gave the .45s and the ranch to his son, Walter Terry.

Walter loved the guns so much that he named his oldest son Colt and Walter had told Colt many times that the guns were to be his when he died.

Colt loved ranching but he thought he wanted more out of life and had headed off to college right after high school, taking the pair of Colts with him.

Walter's second son, Colt's brother Remington, ended up being the rancher and remained on the Bar 90 after Walter died. Colt loved the ranch; he visited it every chance he could get, enjoying the close relationship he had with his brother. He took his Colts with him every time he visited the Bar 90 that their father had given to Remington. His mother, who lived in a small house on the property, smiled when she saw them; knowing the family history of the guns and knowing that no matter how old men got, boys would be boys.

Colt did well in college and got a job in the Phoenix area as a stockbroker. He still enjoyed guns and he carried a concealed weapon—a Colt of course. It was still a .45 caliber, but it was a modern semi-automatic instead of an antique revolver. On this early Monday morning in February Colt knew that the time had finally come to use it.

Colt had come to the Baigs & Beggs restaurant for breakfast to meet with potential clients, Charles and Margaret Bramley. He had never been to this restaurant before but it was recommended by the Bramleys. The front of the menu explained that the name Baigs referred to the bagels they served and the name Beggs referred to the exclusive egg dish they served on a bagel, in several flavor varieties. Charles especially recommended the Salsa Verde Beggs combo plate, complete with chorizo.

The restaurant was in Peoria, a suburb in the northwest part of the Phoenix metropolitan area. Colt had met Charles and Margaret on a cruise to Mexico—one of those quick four-day jaunts out of southern California down to northern Mexico and back. The Bramleys were very good people and had significant assets and investments but had never really connected well with their current broker. Colt was more than happy to meet them for breakfast at Baigs & Beggs.

After Colt had waited for a few minutes Charles had texted him to say that he wasn't feeling well and they would have to reschedule. Colt was already at the restaurant so he decided to just stay for breakfast. He had his heart set on the Salsa Verde Beggs.

Truth be told, Colt had gone on the Mexican cruise with a few friends, hoping to build a closer relationship with Roxanne Beecher, someone he had met a few years earlier at a social event. Colt, at just over six feet tall, had dark wavy hair, broad shoulders and a narrow waist. He would be the ideal hero for a Louis L'Amour western novel. He had dated a number of women but had never formed a lasting relationship. He didn't really know why at first. He had finally concluded that he just hadn't met anyone who had deep enough roots. That sounded odd to him but the more he thought about it the more he realized it was true. He felt deep down that if he made it big as a stockbroker he wanted to retire early and move back to Colorado to run his own ranch. He had not yet met a woman whom he felt would be comfortable on a ranch or have the old-fashioned, rugged-life-style roots that he was looking for. On the other hand he sometimes wondered if he was just being too picky about women.

On the Mexican cruise Roxanne turned out to be more interested in one of the other guys in the group so Colt had reluctantly backed off and let them be together, which actually turned out to be OK. That had given him the opportunity to strike up an acquaintance with other guests on the cruise which was how he met Charles and Margaret Bramley. He expected them to be excellent clients.

Since Charles and Margaret weren't joining Colt at the restaurant that morning he could concentrate on making friends with the waitress who was assigned to his table. She was very attractive and her name tag identified her as Terrie. Telling her that he had been stood up for breakfast made her more solicitous to him.

When she first introduced herself and took his order he noticed the southern accent. It fit her. She was an average size brunette with a beautiful face, nice curvy figure, and a captivating smile. He could just imagine her in a pair of boots, jeans, a checkered shirt, and a cowboy hat. The combination of the accent and the good looks made Colt wonder why she wasn't wearing a wedding ring, or whether she was currently dating someone.

When he had seen her badge, showing the name Terrie, he had chuckled and told her, "Interesting. That's my last name."

She replied, "Terrie?"

Colt said, "Well, actually its spelled T-E-R-R-Y, but it's pronounced the same. My first name is Colt."

She laughed, a delightful sound, and said, "No way! Colt is my last name!"

"Really?" he said in unbelief. What are the chances of that?

She explained, "Yes. Actually, I'm a direct descendant of Samuel Colt, the inventor of the Colt .45."

"I'm not a descendant but my father loved a pair of Colt .45s so much that he named me after the gun that won the west." Colt continued, "Well, Terrie Colt. I am Colt Terry and I'm pleased to meet you."

Between trips back and forth with his food, and with Terrie's need to serve other customers, they continued their conversation in bits and pieces. It turned out that Terrie had grown up in Texas—thus the accent—and was the daughter of a wealthy rancher. She had graduated with a bachelor's degree in veterinary science but didn't have excellent grades and had not been accepted to the graduate school she wanted. Her dad assured her he had the funds to get her into another school but she had had her heart so set on the one school that she hadn't even considered others. She and her dad had been discussing it over the past few days. Changes in life had brought her to the Phoenix area some time back and she was trying to decide what to do next.

Colt worried that she was spending too much time at his table to be pleasing to her employer, especially since the restaurant was very busy that morning. He also noticed that Terrie and two other waitresses kept laughing and joking with each other by the door to the kitchen and had glanced at him during their conversations. He couldn't hear what they were saying but at one point one of the waitresses turned Terrie toward Colt's side of the room and gave her a gentle push as if she were encouraging her to do something that might make her nervous.

When Terrie came to his table she actually sat in the seat across from him and said hesitantly, "I have a ten-minute break . . . and this is silly I know, but I'm doing it on a dare from a co-worker . . . . So . . . I don't see a ring on your finger. Are you currently dating anyone?"

Colt smiled a big smile on the outside and a huge smile on the inside and turned to wave at Terrie's co-workers who were watching from the kitchen doorway. They burst into laughter. Then Colt said to Terrie, "As a matter of fact, I was wondering that same thing about you. I'm not currently dating anyone. Are you?"

"Not right now," and Terrie paused, as if in thought, and looked down at the table. "To be honest with you I have dated different guys but not enough to make my mom and dad happy. I just can't find someone with . . . this sounds crazy . . . and I'm talking to someone I just met . . . I just can't seem to find someone with deep enough roots."

Colt was totally surprised as she said it. He replied, "You know, I have had *exactly* the same thoughts. I've dated many . . . uh . . . I've dated a few women but never felt like they had deep enough roots. That's the exact same word I thought of. I didn't say this yet, but when you mentioned your dad's ranch in Texas . . . well . . . I was also raised on a ranch—in Colorado." He added, "Since you grew up on a ranch I suppose you're not afraid of guns."

"Are you kidding? I've shot all kinds of guns." Then Terrie leaned a little closer and said softly, "I carry concealed here at work. I'm always concerned that some customer could get irate and go ballistic."

"I carry, too. And of course, since my name is Colt, I have to carry a Colt."

"Me too!"

"I have a Colt Defender with me wherever I go."

"A Defender?! That's what I carry in my waitress apron. I like the 9 millimeter."

"I've shot the 9 but I carry the .45. It's not exactly the same round as the gun that won the west but the caliber is the same."

They heard a distant boom—sort of a rumble, but not loud, as if some big explosion had just happened across town. They looked at each other and Colt said, "There was another boom like that about an hour ago."

Colt looked at his watch and realized it was approaching 8:00. He said he needed to get going, but he knew he would come back. He even asked, "Are you working tomorrow? I do eat breakfast every day and there's no reason I can't eat it here."

She smiled that captivating smile and said, "My break's over and I'd better go get your check . . . and yes, I'm working tomorrow."

She started to leave the table but he quickly reached out and caught her hand. "Wait, I'll give you my credit card right now," he said and he noticed that she didn't pull her hand away as he fished with his other hand for his wallet. He didn't mind one bit.

Colt stood when Terrie returned and handed him his credit card and the receipt with her phone number. Gunfire outside interrupted them and they both looked out the window and then at each other as they drew their Defenders. They quickly started toward the door as if following the instructions of a drill sergeant. Since they weren't ready to shoot, their index fingers were laid alongside the gun and not inside the trigger guard.

As Colt and Terrie walked quickly through the restaurant with their guns drawn some people gasped. Others started to pray out loud or with their hands clasped and heads down. Two men stood up from a table, an older man and a younger man. They also drew concealed weapons and pointed them in the air. They waited as Colt and Terrie passed. The older man was holding a 1911, the style of semi-automatic pistol used by the military for many years and now manufactured by many gun makers in more modern versions. The younger man had a semi-automatic pistol similar to many on the market. The two men stepped in behind Colt and Terrie and the older man said, "We're with you."

Colt half turned to the two men as he brushed past and said, "Welcome gentlemen. We appreciate your backup. From the looks of what I've seen out the window there are four gunmen. I hope there's not another wave after the first four. I'm going to give them all I've got." He glanced at Terrie and she looked scared but resolute.

The older man seemed calm, "It's no different than what I saw in Vietnam. Easier actually because we won't be dodging Napalm." He turned to the younger man, "You ready, son?"

The younger man replied, "Yeah, Dad."

The older man said to the other three, "Just stay calm and don't get excited. Shoot quickly, but carefully, as if you were at the range or out in the desert shooting at a target."

Colt and Terrie each took a position on the right side of the entryway, about ten feet back from the door. Colt had motioned for Terrie to stand by the wall and he was next to her, choosing to be more exposed. The older man stood next to Colt and positioned the younger man against the far-left wall. The four were shoulder to shoulder.

The other employees and customers had noticed what was going on and were scrambling to get clear of the line of fire behind the entryway. Some were already dialing 911 and talking to operators. Others had gotten to a safe location and were taking video with their smartphones.

The double doors swung outward as the first two terrorists pulled them open and began to enter. The four inside were ready. The change from the morning light to the interior light of the restaurant temporarily blinded the terrorists and Colt and the others didn't give them any chance to make the adjustment.

Colt fired as fast as he could aim and pull the trigger. He fired all eight shots that his Colt .45 holds—one in the chamber and seven in the magazine. He put four shots into the first terrorist and when that man went down the man behind him was an open target. Colt put four shots into the second man as well.

Terrie also fired all of her eight shots in the exact same manner that Colt did, four into the first man and four into the second.

The two men next to them did the same to the two terrorists on the left. There was a barrage of rapid gunfire from the four people inside the entryway and it was all over. Even though they hadn't had time to coordinate their movements it was a perfectly executed and efficient defense.

The terrorists were caught completely by surprise and didn't fire a single shot inside the restaurant. The first two through the door both fell at the same time, one toppling to the side and hitting the wall and the other dropping into the middle of the entryway. The second two dropped in the doorway, effectively blocking the doors open with their inert bodies.

Colt and Terrie pointed their guns up but maintained their shooter stance. There was silence for a moment.

The older man said, "I'm empty and I don't have a spare magazine. But if more terrorists come, I'm going to be ready." He holstered his gun, stepped forward, and picked up one of the AK-47s that had been carried by one of the terrorists. His son did the same. "We'll cover the door until the police arrive."

When the customers realized the threat was over they started clapping and there were calls of, "Way to go!" and "Glory!" and "Praise God!" from across the room. Those who shot video were already working their phones to send the videos out on social media. The relief on every face was clear and sincere. They heard police sirens in the distance.

Colt turned to look at Terrie. She was gorgeous, standing there with a pistol in her hand. A small smile broke across his face. It was a beautiful sight, accompanied by one of his favorite smells—gunpowder smoke in the air. He holstered his gun in the back of his waistband and turned to her. She slid her Defender back into her waitress apron.

He took her by the shoulders and stepped around her; turning her so that her back was to the bodies. He then slid his arms around her shoulders, partly out of relief that the shooting was over and partly out of admiration for this woman that he had just met and who had shot bravely alongside him. She was a woman he could spend his life with. He could hardly wait to get to know her better. "You okay?" he asked.

She nodded as she put her arms around his waist and leaned in to hug him close. She was shaking from adrenaline and from fear and relief at the same time. She fought back tears because she knew if she started crying she'd fall apart completely. Her thoughts were also racing in anticipation of getting to know her newfound hero, and the thought of being called Terrie Terry crossed her mind. As she hugged Colt she said to him, "I'd really like to get to know you better, Mr. Roots, but do we have to wait until tomorrow? This restaurant will be closed today and I'll have the day off."

9   Celebration and Investigation

A team of law enforcement personnel came through the north-side doors of the Tempe Light Rail train and quickly surveyed the situation. There were three adults and two small children standing there in a group hug, smiling. The first responders said, "We've got to get you away from this bomb." That brought the group back to reality and they quickly got off the train and started walking north, away from the train. The law enforcement personnel walked beside them and pointed out the command center that they could see had been set up some distance away between some buildings.

They saw a mob of news media ahead of them, waiting with cameras and microphones behind the police tape. No doubt video was rolling. The Browning hat guy held up his hands high above his head, holding his right hand with two fingers up in what looked like a peace sign. At the same time, with his left hand he made a fist with his thumb placed upward alongside his fist, instead of the thumb curled along the front of his knuckles. He held his hands high for perhaps ten or fifteen seconds in that pose as he walked and then dropped his hands back to his side.

Jared noticed the gesture and just as they reached the first reporters Jared said to Mr. Browning, "What was that?"

Mr. Browning replied, "My wife is a professional sign language interpreter and also a gun owner like me. I imagine she's watching now or will at least see photos or video from this event later. She and I have used that gesture with each other many times. It's mostly between us, although some others may realize what it says. The peace sign is a 2 and the left-hand fist with the thumb alongside is the American Sign Language symbol for the letter A. I held up a 2 and an A. I'm reminding her of the Second Amendment. That saved us today, you know."

A reporter from Fox 10 News in Phoenix had caught the explanation on a microphone while the cameraman got it all on video. Other reporters were nearby with cameras and mics and also heard the explanation. The crowd where the reporters were standing also included many people who were taking photos and video with their smartphones. Within minutes that two-handed symbol of the Second Amendment would go viral on news feeds and through social media. A hero who had just survived a brush with death and saved many lives with his concealed weapon raised his two hands in the air to signify the Second Amendment. The image spread rapidly along with the story of how that man helped another man and a woman stop a cell of terrorists with guns and bombs. By the end of the day the image and its meaning had reached all over the globe.

*   *   *

Alan Clevenger saw the police escorting two men and a woman toward the command center and was told that they thought those three were the ones who shot the terrorists. Alan said that he needed to interview them but he also asked one of the officers how soon he could see the terrorists who were dead on the train. He needed to try to identify them if he could. The officer said they didn't know yet but would let him know as soon as the bomb squad said it would be safe.

Alan's phone rang; it was Victor Pilchick. "Alan, there was another bomb blast behind a hotel in downtown Phoenix. Apparently, only terrorists were killed this time. One guy happened to be there with his AR-15 and took out several terrorists. Apparently his wife fired the first shots with her revolver and took out two terrorists herself. We have the Phoenix site under control. Stay there in Tempe."

Alan replied, "Just make sure to get good photos of their faces—if there are any faces left. We need to figure out who these guys are, and sooner rather than later."

Alan and some detectives began questioning the two men and the woman who had ended the standoff on the train. They needed to find out the whole story. Their names were Jared Anderson, Spencer Freeman, and Dana Sheering. Alan pulled out his phone and he opened an app with a voice recorder. About that time someone arrived with his Arizona Cell file. They started interviewing the three citizens who had shot the terrorists. The three people began relating the story, each adding comments here and there but Jared Anderson did most of the talking.

Alan and the detectives asked questions from time to time to clarify facts or get a better explanation.

A few moments into the interview, Jared Anderson was approached by a woman, apparently his wife, and Alan watched their happy embrace. He suddenly thought of Cindy. Again, he couldn't stop to text or call her, but he made a mental note to text her when he had a moment. Dana Sheering's husband also came and they all witnessed another happy embrace that included the children. They worked their way through the timeline of the event several times, all with the recorder running. At one point Mr. Sheering took the baby over into the restroom of a nearby building for a diaper change while his wife remained in the interview.

Alan's phone rang again and Victor told him about another terrorist incident on the far side of town in Peoria. In that case an elderly couple was killed. Victor reported that four people in the restaurant gunned down four terrorists as they tried to come through the front doors. Alan just shook his head in gratitude for quick thinking citizens with guns. He thought to himself, *armed law-abiding citizens are going to save our country*.

The interview took the better part of an hour before Alan and the detectives felt that they had enough information and completely understood the events. When they finished they had to take the weapons from Jared, Spencer, and Dana as evidence for their investigation. Alan apologized for leaving them unarmed and all three said they felt naked without their weapons. Alan said he understood but they had to get photos and run ballistics and he said that they would give the weapons back as soon as they could. The three left, two with their family members, grateful that they were able to save so many lives.

As they left, Alan thought to himself how he would feel without his service weapon, a Smith and Wesson M&P 9mm. He could have had the .45 but he was plain clothes and not usually in the direct line of fire, so the 9 was easier to wear under his coat. He also liked the fact that he could carry more rounds with the 9 than with the .45. He admitted that without a weapon he would feel naked and helpless too.

*   *   *

After Jared and his new battle buddies finished the interviews with the FBI and police, Jared gave a business card to Spencer Freeman. They both gave their phone numbers to Dana Sheering and she gave them the number to the now-famous cell phone that had triggered all the shooting. They all promised to get together at Jared's house in a few weeks for an evening together with their families.

Jared called his boss and said he wouldn't be coming to work. His boss agreed and said they wouldn't expect him back to work for a few days.

Jared was so glad to just hold Vicky's hand as they walked to the car. Jared called and talked to Kristi and then called Michael. Now he was ready to go home and just sit and relax and let his emotions settle. He did note that there were still ambulances leaving the demolished train car as new victims or bodies were found and pulled from the tangled mess. Jared was grateful that he was alive for another day and he thought of the families and friends who would be affected by the deaths and injuries in that car.

The earlier stress followed by the quiet ride in the car and an adrenaline crash put Jared to sleep within minutes. Vicky always teased him that the word "butt" stood for the button which was pressed when Jared sat down in church. It put his system into power-saver mode and made him fall asleep. Yes, Jared could sleep in church easily and unfortunately he did it too often. He wasn't in church today but he *was* sitting and pressing the button, and he quickly dropped off to sleep in the car.

When the car stopped Jared awoke. He was surprised to find that they were not at home as he expected. Instead, they were at Pistol Parlour, a gun shop a few miles from their house. As he turned and looked at Vicky she firmly said, "Before we go home, we're buying me a gun. I never opposed you carrying a concealed weapon but today I realized I need to be carrying one too. Maybe I could save the lives of innocent people around me, including my grandchildren or other children. That young mother was a great example to me today. It's time I stopped being a potential victim. If you want we can drive out in the desert tomorrow and you can teach me how to shoot."

Jared said, "Sounds good to me."

Vicky continued, "In fact, as I drove and you slept I have thought about the past years when I watched you carry your gun. At times I thought it was a waste of money, all the different guns and all the ammo you shot up when you went shooting. I thought it was foolish but I just rolled my eyes to myself and let it go. Sometimes I wanted to argue with you about it and I even made negative comments, as you know. I guess I could say that I thought it was unnecessary but I tolerated it—lived with it. Today all that changed. Now I understand. I realize that you were right and you were prepared. I should have embraced it and learned about it and joined you. I'm ready for a gun and I want to learn how to carry and how to be a responsible and safe gun owner."

Jared said, "I'm glad you understand. Let's go buy you a gun. In fact, I don't have one right now, so maybe we'll buy two guns." Jared laughed at his own joke but he was only half kidding.

As Jared climbed out of the car to go into the gun shop he couldn't help but smile at the irony of the emotional roller coaster he had been on that day. The day had been filled with trauma, death, stress, and a bomb that shattered a building and a train and the lives of many people. He had also taken the life of another human being in an attempt to save many innocent people that would have died. He was lucky to be alive. He felt greatly blessed that the second bomb didn't detonate. It was a horrible and emotional day. However, the greater realization was that he was still alive, as were many other people who were almost killed. What's more, the woman that he loved with all his heart had now realized the value of defending herself. It filled him with a different emotion. It didn't take long for him to realize that the feeling was the same feeling he always had when he carried his concealed weapon—freedom. Freedom from fear. Freedom from being a victim. Freedom to keep and bear arms as the wise crafters of the Constitution stated. What glorious freedom that had turned out to be today.

As they walked toward the door of the gun shop Jared let go of Vicky's hand and held his hands up in front of him, the backs of his hands facing away from him. As he made the sign of the number 2 with his left hand and the letter A with his right fist he smiled in gratitude for the Second Amendment.

*   *   *

Partway through the interview with the three armed citizens someone from the bomb squad had come and told Alan that he could go on the train any time. He was almost finished with the interview by then and he sent his photographer to start taking photos.

A few minutes later Alan joined the photographer on the train. Although the photographer had many photos of the entire crime scene Alan wanted some of his own and used his cell phone to take some pictures of the faces of Hamza and the other terrorists. Alan also looked at the inside of their hands but there were no tattoos on palms or fingertips. No Al-Musawi.

Alan tried to match the pictures up with photos in his file but he didn't get a good match out of the three terrorists. One may have been Hamza but the file photo was grainy and he could have argued that it wasn't the guy he was standing there looking at on the floor of the train. He wondered if more terrorists had recently come to Arizona to join the cell or if these were just some that they had not gotten photos of before.

Alan spent the entire day in Tempe, going over and over his notes and the evidence and trying to glean any information he could. At one point he suddenly thought of Cindy and texted her that he was in Tempe and he was fine. The end of his text said, "armed citizens saved many lives."

Investigators found the license plate from the van near where the first bomb had exploded. It was in three pieces. One piece was wrapped around a cable on a bicycle in a bike rack on Mill Avenue. Another piece was mixed in with the rubble of the building that was most heavily damaged by the bomb. The final piece was about 100 feet north of the train tracks, stuck in the bark of a ficus tree alongside Mill Avenue. They started the process of trying to identify any connection the license plate could make for them. They never found the registration for the minivan.

At about 6:30 p.m. Alan called Cindy. They talked for a few minutes, Alan relaying what information he was able to tell her. He also said he was going to have to work at the office that night. He said, "We have so much evidence to go through from the three incidents and I'm trying to see if anything new will tell us what might happen tonight or tomorrow. I'll check in later. I hope to get a chance to come home and shower and change clothes, but who knows if that will happen."

"OK. I love you. Do well in your job. I'm proud of you."

She always told him that at the end of their calls. He loved it. Sometimes that seemed to be the best thing to keep him going.

It had turned out to be a terrible Monday, even as Mondays go. Many people died but many more were saved because of law-abiding men and women who had concealed weapons and were prepared to use them.

By the end of the day, physically and mentally drained, Alan fell asleep on a cot at the office wondering what, if anything was planned next by the Terrorists and wondering if law enforcement could stop them first . . . or if it would take more armed citizens . . . or worst-case scenario, if no one could stop them. He also realized that today may have been a one-time thing but he had a hunch that this wouldn't be over until they got Al-Musawi, if he was the mastermind behind it all like Alan suspected.

10 Shocked

Mansoor Fatik Al-Musawi sat on a bench in Tempe Beach Park. He was still in shock. He slouched on the seat, his photography equipment strewn around next to him and on the ground. It was late afternoon and he was emotionally exhausted.

The day of jihad had begun as planned but then had quickly gone terribly wrong. His bombers ran into problems and the light rail train never left the Mill and Third station. Instead, only a few people were killed. His entire team was killed as well: some by a malfunction in one bomb before they got it out of the van and the rest by armed infidels who had been on the train.

In order to avoid detection by surveillance he had used his cell phone only to keep checking on news updates throughout the day. His other two planned strikes had also failed.

The bomb at the hotel was apparently detonated during a brief shootout between his team and a lone gunman. Well, it was actually not a lone gunman. The gunman's wife shot and killed two of his team and her husband was shooting at the van when their bomb detonated. All of his hotel team was killed and nobody else was even seriously injured.

Further news reports revealed to Al-Musawi that the planned attack at the restaurant in Peoria failed when his four gunmen were shot dead in the doorway of the restaurant by armed citizens. Only two infidels died in that event.

Al-Musawi took no graphic photos to post on social media. He saw no bridges fall. He saw nobody being killed. He had nothing to celebrate. Nothing!

He did see emergency vehicles when he left the bridge and ran down to join the crowd as it watched the events on the train unfold, but it was all he could do to control his anger as he watched and realized his plans had been disastrously unsuccessful. He hoped nobody would notice the photographer who was *not* shooting pictures and who finally just trudged away. He felt literally sick. He had no desire to take pictures that would only remind him of his failure.

At first he was furious! He wanted to scream but he was surrounded by people. In a daze he wandered over to Tempe Beach Park which sat under the south ends of the two Mill Avenue bridges. By the time he got to the park anyone in the park had run over to see the events at the light rail train so Al-Musawi was alone. With superhuman effort he stifled a scream. He still didn't want to attract attention even though he couldn't see anyone around. However, he was shaking with rage. On occasion he opened his palms in front of him to look at the tattoos that inspired him in his commitment to Allah but instead of feeling inspired he merely felt like a disappointment.

Every few minutes he had checked the news on his smartphone and then sat in a stupor. He couldn't believe it! They had planned so well. *What went wrong?!*

As the hours dragged on he continued to check for news updates and grew more and more frustrated and despondent. His cell phone battery finally died sometime in the late afternoon.

He just sat there through the rest of the day, leaving only after the sun set in the west and it grew dark.

11 Sleepless in Chandler

It was just before midnight on Monday night and Cindy Clevenger couldn't sleep. She was worried. She knew Alan would do his best to be safe and try to keep others safe but for the first time in her life she felt very vulnerable. If terrorists could actually carry out attacks in Phoenix, which they obviously had, then they could attack anywhere. It was certainly logical but it had just never registered in her mind like it was doing now. She had been thinking through the events of the day as she went through the motions of taking care of her two small sons. If they had been older the boys likely would have noticed that something was bothering their mom.

She had watched the news about the three attacks that day and that only made her anxiety worse. That was when she had started to shake. She felt cold. She tried playing the piano because that often brought her peace but she was shaking so badly that she couldn't play well and it just frustrated her all the more. She tried singing some hymns and other songs that usually calmed her but it didn't seem to do any good. Alan had been away many times on assignments, some of them dangerous and frightening to Cindy, but tonight was different; tonight that dangerous and frightening assignment was just outside their own door.

Cindy had put the kids to bed a little earlier than normal and then just sat staring at nothing. She finally pulled out her scriptures and with shaking hands she thumbed through some of her favorite stories of God's deliverance of his people. When they were righteous they prospered and were happy and God helped them. When they drifted away from righteousness and stopped believing in God they started having troubles; like wars or being conquered by a neighboring civilization or suffering famine or drought. *You'd think we would learn!*

Cindy read the story of Shadrach, Meshach, and Abednego. She read the story of Daniel being delivered from the lions. She read about Nephi and Ammon and Captain Moroni. Then she read about Moses and Gabriel and David. She happened to notice in Genesis Chapter 14 that even Abraham stormed in with his army of servants and rescued his nephew, Lot. *Gentle, old white-haired Abraham that we see in the paintings? I guess he wasn't always old and saintly-looking.*

She noted that sometimes God fought their battles and other times He strengthened them as they did the fighting with their own weapons. She read about some people who had become Christians and then made a commitment that they would never again take a life; they refused to fight and were willing to just let themselves be slaughtered by their enemies as they knelt to praise God. *What incredible faith and trust!* Thankfully their enemies were stopped before the faithful people were all wiped out.

She wondered if modern America was supposed to let God fight their battles or if they were supposed to fight their own battles. She didn't have too much difficulty trying to decide if, as a nation, the people in the United States believed in God or not. She had read a few studies that suggested that most people believed in a higher power of some sort. But she also knew that there were many non-believers who scoffed at the "foolish idea" that they needed God. *Oh, how much they needed God right now!*

Cindy realized her shaking had stopped at some point and she started feeling better until their dogs suddenly started growling. It was that low growl without a bark, like something was troubling them. The Clevengers lived in an area of acre lots and they had two Airedale terriers, Scooter and Carmel, who always stayed outside. They were well-trained and very gentle dogs. Alan always said a dog is one of the best security systems you can get because they are pretty much four-legged motion detectors and they bark every time they are frightened. Scooter and Carmel finally started barking but after a few minutes they stopped. Even though their noise could be annoying sometimes, tonight she was glad for those dogs and their barking.

Cindy went and got one of Alan's guns. He wasn't a gun nut but he did have several of them. They were all in the gun safe except for his service weapon which he always carried. She knew the combination for the safe and Alan had taught Cindy how to handle guns safely. She particularly liked the Walther PK380; it felt comfortable in her hand and she had learned to shoot it fairly well.

Cindy loaded the Walther, including a round in the chamber. She did not cock the hammer as she walked around the house and made sure all the doors and windows were locked. On her fourth trip around she realized that she was still scared but she felt better. She trusted in her dogs and in the gun in her hand, and she especially trusted in God in Heaven. She hoped if she needed to fight He would either fight for her or He would strengthen her as she fought. She knelt down beside her bed and prayed for His strength and prayed for her husband and her family and prayed for America.

She climbed into bed and fell asleep with her scriptures lying on Alan's side of the bed and the Walther in her hand.

WEDNESDAY

12 Aliens Carry No Cash

Marshawn Tramwell, age forty-two, was one of the nicest guys you could ever meet. Quiet but not shy. Intelligent but very down to earth. Big but gentle. Proud but never one to brag. Competitive but always glad when others excelled. He was just one of those people you enjoyed being around because he was so nice. He got along with everyone. It didn't even rile him when people acted like jerks. He was just a genuine guy. You would never guess that his net worth was over twenty-seven million dollars, and he would never tell you.

Marshawn grew up in the Deep South. His ancestors were slaves, and when freed they became farmers. The Tramwells had a work ethic like no other. They worked hard, they loved life, they especially loved to sing and dance, they loved the Bible and the gospel of Jesus Christ, and they tried to be the best people they could be. They had a fierce pride and confidence in themselves without being arrogant or cruel or rude.

Marshawn was always calm and gentle on the outside but he had a fierce, protective streak in him. Once when he was in the fourth grade some bullies from the sixth grade were picking on Evan Spradling, Marshawn's best friend. By the time Marshawn got there Evan was down on the ground and Marshawn was instantly in the middle of the bullies throwing punches. He was big for a fourth-grader but not bigger than the sixth graders and by the time the teachers broke up the scuffle Marshawn had a split lip and a black eye. "Ha!" he told the sixth graders as the teacher pulled them apart, "My eye was already black to begin with!" He didn't really win the fight but he kept Evan from being seriously hurt, and he especially proved to Evan that he was willing to protect him. The bullies must have gotten some warning message from parents or other kids, or they had their fill because they didn't bother Evan or Marshawn again.

In high school Marshawn excelled on the football team, due to his size and skill. He was one of the most popular students in the school but still remained down to earth and a friend to everyone. Well, almost everyone. When Marshawn was at the prom with Rachel Williams, his childhood sweetheart, the cup of punch she was holding slipped in Rachel's hand and she spilled some punch on the shoes of Gerald, one of the bullies from sixth grade. This time, even though Marshawn was a sophomore and Gerald was a senior, Marshawn was bigger and heavier than Gerald. What Gerald lacked in size and intelligence he made up for in arrogance. He swore at Rachel and shoved her with both hands and she fell toward Marshawn. He easily caught her and stood her up. As he looked into her face the fear and embarrassment in her eyes melted his heart and stirred his anger all at once.

Marshawn turned to the bully and said, "Apologize to her Gerald!" Gerald said, "Make me, sophomore!" and swung a fist toward Marshawn's face. Marshawn was left-handed and he coolly caught Gerald's right fist in his big left hand. Marshawn started squeezing and slowly twisting Gerald's fist back toward Gerald. Gerald's eyes grew larger and larger as the pain traveled down his arm. As Marshawn's hand twisted Gerald sank to his knees to counteract the leverage being applied on his hand and wrist. As Gerald's knees reached the floor Marshawn looked into his eyes and calmly said, "Are you ready to apologize?" Gerald nodded pleadingly. Marshawn eased back on the leverage and motioned with his right hand for Rachel to come over.

Rachel timidly walked over to Marshawn and Gerald, and Gerald said, "Sorry," but it showed no feeling or remorse. It was cold and defiant. Marshawn applied more pressure and said, "You can do better than that; she's a young lady and you need to treat her with respect." Gerald's eyes started to grow large again and he managed to croak out, "I'm sorry Rachel. I was being a jerk."

Marshawn immediately let go of Gerald's fist and offered his elbow to Rachel like a true gentleman. They moved across the room, away from Gerald who was still on his knees, surrounded now by his gathering friends.

Marshawn graduated at the top of his high school class and he and Rachel got married soon after high school and went off to Duke University. Marshawn excelled academically and was recognized by professors and classmates as one of the top students. He studied business and international finance with a minor in Japanese, and then went on to earn an MBA at Stanford on a full-ride scholarship and monthly stipend. Along the way Rachel got a degree in interior design.

Near the end of his MBA program Marshawn got the chance to do an international internship with Kawasaki Heavy Industries. He had excelled in Japanese at Duke, so he was a very good fit for an internship in Japan. He and Rachel moved to Tokyo and loved every minute of it. Kawasaki had many divisions, from ships and heavy equipment, to aerospace and defense, to motorcycles and jet skis, and many others. Marshawn ended up getting the chance to do some exciting things in the few months he was there. While at Kawasaki Marshawn asked if he could work in one of the factories as a production line laborer. Again, his Japanese helped.

Marshawn enjoyed working at the corporate and division level but he *loved* working with the average laborers in the production environment. Some of his Japanese co-workers became great friends. The sound of his name, pronounced as Mar-shawn in Japanese, sounded like the word Martian or Mar-tiahn. Some of them started calling him Martian. He didn't mind the name at all. Eventually, someone called him Uchu-jin, which meant "space creature" or "space man" or "space alien." Uchu-jin became the preferred term of endearment and he was eventually known throughout the company as Uchu-jin. He enjoyed the name and never took it negatively; only adding to their admiration for him. He grew very fond of his Japanese friends and they grew fond of him.

By the end of his stay at Kawasaki, Uchu-jin had identified an opportunity to make a change to a process that made the production of a specific product more efficient. Kawasaki later said that it saved them millions of dollars in production and safety costs over a period of several years. Although they told him they wanted to give him some kind of bonus if they could, he could not be paid individually because he was an intern. Instead they made a significant donation to the internship program at Stanford. After he graduated with his MBA, Kawasaki reached out to him again and offered him a project position to analyze another operation in a different plant.

Again, Marshawn, still affectionately known as Uchu-jin, asked to work on the production line as an average employee. With a skilled problem-solving eye and attention to detail he again identified a change in their process that resulted in a savings of millions of dollars and added safety to the plant workers. This time Kawasaki happily paid him for both breakthrough changes and Marshawn walked away with 135 million Yen, or about $1.2 million in U.S. Dollars. Marshawn used that as seed money, and with a raving review from Kawasaki he started a consulting firm known as Tramwell Analytics. The company logo had a very subtle resemblance to a space alien. His friends at Kawasaki loved it!

The first project for his new consulting company was working for a manufacturing company in Chile, in South America. Marshawn asked to work both in the corporate office and also as a front-line laborer so he could see the company from the highest and lowest levels. With characteristic logic and precision Marshawn suggested a new way to carry out an important step in production and the change saved the company hundreds of thousands of dollars. The company, though vibrant, was cash poor so Marshawn had agreed to accept shares of stock in payment. He had analyzed the company and felt that they were undervalued.

With the cost savings realized by Marshawn's change, the manufacturing company was able to be more competitive in their bids and within just a few months had acquired several lucrative jobs, thus increasing their market share and their stock price. Marshawn cashed out his shares and netted a cool $850,000.

What followed was one project after another, each time ending in success. Each time he took payment in company stock and when the company value rose he cashed out with a significant profit. Marshawn and Rachel moved around the world, spending a few months at a time in each place. Along the way Marshawn's reputation grew and their family also grew. They had four children, increasing their family from two to six. In some of the countries where they went they put their children in private schools; in others they hired tutors. Rachel loved the fact that her children were getting an international and multicultural education.

Marshawn eventually took on two young graduates who showed excellent promise and he began training them in his analytical methods.

Arlinda Marquez was a graduate of MIT. She spoke four languages and was a whiz with numbers. Nicoli Prayogo was a graduate of Texas A&M and was brilliant with technology and computers. Both were similar to Marshawn, possessing excellent soft skills and the ability to relate to people in a positive and down-to-earth manner. The three of them became known as "the analysts who smile all the time." Under Marshawn's mentorship Arlinda and Nicoli began developing the ability to go into a company, work on the front line, and then identify valuable changes that could revolutionize the business.

Tramwell Analytics' approach became legendary: work the production lines, identify opportunities for positive change, take payment in company stock, and when the stock rose, as it almost always did, cash out. Business was great and the positive articles written about them in the trade journals just kept coming, which only served to bolster their reputation and the length of the waiting list for them to do projects around the world.

After a few years Rachel's aging parents moved to Arizona to take advantage of the dry heat for their health, and Rachel felt the need to be close to them. The family settled in the Phoenix area and Tramwell Analytics built a beautiful new building in Scottsdale, an upscale suburb of Phoenix, where they added more employees. They did make sure to include a sculpture of a space alien in one part of the building and Uchu-jin sent photos to his long-time Japanese friends, to their great delight.

With four children of his own and now in a new location, Marshawn was as protective of his children as he was protective of Rachel during high school. However, Marshawn also allowed his children to deal with stress and challenges in their lives to give them character. There was a difference between protecting them from adversity that would make them grow and protecting them from real harm. His children now ranged from a 7th grader to a senior in high school. One of the hallmarks of their family was the love they shared with each other.

With that protective streak in Marshawn it was no wonder that early in his adult life he started carrying a concealed weapon wherever he could. He had carried for many years and never had a need to use it, although he came close a few times. Always armed where possible, Marshawn also stayed alert and ready. He couldn't bear the thought of something bad happening to his family or his employees, so he stayed prepared to defend the people for whom he was responsible.

Then one day came a job that was close to home. Valley Metro, the public transportation company in the Phoenix Metropolitan Area, asked if Tramwell Analytics would help them with a goal. The project was to be completely unknown to the public, of course. Valley Metro wanted to see if it was feasible to take their government-subsidized public transportation company and turn it into a profitable enterprise that required no government funding. Marshawn had had difficult assignments along the way, but this was one of the toughest.

Marshawn and his two budding apprentices did as they always did: they took jobs on the front lines. Arlinda Marquez was assigned as a customer service representative and dispatcher in the Valley Metro call center. Nicoli Prayogo and Marshawn got the special training and licenses they needed and then Nicoli was trained to operate one of the light rail trains and Marshawn became a bus driver on a local route. They would work at these positions for three months, having weekly conferences to begin identifying, analyzing, and discussing ideas for possible solutions. At times they even took the buses and the train as passengers, as part of their analysis. After the three months on the front line they would work in the Valley Metro headquarters for three more months, to analyze the high-level operations of the company. If needed, they would do two more stints of three months each.

Now that he was a temporary bus driver he had the same concern for the safety of his passengers as he had for his family. Per Valley Metro policy Marshawn wasn't supposed to carry a weapon while driving a bus but he did anyway since he had done so for years, wearing a sub-compact Glock 9mm in a holster on his left hip under his vest. Having it on his left side kept it hidden from the passengers and within easy reach of his dominant left hand. The 9mm was not the most powerful gun, but it had proven many times over that it could stop a criminal in his tracks. Marshawn kept his Glock loaded with hollow-point slugs designed to come apart inside the body of an assailant and not exit out the other side to strike innocent people. His Glock could be loaded safely with ten rounds in the magazine and one round in the chamber. Thanks to the Glock's excellent design, the round in the chamber waited safely, ready for firing without having to lever in a round.

Marshawn also carried pepper spray in addition to the gun. He realized that there would be times where making someone incapable of fighting didn't require taking their life. That paid off one day shortly after he started driving when a man who had obviously been drinking came onto the bus brandishing a pair of sharp-pointed scissors, looking for a fight. Marshawn tried to take the scissors away but the man was quick enough to be dangerous. Finally, Marshawn hit the man in the face with a shot of pepper spray and that did the trick. It also served to clear out the bus, and Marshawn and the passengers exited the bus coughing and crying and reaching for anything to wipe their eyes and noses.

Marshawn apologized profusely to the passengers as the police came and arrested the drunk, but after about fifteen minutes of letting the bus air out, most of the passengers thanked him for keeping them safe.

Marshawn took great delight in the sign on the front of the bus above him as he drove: **Driver Carries No Cash**. Marshawn often closed one eye or used his hand as he stretched, to block part of the words so that the sign said, to him at least, **Driver Carries**. He also smiled to himself when he changed the words to **Alien Carries No Cash** or simply **Alien Carries**.

Marshawn prided himself in trying to operate the bus the best he could. Every day he challenged himself to drive as efficiently and safely as a driver could drive, while at the same time looking for and brainstorming ways to turn Valley Metro into a profitable, non-subsidized company. In his non-driving hours he studied as much as he could about the company, using materials and manuals provided by the Valley Metro head office. Arlinda and Nicoli were doing the same and during their weekly conferences they had lively and productive discussions. Marshawn felt like his apprentices and the Valley Metro project were making progress.

It didn't take long for Marshawn to learn that his favorite part about driving a bus was the people. He always loved to meet people. While they didn't often have a chance to talk at length he always greeted them as they got on the bus. He always appreciated it when they called their thanks to him as they were starting to step off. There was just something nice about hearing them call, "Thanks driver!" as the doors bumped open and a passenger stepped onto the sidewalk.

Then one day in February things changed. Marshawn, Arlinda, and Nicoli had been working with Valley Metro for about a month when terrorists attacked Phoenix. The terrorists' first target was the light rail train, operated by Valley Metro. It did not happen to be Nicoli's train and he was completely safe from the situation.

Marshawn and Rachel had watched the news on Monday night; filled with reports about bombs on the Light Rail in Tempe and behind a hotel in Phoenix. There were also the stories about four terrorists being shot dead at a restaurant in Peoria. Someone pointed out that all of the assailants were Middle Eastern. Marshawn was grateful for the realization that some good citizens were prepared and were carrying concealed weapons. There was no doubt that these people had prevented more deaths. In the case of the hotel incident, no one died but the terrorists. The media had surmised whether three acts of terrorism in the same city might signal further acts but, of course, no one knew anything for sure. Intelligence had not detected any threat, at least that's what they were reporting. However, the Phoenix metropolitan area was on high alert.

Marshawn loved the symbol of the Second Amendment shown by the guy walking away from the train. One hand with two fingers held up and the other hand with a fist and the thumb alongside; a 2 and an A. The talk radio people on the AM dial were all discussing it and it was all over social media. By the end of the day Tuesday, some people were already selling shirts and hats with the now-popular sign on them.

On Tuesday nothing happened. No terrorist activity occurred. Law enforcement officials were relieved but still guarded in case anything else came up. They hoped Monday was a one-time thing.

Wednesday morning Marshawn made sure he had his Glock when he started his regular routine. Marshawn had been assigned to bus route #156 that ran east and west along Chandler Boulevard in what was known as the East Valley; on the southeast edge of the Phoenix metropolitan area.

Marshawn's first pass was the westbound route, starting just before 5:30 a.m. On the east end of the line were Gateway Airport, ASU Polytechnic, and some other businesses. He drove west on Williams Field Road, picking up passengers along the way. At Gilbert Road, Williams Field road became Chandler Boulevard as it went through Chandler. Williams Field Air Force Base and the city of Chandler used to be "far apart" back in the 50s and 60s but in recent years it had become city all the way through. Only the change in the street names showed the difference between one city and the other.

Riders got on and off the bus, the remaining number fluctuating nearly every mile. At the far west end of the route Marshawn was south of Ahwatukee in what was within the Phoenix city limits. He waited for a few minutes and then started eastbound again at 7:50. He had gone a few stops, picking up eight riders, and was approaching the Arizona Avenue

69

stop. This stop was right near downtown Chandler, a city of almost 250,000 people. The stop was next to a vacant lot that used to be the home of Tres Toros Cantina.

When they first moved to the Phoenix area Marshawn had heard about the restaurant from some friends and had planned to stop there to eat sometime, maybe with Rachel or with the whole family. Then one day someone with decision-making authority had it torn down, leaving nothing but a patch of empty dirt. Each time he had come to this stop over the past few weeks he thought about missing the opportunity to eat at Tres Toros. Then one day he saw a sign indicating that Tres Toros had moved to a different location in Gilbert. Every time he drove past that empty lot he vowed he would make time to go check out the new location.

As he approached the stop near the vacant lot he saw three men who looked to be Middle Eastern waiting at the stop. Riders such as this were common as the Phoenix metropolitan area was one of the largest cities in the U.S. It had over four million people and boasted a very diverse population. However, Marshawn had learned, even in the short few weeks that he had been driving, who the regulars were and when new people got on the bus. He had never seen any of these men before. Again, that was not unusual, but after the events of this week the red flags were going up.

There were two other passengers at the stop, both women, and as Marshawn pulled to a stop at the curb, the three men got on first. *That* was unusual. The younger generation was not as polite as the older generation, but usually even young men still showed enough courtesy to let the women board first. Not this time. These men got right on ahead of the women, demonstrating to Marshawn that they had not assimilated into American culture very well. More red flags, but not something Marshawn could use to justify keeping them off the bus.

As the three men got on, they didn't have bus passes or money to pay the fare. That was the final red flag. The three were crowded around the fare machine, just an arms' length away from him. Marshawn didn't know exactly what to do but he knew the time had come. This was no pepper spray moment. He started to stand and reach back for his Glock when suddenly there was a quick movement from one of the men and everything went black.

13 Gateway

Celeste Favreau had worked for Heritage Airlines for two years, taking tickets and helping passengers load and unload. She loved her job and especially enjoyed seeing people's bright faces as they prepared to fly off to planned adventures or to visit loved ones. She loved when they returned after a fun time away—well, not all of them. Some were stressed, late or tired and their patience was wearing thin, but she had learned to tolerate that.

Celeste was a redhead with bright green eyes and a bouncy, outgoing personality. She made friends easily and quickly and sometimes by the time a passenger had talked with her for just a few minutes waiting for a flight, they seemed to be old friends. She had a knack for making people feel at ease.

There were four outgoing flights scheduled that Wednesday morning in February, one at 6:00, another at 6:30, a third at 7:00 and the fourth flight at 7:30. All flights left from the same area of the terminal—four gates all fairly close together. Celeste had been checking tickets at the gates with her co-worker, Rhonda, trying to get people ready to board. The Phoenix-Mesa Gateway Airport was small, as commercial airports go, so employees got to fill different roles throughout the day, unlike their counterparts in a larger airport. Celeste and Rhonda moved from one gate to the next helping the passengers as needed.

Celeste looked across the terminal at The Grindstone coffee shop. They served excellent coffee, pastries, fruit, juices, and sandwiches and always seemed to have a crowd. Even though Celeste didn't drink coffee her attention strayed to the shop often. Her interest was in Nick Turcott who worked at The Grindstone. He was a student at ASU polytechnic which held classes right next to the airport. He was not tall, dark and handsome, but two out of three was OK with her. He had dark eyes and wavy black hair and he was very handsome, but he was not tall. He was actually about an inch shorter than Celeste, so since the day she first noticed him she had not worn shoes with heels. They had talked many times and she hoped one of these days he would ask her on a date. She had hinted at it several times but he must have been nervous or shy because he either hadn't caught the hint or if he had, he wasn't taking any steps to do anything about it.

Celeste looked at the crowd of passengers gathering in the terminal and then looked at the time. She picked up the intercom to announce that it was time to start boarding the 7:30 flight out of Gate 8 heading for St. Cloud, Minnesota, but before she pressed the button she heard a steady popping noise outside that sounded like gunfire.

Everyone in the terminal turned to look out the big plate glass windows onto the tarmac toward the plane.

Celeste saw a truck rapidly approaching the plane from the south. A man with a black beard and black hair was standing on the running board shooting a machine gun. With all the things that had happened that week in the Phoenix area, she immediately concluded that they were terrorists. Right or wrong that was her first thought.

Celeste looked quickly to the south of the terminal where Mesa police usually stationed an officer or two with a squad car. Because of the terrorist activity this week, there were two officers. As she feared, the terrorist was shooting at them. They reached for their rifles but were a step behind the threat. One officer went down quickly but the other one got his semi-automatic weapon and returned fire. After just a few moments the second officer collapsed next to the squad car, his rifle landing hard on the ground. Celeste looked at the truck and saw the terrorist fall off the side of it, tumbling along the pavement as the truck continued speeding toward the plane. The officer had eliminated one threat before he was put out of commission.

Some of the shots aimed at the police had struck one of the full-sized windows on the side of the terminal facing the tarmac. Glass and bullets rained into the area causing the passengers to erupt with screams. Cold air began seeping through the holes into the waiting area.

Amid the commotion Celeste felt sick with the reality of the death of two police officers and a terrorist attack on Gateway Airport. However, after a quick glance at the passengers and seeing no apparent injuries, she turned again to see what was going on outside. Everyone was anxiously watching and the noise level rose with obvious fear.

The truck stopped in front of the terminal and seven terrorists, including the driver, jumped out. They stood by the truck as if they were daring anyone to come out of the terminal. One man ran up the moveable ramp into the plane and Celeste heard shots. No doubt the pilot and co-pilot would not be flying that plane and the flight attendants would never again welcome passengers on board. Celeste knew some of the Heritage Airlines flight attendants personally but she didn't know the ones on this flight. It was probably a good thing or she might have been overwhelmed with sorrow. As she watched the scene unfold, her heart was filled with dread at the deaths of good people and at the danger lurking just on the other side of the windows, but she was already formulating a plan.

Celeste still held the intercom mic in her hand. They had talked about these kinds of situations in training and Celeste knew what to do. She pushed the button and said to all the passengers. "This is an emergency! Everyone get down and move to the back wall. Do not panic and do not leave. There could be greater danger outside in the parking lot. Please stay against the wall and wait for further instructions from Security."

People started scrambling to the wall away from the windows, trying to account for all of their belongings and loved ones. Despite the instructions, some started to panic and began to shout or cry. Others attempted to provide comfort to the nervous ones.

Celeste looked over to The Grindstone to see if she could see Nick Turcott. He was standing there and they made eye contact across the room amid the chaos. They had only been friends for a short while, but with the terrorist activity this week, they had spoken about self-defense. Both of them had quietly admitted that they carried a concealed weapon. They knew it was against federal law to have a weapon at the airport but this week was different, and both of them said they were prepared and ready to fight if necessary.

Celeste turned to Rhonda and said, "I've got a gun. I'm going to fight!"

Rhonda said, "Don't be stupid Celeste, you can't outshoot all of those terrorists by yourself." Celeste replied as she looked toward The Grindstone, "I won't be by myself. Nick also carries a gun, and I hope security will be here soon. I'm not just going to do nothing!"

Rhonda stared at Celeste for a few moments and then grabbed the intercom mic from her. She said to the noisy, fearful passengers, "Please remain calm and move to the wall. We will wait for Security to give us further instructions."

Most of the passengers were moving across the room, trying to get as close to the wall as they could. That started some arguments and shouting about not crowding and being more considerate. Others were not thinking rationally and were continuing to struggle with their luggage, slowing down their retreat to the wall.

Nick ran across the aisle, struggling against the passengers. He was swimming upstream but he had to get close to the windows. He fought his way through the crowd and came up next to Celeste. "Ready to shoot if needed?" he whispered.

Celeste said, "Yes, but I'm scared."

Nick said, "Me too."

Two more terrorists joined the one already on board the airplane. Both had a large duffle bag in each hand. They then turned and pushed the loading ramp away from the plane and closed the door. Three men by the truck formed a defensive semi-circle as they stood there, watching the terminal doors and occasionally looking over their shoulders at the plane. The remaining terrorist ran to the push-back tractor and started pushing the plane away from the terminal. He evidently knew what he was doing because he quickly moved the plane out toward the runway and turned it to a ninety-degree angle. He then jumped off the tractor and disengaged the push bar from the front of the plane. He then moved the tractor back toward the terminal.

As he returned to join the others who were standing guard, the plane started moving southeast on to the taxi-way that paralleled the runway and picked up speed as it headed toward the south end of the Gateway runway.

In the past, Gateway Airport was an Air Force base, called Williams Field, and many pilots took their training there during World War II and also long after. It was decommissioned in 1993 and after a few years was converted to a commercial airport. The main carrier that began serving the public out of Gateway was Heritage Airlines. Heritage flew out of Gateway to minor airports all around the U.S., offering a lower-cost alternative to the big carriers and providing access to smaller towns.

The airport runway was about two miles long, running from southeast to northwest. The terminal sat near the middle of the runway, so the newly hijacked plane would need to go about a mile southeast before it turned around to go northwest to take off.

With the plane now safely away from the terminal the four terrorists started walking toward the doors. They did not appear to be in any great hurry but they still held their weapons in firing position.

By now the passengers were mostly gathered against the wall as far from the windows as they could get. Celeste and Nick were the only ones out by the ticket booths. No one could be seen from the shops and restaurants further down the hall in the terminal. Evidently, they were hiding.

Fortunately, right then two security guards came running around the corner. Both of them held rifles, which appeared to Celeste to be AR-15s. She knew all the members on the security team at Gateway and was happy to see them.

Celeste carried a SCCY 9mm. The name was pronounced "Sky" and she loved her Sky. It was purple, her favorite color, and it held eleven rounds. Nick carried a Kimber Ultra Carry 9mm. They already had their pistols drawn and pointed to the roof when the security guards came around the corner. Nick called out, "Over here!"

The security guards looked, and at first did a double-take, seeing someone with a gun. Then they realized it was two employees of the airport that they knew.

Celeste greeted them, "Hi. We're so glad you're here. We were beginning to worry it would just be us."

The two security guards came up to them, and one said, "Please just back away and let us handle this."

Nick said, "No way. With four of them and only two of you the odds are against you. Besides, the element of surprise will help us and if all four of us shoot at the same time we stand a better chance."

The security guard started to argue but then just shrugged his shoulders and turned toward the doors.

There were two doors leading to the tarmac, one marked with a 7 and the other marked with an 8. Both doors led to basically the same passenger area, but they were spaced apart to allow a door for each plane when two planes were loading or unloading at the same time.

Knowing that the morning sun was shining directly onto the glass doors, effectively shielding them from the terrorists' view, the first Security guard felt safe in saying to Nick, "Come with me to the other door." Even without the sun, the windows were tinted, so the terrorists were walking in blind. They were clearly counting on not having anyone oppose them.

Nick and the guard ran to the other door, crouching low as they ran in case shots started flying again.

Celeste and the other guard turned to face the near door. The guard said, "I'll take the one on the right; you take the one on the left." The ticket booth was very near the door and Celeste had stepped over next to it. The Security guard crouched by the small box where passengers could check the size of their bag to see if it was small enough for carry-on. A little bit of cover was better than no cover at all.

Celeste was terrified and knew that life and death were at stake for many people, including her. She was Catholic and wanted to pray, but she realized she couldn't cross herself and still have her gun aimed at the door. In her mind she envisioned her hand making the symbol of the cross in front of her. She started reciting in her mind, "Holy Mary, full of grace . . . ." and the door schussed open.

The door was a bit wider than a regular door, allowing a person carrying or towing luggage to walk easily through. As two terrorists came in together they were shoulder to shoulder with their weapons held in front of them.

Both Celeste and the Security Guard opened up, catching the terrorists by surprise. Celeste had assumed a shooter's stance with feet apart and both hands rigidly in front of her body, leaning forward on the balls of her feet. Her SCCY held eleven rounds, ten in the magazine and one in the chamber. She had also stuck an extra magazine in her back pocket that day, so when she started shooting, she planned to empty the whole thing at the terrorist if needed. She tried to fire as fast as she could and still aim accurately.

The first shot struck the terrorist in the right arm and produced a look of shock on his face. It also effectively paralyzed his shooting arm. She overcorrected on the second shot and her bullet passed between the men without striking either of them. Her third shot caught the man at the base of the neck and his feet stopped moving. Her fourth shot hit him in the torso, low and to his right. Her fifth shot hit him dead center in the middle of his torso. Before she could shoot a sixth shot he fell forward onto the black rubberized doormat, with his gun landing under him. She decided she didn't need to shoot again but stayed ready.

The whole time Celeste was shooting, the security guard next to her was on one knee, firing as well. He was shooting faster than she was because he didn't have to work as hard to re-aim the rifle as she did with her pistol. She knew that shots were being fired near the other door too, but she was too focused to pay attention to anything else. The second terrorist staggered back and then fell, landing with his body on the outside doormat and his legs still inside the sliding door track. With two motionless terrorists by the door, the mechanism tried to slide closed but bumped into the legs of the one man. It open and closed repeatedly. *Bump . . . Bump . . . Bump . . . .*

Nick and the other security guard were successful as well and the shooting was over in mere seconds. Only one terrorist was able to get off any shots, and since he pulled the trigger as he fell, the bullets all went high, hitting the ceiling.

The four airport employees stopped shooting and held their guns ready, waiting to make sure there was no need for further action. The crowd of passengers behind them held their collective breath. Celeste had already switched to her second magazine.

One of the security guards broke the anxious silence by speaking loudly, "Is everyone OK?"

On that cue, the crowd of passengers broke into applause. They started cheering and hugging each other. There were smiles, tears, and looks of relief on their faces.

Celeste turned to look at Nick over by the other door. He was busy looking at something else and she didn't catch his eye. She holstered her SCCY and turned to the security guard next to her.

"Thanks!" she said. "I was terrified."

He returned the gratitude and added, "Glad you were shooting along with me. Two on two was much better than me trying to stop both of those guys at the same time. By the time I was ready to start firing at the one on the left you already had him down." The security guard stepped over to both terrorists, making sure they weren't moving, and then looked out the door toward the departing plane.

Celeste turned back to the ticket booth. As she did so, she glanced toward Nick. She'd have to spend more time trying to get to know him. She was very attracted to a young man who could shoot.

Fortunately, Nick caught her eye and smiled his gorgeous smile, and she hoped he was very attracted to a young woman who could shoot.

*   *   *

By now the alert had gone out that an airport was under attack and a plane had been stolen, possibly with explosives on board. They could hear sirens coming. From the training videos they had watched repeatedly Celeste knew that authorities were already grounding all planes in the Phoenix area. Commercial Aviation and General Aviation were quickly coming to a standstill. Within a few minutes there would be no aircraft flying as each plane out there quickly landed at the nearest airport and all departing flights were delayed. Any incoming flights from distant airports would be rerouted or canceled as quickly as possible. The Phoenix area would be a no-fly zone for as long as was needed to deal with the situation.

The two security guards, seeing that the situation was safe inside the terminal, ran out the doors to see the plane. Celeste saw them looking to the far end of the runway. They just stood there talking.

Before long a couple of police cars came barreling around the end of the building and evidently noticed the uniformed security guards standing there. Pulling up next to them, two officers got out of the cars. They all stood there talking. Finally, one of the security guards turned and walked quickly back to the terminal.

As he came in, Celeste asked him, "What's happening?"

The guard started past her, evidently headed for some business elsewhere. He paused and said, "We can't really tell, but the plane is just sitting at the end of the runway. I'm going to get some binoculars." Then he went down the hall and rounded the corner out of Celeste's sight.

*   *   *

At the south end of the runway the terrorists stopped the plane and left it just sitting there on the taxi-way, facing southeast, engines humming. Then they opened the door and two of them dropped to the pavement below, one of them wearing a backpack. The third terrorist climbed out of the door and held onto the side of the plane. He stood with his toes at the bottom of the doorway and pulled the door closed as far as he could. Without a ramp to help him, he couldn't close it completely. He dropped to the ground next to his companions. Standing next to the plane it was easy to see that the door was ajar, but from a distance it appeared to be closed.

The terrorists didn't know how to fly the plane. Instead, they had been trained only enough to taxi the plane away from the airport. Their goal was to leave it on the runway, thereby raising the alert level around the area and continuing to terrorize America.

The three men ran along the left side of the plane past the front of the nose, and off the end of the taxiway. There was a small road there used for maintenance vehicles and the terrorists began jogging due east, their weapons in hand. After about a half-mile they came near Ellsworth

Road. Ellsworth was a busy, four-lane street with a fence and drainage ditch alongside it. Instead of joining Ellsworth at this point, the maintenance road turned south for another 100 yards. The drainage ditch ended at a retention basin with a drain pipe going into the ground, and the maintenance road curved east around this area before it intersected with Ellsworth.

As they got to the corner where the road turned south, the terrorist with the backpack stopped and turned away from the other two. He ran over into a clump of sparse creosote bushes and small mesquite trees and crouched down in the middle of the brush. Although the bushes were not thick he was fairly well hidden unless a searcher got right next to him. The other two men continued south on the maintenance road.

There was a high chain-link fence all the way around the Gateway Airport area but where the maintenance road met Ellsworth there was a gate, locked with a heavy chain. As the two terrorists arrived at the gate a gray minivan turned off of southbound Ellsworth road. It quickly traversed the 50 feet of maintenance road and pulled up to the gate, well away from the cars whizzing by on Ellsworth.

A man jumped out of the van with a pair of bolt cutters and handed them through a gap in the gate to the terrorists inside. With two quick but powerful snaps, the chain gave way and the gate was pushed open. They stepped outside the gate and then rolled the gate closed and positioned the chain so that from a quick glance it appeared to still be locked. The van had already turned around as they were working with the gate, and the terrorists got in. The van drove back to Ellsworth, waited for a gap in traffic, and then sped off.

14   Pull Cord to Stop Bus

Marshawn Tramwell awoke lying on the floor of the bus about halfway down the aisle. He didn't move. He was groggy and his head hurt. He saw that there was a small pool of blood where his head was resting on the floor. He couldn't figure out where he was until the motion of the bus and loud talking in another language brought him back to the present. He realized that he was on *his* bus, with terrorists in control of it.

He didn't want to make any sudden moves but he knew he had to devise a plan. As he lay on his left side he could tell from the lump under his hip that he still had his Glock. Evidently, they didn't know that he was armed, and that was very good news.

Marshawn groaned even though he didn't feel the need to groan—it was purely an act. He rolled over a little and looked up. A terrorist was standing directly above him pointing a snub-nosed weapon at him. The man commanded him, "No move!" Marshawn held out his hands and pleadingly said, "Can I at least sit up?" The terrorist paused and then said, "OK to sit. Nothing more."

Marshawn sat up and, putting his hand on his head, he groaned again to continue the act. With the terrorist watching closely, Marshawn cautiously and gently felt his head. There was a gash just above the hairline on his forehead that had also produced quite a large goose egg. It was sticky with blood and hurt like the dickens.

Marshawn just sat, watching, planning, and looking at the other passengers. Some of them had terror in their eyes. Marshawn tried to smile reassuringly. He didn't know if it helped.

One of the three terrorists was driving the bus, and not very skillfully Marshawn noted. They just passed stop after stop and Marshawn realized the Valley Metro call center, maybe even Arlinda, was getting complaints about *him*. This was *his* bus and it wasn't stopping.

The terrorists had moved all the passengers to the back half of the bus and two of them were standing between Marshawn and the driver. They kept up a constant chatter in another language while frequently looking at their watches. Evidently whatever they were doing was synchronized to some deadline or event.

The terrorist nearest to Marshawn kept looking at him, then at the other two men as they talked, then back to Marshawn again. Perhaps Marshawn could draw his gun when the terrorist was looking the other way.

Then the middle terrorist turned toward him and Marshawn noticed for the first time that this man was wearing some kind of vest with multiple pockets on it. The pockets looked full and there were wires connecting them. He had never seen a suicide bomber's vest but he imagined that's what one might look like.

The bus lurched around a corner, bouncing up over the curb, and Marshawn noted that the driver had no concern for making a smooth ride for the Valley Metro passengers. The way this man was driving, Marshawn was going to get a lot of complaints.

Marshawn was still seated on the floor but he knew this route well and he could see out the windows to the sky. He realized that they had turned a corner from Williams Field Road and were now headed south.

Marshawn started calculating and knew that two miles away were three key buildings—a hospital, a high school, and an elementary school. He wondered if the terrorists' plan was to detonate the bomb at one of those buildings, perhaps even driving inside the building before detonation.

Marshawn decided the time to act was very soon. As the nearest terrorist turned to talk to the others and look at his watch, Marshawn caught the attention of a woman sitting near him among the other passengers. She was in scrubs and was probably a nurse—if she were a doctor she would likely be driving her own car. He hoped her training and experience had helped her learn to keep a cool head in tough situations.

He mouthed the words "pull the cord" while motioning with his eyes. She seemed to realize what he said and reached for the cord hanging along the side of the bus. As she pulled the cord Marshawn pulled his Glock.

The stop-request bell sounded in the bus and the nurse said loudly, "I have to get off at the next stop!" The diversion worked perfectly. The terrorist turned toward the nurse and was completely focused on her. Marshawn aimed his Glock and quickly put two bullets into the terrorist's chest cavity from the back-left. The slugs were traveling at about 750 miles per hour and they did their job. The terrorist fell against the seats.

Marshawn was already turning and fired three shots at the head of the terrorist with the bomb. The man was fumbling to aim his gun at Marshawn and at the same time reach for something on his vest. Two of the three shots found their mark and the terrorist went limp and fell backward, landing right at the back corner of the driver's seat.

The terrorist who was driving the bus started to point his snub-nosed automatic weapon toward Marshawn, completely ignoring the business of driving a massive vehicle. Marshawn would have preferred not shooting the third man until he could be at the wheel of the bus, but in the current situation he didn't have the luxury of waiting.

Two of Marshawn's four shots struck the terrorist; one in the neck and one in the chest cavity, entering just under the armpit as the man was raising his arm to fire the gun. Marshawn's other two shots smacked into different places on the bus. The terrorist slumped sideways, his raised right arm and machine gun tipping his center of balance toward the aisle, pulling the steering wheel slightly to the right. Somehow, his foot got hung up on the floorboard and twisted downward on the gas pedal, pushing the pedal clear to the floor. The bus veered to the right and the engine revved, although it accelerated slowly because of the bus's weight.

Marshawn jumped up, stumbling a little because of the blow to his head and having to scramble over the bodies of the three terrorists. He looked out the front window to see that they were barreling toward a traffic light. A left turn would take them toward the hospital; a right turn would take them toward the two schools. However, Marshawn instantly had an idea.

With the gradual right turn already started, the bus's trajectory would take it straight into the traffic light pole on the far right corner of the upcoming intersection. The southbound light was red and there were already cars stopped and waiting. If the bus continued on its current path, it would smash into the light pole, but if he yanked it back, he would crash into the cars at the intersection. Marshawn finally got to the wheel with the intention of squeezing between the right lane and the light pole, which meant he would go right on top of the sidewalk. One obstacle stood in his way. There was a single car in the right turn lane.

At the sound of a loud horn, the driver of the car in the turn lane was alerted to a city bus barreling toward him. The car lurched forward and around the corner, leaving the turn lane clear. Marshawn thought, "So far so good." He planned to drive on through the intersection and angle out into the alfalfa field that took up the entire southwest corner of that intersection.

There were eastbound cars on the side street, with a green light in their favor. Marshawn kept one hand on the horn, hoping that traffic would clear for him. He narrowly passed behind someone who had just gone through the light, but the other approaching cars saw him and hit their brakes, a couple swerving to avoid each other. Different pitched car horns answered his.

A fleeting thought came to Marshawn and he smiled: *They didn't teach us anything about this at Duke or Stanford.*

The gap in traffic was just what Marshawn needed but the bus was still picking up speed. Marshawn picked a spot on the corner that would take him over the curb, through a couple of small trees and possibly a cable TV box, and then over the berm at the edge of the field. The collateral damage wasn't nearly as valuable as the people on the bus and the traffic in the streets. The terrorist was still slumped in the seat and Marshawn could only steer. He couldn't reach the pedals nor did he have time to try.

After the bump over the curb there was an instant flash of green as two small trees were whipped against the front window and then dragged under the bus. Marshawn barely registered the screams coming from his passengers as he braced for the next impact. Now came the big earth berm carefully crafted by the farmer and his tractor around the field to contain the irrigation water. Irrigation in this part of Arizona came about every two weeks through a concrete ditch, and the farmer would flood it out onto the alfalfa field. Today there was no water but the ground was relatively soft. As the bus bumped even higher over the berm than it had over the curb, it plowed into the soft earth of the alfalfa field. The constant acceleration and huge mass of the bus kept it moving on the softer surface.

Now there was nothing in the bus's way except for small alfalfa plants and more berms of earth, each running east and west clear across the field to help the irrigation water spread evenly. The berms were made by scraping loose dirt into an A shape about a foot high. The soil on the flat part of the field was a little more firm, but the berms were soft and loose.

The bus was traveling southwest. If Marshawn continued in this direction he would bump over a berm about every 75 to 100 feet, although he didn't know how far apart farmers made their berms. If he turned more to the right and ran due west he had about a quarter of a mile of no berms or bumping before he reached the school. He chose to start west and see if he could slow the bus down but he knew that if he had to, he could turn south.

The bus now rolled steadily and with no more immediate obstacles, Marshawn could concentrate on other things. The loose ground had served to slow the bus a little already. Marshawn yelled to the passengers, "Get ready to get off the bus as soon as it stops! There's still a bomb on here."

83

Suddenly there was someone next to him, pulling the dead terrorist out of the driver's seat. The terrorist's foot was still tangled in the pedals but with a little twisting and yanking, it finally came free. As that was happening, the bus drifted slightly left toward the nearest berm. As the terrorist came out of the seat the left front tire of the bus hit the soft dirt of the berm.

The bus slowed quickly now as it plowed through the foot-high soil. It tried to pull to the left but Marshawn anticipated that and kept a good grip on the big wheel, keeping the bus rolling straight with its left wheels in the soft earth. About that same time Marshawn was able to sit in the seat and finally put on the brakes.

As the bus stopped, everyone lurched forward. Marshawn jammed the transmission lever into park and flung open the front and rear doors, yelling, "Get out quick!" The riders piled off the bus, and after Marshawn checked to make sure everyone was off, he followed them out. They stopped outside but he called out, "Follow me! We've got to get farther away!" He ran across the field toward the sidewalk and then walked to the corner. By now they were at least 100 yards from the bus.

Some of them started calling loved ones on their cell phones. The nurse came over and checked the cut and bump on Marshawn's head. He hugged her and thanked her for her help and her cool thinking. He asked what department she worked in and she said, "Emergency Room." Marshawn smiled, "I wondered if it was something like that."

All the commotion at the intersection and the runaway bus had prompted people on the street to call 911, and Marshawn and the others could hear sirens coming from different directions. Several people were already shooting video with their smartphones.

As Marshawn had anticipated, suddenly there was a loud BOOM and the bus erupted into a ball of flame. Either a timer went off or the bomb was detonated remotely or someone bumped the dead terrorist just right in the mad scramble to get off the bus. Whatever the case, the bomb had detonated and took with it three dead terrorists. The original plot had been foiled by a citizen with courage and a gun. The only real damage was the loss of a bus and some ruined alfalfa and trees, and the residual mental and emotional impact to the passengers and Marshawn.

Marshawn called Rachel and filled her in on what had happened. She said she was going to come find him. He told her about the cut on his head but assured her that he was fine.

Police and fire units came, along with counter-terrorism personnel. Some started investigating the bus, which had been blown apart and engulfed in flames but was now just smoldering. They asked for Marshawn's weapon for their investigation, which he gave to them. They assured him he would get it back. He didn't mind. He had a Glock .40 caliber at home. He would just be a little more nervous without a weapon on the ride home. Fire department personnel treated his wounds but told Marshawn that he would most likely need stitches.

Somewhere during the interviews, Rachel arrived and threw her arms around him. She inspected his head and said, "I prayed all the way here that this isn't the start of another day full of terrorism."

Marshawn said, "I hope it isn't either but I can tell you that God certainly helped me today and He will be with us all no matter what happens."

Marshawn's cell phone rang, interrupting them. It was Lloyd, the Driver Supervisor at Valley Metro. Lloyd was aware of who Marshawn really was but he was intimidated by Marshawn and hardly ever spoke to him. Marshawn was just as friendly to Lloyd as to everyone else, but Lloyd was still nervous around him. Lloyd said, "When we started getting calls that you were blowing past the stops, I knew something was wrong. I knew that wasn't you. Man, am I glad you were on that bus!" Lloyd asked a few more questions and they discussed the situation, and then Lloyd told Marshawn to not worry about the gun on the job. This incident had already caused them to start rethinking that policy. Marshawn knew he wouldn't have been fired anyway since he wasn't really an employee. Just before they hung up, Lloyd told Marshawn to take the rest of the day off.

But the day off didn't happen right away. There was still a lot of investigating to do, which meant many questions and discussions, and Marshawn was the key to it all. They also told him to go over to the nearby hospital for stitches in his head.

As he and Rachel started walking toward the hospital Marshawn looked at the crowd of news media with their cameras and boom antennae on the tops of their vans. Taking his cue from the guy two days ago he held up his right hand with two fingers extended. His left hand was holding Rachel's and he wasn't about to let go of her hand. So after making the sign for 2, he made the fist with the thumb alongside; the sign-language A. With one hand he showed the world the newly popular symbol for the Second Amendment.

As before, the photos of a hero flashing the 2-A symbol went viral within minutes and were again a subject of much discussion in the news. A democratic senator from back east even spoke out against it, calling it "a disgusting display that will no doubt become a much-loved fad at the NRA." Of course, within minutes the NRA came out with a statement that "the Second Amendment is not just a fad."

Word must have gotten around the hospital because when Marshawn and Rachel arrived and were escorted through the halls a few of the people he passed shook his hand and thanked him for his bravery or said how glad they were that he was there. Several people showed the two-handed symbol for the Second Amendment. The nurse from the bus came and found him while he was getting stitched up and he thanked her again for her calm thinking.

Marshawn said, "My dad always said I had a hard head." The nurse laughed, and then in all seriousness and with tears in her eyes she said, "I'm mostly glad that you have a big heart and a lot of courage . . . and a gun." The adrenalin had now stopped pumping and Marshawn suddenly realized that he just survived a brush with death. This high-class, sophisticated business analyst got a lump in his throat and tears in his eyes, and all he could do was nod. He looked at Rachel sheepishly. Rachel calmly said to Marshawn and the nurse, "I've been crying all day, first in fear and now in gratitude. I realized how bad it was all along."

Finally, he was released to leave with Rachel. She insisted on driving since he had been hit on the head and had just been medicated. He thought that was a lame excuse but he kept it to himself and said instead, "OK, but I give the orders where we go." She agreed.

When they approached Williams Field Road, Rachel was going to go straight, but before she reached the light Marshawn instructed her to get in the left lane. She protested but he said, "You agreed I could say where we are going."

As Rachel moved into the left turn lane to wait for a green arrow she said, "OK my hero, then where are we going?"

Marshawn smiled and said, "We are going to lunch at Tres Toros Cantina . . . in their new location."

As she drove toward Tres Toros, Marshawn said, "I feel helpless without my gun. I wish they didn't have to keep it."

Rachel said, "No need to worry, dear," and patted her purse which contained her Springfield 9mm.

15 Whiskey and King

It took more than three hours of surveillance, analysis, and intense discussion for authorities to decide that the Airbus 320 sitting at the end of the Gateway Airport runway was not going to move. No one had seen or reported seeing terrorists leaving the plane. Finally, through high-powered binoculars and from viewing at a certain angle, they realized the door was not completely closed. With no activity for so long and with the door slightly ajar, they determined the plane was empty.

Since the plane had not become airborne, FAA authorities cleared the no-fly conditions and air travel resumed. However, air traffic had been disrupted for nearly four hours and all commercial flights in the Phoenix region were delayed or canceled during that time. It was a huge mess. The terrorists were successful in disrupting America for several hours.

Meanwhile, Mesa police and federal agencies brought in a bomb squad and approached the plane. A large van, the high-tech kind used for crisis management, rolled down the taxi-way accompanied by many law enforcement vehicles. The van stopped about 100 yards away from the Airbus and law enforcement personnel came down the steps of the van onto the tarmac; accompanied by two highly trained bomb-sniffing dogs.

These two dogs were Belgian Malinois, pronounced "mallin-wah." Law enforcement agencies had been using Malinois dogs more frequently in recent years as there were fewer health problems with the breed as compared to German Shepherds, such as the development of hip problems that was a Shepherd trait. The Malinois were about the same size as a German Shepherd and had the same look but with shorter hair. Malinois often had a black face or muzzle and they were very intelligent dogs, with tremendous strength and energy.

Officer Whiskey, a sixty-pound reddish-brown female, was handled by Officer Frank Sapakie, and she had been in service for one year. Officer King, a plain-brown seventy-pound male, was handled by Officer Martha Wallace, and he had been in service for four years. The two handlers knelt and talked to the dogs as other law enforcement gathered around, all of them staying near the van. It was still unsafe to approach the plane but they needed to confirm that there were explosives on board. As the humans watched, the handlers released the two dogs and they ran quickly toward the plane.

When the dogs got to the plane they put their noses to the ground and began moving back and forth around and under it. Suddenly Whiskey stopped right under the door of the plane and sat down. She looked toward Officer Sapakie and just sat there, waiting for further commands. Meanwhile, King continued sniffing and went along the front of the plane and started sniffing in the direction the terrorists had run. Suddenly King let out a bark and started walking quickly down the maintenance road, sniffing the ground and occasionally sniffing the air. He was about twenty or thirty yards in front of the nose of the plane.

Officer Wallace called loudly, "King! Freeze!" King stopped but did not sit down. He stayed in a firm stance looking down the maintenance road, his body trembling as his muscles quivered with excitement.

The commanding officer of the bomb squad, Captain Bart Sossaman, said, "What's going on?"

Both Officer Sapakie and Officer Wallace started talking at once. Then they both smiled and Officer Wallace motioned with her hand for Officer Sapakie to speak. He said, "Whiskey is telling me there are explosives on board. At a command, I can call her back. . . . Wallace?" Officer Sapakie returned the polite hand gesture to Officer Wallace, signaling her turn to speak.

Officer Wallace spoke, "I believe King has picked up a trail. I'm guessing the terrorists left the plane and went down that road. Residue from the explosives would be on their clothes or hands or maybe in a backpack. Those explosives left a vapor wake which King picked up. He is waiting for us to join him or I can call him back."

Of course Captain Sossaman knew all of that, having been a seasoned bomb squad leader, but he wanted to confirm and he wanted the rest of the squad to hear it. He gave some instructions to two officers inside the van and then he called to his squad, "Let's suit up and get our equipment. We have some explosives to retrieve and diffuse." He turned to the regular police officers and said, "We'll need some additional officers with rifles to accompany Wallace and King down that road."

Officer Sapakie called to Whiskey and she ran back to him. He rubbed her ears and her neck and face and praised her for her excellent work. Officer Wallace called out, "King! Stay!" King obeyed the order even while trembling with anticipation.

For the next several minutes, everyone was busy preparing. The regular officers checked their Kevlar vests and all their equipment and inserted 30 round magazines into the receivers of their M-16s, levered shells into their chambers, and flipped their safety levers to "Safe." The bomb squad officers began donning protective Kevlar suits, helmets, and face masks—not just vests, but whole suits—and began gathering equipment. Some of the equipment was technical, like electronics, while other equipment was mechanical, like shields and poles.

When everyone was ready they began approaching the plane. The bomb squad and Whisky reached the plane and stopped near the door. The other group skirted the plane and started toward the maintenance road. Their path of travel caused all the officers to now be in relatively close proximity to the plane.

Unknown to the officers, a terrorist was waiting in a clump of bushes about a half-mile away watching them through binoculars. He was patiently waiting for the opportune moment, his thumb poised over a detonator button.

*   *   *

The terrorist had been sitting there in the bushes and for three hours he had been watching through his binoculars as the police cars gathered near the tarmac and different people came and went. Then he saw a large van and several police cars come slowly down the taxi-way and approach the plane. He saw them stop, he saw them release the dogs, and he waited for the right time to detonate the four duffle bags of explosives that he and his fellow jihadists had rigged up and left on the plane.

As the dogs reached the plane the terrorist just smiled to himself. He knew the dogs would identify that there were explosives and he didn't care, because as soon as the humans came to remove and diffuse the bombs, he would detonate them, killing all of the people and the dogs and destroying the aircraft. He looked toward the terminal and saw news vans with their dish antennae in the air. He had no doubt that they had cameras rolling with telephoto lenses and would show the massive explosion all over the news. He smiled again.

They had planned well for this. His detonator had a range of one mile as long as it was in direct line of sight with no hills or buildings in the way, and if needed they had also configured a second detonator that he could set off by a call from his cell phone. This was going to be glorious!

The terrorist watched the Americans and one dog approach the plane. Some went around the far side of the plane but when they started down the maintenance road near the second dog they would draw close enough that the blast may still reach them, at least enough to injure them if they weren't killed. The terrorist could hardly wait. He got the detonator ready in his right hand while he watched through the binoculars in his left hand.

The first set of Americans reached the plane and began moving equipment around. One of them reached up with a pole to the door of the plane to push it open. About that time the group who had gone toward the maintenance road had just reached the other dog. Both teams were as close to the plane as they would be. In a few moments, the second group would probably move down the road and away from the plane. As the handler stopped and reached down to praise the dog, the terrorist pushed the button on the detonator.

Nothing happened!

He checked the detonator. The light was on, showing it had power. He pushed the button again and again. Nothing! If he didn't hurry, the group on the road would be out of range. He quickly raised his smartphone up and pressed a speed dial icon on the screen. He watched the screen to see the call start, knowing that at the first ring, the entire area would shudder with the sound of a loud explosion, and human body parts and pieces of airplane would fly everywhere.

Still nothing! He hung up and dialed again. Nothing! He was furious. He growled to himself, "Rrrrr!"

That was his first mistake. King heard the terrorist's growl and knew someone was out there, although he couldn't pinpoint the exact location yet. As King looked, Officer Wallace saw the dogs' ears perk up and she said to the others, "There's someone out there. Keep your eyes peeled."

The terrorist's second mistake came next. He pushed the speed dial on his phone that would dial Al-Musawi and waited for a connection. When he heard Mansoor Fatik Al-Musawi answer, he said quietly in a foreign language but with the following meaning, "They have a jammer. They jammed all radio and cell phone waves around the plane and it took out both of my signals. Their van must be well equipped and very powerful. I have to go!"

Unfortunately for the terrorist, King heard the entire conversation although he didn't understand it, nor would he have understood it even in English. However, the conversation allowed King to pinpoint precisely where the sound was coming from. He looked directly at the clump of bushes and detected movement the human officers didn't see yet. With Officer Wallace's permission, King began moving toward the terrorist, pulling Wallace who was holding the leash, followed by the rest of the team.

The terrorist dropped the now useless detonator and pulled up his rifle. He looked up and saw that the group of officers was over a quarter of a mile away. They were still slightly out of range, so he flipped off the safety and waited.

When the group was about 200 yards away, the terrorist decided it was time. He raised his rifle and started firing. He shot a burst of bullets with his fully automatic rifle. Several of the shots struck near the officers but did no damage. That was fortunate because although Kevlar could stop bullets fired from pistols, it was ineffective at stopping bullets fired from rifles. The officers spread out, flanking the terrorist's position, firing back as they crouched and ran. Officer Wallace yelled to the other officers, "Don't shoot King!"

None of the officers could clearly see the terrorist yet due to his concealment in the bushes, so their shots were also ineffective.

The terrorist looked right and left, firing back and forth at each group, but hit no one. At the precise moment that he jammed in a second magazine he realized that a brown hulk of fur was barreling right at him.

He threw his gun up to fire but before he got a shot off, the now airborne animal slammed into him like a freight train, knocking him back into the bushes and biting hard on his right arm. His rifle went flying and landed in the dirt. The terrorist screamed in pain and tried to stand up but the heavy dog was biting his arm and standing on top of him, pinning him to the ground. He tried to reach with his left hand for the pistol tucked in his waistband at the small of his back but the dog moved off of him and pulled hard on his arm. The motion of the dog still locked on his arm, now pulling to the side and almost above his head, sent excruciating pain shooting through his arm and he screamed again in agony and terror. He forgot about trying to grab his pistol.

By that point several officers had arrived and jumped on the terrorist, one grabbing his left arm and two others jumping on his legs. He was more than happy when the woman called commands to the dog and it let go of his arm and backed toward her.

As the police officers rolled the terrorist onto his face in the dirt and short grass, he heard the woman talking to the dog in tones of lavish praise, "Good boy, King! Good dog! You did it!"

16 Extraordinary

It was like a slow-motion replay; similar to a close-up of an Olympic diver on a high-scoring dive slicing perfectly and quietly into the water without a splash. It was smooth. It was subtle. It was pure . . . raw . . . physical . . . with absolute finesse.

But this wasn't water and a finely sculpted Olympian's body.

This was ice cream and a spoon.

She said softly, "Fat equals flavor," as she slowly and tenderly pushed the spoon into the ice cream.

There was no splash.

She was not in a hurry. She was savoring every moment. In fact, the anticipation was almost as good as she knew the ice cream was going to taste.

Her target was just inside the outer edge of the scoop. She liked that heavenly penumbra on the very edge of the sphere that was melting ahead of the other ice cream and was softly resting against the side of the bowl. It was shiny and creamy and a slightly lighter color than the rest of the scoop. She savored the thought of her spoon containing some of the firmer part of the scoop plus that luscious melted edge.

She had always loved ice cream as far back as she could remember. Her parents even told her how much she loved ice cream as a child when she would pound on her bowl or on the table with her spoon until they would give her more or take her down from her high chair while she wailed in despair. She had told people before that she tried to live a good life so that she could get to heaven someday to meet the person who invented ice cream because she was sure the inventor would be there. She was only half-joking.

But this was not just ordinary ice cream. This was Kroger brand Private Selection Black Raspberry Dark Chocolate Chunk. Almost all ice cream lay on a scale somewhere between great and fantastic, but this was a tier above fantastic—heavenly maybe. What's above that?

She had always loved chocolate, but she had an extra affinity for dark chocolate. Dark chocolate was lovely as any other chocolate, but with a bite to it, almost like a dreamy-handsome vampire boyfriend. This Kroger's dark chocolate was in little chunks that were semi-soft. Not as hard as a chocolate chip, but a little softer so they smashed reverently and subtly between your teeth as you slowly bit into them. They were *also* heavenly.

And the Black Raspberry ice cream itself was just as divine. It was smooth, full of flavor, a soft mauve color, with just the right taste of raspberry. Sweet, not tart.

She lightly scraped the spoon against the side of the bowl to get as much of the softened, melted ice cream from where it gently rested between the edge of the scoop and the side of the bowl.

She raised the spoon slowly and deliberately to her lips.

She knew this was not going to be just an ordinary bite of ice cream. This was a sensual, craving, physical, "gotta-have-it-or-I'll-die" bite of ice cream.

But all still in slow motion.

For an extraordinary moment in your life like this one, you don't just put the spoon into your mouth right side up. That's too proper and detached and straight-laced. And who wants to have the hard, tasteless spoon on your tongue instead of the nirvana-flavored creaminess? This was physical, all-in, total, and absolutely personal. She closed her eyes and turned the spoon upside down and pushed it into her mouth.

There was no splash.

She thought again the words she stated just moments before, *fat equals flavor*. This was absolutely *not* low-fat ice cream and she was definitely in it for the flavor. This was a brilliant burst of flavor, like a Girl Scout Cookie on steroids, and the texture was just as wonderful. Smooth. Creamy. Luscious. It subtly enveloped her tongue in comfort, like putting on a pre-shrunk cashmere sweater right out of the clothes dryer on a cold morning, except that was soft and warm and this was soft and cool.

The chilly sensation of black raspberry manna from the gods touched the inside of her lips and flowed across her tongue. She slowly withdrew the spoon, using the tip of her tongue and her upper lip to carefully scrape off any ice cream that tried to stick to it. She wanted all the ice cream in her mouth!

When the spoon passed beyond her lips, she held it up in front of her face and twisted it slightly to examine both sides. Satisfied that she had, in fact, cleaned all the ice cream off, she continued to savor the melting sensation in her mouth.

With the spoon now out of the way the ice cream oozed its coolness across her tongue, onto her teeth and the insides of her cheeks. It slowly melted and flowed to the back of her mouth and she swallowed gently and deliberately as her eyes closed again and then rolled back into her head. She reveled in the sublime flavor of the melted ice cream.

The bits of dark chocolate remained in her mouth, trapped by her tongue, and she carefully positioned them into the space between her teeth. She slowly clenched her jaw and the chocolate smashed softly between her molars. The feel of the slightly firm chocolate blended with the taste of the dark cocoa in her mouth and she smiled. Texture and taste were joined in wedded bliss for a few short seconds in her mouth. It was satisfaction, pleasure, and success all at once. Her smile broadened as her face beamed.

There was no need to hurry. She drew in a breath through her nose with her eyes still closed, like when you first climb out of the car after a long drive to your cabin in the pines and you stop and savor the wonderful smell of the mountains.

Then she said, not loudly but out loud and mostly to herself in total, uncontrolled pleasure, "Oh, my! That is soooooo good!"

Her moment of ecstasy was interrupted by a female voice, spoken in a loud whisper.

"Really, Mandy?! This is a restaurant full of people. You're embarrassing us."

A different female voice said, "Yeah, *stop*! People are staring!"

Mandy didn't care about what the people around them thought. She burst into laughter, "You two fuddy-duddies! You are acting like James in Audit. Where's your sense of excitement and adventure?"

The reference to James broke the tension and made them all burst into hearty girlfriend laughter. James in the auditing department was a quintessential stick-in-the-mud. He had almost as much personality as a potted plant. He never laughed or got excited. They *almost* got him to smile. Once. He was monotone, dull, boring. However, he was an excellent auditor, so the firm kept him on board.

Mandy had been coming to this restaurant in downtown Mesa for several years. She was the front-office receptionist at a mid-sized CPA firm, Phelps & Danaco. She and her close friends from work, Bonnie and Tandi, frequented the Garden Glen once or twice a week. Yes, they had to endure the questions every time they met someone new, "Oh? Mandy and Tandi? Are you twins?" or "Mandy and Tandi! Hey, that rhymes!" They used to reply, but finally gave up and just rolled their eyes and moved on.

They went to other restaurants at times, but they ate at the Garden Glen more than any other place. The entrees were delicious and the staff was very friendly. Now and then a male employee turned out to be a hunk, but sadly the hunks didn't seem to last long enough at the Garden Glen.

One time, about a year earlier, Margo, the owner of the Garden Glen, had overheard them discussing ice cream and Mandy had said how much she loved Kroger Private Selection Black Raspberry Dark Chocolate Chunk. The next time they came for lunch, Margo surprised her with an oversized scoop of Mandy's favorite ice cream. She was delighted. She ordered it often and never tired of it.

It was Wednesday, and they had come for lunch to their favorite place. In spite of the terrorist activity in the Phoenix area earlier that week and even that morning, they felt relatively safe in the quiet downtown area of Mesa.

Mesa used to be a sleepy little town but had since surpassed 450,000 people. As with other towns-turned-city, the downtown area had slumped and then had been revived with significant investment, but it was still a relatively quiet part of town. As they ate they watched the light rail going down Main Street. Engineers had quickly repaired the track in Tempe where Monday's bombing occurred, working round the clock, and the light rail had just started running that morning. They looked down the street toward the beautiful Mesa Arts Center which hosted some of the greatest entertainers of the time and also of the past.

They finished eating and started walking the two blocks back to Phelps & Danaco.

As they approached a van parked parallel to the curb, Mandy noticed that the swinging back doors of the van were open and she could see the legs of someone standing in the gutter behind the open door, but she didn't think anything of it.

As they drew alongside the van a tall man stepped out from behind the van door. He looked like he was from the Middle East and was dressed in black, with a coarse beard and a large knife in his hand.

The man stepped up onto the sidewalk in front of the three young women. Bonnie gasped and they all stopped simultaneously.

The man said fairly loudly, "Who is a Christian?" He spoke decent English with just a hint of a foreign accent.

Other people on the street stopped and gasped too. It happened so fast, no one had a chance to react yet. Clearly, the week's terrorist activity had now reached downtown Mesa and three young women dressed in their professional attire were the first victims.

Bonnie was the first to speak and she said boldly, "I am a Christian."

Tandi replied as well, "I'm a Christian, too."

Mandy looked up at the towering man and looked him right in the eye and said, "I'm a Christian, too; but I feel sorry for you."

The man wagged the knife toward her face and replied incredulously, "Sorry for me? Why? Because I'm not a Christian?!"

Mandy said, "No, sorry for you that you only brought a knife to a gunfight," and even as she spoke, she smoothly drew her Kahr 9mm Black Rose edition from the back of her waistband beneath her jacket and aimed it at the man. Within a split second, she punched three shots into the terrorist. The sound was deafening and he had a shocked look on his face as he slowly dropped the knife and melted to the sidewalk.

There was no splash.

Everyone was stunned! *Mandy did that?!*

As people came running up, Mandy coolly reholstered her Kahr in the back of her waistband and the three young women gave each other a group hug. Bonnie and Tandi were crying, but Mandy was still supercharged with adrenalin. She wasn't smiling but had a look of intensity on her face. It hadn't hit her yet that she was almost killed in a gruesome act of violence, and instead, she herself had killed another human being with her concealed weapon.

After the hug, and as they stood there talking, a police officer came up and said, "Is everyone OK? Who fired the shots?"

Mandy sheepishly raised her hand like a little schoolgirl while Bonnie and Tandi pointed to her.

Bonnie smiled with relief and said, "She's just a normal receptionist, but she's extraordinary in my book."

17   Meet the Teacher

Alison Katz was a kindergarten teacher in a lower-class neighborhood in an older part of town. Alison was also one of the best kindergarten teachers you could ever find. However, right now she didn't feel like one of the best. In fact, she felt terrible. Alison was in pain. She had picked up a cold from one of the kids (probably from three or four of them, actually), and she had an ear infection. She had had ear problems as a child and now she was very susceptible to an ear infection from any cold she ever caught. They always seemed to get worse (the cold, not the kids) and then settled in one or both of her ears. It could be very painful.

She had fought with the cold for a few days, and the pain in her ear got worse and worse so she finally called her doctor. She hated to leave school but she had to get rid of this ear infection or she would miss a full day or more. The doctor had squeezed in an appointment for her in the middle of the day near lunchtime and she was able to arrange to have Mr. Huddlestein, the music teacher, take her class to lunch and then to their music time. If she was lucky she could get to the doctor and the pharmacy and get back before music was over. Hopefully, the medication would kick in before she went to bed. She hadn't slept well for a few days.

It was Wednesday and, as she drove, she listened to the breaking news. The terrorist situations on Monday had put the Phoenix metro area on high alert. However, Tuesday was free from any problems, so they had started thinking that Monday was just a one-time thing. This morning some terrorists had hijacked a bus and blew it up. Fortunately, the bus driver carried a gun and was able to shoot the terrorists and get everyone off the bus before it exploded. It appeared the terrorists were trying to use the bus to blow up a hospital or a school. Other terrorists had also stolen a plane but had left it sitting on the end of the runway and then abandoned it full of explosives. However, bomb-handling personnel were able to keep the bombs from going off and then diffused the explosives. The only casualties were two police officers and four terrorists. Another terrorist had been taken down by a police dog and was in custody.

Alison was relieved that she had her gun with her today. Well, sort of. State law wouldn't allow her to carry her gun at school. She kept it in her SUV in a locked metal case that was attached to the bottom of the driver's seat by a cable. The law said she was supposed to keep it unloaded, but she kept it loaded. *What good is an unloaded gun? That's like a car with no gas!*

She was not what you'd call a gun lover but she was not afraid of guns. Her husband had been trying to get her to carry a gun for years and she had finally given in just a few months earlier. They spent some time shopping and finally bought her a Smith and Wesson Governor. It was a large gun as far as handguns go but she felt comfortable with it. It was a revolver that shot several different types of ammo, but she preferred the .410 shotgun shells with 00 buckshot.

The Governor held six shots, but with the .410 and double-ought buckshot, each round had five balls about the size of a .38 caliber bullet. They could penetrate four to six inches into the human body. Besides, with buckshot you didn't have to be perfectly accurate. That old saying about "close only counts in horseshoes and hand grenades" could also apply to shotguns and 00 buckshot.

Alison finished with the doctor and, thanks to the nurse who phoned the prescription into the pharmacy, made a quick stop at the store to get the medication. As she approached her school she decided she was going to take her gun in and keep it zipped inside her briefcase. She knew it was a risk but with the things that were happening this week, and even just this morning, she decided she would rather be safe than sorry. The belief that the bus may have targeted an elementary school was too scary to be ignored.

At a major intersection about a mile from her school Alison caught a red light. She used the opportunity to quickly turn the SUV off and pull the keys. She unlocked the gun case and even got the keys back in the ignition and started the SUV just as the light turned green. As she drove she put the Governor down into her briefcase and was going to zip it closed when she got to the school.

As was the standard nowadays her elementary school was completely fenced. If the gates were all closed as they should be, the only way into the school was through the front office. However, Alison's room was near the front and right by a gate, so for her it was easy to access and she had a key to the gate.

As she pulled up to the school she glanced at the gate by her room and was surprised to see three men standing there. When she looked more closely she noticed they all had guns that looked like AK-47s. They were dressed in black and clearly looked like the radical Islamists she had seen on TV and Facebook—the kind that are shown beheading people and causing havoc around the world.

As she quickly pulled into the angle parking spot and looked back over her shoulder, she saw the men turn and walk across the front of the school toward the office.

Her face took on a look of determination and she actually said to herself out loud, "Not on your life!"

Alison had taught school for over twenty years. She had taught a few different grades and had even taught Special Education one year, but she loved kindergarten the best. Some of the kids were challenging because they had not learned how to behave in school yet. Some of them had difficult family situations due to this area being a lower-class neighborhood. Kids in richer neighborhoods still had family problems, divorce, death of loved ones, etc., but a lower-class neighborhood had a unique set of problems. The kids had to deal with poverty and hunger, physical or other abuse, parents in prison or being arrested or addicted to drugs, etc. Some of her kids had had significant trauma in their lives and had resulting psychological and behavioral problems as a result.

Another challenge was class size. It was so stressful when she had twenty-five or twenty-eight or even thirty kids. Kindergarteners needed so much help because they hadn't learned to take care of themselves in school yet. Some of them still wet their pants—they were only five years old. Trying to meet the needs of so many young children, even with a Teacher's Aide and with mother helpers at times, was still a tremendous load. By the end of each school week, Alison was completely exhausted. Some weekends she spent hours on Saturday and Sunday just sleeping to recover from the stress from the prior week.

However, Alison knew who she was, and that gave her the strength to carry on week after week and year after year. She knew she was building a foundation that would help them succeed as they continued in school. Because of that, she lovingly but firmly pushed her kids to learn as much as she could cram into their five-year-old heads. If they got out of her class with the ability to read and write, a skill normally learned in

1st grade, then they were that much further ahead of others who had only mastered the alphabet when they were in kindergarten. Sometimes success in school helped them overcome personal and social problems.

Alison had to keep a professional distance, but she also loved each of her students. Now and then they would give her a hug and she knew that meant they loved her. When her former students would see her and say, "Hi, Mrs. Katz!" she felt a powerful sense of accomplishment. She knew from the upper-grade teachers that her kids did pretty well in their classes, and they all knew it was because of the tremendous springboard launch she gave them in kindergarten.

Because of the love Alison had for her kids she was also very protective of them. When a bus driver was rude to a child Alison firmly explained to the driver that such behavior was unacceptable. When an older student bullied one of her kids, she made sure the bully was held accountable. She took anyone to task who was not respectful of her students, always professionally but thoroughly.

So today, when she saw three armed men outside her school, her protective mode kicked in with full force. She had no fear for herself—she was defending the children that were put into her care. She didn't even lock her car or worry about her briefcase. She grabbed the Governor and jumped out the door.

By the time Alison rounded the corner of her SUV two of the men were just starting to go inside the school. The third had lingered near the gate to look at his watch. Her mind was racing and she had the fleeting thought that she was glad she had worn slacks and flats to work that day. She couldn't see herself in a gun fight in a skirt and heels. She shook the distracting thoughts from her mind so she could focus.

Alison ran across the parking lot and as she got onto the sidewalk she heard the voice of Lisa, the front desk receptionist over the loudspeaker. There was an urgency to Lisa's voice as she said, "Lockdown! Lockdown! Immediate lockdown!" and then Alison heard shots over the loudspeaker. It was chilling, but she didn't have time to stop.

The terrorist who lingered behind was just getting ready to turn the corner to the front door. She yelled, "Hey!" and kept running toward him.

He turned to look, and as he did so she stopped, aimed, and fired two shots. The buckshot did its job of spreading out and something connected. The terrorist started to raise his gun but instead got a strange look on his face and toppled forward into the grass by the sidewalk.

Alison reached him as he rolled onto his back and she could see that one of the balls had gone into his neck and blood was pouring from the wound. Another ball had hit him in the face. Blood oozing into his clothing showed her that several other balls had hit him in the body. As she looked at the terrorist she heard gunfire inside the school and her anger increased.

Alison knew this terrorist was no longer a threat but there were two more. She thought about taking the terrorist's gun but she didn't really know how to use it. She didn't even know where the safety was and didn't want to take time to find out. She shifted the Governor to her left hand and grabbed the stock of the terrorist's gun with her right hand. She spun around, kind of like a discus thrower, and threw the heavy rifle as hard as she could. It sailed up onto the roof of the school. She didn't want an unattended gun lying around on the school grounds where a kid could get it.

She switched the Governor back to her right hand and ran to the door. As she ran, the elementary school teacher in her kicked in and she couldn't stop herself from thinking, *If your gun held six rounds and you had to shoot three terrorists, how many shots should you shoot at each terrorist to shoot an equal number of shots at each one?*

Alison smiled wryly and swung open the door with her left hand, her gun pointing into the room. As she stepped inside, she realized she didn't know if it was a good idea to just go barging in but she was worried about who might be fighting for their lives and she knew seconds mattered. She also hoped an element of surprise might work in her favor.

Inside the front reception area she didn't see any terrorists but she saw carnage. The front area of a school almost always had some activity. There were usually a few people coming and going. Today was no different, except that the people coming and going had been in the line of fire.

Alison looked toward the reception desk and saw Lisa lying face down on the floor, covered with blood. Apparently, she had turned off the intercom as she died because only a few shots had been heard. The massacre in the front office was not broadcast to the whole school, thankfully.

Lying next to Lisa was Charmaine, the attendance secretary. She was also covered with blood and was not moving.

Right in front of the main counter was a third or fourth grader and what was probably his mother. Both were lying still, side by side, with the mother's arm across her son in perhaps a last effort to protect her child.

A child and the school nurse lay in the doorway to the Health Center. Alison looked at the child to see if it was a student she knew and gasped in shock. It was Edie. She was one of Alison's students last year and was a beautiful little girl with long, dark hair. Edie had gone through some pretty rough times as a kindergartner due to problems in her family but Alison had been told that Edie was doing very well in first grade. The protective emotion in Alison now increased to include both protection and additional anger that someone would gun down one of the students that she loved.

Two more kids were laying further down the hall. Alison couldn't tell what reason they had for being there, but it was sadly at the wrong time. She didn't recognize them.

It was heartbreaking, but Alison couldn't stop to mourn.

She wondered where Danielle was. Danielle McNeese was the principal and was one of the best principals for whom Alison had ever worked. Danielle's office was near Lisa's desk, but Danielle was nowhere to be seen. Alison feared the worst.

Alison heard a few shots and some bullets smacked into the front doors behind her. One of the terrorists had been down the hall some distance and had seen her as she came through the door. He was coming back and had fired a few shots at her.

Alison jumped over the counter right into Lisa's work area, scattering the items that had been lying on top of the counter. She actually landed on Lisa and it was all she could do to keep from being overcome with grief and nausea. She knew she had only seconds to get to a safe position.

She scooted under Lisa's desk. She realized she was right where the mail slot was at the front counter. The mail basket was sitting on the floor and she pushed it aside and pointed the muzzle of the Governor toward the mail slot.

The reception counter was higher than the level of a regular desk. It was just the right height so that when parents brought their children into the school they could easily fill out the sign-in form without having to bend over. Alison looked out through mail slot just as the terrorist leaned up against the counter to look for her. She hoped her legs were pulled under far enough.

Through the mail slot she could see only fabric and she realized it was the terrorist's pants. His groin and pelvic area were right against the mail slot. The Governor was already in position, pointed out the mail slot, so Alison pulled the trigger.

In the enclosed space, the sound was deafening. However, the damage to her hearing was far less than the damage done to the terrorist.

At ten or fifteen yards, like had just happened outside, the five balls of 00 buckshot could spread apart by anywhere from a few inches to two feet by the time they hit the target. However, right where they came out of the muzzle, all five balls were in a tight formation, almost like one piece of steel. That steel was traveling at about 1,500 feet per second or just over 1,000 miles per hour and it was probably heated to a few hundred degrees by the explosion of gunpowder that caused the .410 shell to fire. In a split second the shot tore clear through the terrorist's body with one hole and came out through his lower backbone as one slightly bigger, jagged hole.

The terrorist roared with pain and fell back away from the counter, shouting something in a foreign language. She looked through the mail slot and saw him writhing on the floor in front of the nurse's office. He obviously had no ability to use his weapon and as Alison came around the end of the counter, she thought about just leaving him because there was no way he would survive.

She had three shots left, but she couldn't bear to see him suffer. He probably deserved to suffer, but she decided she would let God be the judge of that. She pointed the Governor at his head and pulled the trigger again. He stopped screaming and after a few muscle spasms laid still.

Alison grabbed the terrorist's gun and quickly placed it on the floor in Danielle's office because it had a locking door. She made sure the knob was locked and pulled the door closed.

She stepped back out into the hall and looked to see where the other terrorist was. She figured he had gone down the main hall and was around the corner. She started walking that direction and heard a noise to her left. She suddenly realized the third terrorist was down a side corridor only about fifteen yards away from her. Evidently, the screams of his companion had caused him to quickly circle back around to the reception area, approaching from the other hall.

She turned her head and looked into his face. She mentally kicked herself for worrying about the suffering terrorist and the unattended gun.

If she had been more concerned with the third man, she may not have been caught off guard like this.

Alison had walked a few steps down the main hallway already, putting the terrorist in the side corridor directly to her left but also a bit behind her. She was almost looking over her shoulder at him. For her to get a clear shot, she would have to turn her whole body around —a long way when the other person already had a gun pointed at you.

The terrorist's AK-47 was already aimed at Alison but he just stared at her for a few moments, almost as if in disbelief with what he was seeing. Alison wondered if he was thinking, "*A woman infidel with a gun? Can she do that?*"

Alison heard shots and expected to feel bullets tear into her body but she felt no pain. She looked at the terrorist and realized he was no longer pointing his gun at her. He tried to take a step but his knees went wobbly as he collapsed. Alison looked past him and there was Danielle McNeese in a perfect shooter's stance with both hands holding a semi-automatic pistol. Alison didn't know, and didn't care anyway, that it was a Hi-Point 9mm.

Alison said, "Oh! That was close. Thank you!"

Danielle said, "No, that was scary! You were too close to my line of fire. I stepped as far as I could to my left to change the angle, but you were still too close for comfort. I'm glad I wasn't shooting my Taurus Judge with discs or buckshot. This week I've been carrying my 9mm because it holds eight rounds instead of five, and today the buckshot would have been bad."

Danielle continued, "I was not in my office when they came in, but when I heard Lisa over the intercom and heard the shots fired, I ran to my car. If they would only let us carry our guns in school . . . . Whoever thinks a gun-free zone is a good idea is a total idiot!"

Alison said, "I don't think you or I could have saved Lisa and Charmaine or the others who were close to the door, but maybe if they had been armed . . . or better yet, if they were armed and there was *also* an armed guard at the front . . . ."

Alison paused and Danielle could envision the wheels in Alison's head spinning as she thought.

Alison continued. "Well, at least I know this: two of us with weapons stopped three gunmen and if more of us had been armed I can't help but think more of us would have survived. Better yet, if the terrorists knew there were people in the school with weapons maybe they wouldn't have come here in the first place."

Alison paused and breathed a heavy sigh before continuing, "Lisa died bravely protecting our school. This could have been so much worse."

Danielle nodded quietly. Then, being the good leader that she was, she stepped around to the intercom and flipped the switch to reach all areas of the campus, "Teachers and students. This is Principal McNeese. You are safe, but the lockdown is still in force. Please remain in your rooms. We will give you more information as soon as we can. Thank you for your patience." Her voice had been strong but as soon as she finished she looked around her and neither woman could hold back the tears any longer.

The police arrived minutes later to find three dead terrorists, one outside the school and two inside. In addition, they found two women in the front office; surrounded by bodies and each with a gun nearby. One of them was kneeling in the blood on the floor next to her two office assistants; her hands on her knees and her head bowed, sobbing. The other was sitting cross-legged near the wall with tears streaming down her cheeks. She was cradling the small body of her former student in her arms, singing a lullaby in a quavering voice and gently rocking the child as if to help her peacefully go to sleep.

18 The Cowboys

Max and Mel Dahlquist were brothers, and they had been brothers for a long time. Max was eighty-eight and Mel was eighty-six. They had lived and worked together all their lives and had experienced many adventures together. Now in their later years they didn't have a lot to do. Their wives had both passed away and they were retired. They had decided to live together to share expenses and to have companionship. In spite of their advanced age they were very healthy and spry, although they mostly sat around and played cards. They talked a lot about the good old days and about the sorry state of the world and politics and many other things.

They went for walks and stayed active in various ways but most of their exercise was done in the pool at a gym near their house. As their doctor had advised swimming as a non-impact exercise, they would go to the gym every day around noon and swim for about an hour.

That Wednesday in February was no exception, in spite of the events of the week. With terrorist attacks happening on Monday in the Phoenix area, some people had curtailed their usual activity, but not Max and Mel. They still went to the gym that Wednesday.

As they were getting ready to leave, Mel asked, "Got your pea shooter?"

Max replied, "I've got my pea shooter just like I've got my arthritis. It's always with me. Unfortunately, my arthritis isn't near as enjoyable as my gun. Plus, today I got my cannon to go along with my pea shooter. With a week like we have, who knows if my cannon might be needed."

Mel said, "Just checking on you. We are getting old, you know, and we are starting to have memory problems. I got my pea shooter too, as well as my cannon."

Max retorted, "What? I don't remember anything about having memory problems. What did you say your name was?" He intentionally gave Mel a blank look as he said that, knowing that his younger brother knew good and well that Max never forgot to take his gun anywhere. He also knew they both had pulled out their larger pistols to go with the smaller ones they usually carried.

Both Max and Mel carried concealed weapons. Because old guys often had circulation problems and had to work at staying warm, wearing a vest, jacket, or sweater was already easy to do and they both carried their pistol in the back of their waistband.

Since both had fought in the Korean War, they had a great love for the 1911-style weapons that they had used during their service. Their 1911s from the war were collectors' pieces now and they had each bought modern versions of their favorite sidearm for their concealed weapon. Max preferred a Springfield model and Mel preferred a Colt Government model; both guns were .45 caliber.

In addition to their 1911 pistols Max and Mel owned many other guns. Along the way Max had bought a Taurus Raging Bull .454 Casull, which was a very powerful revolver. Not to be outdone, Mel had bought an Arsenal double-barrel 1911 .45 caliber. It was kind of a novelty weapon, with two magazines and side-by-side barrels as a semi-automatic pistol. The double-barrel 1911 shot very well and when the brothers went out shooting with their "cannons", as they called them, they could really throw the lead. Max's .454 shot 250-grain bullets with twice the impact energy as a .44 magnum. Mel loaded his Arsenal .45 with 230-grain bullets, but with two shots fired at the same time he was shooting 460 grains of lead with every pull of the trigger. *Serious lead!*

As they arrived at the gym they noticed that the parking lot wasn't as full as usual. They grabbed their bags from their truck, walked across the parking lot and through the door. They said "Hi" to Mitch and Alyssa, the clerks at the front desk. They knew them so well that they didn't even need to show their membership cards anymore.

Mel said as he passed the desk, "Is the water as wet as yesterday? Yesterday I ended up all wrinkly!"

Mitch and Alyssa both smiled and Max said, "Mel, you are always wrinkly. I don't think anyone could get more wrinkly than you."

Mel said, "Well, you are probably more wrinkly than me since you are two years older."

Max said, "Not me. I always said you should have used Oil of Olay like I did all my life."

Mitch and Alyssa laughed at the banter from the two brothers. One or both of them always had something funny to say as they came in each day.

The gym was designed like a pie, with each area angling out away from the front lobby. The first wedge of the pie, to the far left, was the exercise room, with treadmills, stair steppers, and many assorted versions of those types of equipment. There were TV monitors covering the walls. The gym had glass walls almost everywhere, so you could easily see into each area. The exercise room was usually packed but today it was only about a third full.

As they passed the lobby they looked to the left at the second wedge of the pie. This contained the yoga rooms, with a hallway and several large classrooms, all easily visible due to the glass walls between each section. Not as crowded as usual, there were people doing yoga in one class and others doing Zumba in another class; their brightly colored outfits covering all different shapes and sizes of bodies.

Max said, "Mel, I sure enjoy the bright colors of their outfits."

Mel replied, "I know, brother that it's not the *colors* of the outfits you enjoy, but it's the *shapes* of the outfits that draw your interest."

Max just kept walking, keeping a straight face and making no comment so as not to do any justice to Mel's accurate observation.

Straight behind the lobby was the pool. The area of the pool near the front was mostly a place where people relaxed in the water. Beyond that, turned sideways, was a typical rectangular pool with lane lines and floats for those who wanted to swim laps. Max and Mel often hung out in the front part of the pool for a few minutes before swimming laps.

To the right of the pool was a weight room and to the right of that was the final wedge of the pie—the running area. Runners went into this area but immediately climbed some stairs to the running tracks. In the running area there were actually two tracks, both on the second floor of the gym. One track was indoors so you could run in relative comfort even on summer days in Arizona when the temperature was frequently near 110 degrees and even at 5:00 in the morning when it was often well over ninety degrees. Through the glass, those in the other areas of the gym could occasionally see runners go overhead. The outdoor track was larger and more popular when the weather was nice. It was designed to look like a park. The only places the walls were not made of glass were the dressing rooms.

Max and Mel went into the pool area, placing their gym bags on a bench along the wall. Sometimes if they were coming from some other errand, they went into the dressing room and changed into swim trunks. Usually, like today, they came to the gym already wearing their trunks with sweats over the top and they just peeled off the sweats right next to the pool.

They especially wanted to stay close to their bags today because they wanted to have their pistols nearby if any terrorist activity continued.

On this occasion, as they were shedding their sweats they noticed three young women in the water on the far side of the stairs. As Max and Mel climbed down into the water they moved to the near side, so as to be closer to their bags and their weapons.

Max said, "Good morning ladies. I think I recognize you. Aren't you three usually in the yoga class? How come you're in the pool today?"

One of them replied, "Yes, we usually do yoga but we felt like swimming today."

Mel said, "Could it be that you wanted to be further from the front of the building, what with the terrorist activity and all?"

The three women just looked at each other and then back at Mel. None of them replied. Mel had hit the nail right on the head. Finally one said, "Well, actually yes. It is rather concerning."

Max said, "Well, it didn't keep you from coming."

One of them said, "We talked about it and decided we still wanted to come but we'll be a little more cautious."

Another of the women said, "We see you guys here all the time too, always in the pool. Why don't you ever do yoga?" The three women smiled at each other, enjoying the chance to tease and waiting to see how the brothers would reply."

Mel said, "Nah. We tried it one time, but afterward, we couldn't get Max out of his little spandex outfit. We finally had to cut him out of it. We decided to stick with swimming."

Max said, "Yep. The only problem is that swimming gets us all wrinkly."

The women smiled.

Mel said, "Well, not as bad as that one lady we saw once."

Max said, "We were sitting here the other day and a little old lady walked by. We are in our eighties, but she had to be older than us."

Mel said, "She was wearing a bikini, and after she passed and went into the dressing room, Max said to me, 'What was that?' I told him, 'I don't know, but it sure needs ironing!'"

The three women burst out laughing.

When the laughter died, Max said, as a statement, and not as a question, "So you women are trophy wives."

They all laughed and one said, "You could say that."

"What do your husbands do?"

The woman said, "Well, my name's Veronica, and my husband is a civil engineer." She pointed to the second woman and said, "Becky's husband is a dentist." She pointed to the third and said, "Lara's husband is a mortgage banker."

Mel said, "Any children?"

Veronica shook her head with a smile, "None for me."

Becky said, "I have one in first grade."

Lara said, "I have two; one in kindergarten and a toddler who hangs out with grandma while I come to the gym."

Max said, "Yep, trophy wives. Your husbands make good money and you get to come to the gym a few times a week. Don't get me wrong. I think if you can do that, then more power to you. Congratulations!"

Lara said, "How about you guys? Married?"

Mel said, "Both of our wives have passed on."

Becky said, "I'm sorry."

Max said, "No worries. We'll see them again someday. Besides, if we were still married to them we'd feel guilty talking to beautiful young women at the pool."

The women smiled.

Mel said, "They were sisters. Twins."

Veronica said, "Brothers married sisters? That doesn't happen every day."

Mel said, "Well, that's actually a fun story if you want to hear it." Max just rolled his eyes.

The women said they'd like to hear the story.

Mel continued, "Well, first you need to know that Max and I were cowboys all of our lives. We grew up in Wickenburg and our dad worked on a ranch. He died at a young age, killed in a fall off a horse. We had to start working as teenagers to support our mom and two sisters and we got hired on a ranch out past Wickenburg. One time when we were in our twenties we drove clear into Phoenix to a dance on a Friday night. Back then Phoenix was still relatively small and it was quite a drive from our ranch to Phoenix on the narrow winding roads. When we got to the dance they wouldn't let us in. They said we had to have neckties. You have to understand, we were eighty miles from home. We told the guy at the door, 'Listen, we came clear from Wickenburg and we didn't know we needed ties. Can you make an exception?' The guy wouldn't budge. We dragged our sorry carcasses back to our truck. By now Max had gotten mad and he said, 'We ain't goin' home! We came to dance. Let's find something like a necktie.' We thought of about everything we could think of. If we'd have had one of our saddles in the truck we could have used the cinch straps for leather ties, but we didn't have one. Finally, Max decided we'd use the jumper cables. They were old and beat up and a little rusty on the handles, but we carefully split the two different strands apart with a knife. Max wore the gray one and I wore the black one since that matched our outfits."

Mel winked at the women and they smiled, realizing he was trying to be funny.

"When we got back to the door, the guy said, 'Those aren't neckties!' Max got excited that time, and said, 'Listen, we drove eighty miles to come to this dance. We are just two rough cowboys and we didn't know we needed a tie. These jumper cables are the best we've got. You *have* to let us into this dance!' Well, Max's speech got that guy worked up too and he got a firm look on his face as he held up his index finger as if he was going to wag it or lecture us and show that he was serious. Then the edges of his mouth pulled up into a smile and he said, 'Ok. I'll let you into the dance with jumper cables, but don't try to start anything!'"

Two of the women caught the joke and burst out laughing. Mel said the punchline again, this time emphasizing, "...don't try to START anything." The other woman got it then and they all laughed for a long time.

Mel said, "Actually, that part was a cowboy's tall tale but we did go to the dance. And there we met Mabel and Marge. Twins. Mabel took a liking to Max and I took a liking to Marge, and after about a year of dancing nearly every Friday night, and sneakin' kisses when they'd let us, we had a double wedding. We all moved to Wickenburg and Mabel got hired on as the new camp cook. Marge had worked on a ranch before, even though she lived in Phoenix at the time, and she was hired as a wrangler. She was a better wrangler than the young guy they had earlier and way better than the guy before that who couldn't stay sober.

"We worked for room and board and $30 a month, and after four years of pooling our money, we had enough saved to make a down payment on our own ranch. We found a ranch for sale near Prescott and managed to pull off the deal. We ranched together for purt-near fifty years. As Prescott grew, our ranch ended up being right where some rich city dudes from back east wanted to start a housing development, so we sold out. The sale made us pretty rich and we have been very comfortable ever since. Mabel and Marge died a few years ago, only about three months apart. The twins stayed together clear to the very end."

Becky said, "Ahhh. How sweet."

Max said, "Ranching was lots of fun, and very challenging, but also very rewarding. We loved being outside all the time. We got to hunt and fish and spend lots of time with our best gals. We raised three kids a-piece along the way. But it was hard work too.

Mel took over and said, "One time we went hunting on a friend's land. We left our horses in a corral, with extra feed and a full water trough, and headed off over a mountain. We got lost."

Max groaned and rolled his eyes again as Mel continued, "We wandered around for two days and ran out of water. We finally found a little old town, practically a ghost town. There in the middle of the town was an old-fashioned well with a low stone wall and a bucket with a crank handle. We were pretty thirsty so we hurried and let the bucket down in the well. When we pulled it up it was dry as a bone; not a drop of water on the bucket. Max had some rope in his backpack so we tied that onto the bucket to let it down even farther. It still came up dry. Max tossed a fist-sized rock down into the well, and we listened . . . and didn't hear a sound. That was weird! I got a rock about the size of a volleyball and tossed that down into the well. Still no sound. That was even weirder. We found a big old log lying in the dirt a little ways away. Together we picked up the end of the log and dragged it over to the well. We put the one end up over the little wall and then heaved on the other end and the log went sailing off into the darkness. We waited. No sound. Now it was getting pretty freaky. Suddenly a goat came running lickety-split and ran right between us, bleating frantically as it ran and jumped into the well. This whole thing was getting more strange every minute."

Max was having a hard time containing his smile, so the women knew something was up. Mel's story continued, "Then an old pickup pulled up and a rancher leaned out the window and said, 'Have you guys seen my goat?' We said, 'Well . . . we don't know if it was your goat, but we did see a goat. It ran and jumped into this well.' The rancher said, 'Nah, that couldn't have been my goat. I had my goat tied up to a big old log.'"

Again, the women burst out laughing. This time they had to wipe away tears as they laughed and laughed. This had become one of those situations where someone laughs so much that they get caught up in the moment and everything is extra funny. Their laughter wouldn't stop and their tears just rolled. They realized that at some point Alyssa, from the front desk, had noticed the laughter and had come to join them. The six of them were having a ball.

Mel started right in on another story while Max sighed and shook his head. Mel had a captive audience and he wasn't going to miss the opportunity.

Mel said, "One day we met a city dude in Phoenix. His name was Don. We got to talking about ranching and living in the country and hunting. Don said he always wanted to go elk hunting. We told him if he wanted to, we'd take him hunting. He was pure city and had never owned a gun and hardly knew what an elk looked like but we said we'd help him.

"The next time we came into town we looked him up. He had bought himself a rifle, a license, and all the hunting gear the guy at the sporting

112

goods store could sell him. This was years ago, and you could just go hunt elk as long as you had a license and a tag. You didn't have to wait to be drawn. So . . . we took him elk hunting that fall.

"On opening morning the three of us were standing at sunrise at one end of a long ridge. Max whispered, 'Don, you go right down the top. Mel will be about halfway down on the left, and I will be about halfway down on the right.' Max pointed to the far end of the ridge about a mile away. 'We will take about one hour to walk to that end of the ridge, so don't go too fast. We'll meet over yonder.' Don nodded his head and we all split up and started walking.

"After about 15 minutes, we heard a few shots at the top of the ridge. I quickly walked back up toward where I guessed Don had shot at an elk and I assumed Max was heading up there too.

"I got to a point where I could hear two men arguing but I couldn't make out what they were saying. I came out from behind some trees and saw Don arguing with another hunter who was dressed in fluorescent orange. Don said, "It's mine!" and the other hunter said, "It's mine!" and Don said, "No, it's mine! I shot it!" and the other hunter said, "No, it's mine!"

Finally, Don levered another live round into the chamber of his rifle and pointed it at the man and said, "IT'S MY ELK AND I'M TAKING IT!" The other hunter backed up a couple of steps and held his hands in the air, one hand free and the other holding his own gun. The hunter said, "OK, OK, it's your elk, but let me take my saddle off it first!"

The four women burst into laughter again, but this time the fun was rudely interrupted by an unexpected sound; gunfire. They all instantly stopped laughing and jerked their heads toward the lobby where they saw two men standing there shooting randomly with what appeared to be AK-47s. The men had dark hair and dark beards and wore black clothing, just like the pictures you would see online of radical Islamists in the Middle East. They fired several shots and then walked on past Mitch, who had fallen to the floor.

The two men walked into the first yoga room. They yelled at the women and the instructor to stand against the back wall. Their yelling could be heard through the glass and those in the pool could easily see all that was transpiring, although they were hidden from the terrorist's view down in the water. Only Alyssa was visible and she quickly dropped behind a deck chair.

By now, Max and Mel had both climbed out of the pool as quickly as they could and reached into their gym bags. With the women in the yoga class standing against the back wall, and the terrorists facing them, Max and Mel were to the side and slightly behind the terrorists so they were not noticed. They each pulled both of their pistols out of their gym bags.

The terrorists raised their guns and pointed them toward the women but neither of them got a shot off. Max and Mel opened up with their weapons. Each held a 1911 .45 in one hand and an even more powerful pistol in the other hand as they shot non-stop at the terrorists. The volley of gunfire was deafening as the heavy caliber bullets tore ragged holes in the glass and caught the terrorists completely by surprise. Max and Mel had been shooting guns for over seventy years and they knew what they were doing. They each looked just like the gunfighters in the old movies with two pistols firing at the same time. Only these were two wrinkly old men in swim trunks and their guns were not matching pearl-handled revolvers. They quickly emptied their guns at the terrorists, using up all their ammunition.

One man dropped quickly without firing a shot. The second man was hit, but as he started going down he turned toward Max and Mel. He was only able to shoot one short burst of fire before he collapsed on the floor and laid still.

The .30 caliber shots from the AK-47 came back through the glass at the Dahlquist brothers and one of the slugs struck Mel in the arm. As Max stepped to gain better footing he fell and knocked Mel over just after the bullet hit him. Mel fell back and landed hard on the concrete deck.

The women at the pool were screaming and crying but the danger was over in a matter of seconds.

Max turned, put his .454 revolver into his gym bag and pulled out a spare magazine for his 1911. He replaced the empty mag with the full mag, levered in a round and then uncocked the hammer and laid the reloaded 1911 on the top of his open gym bag. Then Max turned and knelt by Mel, who was laying there in a daze with his pistols still in his hands. The wound in his arm didn't look bad and there wasn't too much blood.

Veronica, Becky, and Lara came over and asked if Mel would be OK. Some of the women in the yoga room were still in there crying but some had come out of the room and, along with Alyssa, had run to Mitch. Mitch was moving and appeared to be talking with the women as they helped him. The exercise room looked empty until people started peeking out from behind the equipment. The sounds of emergency vehicles with their sirens blaring could be heard approaching the gym.

Just then, Mel stirred and looked at Max. He said, "Did I die? Do I get to see Marge now?"

Max said, "No, Mel. You didn't die. You're stuck with me for a bit longer, buddy."

Mel replied, groggily, "But I see three angels in cherub outfits."

Max smiled and said in a consoling tone, "No, those aren't angels in cherub outfits; those are trophy wives in bathing suits."

The three women smiled through their tears.

Mel said, "Did I get shot?"

"Yeah, Mel, but you aren't hit bad. The bullet just went through some of the flabby skin on your arm."

"I used to have muscle under that flabby skin. My head hurts too."

"Yeah, you took a conk on the noggin, but you kept a pretty cool head when you were shooting at those terrorists. I guess it's a good thing that head of yours is so hard from all those years punching cows. Does anything else hurt?" Max was worried that Mel had broken a hip since that was such a common result of falls at their age.

Mel said, "I don't think anything else hurts. You're afraid I broke a hip, aren't you?"

Max replied, "Well, brother, as a matter of fact, I am."

Mel had his eyes closed and he just smiled and said, "It's a good thing I had a Milk-Bone dog biscuit with every meal for my whole life to keep my calcium up."

The three women looked at Max with wide eyes, shocked at what Mel had said.

Max rolled his eyes and smiled as he shook his head gently to let them know Mel was only joking again. They were visibly relieved.

By now the first responders were entering the building.

Mel opened his eyes and said, "Can we come back and see the trophy wives again next week?"

Max replied, "Maybe, but that's up to the trophy wives. Besides, we don't want their husbands to think we're their boy toys."

The women, still wiping tears of stress and relief now laughed again.

Max said, "Why do you want to see the trophy wives again?"

Mel said, "Because they laugh at my stories. You don't laugh at my stories anymore."

Max said, "That's because I've heard them over and over for seventy years."

The women chuckled.

Mel sat up and looked around and then said, "Max, I don't know if we can see the trophy wives again anyway. I don't think this gym will let us come back."

Max asked, "Why not?"

Mel said, "Because we shot their glass walls full of holes."

19 Face the Wind

People who had not fought in a war didn't understand the intense psychological burden that came from the constant day to day struggle to stay alive and keep those around you alive. The mental and emotional pressure was intense. Like many other kinds of stress, some people handled it differently than others. Modern warfare intensified the pressures, including politics, intense scrutiny from the media, and criticism by protestors and other outsiders. Soldiers who came back from war sometimes couldn't fully come back. The deep emotional barriers and defenses that they had to erect to deal with the mental struggles of war stayed with them and became a part of their personality. After their tours of duty some could revert back to civilian life, living with scars on their bodies and in their minds but still maintaining a relatively normal life. Others were debilitated by the scars. The damage to nerves and emotions and behaviors was so severe they could never seem to resume a regular life. Mabry Upshaw was one of the latter.

Mabry had been born on the Fort McDowell Yavapai Indian reservation, on the northeast edge of the Phoenix Metropolitan Area. His veins flowed with both Yavapai and Apache blood and he was proud of his Native American heritage. He went to elementary school and high school in the reservation schools, he played in the desert near his home, he participated in tribal events, and he lived the life of a Native American in a modern tribal setting. Yet, with the close proximity to the Phoenix area he spent many hours off the reservation. He and his family had gone into Fountain Hills, Scottsdale, Phoenix, Tempe, and Mesa many times;

to the mall, to the movies, to sporting events, to 4th of July fireworks celebrations, shopping for anything and everything. He was just as comfortable in the city as he was on the reservation.

His pride in his Native American heritage was fueled by the feisty determination of his small tribe. In 1968 the U.S. federal government unveiled plans to build a dam near the confluence of the Salt and Verde rivers, creating a reservoir that would cover most of the tribal lands. It would be named Orme Dam. The members of the tribe understood the significant benefits from the revenue they would gain from selling their land to the federal government for a large lake, but on the other hand, they decided they didn't want to give up their small patch of real estate. As a people, they stood up and spoke a defiant "No!" After ten years of effort and opposition from the people of the tribe, Interior Secretary James Watt announced in 1981 that the federal government had decided to scrap the plans for Orme Dam. The small nation of Native Americans was proud of their victory and, in celebration, started an annual three-day rodeo called ODVD, which stood for Orme Dam Victory Days.

But their defiance didn't end there. In 1988 the tribe decided to build a casino and it changed their world. The members of the Yavapai nation had mixed emotions. Some were overjoyed for the opportunity and jobs that the casino brought to them. They improved their schools and roads, they built government buildings, and tribal members got better health care and began having opportunities that came only because they had increased income. The casino gave much-needed life to their nation. However, some members of the tribe saw the casino as nothing more than selling their souls and ransoming their culture for money. The casino also brought crime, drunkenness, increased social problems, and exposure to the seedy side of American life.

In 1992 the governor of Arizona decided that all the casinos in Arizona were in violation of the law. The governor ordered all gaming machines in tribal casinos to be seized until the legality of the gaming could be determined by a court. The Fort McDowell Yavapai nation, in a second act of defiance against the government, brought in trucks and cars and heavy equipment and blocked the roads to prevent their gaming machines from being removed from the casino. All the king's men, or at least the governor's men and women, couldn't seize one machine at the Fort McDowell casino. The tribe kept up its vigil for many days until the governor backed down. Their efforts gave courage to the other tribes and eventually a Native American Gaming Compact was signed into law, allowing Native American tribes to continue to operate their casinos, complete with all sorts of gambling machines.

As a little boy Mabry watched his father stand with his tribal members against the various threats to their family and to their small nation of Native Americans. He knew his father was not perfect, but he was proud of him for supporting his tribe and being willing to stand and fight against things that were not in the tribe's best interests. Several times Mabry asked his father about the different threats and he heard the same statement each time. "Mabry, sometimes you have to stand and face the wind." As a little boy he didn't fully understand what that meant but as he grew older he learned.

Once when Mabry was fourteen he went with his cousins to a movie in town. The movie they wanted to see was at a theater in Scottsdale. As they stood in line, waiting for tickets, there were several older teenagers behind them in line who started making derogatory comments about Native Americans. Mabry and his cousins didn't want to cause trouble and ignored it as much as possible. Finally, the boys behind them started getting rough. One of them pushed Mabry's sixteen-year-old cousin, Betty, to the ground. As she was falling she swung at the boy in anger and self-defense, scratching his face with her fingernails.

A younger cousin ran to get security. The bully was outraged and he stood over her menacingly, yelling at her to apologize. She refused and he got more and more angry. The other bullies surrounded them, not allowing any of her cousins to help Betty to her feet. The scratched boy finally threatened to kick her if she didn't apologize. Mabry's patience finally ran out and he plowed in and grabbed the bigger boy and dragged him away from Betty. By the time security arrived, several of the boys had Mabry on the ground and had thrown several punches at his face. The boys ended up getting arrested for disorderly conduct and thanks to the many witnesses standing around, Mabry and his cousins were determined to be without fault and they went home. Unfortunately, they didn't get to see the movie.

When Mabry arrived home with a split lip and both eyes swollen and black, his father listened to what happened and then patted his son on the shoulder. "I'm glad you stayed patient as long as you could and that you stuck up for Betty. Tackling someone who's bigger and stronger than you to defend what is right is what I mean when I say to stand and face the wind. Today you did that, and I'm proud of you, son."

Two years later, Mabry's father lay dying from cancer that was discovered too late. On his deathbed, Mabry's father held his son's hand and reminded him to stand and face the wind. He died just a few hours later.

When Mabry turned eighteen years old he joined the military. Native Americans have served in the military more than any other demographic group in America. Native Americans account for 0.8% percent of the population of America, but at the same time, they account for 1.7% percent of the men and women serving in the armed forces. That statistic, with slightly different numbers but the same overall trend, has been true in every U.S. war or conflict.

Mabry had served three tours as a U.S. Marine in Afghanistan, seeing considerable action and losing battle buddies. Between tours he married his childhood sweetheart, Tennielle, and they had two children. He suffered many physical wounds, some minor, some not so minor, but none serious enough to get him sent home.

Finally, they did send him home. Home to his beautiful wife, Tennielle. Home to his precious five-year-old daughter, Lovinia. Home to his bouncing two-year-old son, Josh. Coming home seemed to him to be more difficult than staying. In the military there was order and structure; he took orders and gave orders. Civilian life also had routines but they now seemed meaningless. He knew each day was important but when he had struggled to survive every single day for months, he now had to force himself to accept day to day life, which seemed mundane and insignificant. And that was when he was awake.

Nights were as terrible as Afghanistan. He would wake up screaming from a nightmare or terrified that one of his loved ones had been killed. Tennielle spent many hours just holding him while he trembled and cried like a baby. He felt embarrassed crying in the night when he was supposed to be tough and rock-solid.

Tennielle told him many times how much she loved him. She had stuck with him for a long time, dealing with his emotional challenges, but she admitted to Mabry that she was starting to worry that he wasn't making progress and she didn't know how much longer she could go on.

Then he had started drinking, and at times he would come home angry and they would argue. A couple of times he had hit her and then he felt horribly guilty. She told him she was about at the end of her rope. She could deal with emotional troubles and strain on their relationship but she wouldn't deal with violence from the man she loved with all her

119

heart. Their marriage was crumbling. Mabry took all the blame. This time it was Tennielle who was standing with her face into the wind. She had been patient a long time but she was starting to worry about the impact on the children.

Mabry had been religious throughout his life, as had Tennielle. They had been married in their church and Mabry had felt the Lord's spirit in his life. Now that he was struggling for emotional survival, he only felt scared, confused, and angry with himself. He had spent many hours in counseling sessions with their pastor. He also spent time praying for help and guidance. Just when he thought he was making progress, something would happen and he would slip again. It was like his mind and heart were stuck in Afghanistan and he couldn't get either of them to come back to the present. Mentally he was trapped in the past, and that destroyed him emotionally. The Marine motto of Semper Fidelis meant "always loyal" or "always faithful," but he couldn't sort out the loyalty to family and the loyalty to country. He wanted to be loyal to both but his mind couldn't seem to figure out how to do that.

When the terrorist activity started up on a cold morning in February it made things worse. It gave his mind something familiar to focus on but it also brought back more of the emotions and stresses of war. He thought of the terrorists and tried to figure out how law enforcement or the military could stop them before they did any more damage. It seemed futile because he couldn't help or change anything. On Monday night after the first attacks his nightmares were as horrific as ever. This time, Tennielle, Lovinia, and Josh were the enemy. He awoke screaming, and when he couldn't calm down Tennielle yelled at him to get out of the house and go sit in the car in the garage. By the time he left, his whole family was awake and crying. He was tempted to start the car and let the exhaust fumes end his pain but he couldn't bring himself to that.

Mabry went to work on Tuesday, tired and in the worst mood he had been in for months. He worked at an auto shop in Tempe, not far from where the train had been bombed on Monday morning. The other guys at work recognized that something was wrong and left him alone. Mabry had a tough day at work and when he got home he went straight to bed. He just laid there awake for hours, tossing and turning and miserable with himself and feeling guilty over what he was doing to his family. When Tennielle came to bed he pretended to be asleep and lay still. She didn't say anything or touch him.

On Wednesday he had to go to the Motor Vehicles Division to get a title situation worked out. He had bought an old pickup from a military friend but it had a salvaged title and he had to get it transferred into his name. At lunchtime, he drove from work over to the MVD office nearby. He was still in a sullen mood.

As he sat there in the rows of cheap, gray plastic chairs, waiting for his number to come up on the display board he kept wondering what to do with his life. The thought crossed his mind more than once to end his life so Tennielle could start over. He carried a concealed weapon, a .40 caliber FNX. He felt the gun pressed against his waist, holstered inside his waistband under his shirt. He wondered about using it on himself but he kept fighting that thought.

Mabry knew Arizona law prohibited him from carrying his weapon in a government building but with a week like this he wasn't about to go anywhere without it. He wondered if anyone else there was also carrying their weapon in spite of the law.

There in the MVD office the chairs were all facing the service counters, with the windows behind the chairs. Although the people were mostly concerned with the service counters, if they looked out the windows they would see out into the parking lot. Mabry was sitting in the back row of chairs by the windows, only paying half attention to what was going on around him. He was miserable and in such emotional agony that it made him hurt physically.

He closed his eyes in pain and anguish and thought of Jesus, who also suffered pain and anguish for the sins of the world. Mabry hung his head and prayed in his heart, "Oh, Jesus, please help me! I don't want to lose my family. You took on yourself my sins and my pain, but it's like I want to hold onto them. I don't know how to hand them over to you. I need you to heal me because I don't know how to heal myself."

Suddenly there was the sound of machinegun fire. He looked to his left, just a few feet away, and there was a man who looked just like the enemies he had fought in Afghanistan. The man had stepped through the doors with an AK-47 and was shooting wildly; spraying bullets randomly back and forth at the people seated in the large room. People were screaming; some falling after being shot, and others ducking to try to avoid being shot.

Stand and face the wind!

Mabry's years of training kicked in without a thought—he was in fully automatic mode, functioning purely on conditioned response. As unthinking as a machine he drew his .40 so fast that the terrorist didn't even have time to react. Mabry was only ten or fifteen feet away from the man as Mabry started firing. He had fifteen rounds to work with. He fired five times and four of the shots struck the terrorist, who fell to the cold tile.

Mabry quickly started looking for other shooters. He had learned that you never accept that there is only one gunman; there could always be more. Sure enough, another man was across the room at a different door behind Mabry. As Mabry saw him, the other man had already identified Mabry and was turning in his direction.

Mabry began firing, but the second gunman was farther away than the first and therefore harder to hit. As he walked toward the terrorist, firing his .40, he decided to empty the gun. If there were three terrorists, Mabry may not be alive by the time a third started shooting anyway so he gave the second terrorist all he had. He was shooting a semi-automatic to the terrorist's fully automatic, so he knew he had to shoot fast and straight. Mabry had trained for hours how to walk and shoot accurately at the same time. He hoped that training would pay off now.

Fortunately, the terrorist wasn't aiming. As he swept his gun from side to side some of his shots missed Mabry. But some didn't. Mabry felt the searing pain as the bullets tore into him but he forced himself to stay focused and he emptied his magazine at the terrorist. When his last shot was fired and the chamber on the FNX locked open, Mabry continued walking toward the terrorist, ready to take him on with his fists if he had to. However, the room started to spin and Mabry started to crumble. His shots had done enough though because the last thing he saw was the second terrorist landing on the floor just before Mabry did.

The last thought he had before he blacked out was his father's voice: *stand and face the wind.*

20 Embarrassed But More Determined

Mansoor Fatik Al-Musawi sat in a stolen car at a convenience store south of an alfalfa field in Gilbert, Arizona. It was 3:00 in the afternoon on Wednesday and he had been sitting there since 9:00 that morning.

With all the excitement in the field nearby he thought everyone was preoccupied and wouldn't notice that he had been sitting there all day.

As had happened on Monday, his Wednesday plans were so carefully thought out and yet had turned to disaster. As had happened on Monday, armed citizens had foiled his plans each time and killed his jihadists. As had happened on Monday, as the day wore on each attack was another failure for his cause.

The first embarrassment was the bus driver who foiled the plan to detonate a bomb at a school. From his location at the QT store, which sat at the south edge of the alfalfa field, Al-Musawi had seen the bus go into the field and then stop in the soft dirt. Since his vantage point was on the side away from the doors he hadn't seen that the people had hurriedly scrambled off to safety until they were on the sidewalk. Al-Musawi himself had detonated that bomb by calling a number with his cell phone. The only thing that prevented him from doing it earlier was that he hoped his fighters were alive and still able to drive the bus to the school. Instead, it was all of the passengers and the driver that survived. Then the driver showed to the news people that childish sign of the Second Amendment, which all of America was now in love with. Well, actually, most of America was in love with the 2A sign; some people protested against it for political purposes.

The second embarrassment was when two women at another school had stopped his men after they had killed only a few people. They had planned to shoot apart the door locks for each classroom and slaughter everyone inside. They figured they could get into six or eight classrooms before law enforcement arrived and then they would die in a gun battle. Instead, they were only able to wreak havoc at the front of the school. What rankled most was that they had been shot by women. Women! Creatures that were only good for serving men and bearing children— preferably boys.

Then there was the attack at the fitness gym, which was stopped by two old men who could hardly walk. Again, only his fighters died.

There was also the embarrassment in downtown Mesa where a young woman shot his knife-wielding cousin Fadhil as he attempted to carry out an attack on people walking down the street. Much to his chagrin and anger, Fadhil didn't so much as scratch anyone with his knife. That one was doubly painful to Al-Musawi because Fadhil was family.

Finally, one lone gunman stopped two of his jihadists at a government building. At least in that situation one of his fighters had shot the armed citizen. The man was fighting for his life in a hospital and Al-Musawi hoped he would die. The American was going to remain a hero either way but Al-Musawi would rather have to hear about a dead hero than a living one.

As had happened on Monday, Al-Musawi was positioned to watch the victory of his team, and instead he grew more shocked and frustrated as the day wore on, leaving him dejected and humiliated sitting there too angry to do anything else. He continued to watch the news reports come in on his cell phone and each report made him more livid. This time he used his car charger to keep his cell phone from dying, so he didn't . . . or *couldn't* . . . end the pain.

A thought came to him of something that was said during one of their early planning sessions. One of the members of his cadre had questioned carrying out the attacks in Arizona. The man said that maybe they should go to a state with stricter gun laws so there would be fewer people who could put up an immediate fight as their jihadists attacked. Al-Musawi had dismissed the comments and commanded the man to be silent. Now he was wondering if the man was right.

As he sat there fuming he looked at the tattoos on his palms and the inside of his fingers but again it just brought him pain like before. He closed his hands in frustration so he didn't have to see the tattoos.

As Al-Musawi sat thinking, a plan began to grow in his mind. He had four more attack teams to work with and they had already planned attacks for four different locations on Friday. Instead, he would use one team to carry out a surprise attack tonight—Wednesday night! Al-Musawi sat there in his car, still embarrassed and angry but beginning to put together the details of a plan that he hoped would help him feel better.

At about 3:30 Al-Musawi picked up his cell phone and dialed a number. Until now he had used his phone very sparingly, not wanting to be detected by any counterterrorism surveillance equipment. Desperate times called for desperate measures.

The person on the other end of the call, an Iraqi named Raiden Najjar, answered and Al-Musawi said, in English, "Change of plans. Bring the team tonight, all ready to play. I'll text you an address and a time. Have everyone ready for a good hard game of soccer. Bring all your equipment."

"Got it," said Najjar. From prior discussions the message and code were clear. They needed to come prepared for a lot of shooting.

Al-Musawi began driving around town. He was looking for a specific place although he didn't yet know where the place was located. He drove up and down street after street, working his way from Gilbert, through Mesa, then Tempe, then further north. At about 5:30 he finally found it in Scottsdale—a Christian church. A *big* Christian church called the Rock Of Christ Arizona, with a marquis sign at the front which read, "Wednesday night Worship and Dinner. All Welcome. 7:00."

Al-Musawi smiled a sinister smile as he thought: *"All" meant jihadists too, didn't it? What better place to slaughter infidels than a Christian church—and they even invited us to come.*

21 Ready or Not

Rob Kerrington had prayed all week for Arizona. He knew he was also praying along *with* the rest of America and probably with many people around the world. He prayed for peace and safety and for the Holy Spirit to heal and help those who had been injured, and he prayed for the families of those who had been killed in this week's attacks. He also prayed for government officials and law enforcement officials and first responders, that they would be safe and effective and do their jobs well. He especially prayed that someone would stop the terrorists.

Rob had been attending the Rock Of Christ Arizona for seven years. He got involved with ROCA when he was thirty years old and he had loved every minute of it. Rob and his wife, Nola, had made good friends, the church finances were good enough to support some worthwhile charities locally and around the world, and there was a very good team of pastors and volunteers. Rob liked their teachings and their approach to the Bible. It was a very gratifying place and an enjoyable time in life for him and Nola and their three children.

Along with his praying, Rob felt like he needed to be prepared to defend himself. He and his brother were gun fanatics. In fact, they had made guns their profession. Rob and his brother, Tanner, owned and operated a small gun shop and shooting range in Scottsdale and also took groups out to a shooting range in the desert at times. They carried several machine guns in their inventory and owned one for their own use, a fully-automatic masterpiece called a Max-11Sk made by Lage Manufacturing just across town in Mesa. Because they dealt with those types of weapons they had Class 3 permits to carry and operate machine guns.

This week there was a group of thirty-four people from back east in town for a corporate leadership conference. They would take them out to the Ben Avery Shooting range in north Phoenix and shoot semi-automatic pistols, and those who wanted would be able to shoot the Max-11Sk. The Lage was a very fun machine gun to shoot.

They also owned many other guns, and with all the terrorist activity this week Rob put his Rock River Arms AR-15 in the trunk of his car. It had a bump stock and he loved the way it shot like a machine gun. He had used it many times at the range and out in the desert and forests of Arizona. He also carried his Steyr 9mm pistol under his vest, which held seventeen rounds. He was determined to be ready and he stayed alert all week.

On Wednesday Rob started thinking about the ROCA activity scheduled for that night. If terrorists wanted to attack Christians a church would be the best place to be . . . or the worst place to be, depending on who you were. He didn't have any feelings or warnings that he felt were from the Holy Spirit but he just knew that it would be a good idea to be well-prepared tonight. His brother, Tanner, attended ROCA too and Rob wanted him there that night but Tanner had to be out with the corporate group. In fact, Rob wanted the machine gun but Tanner needed it.

At around noon Rob texted his four closest gun-nut friends from church. "Hey. Feel like we should have our guns at the worship/dinner tonight. I'm bringing my AR. You in? I'm only telling Nola."

Within an hour all four of his friends had replied. Two of the four couldn't be there but two others, Larry and Travis, said they were planning on attending and would bring their ARs.

As Wednesday afternoon wore on, Rob kept thinking about their situation. The Constitution protected the right of the citizens to bear arms. Rob had done a lot of research and had read the writings of Thomas Jefferson and others of the Founding Fathers who commented on the Second Amendment. It was clear that their purpose for putting the Second Amendment in the Constitution was to give the people the right to have weapons. Although the phrase "well regulated militia" made it sound like the Second Amendment was designed to make sure the country had a military force, that's not what the Founding Fathers meant. They were clear in their writings as to what they intended.

The phrase used to describe a country's military was the term "standing army." The writings of several of the Founding Fathers used that term and said the people had to have a militia to give them the ability to be a check and a balance against the country's standing army. In other words, the government can't have the only military in the land because that gives the government too much power and the Constitution was all about limiting and restricting the power of the government. There also had to be a militia of the people.

In addition, the Second Amendment had absolutely nothing to do with hunting, so when people said, "Why would you need thirty bullets to kill a deer?" Rob knew that was nothing more than political rhetoric. The Constitution was not intended to say anything about hunting and it didn't.

The framers knew that the way to keep the government from becoming too powerful was to utilize the structure laid out in the Constitution: three branches of government to check and balance each other, states to balance the federal government, and the people being able to vote for their representatives. However, if that all failed to keep a dictator from coming into power then the only thing left was for the people to have the ability to stand up and fight against the standing army and to take control of the country away from the dictator.

Rob had thought about it many times and realized it was the only way to keep the power in the people, and if the people chose as a body to give up their freedoms to the government, then by that point they would be too far gone anyway. Rob and his wife prayed that God would help the people trust in Him so that they could stay free. Sometimes, they realized, God allowed or sent calamities to help them remember Him and to stay humble and value their freedom. Sometimes God didn't actually need to send calamities, because mankind in general was pretty good at man-made calamities, mostly in the form of wars and struggles for power. If the people could stay humble they cared about freedom. When they got prideful and thought they didn't need God then they started losing their freedom and had to fight to regain it.

The other misunderstood part of the Second Amendment, in Rob's opinion at least, was the term "arms." At the time of the framing of the Constitution they had a limited variety of weapons. They mostly had pistols, rifles, swords and knives, and cannon. Their technology was archaic but it was quite easy for the people to have the exact same technology as the government. People had the same guns as the government, and although the government had most of the cannon, people could have cannon for themselves. There were wealthy merchants who owned ships that were armed with cannon to protect themselves against pirates.

As technology changed so did the weapons gap between the people and the government. Rob had thought a lot about that as he had seen weapons technology change over the years. He and Tanner both had Class 3 weapons permits so they could own and possess machine guns but that was about as high in technology as the people could go. People could get explosives, but not many, and they didn't own jet aircraft, heavy artillery, tanks, missiles, helicopters, ships, and other massive and powerful weapons. Rob supposed there were wealthy people who could afford the more powerful weapons if they wanted.

Although Rob was immensely grateful for the sophisticated weapons that the U.S. government had, which is why they were able to win wars and maintain freedom, he believed that it was actually a problem that the people didn't have access to those kinds of weapons too. Clearly, the government had superior weapons compared to the people. When technology changed, those who wanted to restrict the people passed laws to limit the amount of weapons technology the people could have.

Machine guns and bump stocks were prime examples. Why did the people need to be controlled to not own machine guns? Why would there need to be laws to control or prohibit bump stocks? The anti-gun crowd said it was because the average citizen didn't need a machine gun for sporting purposes but they were ignoring the whole purpose of the Second Amendment. It wasn't about hunters and sportsmen; it was about the people having the opportunity to have as much power as the government.

What the people had going for them, if push came to shove, was greater numbers as compared to a standing army. Also, those who could operate the sophisticated weapons that the government controlled were actually *among* the people. If the time ever came when the government wanted to oppress the people as a whole, Rob hoped that enough of the people who worked for the government would feel the need to turn against that tyrannical government and instead of using the weapons against the people, to use them *for* the people. Fortunately, they hadn't gotten to that point yet but at times some in our country would probably argue that we were close.

As technology developed, Rob was glad that ordinary people were able to obtain some of that advanced equipment. An AR-15 was certainly a far more innovative weapon than a single-shot rifle and also much better, for speed at least, than a bolt-action or a lever-action rifle. When it came to needing to fire many rounds quickly, an AR-15 was far superior to older firearms.

The same went for the high capacity magazines, which really weren't "high capacity" at all. Thirty rounds was a normal capacity. While a citizen didn't have a pressing need for that technology, the fact that they could get that technology kept them on a more level playing field with the government. A level playing field was what the Second Amendment was all about. Rob feared the day that the government ever got so powerful that it took those kinds of things away from the people.

As Rob heard people debating the issues surrounding gun control he often thought of those two points of the Second Amendment: the militia versus the standing army and the weapons gap. As long as the majority of the people understood the Second Amendment he felt like they stood a chance to maintain freedom.

Finally, the afternoon passed and Rob headed home from work.

As he and Nola got ready for the worship service and dinner that night, Nola stopped him all of a sudden, took his hand and said, "We need to pray. Now." He didn't tell her he had been praying all day. They held hands as they knelt by their bed, bowed their heads and Nola prayed for strength, for wisdom, for good judgment to make the right decisions if and when needed, and that they would be safe from the terrorists and their worship service would be uninterrupted.

When she finished, she told Rob, "Now, don't worry. Get your guns and trust in God; do what He needs you to do and everything will be fine. There may not even be anything to worry about tonight."

Rob kissed her and said, "I know. I do feel foolish for worrying about it. Probably nothing will happen. But I'm so grateful for a faithful wife who fears God and no one else."

She looked into his eyes and smiled and said, "What gave you the idea I'm not afraid?"

*   *   *

At 5:40 p.m. Mansoor Fatik Al-Musawi sent a text to Raiden Najjar. It said "7:20" and gave an address. It was, in fact, the address to the bank next door to the ROCA church building. There were no cars in the parking lot, the bank having recently closed for the day. There were no other businesses or homes next to the bank so Al-Musawi was unnoticed as he sat in his car behind it. On occasion a car would come to the 24-hour ATM machine at the side of the bank but nobody paid attention to Al-Musawi's car.

At about 6:00 as it was starting to get dark Al-Musawi drove through the parking lot of the church and looked at the layout. Satisfied that it would be easy to get into so that they could do the damage they wanted to do, he drove back to the parking lot behind the bank.

Al-Musawi's jihadists arrived right at 7:20. They pulled up next to his car and Al-Musawi gave brief instructions through the open windows.

They quietly but excitedly reviewed their plan. At 7:30 they would quickly drive next door, jump out of their cars with their weapons and run into the church. Al-Musawi had determined from his investigation earlier that they could pull up right at the curb next to the front doors on the northeast corner of the building. They could go through the doors, shoot as many people as they could in a short time and then retreat back to the cars, thus slaughtering many Christians and remaining undetected by law enforcement.

They had already built onto their cars a mechanism to press a button while driving which would rotate their car license plates on hinges on the bottom of the plates. They had a box-shaped framework about three inches thick that fastened to the car, and the license plate was fastened to the framework. The three inches of the framework allowed room for a small motor which was built into the framework, along with the wiring that was hooked to the car to power the motor. When they pressed the button the top of the plates would swing outward and down, like the tailgate of a pickup, causing the plate to lie flat, parallel with the ground. That would prevent anyone behind them from being able to read the plate. With luck, the car's make, model, and color wouldn't be sufficiently identified as they drove away and for sure the license plate couldn't be read. Then later they could swing the plate back up to a vertical position so as not to attract attention. They still had another job to carry out on Friday night.

By the time Al-Musawi had given instructions and they had discussed a few questions it was 7:26. He sat in his car, preparing mentally. He looked down at the tattoos on his hands and repeated some of the words for inspiration.

At 7:30, he started his car. The time had come.

*   *   *

At 6:40 Rob and Nola arrived at the church to help prepare for the evening. Rob's AR-15 was in his trunk. He didn't want to arouse suspicion. So far, only Nola, Larry, and Travis knew that he would be armed, along with the other two friends who couldn't be there that night, but they had not told anybody.

Rob had two sixty-round magazines and four thirty-round magazines. With his AR having a bump stock he could go through shells very quickly if he wasn't careful. Of course, if they were attacked conserving shells was not the goal. If anything happened he'd have 240 rounds to work with. Probably nothing would happen anyway; nor did he want it to happen. Rob had carried concealed weapons for years and never had to use one in defense. He hoped it stayed that way. Similarly, he always wore his seatbelt and hoped he never had to rely on it to save his life. His business had several fire extinguishers that they hoped they never had to use but they kept them fully charged and always close at hand in unlocked cabinets.

Rob's Steyr 9mm was in a holster in the small of his back under his vest. Rob enjoyed cooler weather because it made it more natural for him to wear a vest which covered his concealed weapon. It was awkward to wear a vest when the temperature in Phoenix was 114 degrees Fahrenheit.

Rob started to help set up for the events of the evening, moving chairs, helping arrange sound equipment. Suddenly he realized he was in the back of the room instead of near the doors and he changed to a different task. As it drew closer to 7:00 he went outside. He saw Larry and Travis standing by Larry's pickup under a light in the parking lot. Rob casually strolled over to talk to his friends.

Rob gave the usual greeting "Hey."

They both replied, "Hey." They were subdued and quieter than normal. Larry and Travis had the tailgate of the truck down and their

ARs were lying on a blanket spread in the bed of the truck. There were several magazines already loaded.

Rob said, "I don't even know if anything's going to happen. Maybe it's crazy to think about it . . . ." he stopped, not knowing what else to say. Then he continued, "I'll feel like an idiot if nothing happens."

Travis said, "No, I think it's a good idea. I figured I'd just hang around outside all night. I asked Sondra to bring me a plate of food. Hopefully it will be quiet." Travis smiled weakly like he wasn't even very convincing to himself.

Larry said, "I've been sitting here wondering if anything will happen. The other attacks were at random, weird places, so why not here? I suggest that when everyone has gone inside we get our guns and stand by the two pillars in front of the main doors. If there is trouble they will offer us some cover.

"I agree," said Rob. "I've also wondered about the north door. The four main doors facing east will be obvious, but if someone wanted to be sneaky and came through the north door while we weren't watching, we wouldn't be able to get to them until they had already started shooting."

Larry said, "Yeah, that's right. We should probably stand . . . or . . . maybe have *one* of us stand slightly around to that side to watch the door."

Travis said, "Rob, don't you have a bump stock?"

Rob said, "Yeah. I added it after I bought the gun. It's really nice."

Travis replied, "The beauty of owning your own gun shop. You have to do research on your products, don't you?"

Rob smiled and said pleasantly, but sarcastically, "Yeah. One of the worst parts of my job."

The others smiled, but nobody was in the mood for laughing.

They stopped talking and Rob walked over to his car and pulled out his AR and the six magazines. He held one of the sixty-round mags and jammed the other mags into various pockets. He walked back to Larry's car and after checking to make sure his action was empty, he laid the mag and the gun on the blanket near the other rifles.

As they stood there by Larry's truck talking, many members of their church arrived and went inside. Some were carrying dishes of food. Several of the men walked over to talk to Rob, Larry, and Travis, and some of them, after spying the weapons, commented on the wisdom of being prepared this week.

At 7:00 the band started playing and the three men in the parking lot could hear some upbeat hymns as the people inside all started singing. By now, there were only a few stragglers coming late. Rob and his friends continued to talk and buy time, all the while keeping a watchful eye for anything suspicious.

Finally, at about ten after the hour, Rob said, "Well, now that everyone is inside and I won't be as embarrassed about what I'm doing I may as well get completely ready." He picked up his AR and shoved the sixty-round magazine into the bottom of the gun and pounded it to make sure it seated completely. He pulled back the loading lever and pushed the button to snap the action shut and lever in a round. Then he flipped the safety lever to the "Safe" mark.

Sometime in the past, Rob had used a fine-point Sharpie marker and next to "Fire" he wrote "Pew" and next to "Safe" he wrote "No Pew." As he flipped the lever to "No Pew" it usually made him smile, but not tonight. He was a swirl of emotions—embarrassment and foolishness mixed with fear and adrenaline. Tonight would hopefully just be a quiet night with nothing but worship, food, faith, and friendship.

After he finished preparing he walked off toward the north door. He wasn't in the mood for any kind of joking. As he left, Larry and Travis picked up their ARs, inserted magazines, and levered rounds into their guns too. They walked over by the main doors and stood behind the columns, one behind each column.

Rob stood there around the corner from the main doors and partway down the sidewalk that ran between the building and the parking lot. He could see the north door about twenty yards away, illuminated by a light hanging off the side of the building above the door. He stood there for ten or fifteen minutes and suddenly Pastor Bruce stepped out the door. He was one of the senior pastors and knew Rob well. He had a Big Gulp cup in his hand and he threw a slosh of water and ice out into the parking lot. His other hand hung onto the door to keep it from closing. He caught a glimpse of Rob out of the corner of his eye and did a double-take, almost dropping the cup.

"What are you doing, Rob?"

"Just . . . uh . . . watching."

"I have to hold this door open because there's a baby playing right here by it, but can you come over here to talk to me?

Rob walked over, his gun held ready but pointed away from the pastor.

"What's with the gun?"

"Well, I just . . . thought that . . . maybe with all of what's going on this week we should be a little more . . . prepared than we usually are. Larry and Travis are around the corner by the main doors." Rob was trying to make it sound like he wasn't the only one with a crazy idea.

"Rob, I get the feeling you are embarrassed about bringing your gun to church." Pastor Bruce raised his shirt and revealed a semi-automatic pistol in a holster strapped around his waist above his beltline. "I don't think it's crazy at all. In fact, the Lord's people have had to defend themselves throughout history. Jesus taught that those who live by the sword die by the sword, but at other times God supported his people who had to battle with the sword against their enemies. You are doing a good work, Rob. Don't ever be embarrassed for protec . . . ." but he never finished his sentence. Semi-automatic gunfire from the area by the main doors interrupted him. It was followed immediately by automatic gunfire.

Rob didn't say another word to Pastor Bruce, just whirled and sprinted toward the front of the building. As Rob came around the corner there were Larry and Travis by the big columns about 15 yards away. They were shooting with their semi-automatic rifles but there were two men with automatic rifles shooting back at them. Rob thought there were one or two other men already on the ground but he didn't take time to think about that. His gun was already coming up toward the intruders and he flipped the lever to "Pew".

Rob pulled the gun to his shoulder and aimed at the men. The two gunmen were already focused on Travis and Larry so it gave Rob a slight advantage. He needed it since the two men had machine guns.

The Rock River .223 did its job throwing lead and the bump stock did its job of using the recoil to rapidly trigger the next round without Rob having to pull the trigger for each shot. It worked just like a machine gun and Rob's shots tore into the two men, mowing them down. The gunmen had been shooting into the two columns where Larry and Travis were, some of the shots going past the columns and into the double doors and foyer area, but Rob was a step ahead of them as they turned toward him and he was already firing. If he had only been shooting a regular semi-auto he would have gotten maybe one of the gunmen, but with the bump stock he put out so many shots so quickly he kept the slight advantage that he had, and shot both terrorists before they were able to connect their shots with anyone else. The two men had thrown some shots wildly in Rob's direction but only as they were falling to the ground.

As the gunmen fell and stopped shooting, Rob popped out his first magazine and jammed in his second sixty-round mag. The first mag fell to the concrete and Rob didn't pay any attention to it. He wanted to stay completely ready; he could come back for the mag later.

Suddenly Rob noticed motion in his peripheral vision and as he looked he saw another man coming around the corner of the building right under a light on the side of the church. The man had a rifle and was starting to swing it toward Rob. Rob threw his gun to his hip again, not taking time to go into a shooter's stance, and started firing toward the gunman. Rob actually started pulling the trigger before his gun was on target, so bullets sprayed along the sidewalk as he got the man in his line of fire. Suddenly the gunman jerked and dropped his weapon, jumping back behind the corner of the building. Rob thought he saw the gunman's open hand, but it looked dark and it puzzled him why the man's hand looked so odd. Rob decided one of his shots must have hit the man in the hand and it was covered with blood. The rifle still lay on the sidewalk near the building under the light.

Rob and Larry ran toward the corner where the man had been standing, although they skirted wide so as not to be surprised if the man was standing right by the corner. As they got around the corner, albeit out into the parking lot forty or fifty feet, they heard the screeching of tires and saw a car speeding off through the parking lot. It squealed around the corner, sped down a side street, and was gone. They didn't even get a good look at it.

They heard sirens in the distance, apparently first responders coming their way. Rob and Larry walked back to talk to Travis, who by now had been joined by Pastor Bruce and several other men and women with their drawn pistols in their hands, pointing them into the air. It was an awesome sight! He loved this congregation!

As they stood over the four downed terrorists, all carefully guarded by Travis, the first police cars came speeding into the parking lot. Pastor Bruce reholstered his gun and walked out toward the police cars with his hands safely out to his side. He said, "Welcome officers. We have it taken care of for now but we would really love to turn it all over to you."

All of those in the church who had guns put them away and the officers started breathing a little easier. They did not confiscate guns this time, but clearly identified Rob, Larry, and Travis as the ones who had done the shooting.

As the next four hours wore on, police and FBI agents did their thorough cleanup and investigation. Most of the people in the church eventually went home. At some point along the way, Nola brought Rob a plate of food, but he wasn't hungry and she eventually went home with the kids. Rob said he could get a ride home with Larry.

Somewhere along the way they were introduced to FBI Special Agent Alan Clevenger. Special Agent Clevenger was head of the counter-terrorism task force and wanted to interview the three men who had done the shooting. He had them explain the whole evening several times, his phone recording app running constantly.

They explained to Special Agent Clevenger that around 7:30 when Rob had been around the corner for a few minutes Larry and Travis had noticed a car pull up at the curb instead of into a parking spot. That was slightly odd, but then they noticed four men get out of the car with weapons and start walking toward the church. Larry and Travis had been behind the pillars and were not easily seen. They didn't wait for the men to get closer before they started firing with their semi-automatic AR-15s, and two of the terrorists immediately went down. In that split second, the remaining two men started firing back with automatic weapons so Larry and Travis had to pull back behind the pillars.

Right about that time Rob came around the corner and saw the terrorists and took advantage of their focus being elsewhere. He started shooting at them before they could return fire in his direction.

Then Rob saw the fifth gunman and shot at him, and that was really all of the shooting.

When they talked about the lone gunman back by the corner, Special Agent Clevenger asked if they could describe him. They said they didn't really get a good look at him. When Rob shot, the man quickly dropped his gun and retreated.

Special Agent Clevenger said, "Did you see anything unusual about his hands?"

Rob said, "As a matter of fact, I did. When he dropped his gun I saw his open hand and it looked dark. I thought maybe there was blood on it but we didn't see any blood on the sidewalk or on the rifle."

Agent Clevenger smiled with relief and said, "Actually, we believe this cell of terrorists is being led by an Iraqi named Mansoor Fatik Al-

Musawi. He has tattoos on the inside of his palms and fingers. Could it be that what you saw were tattoos?"

Rob said, "Now that you say that, I think that's exactly what I saw. He was right under the light and his open hand looked so odd. I just knew it was dark, but when you say tattoos, that makes perfect sense."

Agent Clevenger said, "That's the first break in this investigation that points to Al-Musawi. I hope you are right. I hope we can get some fingerprint evidence from the rifle too. At least we . . . or I should say . . . you . . . you three . . . stopped another attack. Three armed, law-abiding citizens saved many lives tonight. I think more of us are going to start doing better at protecting our churches."

The questioning and investigation wore on and the adrenalin wore off. By the time Larry dropped off Travis and then Rob, they were all subdued again. It had sunk in how close they had come to death and that they had killed other human beings. They talked about it a little in the car, but again, they didn't feel like saying much. Larry told Rob good night and drove off. As Rob got inside his house and set down the weapons and ammo that he had with him, Nola threw her arms around him and just held him while he cried quietly—for a very long time.

22 Helpless

Cindy Clevenger felt so helpless the whole week. Monday was a nightmare with all the violence that went on. Alan came home for a couple of hours on Tuesday. He showered, shaved, ate, and headed back to work. She wanted to know what was going on but she had learned that if he could talk about it he would. This time he didn't. She guessed that there was still no intelligence that he could use to help figure out these terrorist attacks. He was quiet and she did what she could to help him recharge and get back to the office, but there wasn't much interaction. He was under a lot of stress.

As he drove away, she prayed for him and for America, and there was nothing more she could do. She couldn't stop the terrorists. She couldn't help her husband. She couldn't really change anything.

Late Tuesday afternoon Cindy got a call from the jewelry store in the mall, telling her that the ring she had ordered was ready. In preparation for their anniversary she had ordered Alan a new ring. When they had bought his wedding ring they hadn't spent a lot of money on it and she had always wanted to get him a better one. Also, his ring had edges that were kind of sharp due to its design. A few times he had caught it on something and it cut into his finger.

Once when they were walking around the mall on a Friday night date, she asked him to try on a few rings. He really liked a certain design and she paid attention to the size, vowing to get it for him someday. That was months ago.

As their anniversary approached she had gone back to the jewelry store to buy the ring. They didn't have it in stock right then but they said they would call her when it came in. On impulse, she asked them to put an inscription on the inside, "Love my G-Man." When they called on Tuesday, they said it was ready. She decided she would go get it on Wednesday.

On Wednesday morning, a bomb attack on a city bus was thwarted by an armed citizen. Cindy watched the news about it and looked for any sign of Alan doing his work. While reporters from a distance told what they knew, the ragged, scorched remains of a smoking bus sat in the background with law enforcement searching through the wreckage. She didn't see Alan, although she figured he was probably there somewhere.

Wednesday around midday three more terrorist attacks occurred. One was at a school, one at an MVD office, and one at an exercise gym. In each case, gun-toting citizens shot the terrorists, saving many innocent lives. At the MVD office, the citizen was also shot and was fighting for his life in a hospital. One of the employees of the gym had been in critical condition but was later upgraded to serious condition.

By Wednesday afternoon Cindy Clevenger was a nervous wreck. She paced the floor. She played with the kids. She mindlessly cleaned the house. She watched one of her favorite movies. She read an eBook she had just bought called *Emancipation Expedition* about a couple who were trying to hide from corrupt FBI agents. That just reminded her of Alan and she prayed that he would never betray his position in law enforcement with a turn to crime or corruption. She couldn't stop thinking about her husband and the fact that she could do nothing for him; nothing except take care of their home and children and pray unceasingly. Somehow it didn't seem like enough.

As she continued to worry she realized that a big part of life was learning to wait. And wait. And wait. Learning patience took time and was certainly difficult.

She thought of a quote she heard from someone who said, "It won't always be this way." Whether things were bad or good, they would always change again. She hoped things would change for the better sooner rather than later. This week was nerve-wracking. She thought about turning on the news but it had been so frustrating she decided to leave it off tonight.

She barely held on to her tears when, as she was giving the boys a bath, one of them asked about Daddy. She explained that Daddy was busy working and that they would have to go to bed without his goodnight kiss. As she was getting herself ready for bed after 10:00, she thought of the ring that she was supposed to pick up that day and that added to her frustration. She was so preoccupied with the day's events and thoughts of how to clear her mind of worry that she hadn't even thought about the ring at the mall.

It was too late by then and, again, she felt powerless to change things. It took her a long time to go to sleep that night; as she had many troubling thoughts running through her head. She tossed and turned for so long, she finally gave up, turned on the light, and continued reading her book. She read clear into the wee hours of the morning before she gave up, and then was finally able to fall asleep.

23   Hurt and Enraged

Mansoor Fatik Al-Musawi barely made it home without passing out. He realized after he got into his house that he had forgotten to push the button to flip down his license plate. He was in pain, intense pain, and he was even angrier than before.

Again his plans were completely ruined by armed citizens. *Why did this city have so many people with guns?*

They had arrived at the church as planned. But just before they stopped, Al-Musawi had wondered about the south side of the building. He hadn't looked at it as closely when he drove through the parking lot earlier. He pulled to the side of the drive area and jumped out to look quickly along the south side of the building. Just as he did that, he heard shots from semi-automatic weapons followed by shots from automatic weapons. He ran along the side of the building and just before he turned the corner the shooting stopped. As he stepped around the corner someone by the main doors started shooting at him with an automatic weapon. He didn't think America allowed citizens to have machine guns. As he was stepping back away from the corner one shot struck him in the left forearm, and as the bullet passed through his arm, it knocked his rifle out of his hand. He tried to grab the gun with his right hand but he missed and merely swung his hand through empty air. His left arm started burning with intense, searing pain.

Al-Musawi quickly realized that this attack had failed just like the others and he ran to his car which still had the door open. With his right hand he awkwardly closed the door, jammed the transmission into reverse, and backed the car around to get it turned toward the exit. Then he threw it into drive and sped out of the parking lot as fast as he could. His left arm throbbed with pain, although it bled very little. He wondered if the bullet that pierced his arm had been so hot that it cauterized any blood vessels.

By the time he got home to his apartment, his arm had started to bleed a little and it was throbbing with pain. He got inside, unseen by any neighbors, and slammed the door behind him. He rummaged around and found some rubbing alcohol, and while he held his arm over the kitchen sink he poured the alcohol on the wounds, one on each side of his arm. He screamed with pain, but he also knew it was partly out of frustration, yet again.

Al-Musawi had no family. He was totally committed to jihad and had no time or place for a woman or children in his life. He could make as much noise in his home as he wanted and he did, not worrying at all about the neighbors. He was bellowing because he was so enraged. Every one of his plans had failed! He had three more attacks scheduled for Friday night, which would have been four until he lost a whole team tonight; and he still had the final attack to prepare. However, that one was not in Phoenix and he couldn't think about that one right now. He was too consumed by the physical and mental pain. He roared again just to let out tension. Suddenly he realized that he had to be healthy enough to lead his team through the final attacks on Friday. He needed help immediately.

He picked up his phone and dialed a number. Still speaking only English to avoid surveillance, he said in response to the answered call, "I need stitches. I'll be over in a few minutes." He abruptly hung up. He didn't know if he needed stitches or not but the person on the other end would know what he needed and would know what to do. He just needed to get there soon.

As he drove, he was too embarrassed to open his right hand to see the tattoos. He had wrapped his throbbing left arm in a towel but that was not his greatest pain. The embarrassment and sense of failure hurt more than the pain in his arm.

He was failing.

THURSDAY

24 Council of Chiefs

"Good morning ladies and gentlemen. I think you all know me, but for the record my name is Elise Maldonado. I'm the Maricopa County Sheriff. I'm going to speak for a few minutes and then we will hear from many others. Let me lay some groundwork for why we called this meeting and then I'll make some introductions.

"The Maricopa County Sheriff's Office and the Phoenix Police Department are the largest law enforcement organizations in the state of Arizona. The MCSO has approximately 3,300 law enforcement personnel and support staff and the City of Phoenix has even more than that with 3,900 law enforcement personnel and support staff. MCSO handles county issues and supports Phoenix and the many other smaller cities and towns around the county to provide law enforcement to those locations. I use the term "smaller cities" carefully, because although Phoenix has 1.6 million people, the next five cities; Mesa, Chandler, Glendale, Scottsdale, and Gilbert each have populations of from nearly 250,000 to almost 500,000. The population of all of Maricopa County is over 4.6 million. It is the fourth most populated county in America. We have here with us today chiefs of police or their senior deputies from almost all of the cities and towns that make up the Phoenix Metropolitan area.

"This meeting grew out of a face-to-face discussion I had late yesterday with Michael Kirby, Director of the Department of Homeland security. Director Kirby flew into town on Monday after the initial terrorist attacks, and he and I were discussing a certain aspect of what's been going on this week in Phoenix. In that discussion, he asked me to make a certain announcement to the general public and I refused. In the ensuing debate between the two of us we finally reached somewhat of a compromise. I offered to put the issue to a vote of all of the chiefs of police in the Phoenix area, and we would see what they say. Director Kirby agreed to accept the verdict of the vote.

"I contacted the police chiefs of the different towns and cities late last night and asked for this meeting. Thank you for your willingness to be here on short notice; we have twenty-three organizations represented. I appreciate everyone's sacrifice. I know many of you had to make great efforts to cancel other meetings or rearrange business and personal schedules. Chief Wong, please let your husband and daughter know that I offer a personal apology for interrupting your daughter's wedding rehearsal dinner last night. I also thank you for the photo of your daughter in the text you sent me. She's a beautiful bride, and congratulations to the happy couple.

"We asked for special permission to hold this gathering in this little-used assembly room in the state capitol complex because it has room for speakers sitting in two semi-circle rows facing the audience. When I first decided to have this meeting I thought of using this room. There's something important about it. It's not set up like a legislative room, with the two houses of the legislature facing a few people in the front and the general public behind the legislators. This room is designed so that twenty-five leaders sit *facing the public*.

"I personally believe that too many decisions these days from government agencies and elected officials are not done with the attitude that the leader is facing the people to make that decision. Sometimes the leader has little thought, I believe, for the public impact as a result of the decision. Sometimes, too many times, the leader doesn't even want to face the public about the decision and hopes the decision or action will go unnoticed. The floor plan of a legislative room seems to me to have it all wrong. It looks like the attitude of 'We are the leaders and you are the people. We are leading so you are behind us.' This room takes the opposite approach—and I like it. We are the leaders and we are having a discussion in front of the people who gave us the power by their votes and their taxes, and those same people will hold us accountable for the critical decisions we are making.

"You will also notice that I am the only elected official in this group. No one here except me has to worry about being re-elected, and quite frankly, I am more worried about public safety right now than my own re-election. Unfortunately, the issue of re-election has had a catastrophic impact on the decision making in this country. The reason I wanted us to meet with the chief law enforcement leaders is that I didn't want a meeting tainted by politicians worrying about getting re-elected, which could happen if we met with the mayors this morning. I'm probably going to take heat for that but I'm telling it like I see it.

"I think this hall seats about 300 and it's maybe half full, but others are joining us as I speak and I imagine we will get more throughout the meeting, which is just fine. My sincere thanks to the administrators and security team here at the Arizona Capitol for accommodating us on the spur of the moment.

"I have also invited the media and we welcome you. Several of us debated how to include the media and spectators in this meeting. We knew if we did not include you, you would be able to file Freedom of Information Act requests to get the transcripts later, which we would not oppose. We also knew that we did not plan to discuss anything of a secure nature in this meeting. We decided to include you in the meeting so you could witness the proceedings first-hand. We are glad you are here to observe but there's a caveat, which involves what we were most concerned about. We ask that you behave.

"There is a trend in our society these days to protest loudly and to disrupt the normal course of business and government. We will not tolerate any of that. We *will* maintain order in this meeting, and if anyone in the media or audience interrupts we will escort you from this room. You may have noticed the many deputies we have lining the walls of this room. They are standing by to remove anyone who is disruptive. When my children on occasion said they didn't want to go to church and argued that they had freedom of choice, my husband would tell them, 'Yes, you have your freedom of choice. You can go to church willingly or unwillingly, but you are going to church.' That same principle will apply here today. If anyone disrupts this meeting, you will leave willingly or unwillingly but you *will* leave this room. I insist that we have decorum and order. Also, this is not a press conference and we will not be fielding questions from the media.

"I was going to introduce everyone but with twenty-three cities and towns represented here that would take too long. Most of the chiefs of police here in the Valley know each other. Let me just introduce three people that you might not know.

"On my immediate right is Director Michael Kirby of the U.S. Department of Homeland Security. We are glad to have him here in Phoenix this week. He flew in immediately after the three attacks on Monday morning.

"Next to Director Kirby are Alan Clevenger and Victor Pilchick, both with the Phoenix office of the FBI. Special Agent Clevenger is head of the counter-terrorism task force and Victor Pilchick is the Agent in Charge of the Phoenix Field Office. For those who aren't aware, that means he's the top dog. AIC Pilchick and my team have worked together on many occasions and he has been extremely supportive in the challenges we are facing this week. He asked Special Agent Clevenger to come to the meeting because of his intricate knowledge of the people we are dealing with this week.

"As we have our discussion this morning, I ask that each police chief please identify yourself as you speak, including the city or town you are from, so all in attendance will know who is speaking.

"I'm glad to see that we have been joined by so many people today. As you well know, the Phoenix Metropolitan Area is under attack from radical Islamic terrorists. Monday was bad, with three attacks, and yesterday was worse, with seven attacks. We anticipate more attacks, although we must admit, and again I'm facing the people when I say this, we are struggling for intelligence. The FBI and all of us have been working extremely hard to find out what's going to happen before it happens. We wish we had a crystal ball but we don't. That brings us to our discussion.

"Yesterday Director Kirby asked me to hold a press conference to announce to the public that the risk is too high when average citizens use their weapons during a terrorist attack and that we should instruct the people to refrain from engaging and instead to hide or flee until law enforcement arrives."

. . . .

"Order!"

. . . .

"Order!"

145

. . . .

"We must have order! Please!"

. . . .

"Thank you.

"Director Kirby, I'm sorry, but I warned you that the people of this valley and the heads of the law enforcement agencies would likely react exactly as you just witnessed.

"Let's turn it back to a discussion instead of a melee. I'd like to start with Chief Bailey Treseder, Chief of Police for the city of Peoria, where the attack happened in the restaurant on Monday. Chief Treseder."

"Thank you, Sheriff Maldonado. I am not surprised that someone from outside of Arizona would feel the way Deputy Kirby does. I'll tell you now, the people of Peoria won't do it. You expect our armed adults to stand down while innocent people are slaughtered for five or ten minutes until my officers can get there? Our people won't do it. My vote is an absolute No!"

"But not everyone in Arizona feels that way. . . . Sorry, I'm Graham Fenton, Chief of Police in Tempe. The City of Tempe has always stood for the reduction of guns in society. I can't have people carrying concealed on the ASU campus and at the downtown Tempe block parties and at the Tempe Town Lake fireworks show or music festivals. Tempe has too many events with large crowds, and consequently, law enforcement in Tempe is a huge challenge. My vote is to have the armed citizens stand down."

"I am Senior Assistant Police Chief Donovan Rascon of the Chandler Police Department. Chief Saylor Krahn is on a skiing trip with his family in Utah for this whole week. I spoke with him last night. In Chandler we also have large-crowd events but we want our armed citizens to be ready and well-trained and able to help stop a threat because we know we cannot always get there in time. Chief Fenton, without those three gun-wielding individuals who stopped the terrorists on the light rail on Monday, you would have had a whole train of people killed in your city instead of only half a train. My vote is to let the good, armed, trained citizens use their weapons until our law enforcement officers can get there. I train my officers to be able to handle the situation when they arrive, expecting an armed citizen to be there, and in every case we've had so far, the citizens quickly turned it over to the police without incident. They drop their weapons, lie down on the ground, and let us know they are not the threat. In fact, many times the threat is over

146

by the time we get there, just like every terrorist attack this week. Part of the problem is that, outside of this week, the news media does not report the good-guys and gals who stop violence before the police get there. Those accounts don't make the news. All we hear are the horror stories and to tell you the truth, it really aggravates me when the media does that."

. . . .

"Order!"

. . . .

"Order Please!"

. . . .

"Thank you."

"I agree with Tempe. I am Brendan Kanegan, Chief of Police in Scottsdale. Scottsdale also prefers for the citizens to stand down. They are not trained to handle the complex aspects that arise in an active-shooter situation. We prefer them to leave it to the highly trained law enforcement officers."

"No, no, no! I am Carson Arlo, Chief of Police, City of Glendale. My niece, Sabrina, was inside the Peoria restaurant with some friends on Monday morning at the third terrorist attack. She was sitting near the front doors. There is no doubt in my mind that if the four armed citizens had not stopped those terrorists as they came through those doors, Sabrina would have been killed or injured. I'm sorry Chief Kanegan, but the citizens are sufficiently trained and sufficiently intelligent to be able to stop a threat. They do not need to wait for law enforcement. They CANNOT wait for law enforcement!"

. . . .

"Order!"

. . . .

"Order."

. . . .

"I am Keenan Thibaudeau. Chief of Police in Carefree and I also represent the Cave Creek area. We prefer the citizens to stand down as much as possible. I'm persuaded by the urgency of a threat or an active shooter situation, but we prefer the citizens to follow the training that says Run, Hide, Fight, in that order. Fighting should be the last resort."

"I disagree. The Run, Hide, Fight training is flawed."

"That is Megan Singh, Chief of Police from the city of Avondale."

"Oh, sorry. Yes, I'm Megan Singh, as she said. . . . Run, Hide, Fight,

147

was our thinking at one point, and I should add that it still is for some cities and states, and I'm especially referring to California where the government wants to go overboard taking care of its citizens. The problem is, Run, Hide, Fight is too often perceived by citizens as the order that they are supposed to handle a situation. They think they are supposed to Run to somewhere, and then Hide, and then when the situation finally reaches them, only then do they Fight as a last resort. That's flawed thinking. Sometimes the best choice is to Fight immediately, which often catches the assailant completely off guard because they are expecting everyone to act like a victim. The more current thinking is that if an active shooter situation begins in a crowd, the better outcomes are for the crowd to attack the shooter. Gang up on him. Yes, some of the people who run to the shooter will be shot, but they would likely have been shot anyway. I'm sorry if that sounds callous but this is reality we are dealing with. When the crowd attacks the shooter the reality is that they overpower the assailant and more people survive. In fact, one expert on the subject says that when an active shooter situation is stopped during the shooting, two out of three times the shooter is stopped by armed citizens. That means only 33% of the time does law enforcement stop an active shooter. The news never reports that. In Avondale, we don't want people to think of themselves as victims. We want them to take action. If Run is the best approach, then run; but if Fight is the best approach, then Fight should be the first response and not the last resort. People are mature and intelligent and they don't need the government to be their nanny."

. . . .

"Order"

. . . .

"ORDER PLEASE!"

. . . .

"WE MUST HAVE ORDER!"

. . . .

. . . .

"I thank you for your support and your input, but please, we must have order."

"I am Joseph Willis, Gilbert Chief of Police. An additional problem with Run, Hide, Fight, is that when the citizens expect the government to take care of them, then they don't have a Fight mentality to begin with and they don't have a weapon. Then when they do decide to fight, they have a stapler or a fire extinguisher, a paperweight or a letter opener. In Gilbert, we are much like some of the other towns in the outlying areas of the Phoenix Metro area. We still have people who spend all day on their farmland. We still have people who carry a knife or a gun to church. We are now a population of over 230,000, but many still have a farm-town mentality. Others are owners of some of the most modern, high-tech companies on the planet. We have whole neighborhoods with million-dollar homes. Regardless of their lifestyle, on both ends of the spectrum, our people like their freedom. They like their guns and they are lawful gun owners. They will stand and fight. They won't wait for law enforcement. They stop the threat before my officers get there and my officers and I are OK with that. That has already happened many times, and no, it doesn't end up on the news as it should. Often times they stop the threat so fast there is no shooting."

"I am Trenton Carr, Chief of Police for the City of Phoenix. I admit that I am torn. Phoenix is a large and still growing city. As one of the country's largest cities we at the Phoenix Police Department take our responsibility seriously to keep the peace. We don't encourage or recommend our citizens to take the law into their own hands. We prefer that they let us do the policing. On the other hand, I support the fact that Arizona has a tradition and a culture of openness when it comes to gun ownership. I believe Arizona was the first state in the Union to allow concealed carry without a permit. Be that as it may, I prefer that our citizens wait for qualified law enforcement personnel to be the ones to stop the terrorists."

"I am Alejandro Valente, Chief of Police for the City of Mesa. I'm standing because I cannot sit here and listen to community leaders tell their people to let themselves be slaughtered while they wait for law enforcement to arrive on the scene. In every one of the ten attacks so far the armed citizens have been extremely effective. You expect them to run away like little children when they are grown adults who want to protect their loved ones and other innocent people? You expect them to hide somewhere hoping a gunman doesn't find them? No! They are adults who can take care of themselves and that includes using a gun.

"The Minute Men at Lexington and Concord and who helped this country gain its freedom were not formally trained, but many of them had been shooting all their lives, and against the British, they were fighting for freedom. You expect our citizens now to not fight for their freedom and their survival? Since when are we a nation of sheep?! Since

149

when do we let bullies get away with being bullies?

"When we have a fire, we expect every single adult to be able to handle a fire extinguisher. We don't make them get permits to use it. We don't make them take training and restrict them from using one unless they have passed a rigorous training course! No way! We put those fire extinguishers on the wall, within easy reach of everyone, and we expect them to use it responsibly. We teach our children that it's not a toy. A fire extinguisher can be used as a weapon. In fact, a video put out by LA County shows a person using a fire extinguisher to stop an active shooter by spraying the gunman in the eyes. If they are that dangerous, why don't we lock up all fire extinguishers and not let people use them? Why don't we tell people, 'Don't use the fire extinguisher if there's a fire; just wait for the firefighters to arrive.' That's ridiculous!

"We aren't afraid of fire extinguishers. We shouldn't be afraid of *gunfire* extinguishers, which is nothing but another gun in the hands of a law-abiding citizen. Used responsibly, a gun is as safe as a drill or a nail gun or any other power tool that we use to make our lives better.

"I note that in our discussion today you have seen the results of the demographics of the Phoenix Metro Area. We in the outlying towns and cities are a bit more rural; less like the big city. On the other hand, Tempe, Scottsdale, Phoenix, and the other inner-city areas are more like the big city. Big cities have a different attitude about guns. They don't understand them and don't like them and therefore they think guns are bad. Those in the country, if I can call it that, are not afraid of guns. Heck, the kids in the city don't even know where milk comes from or what a carrot really looks like. They think carrots are those little short stubby things we all eat now. Too many people in the cities have lost touch with what life is really like. They think their sheltered, distorted view of life is reality. They are too often wrong.

"One of the biggest realities of life is that there are bad people that the government can't control. It's impossible for the government to always protect you just like it is impossible to always prevent fires. So, when a fire erupts, you as the citizen have to use your fire extinguisher to put it out or control it before the fire department arrives. When a bad person comes with a gun, you as the armed citizen have to stop or control the bad person from shooting innocent people.

"Director Kirby, with all due respect, we don't need you here in Arizona telling us that we should act like the leaders in Washington D.C. or California who are afraid of guns. We are not afraid of guns. Guns in the hands of average, ordinary citizens have saved many lives this week. I am NOT going to tell the citizens of Mesa to stand down and allow themselves to be slaughtered! NOT ON MY WATCH! NOT IN MY HOUSE! IF YOU DON'T LIKE THE WAY WE TRUST OUR PEOPLE, THEN GET OUT OF OUR STATE AND STAY OUT OF OUR STATE!"

. . . .

. . . .

. . . .

"ORDER! ORDER! ORDER!"

. . . .

. . . .

"ORDER! PLEASE!"

. . . .

. . . .

"WE MUST HAVE ORDER!"

. . . .

. . . .

"Please sit down."

. . . .

. . . .

"Sit down please. Order."

. . . .

. . . .

"OK."

. . . .

. . . .

"Thank you.

. . . .

. . . .

Do any of the police chiefs have anything further to say?"

. . . .

. . . .

"Then by a show of hands, how many wish to have us instruct the citizens to stand down?

. . . .

"I see six hands.

. . . .

"How many are willing to have the citizens continue to do as they have been doing?

. . . .

"I see seventeen hands.

. . . .

"I believe, Director Kirby, that you have your answer.

. . . .

. . . .

"Order!

. . . .

. . . .

"Order Please!

. . . .

. . . .

"You may be seated.

. . . .

. . . .

"Please be seated.

. . . .

. . . .

. . . .

"Thank you.

. . . .

. . . .

"Thank you. We appreciate your support. Let me add a note of instruction to the citizens. We do not need people looking for a gun battle and we do not need people who don't know what they are doing to try to get involved. It has been evident from what we have seen so far that the people who have used their weapons had a measure of proficiency and good judgment. Please don't go out and buy a gun and think you are ready to help. I'm not saying you have to be trained as well as a law enforcement officer to be able to stop a terrorist threat, but you do need to know what you are doing and you do need to have proficiency with a weapon.

"With that, I will end this meeting. May God bless America, and especially this week may God bless the State of Arizona."

25 Return

Mabry Upshaw was standing in grassland. It reminded him of some of the places he had hunted in Arizona except there was no cactus. There were rolling hills covered with coarse, dry, pale-green grass. The sky was mostly clear with a few wispy clouds and he saw hazy, blue mountains far in the distance. The air was cool and comfortable and there was a slight breeze which swept the grass now and then. He felt the coolness ruffle his hair and brush his cheek. The area was expansive and beautiful and he felt completely free; at peace.

He heard someone call his name from behind and he turned around. There was a man in a brilliant, white robe, with a beard and shoulder-length, flowing hair. Mabry immediately knew it was Jesus. He wasn't sure how he knew; he just knew. Jesus was just standing there some distance away, his hand outstretched. Mabry tried to walk toward Him but he couldn't seem to move his feet.

Mabry called out, "Jesus! Help me!"

The Savior didn't speak but continued to hold out his hand toward Mabry as if beckoning him to come.

Mabry continued to try to walk, and finally, after making a tremendous personal effort he slowly and laboriously moved toward the Savior until they weren't far apart.

Mabry remembered the shooting in the MVD office and said, "Am I dead?"

The Savior of the World spoke to Mabry in a soft, but penetrating voice. "Yes and no. Yes, you died but you won't stay here long. You are going back."

"Back to my life on earth?"

"Yes and no. You are going back but I need you to come back, too?"

"I don't understand."

Jesus said, "Mabry, you are not making progress on earth because of the choices you have made. You have drifted away from me and therefore I need you to come back."

Mabry haltingly said, "So . . . I go back to earth, but . . . you need me to come back . . . to you?"

153

"Yes, Mabry, that is right. You have been through some very difficult things but you need to leave those things behind. You are too focused on yourself and on your trials.

"Mabry, on earth your body is in the present but your mind is stuck in the past. You have a loving wife and beautiful children who need you. But you are not moving forward because you will not let go of your former life. Like you just realized, you only drew closer to me after making an intense effort. On earth you have allowed your challenges to prevent you from making sufficient effort to move forward. You are using them as an excuse, thinking that you deserve a rest because of the sacrifices you have made."

"But I don't know how . . . and I've tried. I've even asked for help from your servant and I've asked for help from you in prayer—many times. I can't seem to make any lasting progress."

"Mabry, what you see depends on your focus. Remember when Peter walked on the water to me on the Sea of Galilee? When his full attention was on me he was safe and made progress. But when he shifted his gaze and saw the turbulent water he started to sink. When all of your mental energy is on the last few years that you have been a soldier you lose focus on the good things around you. Mabry, you have to change your focus."

A look of pain and sorrow clouded Mabry's face. His military training influenced even the way he spoke to the Savior. He said, "Yes, Sir. I know you are right. I spend too much time wishing for the structure and order of military life. I miss my buddies and I feel guilty that some of them were killed and I'm still alive."

"Mabry, you must look forward and outward. You have concentrated so much on your own pain and frustration that you have stopped thinking of those around you. In fact, one of the best ways to focus outward is to serve others. Mabry, when was the last time you did the dishes in your home or swept the floor or changed Josh's diaper?"

Mabry just looked down at the ground in front of him. His guilt prevented him from being able to look at Jesus. They both knew the answers to the questions. Mabry had done nothing but wallow in his own misery since coming back from his last tour. Finally Mabry looked at the Savior.

Jesus's gaze got very penetrating. "Mabry, your other problem is your drinking. It is destroying you and your family and it pulls you away from me. You have excused yourself by thinking you deserve to drink as an escape. It is not an escape, it is a trap. It is like continuing to walk into danger with your eyes closed; feeling that because you cannot see the danger it somehow will not harm you." If it was possible, Jesus's expression got even more forceful. "And the violence it inspires is sinful. If you stop drinking you can succeed, but it will take strength and determination."

Mabry quietly said, "Yes, Sir. I know you are right. I understand."

Jesus's look softened, "Mabry, these instructions are for you. They may or may not apply to others in your situation. They have to find their own way but they can if they will not give up."

Just then, Jesus started moving away from Mabry but neither of them was walking. They were drifting apart.

Mabry held out his hand and called, "Jesus, come back to me?"

"No, Mabry. You come back to me."

Jesus's words burned into Mabry's conscience like the bullets that had torn into his body. He knew Jesus was right—and it hurt. Jesus didn't leave Mabry; Mabry had left Jesus. That's what was keeping Mabry from repairing his relationship with Tennielle and being a better husband and father—the drinking and the self-centeredness, and drifting away from the one who atoned for his sins and weaknesses.

Jesus was some distance away now and still moving. He said, "Mabry, come back to me by changing your ways."

Mabry was searching his heart. He knew that's what he had to do.

Jesus said one more time, "Come back to me," but somehow even though Mabry knew Jesus was talking the voice had a higher pitch. As Mabry called, "I will!" he felt a soft hand touch his.

Jesus was far away now but the feminine voice was close. It softly said, "Mabry?"

"I will!" he called to Jesus with more firmness and conviction.

His loud cry woke him. He was in a hospital room, covered in bandages and connected to several machines. His eyes darted around the room as much as possible without moving his head too much. He was receiving oxygen through his nose and an intubation tube was down his throat. It prevented him from speaking. His call of, "I will!" had been muffled and distorted. He realized that the feminine voice that said, "Come back to me," was Tennielle's and that it was her soft touch on his rough hand that helped awaken him.

He looked into her eyes and she leaned down to kiss him gently on the forehead. That was about the only place she could kiss because of the tubes and tape. Tennielle said shakily, "I'm so glad you came back. I thought I'd lost you. I'll tell the nurse that you are awake."

Tennielle pushed the call button and a nurse appeared quickly. She saw that Mabry was awake and said that she would call the doctor to see about having the tubes removed.

Tennielle held Mabry's hand while they waited and Mabry just laid there with his eyes closed. From time to time he would squeeze Tennielle's hand.

After a few minutes, the doctor and nurse came in and removed the tubes. After everything was cleaned up they left Mabry and Tennielle alone. She helped him get a drink of water and then leaned over and kissed him on the lips.

Mabry's voice was scratchy and it took effort to speak. He said, "You said you thought you lost me. Well, actually, you did lose me; for a few years and for a few minutes. I'm so sorry, Tennielle. . . . I even lost myself. But I think I'm found now, thanks to Jesus . . . and to you. I'm ready to change. Will you still have me?"

Tennielle started crying and said, "Of course I'll have you. I have always believed in you and I have been praying that somehow you would figure out what you need to do to come back. Did you see Jesus?"

Mabry nodded and just sat quietly and she gently caressed his hand. He seemed to not want to talk about it yet.

He looked around the room. "There was a shootout. Is that why I'm here?"

"Yes. You were shot by a terrorist and spent a long time in surgery. You almost didn't make it. They said you died on the operating table." Tennielle paused in painful memory, closed her eyes, and shuddered briefly. Tears squeezed out from under her wet lashes and trickled down her cheeks. She sat quiet and still for a few moments with her eyes closed, trying to control her emotions. Mabry just lay there resting.

Tennielle opened her wet eyes and said in a halting voice, "Mabry, I was praying that God would bring you back to life and back to me. I know He always hears our prayers but I also know He doesn't always answer the way we want. This time I guess He did."

"What day is it?"

"Thursday. Thursday afternoon. You were shot on Wednesday."

"What's with all the balloons and flowers? From what I can see, the room must be full of them. And there are even a couple of banners with that Second Amendment symbol so many people seem to love now."

156

"Well, you saved a lot of lives and people have sent gifts and wishes for you to get well. Also, the news agencies have been anxious for you to wake up so they could talk to you and take pictures. All of America is proud of you and so am I. It's been a rough week and you are now one of the heroes."

"I don't really feel like a hero. I feel like a jerk for the way I have been acting for the past few months. But Jesus told me some things that will help me clean up my act. I'll need your help, and I must ask for your forgiveness."

"I forgive you. I will do all I can to help you, but you know *you* have to make the changes or it won't work."

"I know. That's basically what Jesus told me."

"Did you talk to Him?"

"Well, I may have talked to Him or I may have just dreamed that I was talking to Him; I'm not sure. But I *am* sure that He expects me to change."

"Well then, let's make it happen. Are you ready to talk to America? They all want to hear from you. What are you going to say?"

Mabry thought for a few moments and then said, "I'm going to tell them I know Jesus lives and loves me. And I'm going to tell them I'm grateful for my wonderful wife and children. And . . . I'm going to tell them I'm glad I had my gun."

26   Tough Case to Crack

By the end of the day Wednesday, the Phoenix area had undergone ten terrorist attacks in three days. Many innocent people were killed and most of the terrorists. A few of the terrorists survived and were recovering in local hospitals, closely guarded. One terrorist had gotten away. Armed citizens had saved many, many lives and performed heroically. In every case the citizens had done all the work of stopping the terrorists. So far, law enforcement had not fired a single shot.

At least this time, finally, top government officials and the media started calling it terrorism right from the start. They didn't avoid the term or call it something else. It had always bothered Alan Clevenger that they called things like this everything *but* terrorism, even when they knew that's what it was. Sometimes the politics was the worst part of law enforcement.

In each terror attack that week Alan participated in the aftermath investigation. In the first event he got a possible match on the terrorist named Hamza who looked kind of like one of the faces in a picture he had from his file. However, he was not able to match even one more face to any names of known terrorists. He found no evidence of Al-Musawi and he found no evidence of tattoos on the inside of anyone's hands until the shooting at the church. Boy was he glad that guy saw those tattoos!

By now, twenty-eight terrorists had been killed, or at least they could count twenty-eight. In the two instances where bombs went off in vehicles, at the train station, and behind the hotel, there could have been another terrorist or two that was completely obliterated by the blasts. They didn't think there were others but they all acknowledged the possibility.

The death toll among innocent civilians currently stood at fifty-three, with many injured still fighting for their lives in hospitals around the valley. The death toll would have been hundreds or thousands more if not for the people who carried legally concealed weapons and who bravely stopped the attacks. One of those people had been critically wounded and almost died.

There were still no indicators from their intelligence sources that even hinted at upcoming attacks, either as to timing or location. Alan was supposed to be so sophisticated and in control, and yet he felt as if he was wearing a blindfold and earplugs. He could see nothing and he could hear nothing that gave him anything to work with. It was excruciatingly frustrating.

Alan had started thinking . . . when was it . . . one of the days this week, that if he found Al-Musawi among the dead terrorists, that might indicate the end of the attacks. That was just another hunch. In fact, maybe it was nothing more than a hope.

Alan hadn't been home since Tuesday afternoon. He worked right through Wednesday, with all the aftermath and investigations from that day's attacks. After his investigation at the shooting at the church he then worked through the night. He slept for a couple of hours on a cot in one of the rooms down the hall from his office. He then went back to work, poring over the information from their investigations. He and Victor Pilchick, Alan's boss, had gone to the meeting with the police chiefs on

Thursday and then after that Alan plowed into his work again. He was making no progress but was determined to not give up.

Early Thursday afternoon, Victor came into Alan's office and said, "Alan, I had another thought about that meeting with the police chiefs this morning. I guess I hadn't thought so much about it before but the observation from Chief Valente was accurate. Yes, I know the interior cities in the Phoenix area are more liberal politically but I had never made the connection that it was mostly influenced by a more rural atmosphere or mindset in the outlying cities and towns. That same demographic difference exists among the whole country with the differences between the cities and the flyover country, but I hadn't made that connection of it happening right here in the Phoenix area. Chief Valente hit the nail on the head."

"Now, Alan, I want you to go home."

Victor was tall and commanding, with thinning hair starting to gray at the temples. Victor had been an excellent Special Agent in the field and was a well-respected Agent in Charge. He was athletic and could still beat all of them on the basketball court, even matched up against younger agents. He was tough and fair and didn't take unnecessary risks and he was a domineering leader. He was feared but also respected and his personnel followed him loyally. However, Victor also expected his team members to challenge him and speak up when they had ideas and comments worth making. He expected them to know what was worth speaking up about, and if they were wrong he called them on it. It forced them to think and analyze, but the exchange of ideas followed by dutiful execution caused them to work together as an effective and powerful team.

Alan replied, "I can't go home yet. I still can't crack this puzzle and I have a few things I need to go over . . ."

Victor cut him off. "No, Alan, that was not a suggestion. I'm telling you. Go home. Go home now! That's an order from your superior. You can come back tomorrow. Your wife is probably a basket case and working nonstop dulls your ability to think clearly. No terrorist activity is happening today. You go home for the rest of the day and then tomorrow we'll hit it bright and early again."

Alan reluctantly shut down his computer, picked up his briefcase, and headed home—all with Victor standing there watching him to make sure it happened.

27 The Ramjets

As Dr. Paul Kershaw opened the door to his classroom for his 2:00 class on Thursday, the first thing he heard was a loud, angry shout from a voice he recognized.

"WE SHOULD ROUND UP ALL OF THE MUSLIMS, INCLUDING THESE TWO, AND SEND THEM BACK WHERE THEY CAME FROM!"

The voice was Daniel Barton's, the most outspoken and opinionated member of the class.

The students were angry and some of them were standing around Lalzari and Aaeesha, two Muslim young women who were enrolled with about forty other students in the class. Dr. Kershaw had been teaching the Religious History of the United States course for a few years at Scottsdale Community College and it was frequently mentioned in student surveys as one of the favorite classes on campus.

Daniel Barton was standing right in front of the girls, pointing menacingly; his face red with anger as he shouted at them. Their faces showed fear and embarrassment.

Most of the students were so focused on the two young Muslim women that only a few noticed Dr. Kershaw enter.

Paul Kershaw was a tall, gentle man who was always dignified and soft-spoken. He wore a suit coat or jacket most of the time wherever he went. Despite Dr. Kershaw's professional, gentle demeanor he could deliver when needed.

During his twenty years of teaching he had learned to project his voice very well and as he interrupted the disturbance he spoke to the students in a commanding voice. The tone and volume were not artificially added by Dr. Kershaw since he was furious over what was going on in the class. He boomed out, "NO ONE WILL GET RID OF ANYONE, AND MR. BARTON, IF YOU DON'T GO TO YOUR SEAT IMMEDIATELY, SO HELP ME I WILL *DROP* YOU FROM THIS CLASS WITH A FAILING GRADE AND I WILL *PERSONALLY* SEE THAT YOU ARE EXPELLED FROM THIS COLLEGE, NEVER TO RETURN!"

The mob quickly dispersed and the students, sheepishly but quickly, went to their seats, except for Daniel Barton. He slowly walked across the room and plopped himself angrily into his chair.

Dr. Kershaw was now in full control of the class and he immediately went to where Aaeesha and Lalzari were sitting. Their faces were now turned down and they were staring intently at the floor.

Dr. Kershaw knelt on one knee in front of their desks and in a gentle voice said, "Ladies, I am so sorry for the behavior of this class. You deserve better than this. I sincerely apologize on behalf of this college. Are you OK?"

Both girls nodded almost imperceptibly and kept their eyes down.

Dr. Kershaw stood and raised his line of sight and glared at the class. He didn't speak for at least thirty seconds as his eyes went from one student to the next until he had looked at every person in the room. Some met his gaze; some were too embarrassed. Daniel Barton was still angry and he stared back at Dr. Kershaw defiantly.

Dr. Kershaw's demeanor softened as he spoke to the whole class again, this time in his customary gentle tone. "I can see that it's time. I normally save this lesson for the last day of the semester but with what has happened this week I can see that the students are ready so the teacher must teach. We will save my planned discussion about the influence of East Asian religions on American society for another day."

Dr. Kershaw paused, then stepped over and sat on a tall stool at the front of the class. "I want to tell you all a story. In fact, it's *my* story. I tell it in hopes that you will see why your behavior a few moments ago is absolutely unacceptable and is not based at all on anything close to reality."

"As some of you may know, and as we have briefly mentioned at times in this class, the Soviet Union and the United States at one point were involved in what was called The Cold War. It started back in the late 1940s or early 1950s and ended around 1990 when the Soviet Union dissolved.

"The Cold War was called that because the mistrust that the countries had for each other and the angst against each other never heated up into an actual war, but they continued to jockey for strategic position and tried to embarrass each other and snub their noses at each other politically.

"The strategy employed by both countries to avoid a war was to arm themselves with nuclear weapons so thoroughly that neither side dared

161

start any conflict of great significance. They counted on the expectation that if one country launched nuclear missiles at the other country, the second country would realize, through their sophisticated radar equipment, that they were about to be destroyed and would immediately launch *their* nuclear missiles back at the first country in a counter-attack. It takes about thirty minutes for nuclear warheads to be launched and eventually fall onto a target, so logically speaking, the two superpowers could each have time to launch all their warheads toward each other, thus annihilating each other and causing widespread radioactive destruction around the planet. That avoidable event was termed MAD or Mutually Assured Destruction, and as you can see, the acronym is very apropos.

"The US hoped Russia would see the futility of nuclear war and Russia hoped the US would feel likewise. By threatening each other with annihilation it caused each country to always stop short of the ultimate act, thus avoiding world destruction. In fact, if any of you need extra credit to save your grade . . . ," and he turned to face Daniel Barton, looking directly at him as he continued, "I invite you to watch the old movie called War Games with Matthew Broderick. It's a very entertaining film and hits to the heart of what I just described about Mutually Assured Destruction."

He was still staring at Daniel as he said, "If you do watch it, I want a two-page, single-spaced, written report on it. Also, I hope you will notice the level of technology that was available to us in the 1980s, which is comical now, and I also apologize for the language. Some of you won't care or won't notice, but I had forgotten how the language was until I watched it again recently. In its day it was rated PG, but nowadays it would be PG-13 solely for the language.

"Well, to continue . . . one way that the US 'fought' the cold war," and he held up his hands and made quote marks in the air as he said the word *fought*, "was to establish and arm the Titan II missile system. We dug deep holes in the ground, called silos, and put nuclear missiles in them and we told the Soviet Union all about it and even told them where each missile was. We wanted the Soviets to know what kind of power we had and we didn't hide it at all.

"The Titan II missiles could be launched in just minutes and there were a total of 63 missiles scattered across Arkansas, Kansas, and Arizona, each with a nine megaton warhead. For perspective, the atomic bombs dropped on Hiroshima and Nagasaki, which prompted Japan's surrender in World War II, were fifteen and twenty-two kilotons, respectively. The nine-megaton warhead on each Titan II missile was forty to sixty times more powerful than what the U.S. had in World War II.

"For additional extra credit . . . ," and he again stared at Daniel Barton, "I recommend visiting the Titan Missile Museum, which is just south of Tucson right on the I-19 freeway. It has the last surviving Titan II missile, which is, of course, disarmed but still in the underground silo. It's a fascinating way to spend a couple of hours for about a $10 entry fee.

"That's the part that was known. My story comes from the part that was unknown and was a very well-kept secret. My father told me all about it many years later just before he passed away. It has been officially declassified now but good luck finding anything about it online because those involved still want to keep it a secret.

"In 1967, when I was six years old, my father worked as a technician on a radio communication tower on a hill in northeastern Wyoming in a tiny town called Pine Bluff. Seven other families also moved there at the same time my family did. For all that anybody knew, they were there to operate and maintain the newly erected radio tower. However, as my father told me later, it was all a facade. Actually, there really was a working radio tower and they did operate it but there was much more to the story.

"Pine Bluff was an hour on a small, two-lane road from the nearest town and that town wasn't much bigger. We were two hours from Belle Fourche, South Dakota and about three hours from Rapid City. Those were the nearest towns of any size.

"Pine Bluff had a population of about 1,200, mostly ranchers and farmers, but also some others. There were two gas stations, a small general store which included a soda fountain, a diner, an elementary school with grades one through eight, and a high school with grades nine through twelve. There were several other small businesses of different kinds; a feed and tack, a clothing store that didn't have much more than overalls and cowboy boots, etc. There was a small hotel that changed owners every few years because they could never get enough customers to stay in business.

"When my father went to work he drove to the radio tower building which was a little bit outside of town. Four technicians had to man the station around the clock, so of the eight technicians, there was always someone coming and going and staying, overlapping shifts. From time to

163

time, one of them would come outside the building dressed in a protective suit that looked like it was made out of aluminum foil. The information was passed along to the whole town that the radio waves generated some kind of dangerous radioactivity in a circle around the tower and the technicians had to wear special suits all the time they were in the building to protect themselves. That was actually a well-protected lie which was necessary for national security. The tower didn't generate any such thing, but because everyone thought it did, and they saw the men come out every now and then looking like spacemen, they stayed away from the building and allowed the technicians to be completely undisturbed. The reason for all that was because they weren't just radio technicians.

"Unknown to anyone else, the radio tower building was connected by a mile-long tunnel to a nearby missile silo. When the technicians arrived at the radio tower building, some of them would open a locked cabinet which turned out to be the door to a staircase that led down five flights of stairs to a tunnel below. The technicians would ride in an electric golf cart down the tunnel for a mile to a place beneath a barn at the nearby N Bar Z Ranch.

"What looked like a dilapidated old barn was directly over a 200-foot-deep missile silo containing a warhead capable of obliterating a large city. The ranch had been there for over forty years, but in the 1950s, when a horse trailer or a load of cattle or hay pulled into the barn, it wasn't always horses or cows or hay but was instead equipment or building materials coming in or dirt going out. They dug and then built an entire missile silo and stocked it with a nuclear warhead and the liquid rocket propellant to launch the missile, all disguised as the normal operations of a cattle ranch. One of the most difficult parts was making the liquid propellant tanks look like a horse trailer identical to the regular horse trailer that came and went at other times.

"The missile was built, maintained, and operated around the clock by the eight men who were called technicians but were actually rocket scientists and Air Force employees. Sorry ladies, but they were all men. Women's rights were just starting to develop in those days and in spite of what Hollywood tries to show you there were no women in that part of the workforce at the time."

At that comment, several of the young women in the class shook their heads or mumbled under their breath regarding the lack of civil rights and equality.

Dr. Kershaw continued, "The rest of us never knew what really went on. The cattle ranch operated right above the rocket, the tunnel shuttled scientists back and forth to the radio tower, and the radio tower provided the logical reason for the vans to come and go at all hours. The government had built eight homes, side by side, for the families. Us kids didn't know it, but the homes were connected by underground tunnels so the fathers could sneak in and out to and from the vans as needed.

"Now comes the part where I fit in. All eight families had a little boy about my age. They had other children too, and there were seventeen children in all when the eight families first moved there, but the hope was that because each family had a boy about the same age that it would help pull the families together. It wasn't a completely smooth ride, getting us all to exist happily together, but it worked. Of course, there were boys and girls our age in the town too.

"I suppose that if they had found eight families with little girls all about the same age, they would probably have selected those families. I don't know that there was anything magic about it; they just found eight families with at least one child of the same age and gender.

"My family was Catholic and we were from Nebraska.

"Michael Ostenson's family was from Minnesota and they were Lutherans.

"Enrico Mendocino's family was Catholic and Hispanic. They were from San Antonio, Texas.

"Owen Huish's family was from Arizona. They were members of the Church of Jesus Christ of Latter-Day Saints, commonly called Mormons.

"Clifford Johnson's family came from Mississippi. They were Southern Baptists. I heard Clifford tell me how surprised they were when they arrived in Wyoming that first night. Here was an African American family in a station wagon at a time when African Americans were viciously and violently discriminated against in the South. When they arrived in Wyoming their father was an Air Force employee. He was extremely qualified as a rocket scientist but could not get the official credentials because it was still only the 1960s. Anyway, Clifford's dad asked a gas station attendant what hotel they could stay in for the night. The attendant was puzzled by the question and said, "Sir, you can stay at any hotel you want." Mr. Johnson had never been called "Sir" by a white man in his whole life. He was completely surprised. It took quite a bit of conversation before Mr. Johnson could accept the fact that in Wyoming in the 1960s, an African American family could stay about anywhere

165

they wanted to stay, instead of the culture they had just come from where they could only stay in hotels that were designated as "Colored Only."

Dr. Kershaw continued naming the boys. "Benjamin Eisenbraun's family was Jewish, from New York City.

"Rasmi Kassab's family was from Saudi Arabia but had lived in the U.S. for some time before being put on this assignment. They were Muslims. Mrs. Kassab had studied medicine and was a doctor in a hospital in Florida before they were assigned to Wyoming. She and her husband had to sneak out of Saudi Arabia so that she could become a doctor. America would let her do that, although that had just started to be acceptable. However, the society where she came from would not allow her to be a doctor. Mr. Kassab was a rocket scientist.

"And last, but certainly not least, Ichiro Matsuzawa's family was Japanese, from Seattle, and they were Buddhists. I heard Ichiro tell about how his father, as a young boy, was kept in a Japanese internment camp during World War II. As you may know, America was afraid of the Japanese people living in America at that time and they incarcerated over 100,000 of them in what was basically prison for families. The Matsuzawa family had lived in the U.S. for over thirty years by the time World War II broke out and they were full-fledged American Citizens, but they were still feared as having the potential of fighting against America.

"So, eight families were brought together because of two common characteristics: they each had a little boy and they each had a rocket scientist father who posed as a radio tower operator.

"When we first got to Pine Bluff we didn't blend together very well. Most of us boys became friends quickly, as kids often do, but some of the parents were still unsure and slightly aloof until three things happened.

"The first event happened not long after we got there. Ichiro, the Japanese boy, and Rasmi, the Saudi, were playing one day and wandered off, getting lost. As it got dark the adults realized it was going to be a cold autumn night, and remember that this was northeastern Wyoming where it didn't just get cool, it got cold. In addition, a big storm was brewing. When we heard that two of the boys were lost, the adults all went searching, everyone pairing up with a partner so that no one was searching alone.

"The wind continued to get worse and it started to rain. About 10:00 p.m., Mr. Eisenbraun and Mr. Ostenson came in with both boys. They were all cold and wet but they were OK. In fact, Rasmi had fallen asleep in Mr. Eisenbraun's arms. My mom told me that it was a beautiful sight to see Mr. Eisenbraun, the Jewish father, handing the sleeping Rasmi over to his Muslim mother as tears streamed down her face. Mr. Kassab was still out searching with Mr. Huish but they came back around midnight, both soaked to the skin. You can imagine the relief that Mr. Kassab felt that his son had already been found. In spite of their stark religious differences the Kassabs and the Eisenbrauns were good friends after that.

"Only a few weeks later, the second thing happened that helped pull us together. Owen Huish and I were playing and we found the hood of an old car near the top of a hill. We decided it would be a good sled with the newly fallen snow so we climbed on and started pushing it. We thought it would slide gently down the nice, clear road covered with six inches of snow, but instead, it slid off the side of the road, careening down through the rocks and bouncing off trees. When we finally came to a stop I had been knocked unconscious and at some point my arm had hung over the side of the hood. I was probably trying to hold on but I don't remember any of it. My coat sleeve was ripped off and my bare arm was nearly severed by the hood of the car.

"Owen was pretty banged up but he was OK enough to run for help. They carried me quickly to Mrs. Kassab. With her medical training she was part of the reason the Kassab family was sent to that remote part of Wyoming with us because we needed a doctor.

"By this time, I had lost a lot of blood. Mrs. Kassab skillfully cared for me and controlled the blood loss while my parents drove me the three hours into Rapid City. I almost died, but thanks to Mrs. Kassab I survived with only a few lingering effects."

At this point, Dr. Kershaw held up his left hand for all the class to see that he was missing his pinky finger and his ring finger. Some of them had never noticed that he was missing two fingers.

"From then on, my mother and Mrs. Kassab were best of friends.

"The third thing that pulled us together happened six weeks after my accident. I was due for a doctor's checkup in Rapid City, South Dakota. Some of the moms realized that we all needed measles vaccinations, so my mom and Mrs. Kassab took us into town on a Friday afternoon. I don't remember what year that was, but the measles vaccine was first introduced in 1963, so it was sometime thereafter. For some reason they didn't take all our siblings. I presume they only took part of us because of the difficulty of getting all seventeen of us together.

We all piled into our station wagon to go, and I know what you're thinking: *not enough seat belts*. Back then hardly anybody wore seat belts and some cars didn't even have them. Besides, our station wagon had something in the far back that the little kids thought was really cool. You could pull up two panels in the floor to reveal two large seats that faced each other. Four kids could sit back there and it was the best because you were knee to knee with the guy across from you. We always argued about who got to sit in the back.

"I forgot to tell you that Mrs. Ostenson was a school teacher at Pine Bluff Elementary. Because of the timing of our birthdays we were spread across two grades and Mrs. Ostenson taught one of those grades. It was no problem for us in Pine Bluff to miss a day of school, since we made up a big portion of the kids in the school. In fact, the two grades of school got canceled for that day because we were almost all the students in those two grades. The other students were delighted, of course. So, on that Friday afternoon we went to town for our shots—and my checkup. Our siblings got their shots later if I remember right.

"At the last minute, my doctor in town had to help with an emergency, which caused a long wait at the clinic and delayed my appointment. Meanwhile, the other boys got their shots and were playing at the park in town. The seven of them ended up behind the maintenance shed and were confronted by five of the bigger kids from town. These five boys started making fun of Clifford and Ichiro, calling them racial slurs and pushing them around. Not everyone in Wyoming was as accepting as the gas station attendant.

"Well, Benjamin, Owen, Rasmi, and Enrico wouldn't have it, and lit into the bigger boys, defending Clifford and Ichiro. Clifford and Ichiro also joined the fray and the six little boys fought the five big ones while Michael ran for help. By the time some adults got there our group was sporting bruises, black eyes, split lips, and torn shirts. They looked like they had taken on a whole platoon. The adults chased the big boys off with plenty of threats about how much trouble they were in, and then the parents asked the little boys what happened.

"Ben said, 'They made fun of Ichiro and Clifford and we didn't like that, so me and Owen fought 'em all.' Then he smiled proudly and said, indicating the other boys, 'And they fought too, and they're good fighters!'

"After a little more medical care for the minor injuries from the fight, and a stern lecture about not fighting, and after my doctor's checkup ended, we all headed back to Pine Bluff. As the boys talked about the fight I actually felt jealous that I hadn't been involved.

"From those three events, our families, and especially us as boys, bonded together very tightly. We had our scuffles and disagreements, but for the most part we got along very well, as did our parents. We became a very close-knit little group.

Dr. Kershaw smiled, "Well, we weren't always perfect. If you've never been chewed out in Spanish you're missing out. One time, Mrs. Mendocino caught Enrico and me just after we finished scratching our names on the back door of their house. I didn't know a woman could talk that fast, and I didn't understand one word of her Spanish, but I assure you I knew I was getting a tongue lashing and I vowed to stay on Mrs. Mendocino's good side after that."

The class laughed and even Daniel Barton cracked a smile.

Dr. Kershaw continued, "One day when we were around nine or ten years old, two of the moms decided we needed to form a Boy Scout troop. Actually, at first it was Cub Scouts because we were still young, but as we grew it changed to Boy Scouts. Eventually, at about age fifteen or sixteen, we all earned the Eagle Scout rank together. If there had been a local paper we would have made the news, but we were too remote for that. Since the requirement for Eagle rank is to do a leadership project that benefits your community, and our community was very small, we got pretty creative about our projects.

"Also, each boy earned the religious award for his faith: Clifford Johnson, the Baptist, and Michael Ostenson, the Lutheran, earned the God and Family award. Ichiro Matsuzawa, the Buddhist, earned the METTA award. Enrico Mendocino, the Catholic, earned the Parvuli Dei award. Owen Huish, the Mormon, earned the On My Honor award. Rasmi Kassab, the Muslim, earned the Bismillah award. Benjamin Eisenbraun, the Jewish boy, earned the Aleph award. As a side note, I would not normally remember the names of all those awards but for the fact that I have looked them up two or three times each year to tell this story to my students. Over the years I have memorized the names of the awards.

"At some point along the way, and maybe it was because of the scout troop, we picked a name for our gang. Back then gangs were often good and didn't have a negative connotation like they do today. We loved to

169

watch a popular TV cartoon called Roger Ramjet, about a not-so-smart superhero who always saved America and the rest of the civilized world. It was about the caliber of cartoons like Phineas and Ferb or maybe Gumball or SpongeBob Square Pants that you are all familiar with.

"Somewhere along the way our group of eight boys started calling ourselves "The Ramjets" in honor of our favorite superhero. That name has stayed with us through the years.

"Our families did everything together because we were all we had. Actually, sometimes we did include the rancher's family, by the name of Nelson. They had a couple of girls but no boys. We also included some of the kids from the town.

"Most of the time each of the eight families held its own worship service on their chosen day, Saturday or Sunday or whatever. Then for big events and celebrations, we invited each other to join in and we did. We all went to the Christmas Program. We all helped celebrate Hanukah and Ramadan. We all celebrated when Owen Huish and later his little sister were baptized at age eight in Pine Creek just outside of town and when Ben Eisenbraun had his bar mitzvah when he turned thirteen.

"We became very close religiously, even though we all had different faiths. Mrs. Johnson, from Mississippi, had a beautiful singing voice and I loved to hear her sing the African American spirituals. Even as a young boy I would get goosebumps because of how moving and beautiful she sang "Sweet Little Jesus Boy." She would close her eyes and lean her head back and sing . . . and oh my, it was stunning! We learned about each other's faith and learned to accept each other the way we were.

"Sometimes we ended up at each other's house during the other family's scripture time or prayer time. I've prayed and studied scriptures in all those different faiths and they did the same with me at my house. It didn't hurt us a bit, and I assert that in fact, it made us better. Better because we learned from each other religious truths and how to behave, and better because we learned to respect each other's beliefs. In spite of each family's individual beliefs each of us boys had a very broad religious foundation.

"The concept of social diversity had not even been invented yet but we had it growing up in Pine Bluff. We wouldn't think of stifling another family's right to practice their religion. I'm saddened by the way diversity today has become a way to repress or nullify all differences instead of celebrating them. We all told each other "Merry Christmas" or "Happy Hanukah" or "Ramadan Mubarak" or whatever cultural holiday each was celebrating at the time. We celebrated our differences together. That's what diversity is all about.

"We grew up together and eventually we grew old enough to move away, even while our families stayed in Pine Bluff. Owen Huish went away to serve his church as a missionary in, guess where? Japan! Ichiro's parents were delighted. When he came home two years later he spoke fluent Japanese and they talked at length in their native tongue.

"I went away to study for the seminary but instead of becoming a priest; I ended up teaching Religious History of the United States at a community college, and I'm very happy.

"Enrico was the best athlete among us and ended up going to Florida State on a baseball scholarship. I guess all those days where we all played baseball on a makeshift field for something to do gave Enrico a good foundation in baseball. I also wonder if his father being a rocket scientist somehow passed down into his genes because by the time he was sixteen or seventeen, he had a rocket for an arm and his home run hits were like missiles sailing into orbit. We had to expand the size of our field because we, mostly Enrico, outgrew it.

"Clifford joined the military and was killed in an accident at an airshow in Germany in 1982. That crash claimed the lives of 46 people, including paratrooper Clifford Johnson. It was a very sad day for the Ramjets, and everyone who could possibly be there attended the military funeral. Mrs. Johnson was too emotional to sing but she hugged us like each one of us was her son. She told us how blessed she was to have such good boys for her son to grow up with. I assure you that none of us Ramjets who watched Mrs. Johnson accept that folded U.S. flag from that Marine's white gloves have any sympathy for these spoiled athletes who take a knee during the national anthem. There are more appropriate ways to share your opinion and exercise your First Amendment rights.

"Over the years the Ramjets kept in touch. When my wife died a few years ago I went through some serious loneliness or maybe even depression. The Ramjets took turns calling me every week and they helped pull me through. There have been many other times when we helped each other. We manage to get together every other year or so for dinner and we love to sit around and reminisce about the good old days.

"And here's what I've learned as I've thought about Pine Bluff and the Ramjets over the years. It was our faith that made us behave the way we did. Each of us was well taught and we were well behaved. We loved each other for who we were and are. No one has more respect for different faiths than the Ramjets.

"All of the terrorism that has gone on this week has *absolutely nothing* to do with religion. Instead, it has absolutely everything to do with how one behaves. You aren't good or bad because of your faith tradition. You are good or bad because of what you do.

"All religions and faiths have good people and bad people as members. Hopefully, there are way more good people because that's what religion and faith are all about: helping bad people become good and good people become better. But just because some people of a certain religion are bad doesn't mean the religion itself is bad or that all people who practice that religion are bad. It is a completely false concept if you think religion makes people evil. It's the behavior of a person or group that makes them evil, not their religion.

"I have read the Bible, the Quran, the Book of Mormon, each in their entirety, and I've read from many Buddhist texts. All eight families in Pine Bluff used their own scriptural texts as a major part of their family life. We all studied our unique scriptures, but from what I have found and read, all of those scriptural works have many similarities and all of those works teach their believers to fear God, to love their fellow men and women, to strive to do what is right, and to be good citizens.

"Interestingly, all of those scriptures also talk about war and defending the followers of your faith from oppression, from slavery, and from destruction. The Christians sing "Onward Christian Soldiers" and "We Are All Enlisted." The Old Testament tells stories of the Children of Israel attacking the wicked inhabitants of the Promised Land to cleanse it before they entered. You may hear from some misguided people that the Quran tells Muslims to fight against the infidels but the way I read it, it says the Muslim people have it as their duty to defend themselves when attacked and threatened. Nowhere in any of those religious works have I seen anything that condones attacking offensively except for those Bible passages I just referred to.

"Our eight families are proof that people of different religions can and do get along very well and they can all love each other and watch out for each other. If anyone wants to fight against other people in the name of religion it's because they are misguided and have twisted their scriptural directives to the extreme and distorted their faith. If someone disobeys the law and attacks or threatens others then the others have the right, by law *and* by their religious teachings, to defend themselves."

172

Dr. Kershaw paused.

"So, that's my story. What I hope you learn from it is to respect all people *because* of their religious beliefs, and that if you get angry about bad people, get angry because of their behavior and not because of their religion.

"Before we finish, let me teach you a little bit about Muslims in America. Many people think that Arab Americans are all Muslim. I'm using the term Arab Americans to include all the ethnic groups from the Middle East. In fact, 63% of Arab Americans are Christian and only 24% are Muslim. For those who aren't clear, a Muslim is generally a person who identifies with practicing the religion of Islam.

"Many of the Muslims in America immigrated here, just like the pilgrims on the Mayflower and the many, many others who have come here throughout U.S. history. Also, many people have converted to Islam from another religion or no previous religion. In addition, many Muslims are second, third, or even fourth-generation American. Their ancestors immigrated to America and they have now grown up here too, one generation after another."

Dr. Kershaw looked toward the two Muslim young women, who were still sitting with their heads slightly down. He smiled, closed his eyes and bent his head forward slightly, tapping the top of his head several times with his index finger.

He looked up and continued. "In fact, this old brain doesn't retrieve data like it used to. I met Lalzari's mother a few weeks ago at a community leaders networking event. Lalzari, I forgot to tell you."

Lalzari raised her head for the first time and looked at Dr. Kershaw.

"Lalzari's mother is a delightful and intelligent woman. She is an attorney here in the valley, has raised a good family and is a great strength to this community. And . . ." Dr. Kershaw paused for effect. "She was born and raised in Queens, New York in the same house where her father was raised.

Dr. Kershaw raised his hands and used his fingers to make quotes in the air. "To think that all Muslims are "*from*" a Middle-Eastern country is completely false. That would be like saying all Christians are "*from*" Europe where the Catholic Church began or "*from*" Israel where Jesus Christ lived. We wouldn't think of telling Christians to "go back home where you belong" expecting them to go back to Europe or Israel. We wouldn't think about telling the Jewish people to go back to Jerusalem where they are "*from*" when they have been in the U.S. for many, many years. This *is* where they are from.

Dr. Kershaw paused again and looked around the room. Then he continued, "All right. That was a long lecture and was very personal to me but it was a message for you. If I as the teacher cannot take from my experiences and education and successfully pass good principles and ideas on to you as a student, then I have failed in my role as a teacher and you have failed in your role as a student. I hope you learned something about those around you by hearing my story and by thinking about things differently than you did before today.

"I also hope that each of you, and especially you, Mr. Barton, will apologize to Lalzari and Aaeesha for mistreating them today. And I encourage you to do it on the way out of class. Don't wait. What if you didn't apologize to them today and then something happened so that you couldn't, especially with a week like we are having here in the Phoenix area? How would you feel the rest of your life?

"In addition, please try to see people for how they behave and accept what they believe.

"Again, I apologize to you two young women. We want you in our class and we want good people like you in our country. We are sorry when anyone, be they in this class or outside of this class, mistreats you or looks down on you because of your religion."

With that, Dr. Paul Kershaw turned quietly but abruptly and left the room.

With class over, all the students filed past to apologize to Aaeesha and Lalzari. Some of the young women in the class even gave them hugs. A few wiped away tears. Daniel Barton offered a very humble and sincere apology.

As Dr. Kershaw headed home after class he was thinking about the events of the day. These were difficult issues for people to deal with; especially those who were younger and those who let themselves get caught up in politics or emotion without thinking things through.

When he was almost home, he suddenly remembered that his daughter, Belinda, was coming over that evening and bringing her two children, Micah and Sylvia. He always liked to have a treat for them. When his wife was alive, she always had raspberry chocolate chip cookies and she went to great lengths to find raspberry chocolate chips. Now that it was just him, he resorted to candy. Belinda loved red licorice and Micah and Sylvia liked pretty much anything that was sweet.

174

Just before he arrived home he stopped at the corner convenience store and gas station. He had stopped there many times and had gotten to know the owner fairly well. His name was Wisal and he was a Muslim from Iraq who had fled the oppressive regime of Saddam Hussein years before. In fact, his father and an uncle were tortured and killed by Hussein's henchmen before the rest of the family escaped. Wisal was a very devout man who was very kind and friendly. Wisal had gone through the whole immigration process and had taken his oath of allegiance to the United States in a citizenship ceremony several months earlier. He invited Dr. Kershaw to the ceremony where he became a U.S. citizen, and Dr. Kershaw was honored and pleased to be there.

It was busy in the store so both checkout counters were running, with several people waiting in both lines. Wisal was running one cash register and his cousin, Aland, was running the other. As Dr. Kershaw got to the counter, he said "As-Salaam-Alaikum" to Aland and then looked over and said the same thing to Wisal at the other register. That was the traditional Arabic greeting that Muslims say to each other around the world and it means "Peace be unto you." It is similar to the way people say "Aloha" to each other in the South Pacific. The two men responded to Dr. Kershaw with the traditional reply, "Wa-Alaikum-Salaam," which means, "And unto you, peace."

Suddenly, the peace in the room changed to chaos as a young man who was at the other register pulled out a knife and pointed it at Wisal, yelling loudly, "It's you and your disgusting Muslim friends! We had peace in this city and then all of you radical Islamists started moving in and now it's completely out of hand and someone's got to do something! Why don't you get out of our country and go back where you came from!"

Wisal was standing there with fear on his face, not knowing what to do as he stared at the shining, menacing blade of the knife. Some of the people in the store screamed and others didn't really know what to do. It happened so fast.

Wisal held up his hands as if he were being robbed. He cried, "Don't hurt me!"

The young man started to climb up on the counter to get closer to Wisal. But before he could do that, Wisal backed against the wall. The store had four-foot-high counters and the young man had to struggle a little to get far enough across it to reach for Wisal, who was about three feet away. It must not have crossed Wisal's mind that he could have turned and run toward Aland and out the open end of the counter to his right.

However, before the young man could actually get to Wisal with the knife, Dr. Paul Kershaw reached with his long arm and hit the young man in the side of the face with a blast of pepper spray. The cash registers and customer counters were about six feet apart, with displays of merchandise and the cash register monitors, but Dr. Kershaw had reached over the items and sprayed the young man with the pepper spray from a range of about two feet.

Dr. Kershaw carried a Charter Arms Pathfinder .22 magnum revolver concealed in a shoulder holster beneath the jacket that he always wore, but because of the proximity of the young man to him and because he had a knife instead of a gun, Dr. Kershaw chose to use his pepper spray. Many people who carried concealed weapons also carried other means of disabling a threat. Pepper spray or an intensely bright flashlight could be used in the right situation as a first option, with the deadly weapon used as a last resort. At times the weapon was the first choice, depending on how close the threat was, who else was around, whether the situation was indoors or outside, and the type of threat. A non-lethal method to stop a threat would be used out of a desire to not cause a death that could be avoided. Another very valid reason was the risk of prosecution or a personal injury suit against the defending person. There had been many instances where someone used their weapon to stop a threat, only to be charged with murder or manslaughter because the situation didn't necessarily call for lethal force. In many cases the family members brought a wrongful death lawsuit.

All of those thoughts ran quickly through Dr. Kershaw's mind in a split second and he opted for pepper spray instead of his weapon. His choice turned out to be the right one for the situation. Dr. Kershaw had tried to reach out in front of the young man as much as possible so as to hit his eyes and nose. The active ingredient in the pepper spray, Oleoresin Capsicum, derived from hot cayenne peppers, produced its desired effect and the young man immediately stopped thinking about harming Wisal.

The young man screamed and dropped his knife. He grabbed at his face with both hands, thereby rubbing the pepper spray even more completely into his eyes. Then he jerked back, using his legs for leverage, and his whole body squirmed off the counter. He fell backward to the floor in front of the other customers, writhing and screaming with pain. It was then that Dr. Kershaw saw a woman behind the young man lower a bottle of beer. She had obviously been thinking about hitting him with it but didn't have the right angle. They looked at each other and nodded solemnly.

The pepper spray in the air caused several others to start coughing while their eyes watered. Many of them had to quickly go outside to breathe fresh air. A few of them backed up, coughing, but made sure the young man wasn't going to try to go anywhere. It was obvious he was in no condition to do anything; he was completely incapacitated by the pepper spray. He lay there moaning loudly and cursing.

A little of the pepper spray had drifted over to Wisal, who was still backed flat against the wall. It was enough to make him cough and wince and tears flowed down his cheeks.

Amidst his own coughing, Dr. Kershaw said to the hacking and crying customers standing there in awe, "I'm sorry, but no one has the right to attack an innocent, unarmed man regardless of his religion."

People had already called 911 on their cell phones and the sound of sirens could be heard approaching the convenience store. Others were using their phones to take video of the situation. Dr. Kershaw walked around the counter and saw that Aland was sitting quietly in a daze on a stool near the wall. Dr. Kershaw went over to Wisal who had pulled a handkerchief from his pocket and was standing there against the wall wiping at his eyes.

Smiling gently, Dr. Kershaw said, "It's OK. You are safe now."

Wisal looked Dr. Kershaw in the eye and then reached out and embraced him with tears streaming down his face and a smile of relief on his lips. As he did so, he said, "Thank you, my friend . . . my brother."

28 Family Time

On Thursday morning, Cindy Clevenger awoke and lay in bed for a while to plan her day. Curtis had preschool that morning and then in the afternoon Cindy was going to take the boys to the mall to get the ring at the jewelry store.

Curtis loved preschool. Cindy could hardly pull him away each time he went. Thursday was no different. On the way home he talked non-stop in his four-year-old vocabulary about everything they had done and all the fun they had.

Cindy fed the boys lunch and put them down for a nap. She had not had the desire to do anything except read and she glanced at the dirty dishes in the kitchen sink. She almost turned to do them but she just couldn't muster the energy. Instead, she laid down on her bed and finished her eBook about the Arizona couple hiding from the corrupt FBI agents. She admired the young mother for her ability to use guns to protect her family when needed. Cindy didn't think she could do that. She had always felt like Alan would protect them. However, she realized after this week that maybe she was starting to change.

About 1:30 she heard the garage door open. Something about the way it was designed or installed made it so that you could hear it through the entire house. It wasn't loud but you knew it was moving. She wasn't expecting Alan. She grabbed the Walther, which had now become a closer companion than in the past, and sat on the bed watching the open door, waiting. She heard the door from the garage open and Alan's voice called, "Cindy? Are you home?" Of course he knew she was home because her car was parked in the garage but he always called out anyway.

She quickly hid the Walther under some clothes on a high shelf in their closet. She didn't want Alan to see her feeling anxious, and the shelf was completely out of reach of the kids. As she came out of the closet Alan was just coming into the bedroom.

She ran to him and although she didn't intend to act scared, she threw herself into his arms and hugged him tightly. She held him for a long time with her face buried against his chest. He tried to pull back a few times but she just clung fiercely to him. Finally he just kept his arms around her and enjoyed her embrace.

She released him, looked into his eyes, and said, "Wow! I knew I missed you but I didn't realize I missed you that much. Why are you home so early in the day?"

Alan explained the order from Victor and said he was very tired and glad for the break.

They spent the afternoon together, alone while the kids finished their naps, and then playing with the kids in the back yard. They went out for fast food and after that they watched one of Curtis's favorite movies, Spirit, about a horse that lived in the 1800s in the American West.

Alan didn't want to talk about work, although he did tell Cindy that he had made no breakthroughs in the dead air in their intelligence. He said it was very frustrating.

All afternoon she kept thinking about the ring but she knew she wouldn't be able to go get it today. She'd have to go to the mall tomorrow. She did ask Alan about their planned date on Friday night but he said he didn't know and that they'd have to play it by ear.

They had a very nice day and evening together. They had so much fun that they put the boys to bed later than normal. They would be tired and probably sleep well into the morning tomorrow.

As Alan and Cindy knelt to pray before going to bed she asked if she could pray this time. Usually, she waited for Alan to either start praying or to ask her. Sometimes, probably too often, she hoped he wouldn't ask her or she would be a bit exasperated when he did. Not this time; she was intensely grateful he was there and she also wanted to do all she could to ease his burden.

In the prayer, she prayed for safety for their family and friends and for all the people in Arizona who were exposed to the terrorist attacks. She prayed for the people who had been injured and who had lost loved ones and she prayed for the many people who were the first responders. She asked God to bless the many people whose lives had been shattered and changed by the attacks this week. She also prayed for Alan. She asked God to inspire and guide him; to help him know what to do and where to look to figure out how to stop the attacks. She prayed that law enforcement would be in the right places at the right times. She gave thanks for the armed citizens who had done so much to save so many lives. She ended by thanking God for the righteous people who had given their lives to establish and preserve freedom in America.

Like other righteous people throughout history, they prayed hard, they worked hard to do all they could do, and then they entrusted themselves to the love and power of God.

*   *   *

The next morning Alan awoke and looked over at Cindy. She appeared to be sleeping peacefully. He stirred and then turned over to climb out of bed but her hand caught his arm. She pulled him toward her

179

and then into her arms. She said, "Where do you think you are going, my love?"

"I've got to get back to the office. Victor only gave me a temporary reprieve. I must say that a good night's sleep has really been helpful."

"I'm glad. You know I'll be praying for you, as I have all week."

"Thanks. It means a lot even if I don't always take the time to tell you."

Just then eighteen-month-old Carlton started crying and Cindy said, "You go get ready while I get the boys. They are up early for going to bed so late, but at least they will get to see their daddy for a few more minutes. I have a feeling that with the way the week has been going and with no end in sight, our date and weekend are officially off."

"Probably. Sorry."

"That's OK. Our love is forever, so I can take you on the date in a few days or a few weeks when this all ends . . . hoping this all ends. You'll still love me in a few weeks, won't you?"

He kissed her and said, "Absolutely!" and rolled quickly out of bed and headed for the shower.

FRIDAY

29 Cuss and Discuss

Alan had a frustratingly long morning at work on Friday. He pored over the evidence in the ten cases they had to that point. He tried to analyze them one by one. He tried to compare them. He tried different combinations of them. He could see patterns in several places but he just couldn't find anything that gave him clues about where they would strike next. He felt sure it was Al-Musawi, especially after talking with the guy at the church, but he didn't have anything concrete. They had checked out all of Al-Musawi's previously known locations and those of other members of his cell. Al-Musawi had seemingly vanished and Alan didn't know where else to look to try to intercept him. Alan's team continued to watch all of their sources and reach out to anyone they could think of, with nothing but dead ends and no helpful information.

About 12:30 Alan suddenly had the urge to pray. He had been praying off and on all day—all week in fact. But this was a sudden, new feeling of the need for additional prayer. He bowed his head and prayed.

When he finished he still had the urge to pray. This time he got up, closed and locked his office door, and then knelt by his chair, pouring out his heart to the Lord. He said he had tried to do his best and he was willing to do whatever he needed to do. He pleaded and asked for direction and inspiration. He finished his prayer and remained kneeling for a while, just waiting and listening for an answer. Nothing!

Alan was very faithful and trusted that God would answer his prayers according to His will and time table and Alan had learned to not get discouraged when answers to prayers were harder to come by. He finally got up, walked to his door and opened it.

As he turned to go back to his desk a strong thought suddenly filled his mind: "Take a team to Roosevelt Dam now!" It was very intense, very clear, and he felt like it was some kind of message from God. No, actually he *knew* it was a message from God; it was not something he would think of on his own. After Cindy's prayer last night and now this impression that was so specific, he knew it couldn't have come from any other source.

He called Cindy. "Your prayer was answered, at least in part. I just had the distinct feeling that something is going to happen at Roosevelt Dam and I have to take a team there."

"The one way up the river?"

"Yes. It is old but strong and it holds back a lot of water. If the terrorists could figure out how to break it, it could be catastrophic! There are three dams below Roosevelt, each with a sizeable lake. They could break under the increased pressure and the whole valley would be flooded. I can't even begin to imagine the damage and loss of life."

"Could someone break a dam like that?"

"Probably not, unless they had a nuclear bomb or by using heavy machinery for days. I don't think the terrorists could get a nuke in there but maybe they are going to try. I just know that last night you prayed that Heavenly Father would give me inspiration and direction, and I was just given the impression to take a team to Roosevelt Dam. I don't know when I'll be home. And now I have to figure out how to convince Victor."

"Well, knowing what you have told me about Victor it will be like Moses telling Pharaoh to let the Children of Israel out of Egypt." She laughed in spite of the tension in the situation.

"Yeah, I will just march in there and say, 'Victor, God told me to take a team up to Roosevelt Dam.' He was so against my earlier hunch."

"But the events proved that you were right. Maybe he'll see it your way this time."

"Maybe so. I need to get going."

"OK. Good luck with Victor and at the dam. *Please* be safe! I'll be praying for you."

Alan hung up the phone, got up and walked down to Victor's office. He didn't know what he was going to say.

Victor was sitting at his desk.

Alan said, "Victor, I got a tip. I need to go to Roosevelt Dam. With a team. Now."

"Where did you get the tip from?"

"From one of my sources."

"No one else mentioned anything from a source."

"I know, but I got the tip, and we need to go to the dam."

"That's two hours away, maybe three. What makes you so sure that's where we need to go."

"That's what the tip said."

"Who was the tip from?"

"I'd rather not reveal the source."

"Alan, you expect me to release a team of our people at a critical time based on a wild-goose-chase of a tip, and you can't even tell me who the tip is from?"

Alan just stood there looking at Victor. Victor glared at Alan. Finally, Alan spoke softly.

"I didn't say I can't tell you; I said I'd rather *not*. Victor, you know I had a hunch that something significant was going to happen but we couldn't put our finger on anything to support any action. Well, "significant" doesn't even *begin* to describe what has happened, just like my hunch."

"Not just like your hunch. You didn't know any details."

"But I knew something was going to happen and everyone dismissed it."

"Who's the tip from?"

"I said I'd rather not tell you?"

"Then I'm not authorizing anything. You can go back to your desk and look for a tip from a more reliable source."

"Oh, there's no source more reliable than this source."

"Well then tell me who it is before I start swearing. I'm working very hard to hold back because I know you don't like me to swear around you."

"Victor, I never said you couldn't swear around me."

"I know you never said it . . . but I just don't because I respect you."

"Well, thanks, Victor. I sincerely appreciate that."

"But I am losing my patience . . . the little bit that I have left this week. Who is the source?"

"OK, but there's some background before I tell you."

"I'm starting to wonder if I know where this is going."

"Probably. When you sent me home yesterday . . . well, last night when I was talking to Cindy . . . well, when Cindy and I were praying last night . . . she prayed that I would be inspired to know what to do or where to go. I've been trying to figure it out all day and a few minutes ago I felt like I needed to pray again. Afterward, I got an intense, overpowering thought in my mind: Take a team to Roosevelt Dam. I can't get the thought out of my head. In fact, it keeps getting more intense and . . . pressing . . . as the minutes tick by."

"Alan, you expect me to release a team of people to drive three hours away from Phoenix when Phoenix is under attack, based on a tip from a source you and I can't talk to anyone about? Request denied! And that's final. Now get out of my office."

Alan glared at Victor as Victor glared back. Alan had no more to say. He turned and trudged out the door and down the hall to his office. He plopped down in the chair at his desk and turned to look out the window. He knew something was going to happen at Roosevelt Dam, but he didn't know what. And worse, he didn't know how to convince Victor to let him go. Alan closed his eyes and prayed in his heart, "Heavenly Father. I tried to do my best. I'm sorry I failed. Please help me know what to do or help Victor to accept my . . . your . . . request . . . instruction . . . command."

Alan opened his eyes and continued to look out the window. He felt the impression that he needed to start preparing. He didn't even have permission to go but he knew he needed to prepare. He turned around and started typing a list of what they would need and who should go. After he had typed for about five minutes Alan saw motion out of the corner of his eye and he looked up to see Victor standing in his doorway.

"I didn't hear you come in."

"Well, I just got here . . . and I don't . . . ."

"What?"

"Alan, go. Get a team together quickly and go to Roosevelt Dam."

"What changed your mind?"

"I . . . I can't explain it. I just suddenly had this gut feeling that it's really important for you to take a team to Roosevelt Dam. I know it has to be done even though I think it's crazy. I also feel like you need to take the two armored vehicles."

"As a matter of fact, Victor, I just finished my list of who and what to take. And I also thought about the armoreds."

"Go, keep in touch . . . and may God go with you."

Alan realized that was the most religious thing he had ever heard Victor Pilchick say.

30 The Ring

On Friday morning after Alan Clevenger left for his office at the FBI building, Cindy Clevenger planned her day. She had some things to do that morning but she vowed that right after the boys had lunch and naps she would go to the mall and get Alan's ring. She called the jewelry store mid-morning to confirm that she would come that afternoon.

She had felt like such a victim all week. It surprised her a little how vulnerable she felt. She thought with a husband in the FBI she would feel more secure. She knew now what would make her feel more secure— carrying a gun of her own. She wondered what Alan would say when she told him that she had been thinking about carrying the Walther or some other smaller gun.

She decided to feed the boys an early lunch so she could lay them down for a nap. Since they were up late the night before and woke up relatively early that morning, they would go to sleep for an earlier nap. She had another book—the sequel to *Emancipation Expedition* that she finished the day before. *Emancipation Expedition* was awesome! The sequel, *Emigration Expedition*, promised to be about another journey of freedom. She couldn't wait to get into it, but she had to get the boys down first.

Just after the boys dropped off to sleep her phone rang. It was Alan and he told her about the impression to go to Roosevelt Dam. After the call Cindy knelt beside the bed and prayed for her husband and for all law enforcement personnel and for Arizonans and Americans in general.

When she finished she climbed back on the bed and started the novel. Suddenly she remembered that she was supposed to teach a

Sunday School lesson to the 14-year-olds on Sunday and she hadn't started preparing. She got up and printed the lesson from the internet, got her scriptures and started reading the lesson.

The next thing Cindy knew, little Carlton was crying. She looked at the clock and was surprised to see that it was 4:30! She had fallen asleep. The boys usually napped for less than two hours, but today they slept for three and a half hours and they all overslept. She made a mental note to not disrupt their normal routine from now on.

She jumped up, got the boys and started preparing dinner. By the time she had some mac and cheese ready, along with some fish sticks, mixed vegetables and juice, it was 5:15. After they ate and she got the boys cleaned up and made herself presentable to go to the mall, it was just after 6:00.

As she gathered their things to head for the mall she thought again about being a victim and she grabbed the Walther. She tucked it deep into one of the pockets of the diaper bag. She didn't know how to handle the tactical aspects of a situation if she were to get into one, but she could shoot and she was not afraid to use the gun if needed. She wasn't going to be a victim anymore. She had researched online sometime this week that in Arizona anyone twenty-one years or older could carry a concealed weapon even without a permit. She had talked about that with Alan before but she wanted to be sure. With that knowledge, she was comfortable that she wasn't breaking the law by hiding the gun in the diaper bag. She thought about the woman on the light rail train on Monday. The woman carried a concealed weapon, perhaps in her diaper bag, and if she could do it Cindy could too.

As she walked out the door, she thought of a quote she heard once from a motivational speaker named Les Brown. She wasn't sure if it exactly fit because she didn't consider a gun battle an opportunity, but the concept was right, "Better to be prepared and not have an opportunity than to have an opportunity and not be prepared."

When they got to the mall, Cindy noticed that the parking lot wasn't as full as she expected for a Friday night. She knew that because of the terrorist activity many people had stayed home. The news media and talk radio programs she listened to while driving had discussed whether or not people should stay home this week. They debated what was best to show to the terrorists. Should people keep living their lives as normal to show that they would not be intimidated by the terrorists, or would people cower in the corner, so to speak, and just stay home? Evidently, while she was showing her courage others were showing their fear. She did feel comforted knowing she had a weapon so she could at least fight back if needed. She also realized the chances of being in the same location as a terrorist event were probably about as great as getting in a car wreck just driving around town.

Once inside the mall the first thing they saw was the play area. Curtis loved to ride the toys that moved or rocked if you put in enough quarters. Cindy had learned to hoard quarters and put them in the diaper bag so she always had plenty when they were there and had time to stop. It wasn't even 6:30 and the mall didn't close until 9:00 so they had plenty of time. Eighteen-month-old Carlton enjoyed riding behind Curtis on the horse as long as Cindy held him while the horse smoothly and gently rocked back and forth.

After a few rides they headed toward the jewelry store. As luck always had it they passed the food court and had to stop for a "Cream Cone," as four-year-old Curtis called it. When he was first learning how to talk he left off the "ice," but it was so cute they let it go. They knew he would learn to say it correctly at some point. His pronunciation was good and that was of greater concern to them; the vocabulary change could come later.

While Curtis had his mini cone Cindy shared her regular cone with Carlton. The next stop was the restroom to wash off the stickiness from the ice cream.

They finally arrived at the jewelry store. The ring was beautiful and Cindy was so glad to finally have it. She put the ring box deep in the diaper bag. As she was getting ready to leave, some comment was made about the small crowd in the mall for a Friday.

The clerk said, "Yeah, it's about like a Tuesday or Wednesday. Some people are cautious. I wasn't sure I wanted to come to work either but you can't stop living your life."

Cindy agreed.

The clerk said, "Somewhere in the process of ordering and getting this ring I thought I heard you say that your husband works for the FBI."

Cindy said, "Yes, but we don't talk about it much for safety reasons. He's been out trying to fight this terrorism all week."

"Does it make you feel safe having a husband in law enforcement?"

"Actually, sometimes it makes me feel more vulnerable because he's always gone when something happens. And there's always the risk that he won't come home. I try not to think about it, and I pray. A lot!"

"I can see what you mean. I've been praying a lot this week too—more than usual."

Cindy leaned across the counter a little and said quietly, "I've started carrying a concealed weapon. You'd be surprised how much better you feel, knowing you at least have a fighting chance if something happens, instead of feeling like a helpless victim."

The clerk said, "I know what you mean about that too. I actually have a concealed weapon that I have been carrying for a few years, but especially this week it helps me feel much better."

Cindy smiled in acknowledgment, but deep inside she couldn't stop worrying about Alan.

31 Roosevelt Dam

Alan and his hand-picked team left for Roosevelt Dam by 2:30. There were ten of them in two vehicles. Alan and Esmerelda Carrasco, one of the regular members of his team, were in a Tahoe, accompanied by three others from the counter-terrorism SWAT team. One of the members of the SWAT team was driving the Tahoe, which was loaded with gear, camera equipment, files, surveillance equipment, and of course many firearms of different types along with the necessary ammo.

Ezzie spoke fluent Spanish, having grown up in Cuba, and was a great asset to the team. She was very smart and full of energy. Her Spanish wasn't always needed, like for this mission, but it had been very helpful to their team many times.

The other vehicle was a Suburban, with Evan driving, and Bella and Quinn riding along. Those three were also on Alan's team. They were accompanied by two others from the SWAT team. The Suburban was also full of gear and weapons. They didn't know what they were going to find but they had been thoroughly briefed by Alan that they were following a tip and they needed to get there as quickly as they could, within reason. So far that week the terrorists had struck in teams of three or four, with up to as many as eight, so they expected that a team of ten would be enough; at least they hoped that would be enough.

188

Included in the Suburban was Scout, a bomb-sniffing dog belonging to the FBI. Brian Crandall, one of the SWAT officers, was Scout's handler. Alan's team had worked with Brian and Scout many times before.

Both the Tahoe and the Suburban had extra armor. They had been sent to a company in San Antonio, Texas that dismantled them and then put them back together with "bulletproofing." They had three-inch-thick windows, Kevlar in the door panels, electric shock capability in the outside door handles, and even a smoke screen that could be released out the exhaust pipe and tear gas canisters built into each corner that could be utilized for protection of the vehicle. They also had two batteries in case one failed and tires that would deflate if shot but remain intact and allow a getaway. It was kind of James-Bondy and sexy, but it worked, and it was designed to protect the Special Agents and allow for a quick escape in an ambush situation. The company in San Antonio had armored many cars that were used all around the world and had even built the Popemobile.

Alan had called ahead to the Pinal County Sheriff's office in the small town of Globe, population less than 8,000, and also to the Department of Homeland Security, the agency in charge of security at the dam, as well as the Salt River Project engineers. He informed them that they were following up on a tip regarding the terrorist activity this week and that timing was critical. That got their attention.

Alan's team ran with their emergency lights on, but even then, it was almost 5:00 by the time they reached the Sheriff's office in Globe.

Pinal County Sheriff Emelio Concepcion met them at his office. A stocky and solid man in his late 40s, with pearl-white teeth and jet-black hair, he had grown up in Globe and had been in law enforcement for a long time. He had a very capable and experienced team. Sheriff Concepcion had six deputies with him at the office to join Alan's team. That was all he could spare as the rest of his officers were on patrol across the county.

Sheriff Concepcion was a cheerful man with a good sense of humor but he had a reputation for being very tough when he needed to be. Alan felt comfortable with the man as he had worked with him on assignments before. In the Ready Room, Alan told them that they had received a tip that something was going to happen at Roosevelt Dam but they didn't know what or when. They discussed possible scenarios as they waited for the SRP engineers to arrive. They arrived within minutes and a discussion ensued concerning what a group of terrorists could do at the dam.

Roosevelt Dam was the uppermost of four dams on the Salt River, east of the Phoenix metropolitan area. Back in the early 1900s, a co-op of farmers started the Salt River Project, or "SRP," to help them farm. The quasi-government entity built a series of dams along the Salt River to control floodwater, capture and store spring runoff in reservoirs, and generate power. There were two other dams to the north on the Verde River which were also part of the SRP system. Roosevelt Lake was about two miles wide by twenty-two miles long and contained over 1.8 million acre-feet of water or over 586 billion gallons.

Although Roosevelt Dam was built in the early 1900s, the strength of the dam and capacity of the lake was increased by an improvement project that was completed in 1996. Roosevelt Dam was now almost 200 feet thick at its base and over twenty feet thick and 350 feet high at the top. The dam was a curved concrete structure, only 1,200 feet long, as compared with other earthen or concrete dams that were straight and much longer.

If Roosevelt Dam could be breached, releasing Roosevelt Lake, the deluge would flow to Apache Lake and then on to Canyon Lake and then to Saguaro Lake. It's possible those other dams would contain some of the water from Roosevelt Lake but they couldn't contain it all. And if one or more of the lower dams also broke, the resulting flood would add to the devastation in the Phoenix metropolitan area.

To damage or breach Roosevelt Dam to the point of failure would be extremely difficult. It would take a significant amount of very powerful explosives placed with extreme engineering skill to cause it to fail and that would take many hours of work. The terrorists could also attempt to damage the spillway mechanism or the dam gate system to allow water to rush down the river but that would only be a slow release.

Taking out Roosevelt Dam was a long shot, but taking down the twin towers of the World Trade Center or sinking the Titanic were also long shots—until they happened.

There were several scenarios that Alan and the others could think of, but they didn't consider any of them to be very feasible or likely. Nonetheless, with the tip they received they would try to stop whatever was going to happen, even if just for the sake of controlling the cost of repairs.

When Alan first alerted Sheriff Concepcion earlier that day, the Sheriff had dispatched some deputies to go watch the dam and the area around it but they had not reported anything suspicious.

The dam was about forty-five minutes north of Globe, but with their lights and sirens on they made it there in just over thirty minutes; arriving just after 6:00 with the sun going down. In spite of it being "winter," there was no snow at the dam like there was on nearby Aztec peak and also far in the distance on the Mogollon Rim. The temperature was 48 degrees Fahrenheit. That was chilly for Phoenicians in February, but it would have been very comfortable for other parts of the U.S. The overnight low would probably be around thirty-five to forty degrees.

On the south end of the dam, the east end of the Apache Trail highway twisted through the canyon and between rough, rocky cliffs. Right at the end of the dam there was a widened area in the two-lane road with a concrete wall separating the end of the dam from the road. Immediately east of that point, the road cut between a high cliff on the south and a thumb of rock which jutted up about fifty feet.

Less than two miles southeast of the dam, in the tiny town of Roosevelt, there was a sheriff's office substation but Alan and his team did not stop. Instead, they went directly to the dam and pulled up on the south end in the widened area of the road. A car passed slowly by; the occupants staring with curiosity at the many vehicles and personnel milling around under the lights by the road and atop the dam.

The deputies on watch told Sheriff Concepcion that it was quiet and nothing suspicious had occurred.

Leaving some of the team at the top of the dam on watch, Alan accompanied the Engineers and Sheriff Concepcion down into the dam. They inspected the structural integrity, all the gates and control systems, and everything they could think of. Scout, the bomb dog, was intent throughout the inspection, sniffing for any scent of explosives. The dog showed no sign of finding anything.

At the same time, on the top of the structure, those stationed there inspected the dam and all they could see in the surrounding area. They glassed with regular and night-vision binoculars at the hills, cliffs, and roads around the dam. They looked over the east-facing side into the water of Roosevelt Lake and along the shore, looking for anything out of the ordinary.

With their binoculars they inspected Roosevelt Lake Bridge about a quarter of a mile east of the dam. The original road crossed the top of the old dam. That road was narrow and required very slow speeds, but that changed in 1992 with the addition of the bridge. Roosevelt Suspension Bridge spanned the end of the lake and allowed travelers on state highway 188 to breeze smoothly past the entire dam area. The bridge was just over 1,000 feet long and when it was finished it held the honor of being the longest two-lane steel-arch suspension bridge in North America. The road level of the bridge was between fifty and 100 feet above the water level, depending on the volume of the lake at any given time. Because of the proximity of the dam and the bridge, less than half a mile apart, a visitor to one could easily see the other. The law enforcement personnel inspected the bridge with their binoculars from end to end and saw nothing suspicious on or around the bridge.

They looked over the downstream side of the dam to the Salt River below and they even sent a team down the Apache Trail highway to the maintenance road that provided access to the power plant at the base of the dam. Still nothing.

Alan was embarrassed and frustrated. He was in charge of this operation and he felt responsible for all the personnel and equipment. He knew he was instructed to bring them there but he couldn't figure out why everything was so normal and undisturbed.

He stepped over to the upstream side of the dam, a little bit away from the others, and looked across the water at the bridge and the rugged mountains across the lake in the distance. He briefly closed his eyes but didn't want to make a scene so he opened them again and prayed in his heart.

"Father in Heaven," he thought to himself, "I'm trying to do what I was instructed to do. I brought a team here and even Victor supports this mission. However, nothing seems out of place and some of the others are thinking this is a waste of our time. Please help me know what to do and . . . ."

Alan paused before continuing and suddenly his phone rang. It was Victor Pilchick.

"Hi, Victor. We are at the dam but have found nothing so far."

Victor replied, "The terrorists have just struck in several places around the valley. I don't have many details yet, but I'll let you know as soon as I do. Stay there until I give you further orders."

32 Predator Hunting

Ralph, Waldo, and Emerson were brothers. Their last name was Thornton. Their mom, Margaret Thornton, was an English teacher, and she couldn't resist naming her sons after her favorite literary figure. The three brothers were each two years apart in age. Each one had a son and the cousins were also two years apart. Ralph's son, Kyle, was the oldest cousin, at seventeen. Waldo's son, Jacob, was fifteen, and Emerson's son, Porter, was thirteen.

While they loved their mother, the brothers did not want their own sons to live with the kind of name association they dealt with growing up. They didn't hate their names, but they didn't care for the attention and comments the names generated. As adults, they intentionally chose names for their children that they thought would not lead to any unusual remarks.

All six of them, the three sons and *their* three sons, did gain from the influence of Margaret Thornton. All were intelligent and well educated and the younger boys already had their sights set on college. However, they were also well-rounded, with interests in sports, music, and electronics.

They also loved the outdoors. They loved to hunt, fish, camp, and hike. The six "Thornton Boys," as they came to be called, spent a lot of time in the outdoors together.

It was no wonder that on a Friday night in February they were going predator hunting. Coyote pelts were best in January and February due to the animals' fur being so thick in the coldest months of the year. Arizona had also changed its law in the past few years to allow coyote hunting at night if hunters used a light and the light was not attached to a vehicle. However, they could only hunt in certain areas of the state.

They were aware of the terrorist attacks that had been happening that week around the Phoenix area. They were saddened by the number of innocent people who had been killed, including some young children at a school. However, they were also very proud of other armed citizens who stepped up and stopped the terrorists.

The Thorntons had been planning this trip for weeks and the terrorist activity did not cause them to change their plans. They would drive a few hours out into the desert where the Arizona Game & Fish Department had opened a certain hunting unit for night hunting of coyotes, and they would do some varmint calling in the dark. They had done it before and they loved it. They all went together in Waldo's four-door pickup. When they reached the desired location, they got all bundled up to stay warm, even though the night-time temperatures in the desert were usually only in the thirties or forties. They would hike quietly away from the truck for a half-mile or so, do some varmint calling for fifteen or twenty minutes and then turn on their spotlights. Sometimes they saw nothing and other times they would see one or more coyotes or other predators. Then they had lots of fun and lots of action shooting as the coyotes tried to get away or hide. Game & Fish had opened these areas precisely because there were too many coyotes, so they were doing their part in controlling the predator population and helping manage the state's wildlife. Proper game management was no different than only having so many fish in your fish tank or so many cows in a pasture. Optimum management meant optimum health and well-being of game populations and individual animals.

With the recent advances in spotlight technology, they could take very powerful spotlights out away from their truck. The lights wouldn't run for a long time on battery power, but for sure they would run long enough for each calling session. They would hunt all night, laze around in camp on Saturday morning, and then head back home in the afternoon.

The three brothers liked AR-15s, and the younger sons were allowed to shoot semi-automatic .22s. The Ruger 10/22 was the gun of choice for the younger ones. This year, however, since Kyle had turned seventeen, his dad had agreed that he could shoot an AR-15. Kyle had an Olympic Arms .223, and Ralph, his dad, had a Beretta .223. Waldo had a 7.62 PredatAR from LaRue Tactical, and Emerson had a Livewire .308 from Spike's Tactical. All of the weapons were semi-automatic so that a shot was fired for each pull of the trigger. The faster you could pull the trigger, the faster you could fire another shot. Four AR-15s and two 10/22s could throw a lot of lead at a coyote that was picked up in a spotlight. It was great fun for the six of them.

One time a guy at work who was politically liberal asked Waldo why he needed an AR-15. Waldo calmly replied, "Why do you need that quad you ride on weekends? Why does Linda need a horse? Why does Nicholas need a boat? Why does Monica need so much jewelry? We all have our hobbies and forms of entertainment. Owning one piece of property for fun is no different than someone else owning another piece of property for fun or spending money on some other type of entertainment. But there's one very critical difference. If our government ever went rogue and turned into a dictatorship, Monica, Nicholas, Linda and you can't use your property to protect those around you from oppression or to fight for freedom if needed." Waldo turned, walked away, and no more was said.

By the time the dads got home from work on that Friday night in February it was after dark. They needed a little more ammo and Ralph wanted to buy a new spotlight, so they stopped at the sporting goods store that was right by the mall. After that they planned to find some fast food on their way out of town. They were all dressed in camouflage, of course, but mostly for fun and not because it was needed.

They all went into the sporting goods store, and after finding what they needed, they were heading out the door. Right at the last minute, Ralph looked more closely at the spotlight he had just purchased and noticed that it had a big crack clear across the glass. He headed back into the store, told the others to go to the truck, and he would come out as quickly as he could.

When they got to the truck they started loading their magazines to be completely ready when they arrived at the hunting area. They all had thirty-round magazines for the ARs and also some twenty-round and some ten round magazines. However, when they hunted coyotes they preferred the thirty round mags. If three or four coyotes showed up in the spotlight and everyone else was still shooting, it was no fun to be the one person who only had a ten-round magazine.

The Ruger 10/22s came with a ten-round magazine, but there were several fifty-round mags on the market that were inexpensive. For the .22 caliber guns, a fifty-round magazine could hold a whole box of shells and the cost of all those shells was actually very inexpensive compared to the AR-15 shells. It was difficult sometimes to find .22 ammo, but they worked hard at it and found enough.

As they sat there in the truck, loading their thirty-round and fifty-round magazines and talking about their trip, thirteen-year-old Porter asked, "What if some of the terrorists did something close to us? Would we go shoot at them?"

Porter's dad, Emerson, wanting to help his son learn their family's commitment to freedom, said, "Porter, the founding fathers and the minutemen fought for our freedom back in the 1700s, and some of them even gave their lives for our country to be free. We are grateful to them

195

and we also feel like it is our duty to fight for freedom and to protect innocent people . . . at least I feel that way. Your uncles and I carry concealed weapons to protect innocent people, and I suppose if we had a chance to stop terrorists, we'd take that chance."

Fifteen-year-old Jacob said, "It would be really scary. What if we got shot?"

Waldo said, "That could happen. Many of our ancestors fought for freedom and some of them got shot. In fact, some of them were about your age. Do you think you could be brave enough in a situation like that to shoot someone?"

Seventeen-year-old Kyle said, "I don't know if I could shoot someone."

Emerson said, "I remember an uncle of ours who fought in the Viet Nam War who said he wasn't sure he could shoot someone either. But he said that when his friends got shot right next to him it caused him to become angry—more defensive—and then he could do it."

Waldo said, "That bus driver on Wednesday and even those two women at the school . . . they were able to do it. Their motivation was to protect the people around them. We have lived for so long in a peaceful society we have pretty much forgotten what it's like to have to fight for freedom. Our military forces serve in faraway countries that we will likely never see, so it can be hard for us to visualize. I remember a song that said something like 'Freedom isn't free: you always have to fight for it'."

Emerson interrupted, "What's taking Ralph? Did he have to go build a new spotlight from scratch?"

At that moment, gunfire interrupted—lots of gunfire. The sound was coming from the area where the movie theaters were located in the mall. It sounded like automatic weapons fire from multiple shooters.

Waldo grabbed his AR as he said, "I'll bet its more terrorists. I'm going over there. Who's coming?" He had three fully loaded magazines for his weapon.

He jumped out of the bed of the truck and started running toward the theaters. He jammed one magazine into the bottom of his .308 and tucked the other two into a pocket as he ran. He pounded the magazine with the palm of his hand to make sure it seated completely, and then levered in a round and flipped the safety to SAFE.

He turned to look, and there were Emerson and all three boys, loading magazines into their guns as they ran.

196

Waldo called out as they ran, "Be careful. We don't want to shoot each other or an innocent person. Watch your safety and your muzzle."

Just then Ralph came out of the store, heard the shots that were being fired, and saw his family running across the parking lot with their guns. He hadn't loaded any magazines and he had an uncharged spotlight in his hand. He dashed to the truck to grab his gear, but by then, the others had disappeared around the corner of the store and were probably at the big open area in front of the theater box office.

As they ran around the corner of the building into the theater area, they ran past the Code of Conduct Sign which told moviegoers how to behave at the theaters. Waldo thought about the paragraph on the sign that he had read in the past that said no weapons were allowed in the theaters, including pepper spray or even any small knife or stick that could be used as a weapon. He almost laughed at the irony of a silly sign that only served to cause timid people to feel safe when the safer approach would be to allow law-abiding citizens to carry their weapons. A lot of good the sign did right then, with terrorists on a shooting rampage. *Didn't the terrorists read the sign?!*

Those thoughts made Waldo smile and shake his head, but then he turned his attention back to the situation at hand. He and Emerson were looking for terrorists. They saw no gunmen, but they did see several people lying around covered in blood. Some people were frozen in terror while others were screaming; some seemed unharmed but were in shock. Others had already started helping the injured. One woman looked up at them and her face showed a look of horror.

"Don't be afraid; we're here to help! Where did they go?"

The woman said nothing but pointed into the theaters. Suddenly they heard gunfire from inside and Waldo resumed his pace. Beside him was his brother, a seasoned hunter, but neither of them had ever had any combat training. Behind them were three scared young men, who weren't sure if they wanted to be there, but were determined to follow the leadership of their fathers.

Some of the gunfire inside stopped.

Waldo paused at the door. "Probably reloading." He said to Emerson, "Ready?"

Emerson had a determined look on his face as he responded, "Let's do it! But we have to aim for the head. If they're wearing bombs we don't want to shoot a bomb. You go left, I'll go right."

Waldo said, "Porter, pull open the door so we can run through ready to fire. You boys can follow us in if you like. If not, wait out here, but be ready to surrender to any police. We don't want them thinking you are the bad guys. Go, Porter!"

Porter met his dad's eye and received a reassuring nod before he yanked open the door. Waldo charged in, his gun pointing forward with the safety now on FIRE. He didn't know anything about tactical fighting but he wasn't about to let anyone kill innocent people without trying to stop them, even if he risked injury or death. He was going on pure adrenalin.

Trusting that Emerson had the right side covered, Waldo looked left as he entered. He saw a guy standing in front of him about fifteen feet away, at a clock-position of about 10:00. The man was dressed in black and was just raising his gun to shoot at some people to the left of the doorway. Waldo noticed a crowd of people running from the terrorist and he didn't want to accidentally shoot any of them if he missed, so he knelt down on one knee. At that angle, if he did miss his shots would go over the heads of the others. Waldo aimed at the man's head and pulled the trigger three times. One of the shots connected and the man's head tipped sideways a little before he dropped like a rock.

On the right, Emerson had identified another terrorist at about 1:00. The man was looking away from him and was in the process of reloading a magazine into his AK-47, which was held a little to the side as he worked the magazine. Emerson aimed and put a bullet into the back of the terrorist's head. He also dropped without a sound.

Kyle had followed his uncles inside, his gun at his shoulder. He saw that a third man was farther to the right and had started to point his AK at them. Kyle didn't know why he was so calm and collected, but he quickly aimed at the terrorist's head and started firing. After two shots, the man fell sideways onto some moviegoers who had already been shot.

Suddenly they heard frantic knocking on the glass door. Jacob and Porter were crouched together outside the door, pointing at four more terrorists who had just come around the corner of the building into the theater area, opposite from the position of the sporting goods store. The boys had as yet not been noticed as a threat and they had not fired a shot.

As Waldo, Emerson, and Kyle stepped back outside, Emerson spoke to the boys, "Stay down, but help us shoot."

The terrorists had started firing at other people but one of them noticed the five Thorntons by the door. He hollered something in a foreign language.

Waldo, Emerson, and Kyle stood around and above Porter and Jacob, who were kneeling, but just as the terrorists turned their fire toward them, an intensely bright light shone from the south corner of the building. Evidently, Ralph had finally arrived with one of the older, but still powerful spotlights.

The sudden light distracted and blinded the terrorists, giving the Thorntons a huge advantage. Emerson yelled, "Aim for their heads!" as they all started shooting. Three AR-15s and two .22s were blazing away at the terrorists. The few-second advantage made all the difference. A window behind them exploded as the terrorists only got off a few wild shots before the barrage of gunfire from the Thorntons mowed them down. Fortunately no one detonated a bomb, if there was one.

They heard more gunfire from inside the theater. As they turned to step back inside, Emerson moaned, just now noticing that he had been hit. His left leg crumpled beneath him and the others saw blood soaking his pants near his knee. As he carefully maneuvered himself to the ground he said in a strained but strong voice, "I'm okay. Go!" Waldo huffed out a breath and said, "Reload if you need to." He turned a quick look of concern to his brother as he led the boys back inside. Porter opted to stay with his father.

Kyle and Waldo popped out their magazines and quickly jammed another into the receivers on their ARs. Jacob's fifty round mag still had plenty of ammo left.

Ralph turned off his light and ran across the courtyard, going in the theater through the exit doors on the far side of the ticket booth. He had the spotlight in his left hand and his Sig Sauer 9mm in his right hand. He didn't know what he would find but he figured the other five had the entry door well covered.

Waldo, Kyle, and Jacob found three more terrorists coming back into the lobby from the right hall that led to the theaters. The terrorists were firing randomly at the moviegoers. The Thorntons opened up and delivered a barrage of bullets, catching the three men off guard and quickly killing them.

They stopped shooting, then suddenly they heard three shots that sounded different than any so far. A bright light bounced across the lobby to their left and they saw Ralph firing at someone on that side of the lobby. By coming through the other door he had noticed another terrorist hiding behind the wall, preparing to shoot from his concealed position. Ralph shot three times at the gun as it was sticking out past the wall. That served to stop the terrorist from shooting, but because he was still hidden Ralph couldn't get in a kill shot until he was closer. Running across the lobby was difficult because of the dead and wounded who were lying on the floor but he managed to do it. With the spotlight blinding the terrorist, Ralph fired three more times at point-blank range. He was glad his Sig had a fifteen-round magazine.

The shooting stopped. The gun battle appeared to be over.

Ralph said, "Shall we split up to make sure there are no more, or just wait?"

Kyle said, "I move we wait."

Waldo said, "I second the motion. I'd hate to have one AR or a 10/22 come across four terrorists. Those are bad odds."

Ralph said, "We wait then."

They stayed alert, watching and trying to listen, which was no easy feat because of the number of people around them who were calling for others or crying out in pain.

Ralph yelled over the noise, "We are watching for terrorists. It's safe now. Start helping the wounded!"

People who had not been shot or who had only been slightly wounded started helping anyone they could. Employees of the theater appeared from behind the concession counter.

In the distance they heard sirens.

Kyle moved to stand by his dad, who lovingly punched his son's shoulder with the back of his hand while still holding the spotlight, "Great job, guys! Is everyone OK?" The others nodded in consent as Ralph noticed he was missing a brother. He asked, "Is Emerson still covering the door?"

Waldo answered, "As well as he can with a bullet in his leg." Ralph's eyes widened as Waldo assured him it was only a flesh wound.

Ralph then said, "The police will be here any second. We are going to be questioned and probably thrown to the ground and arrested. Just stay calm and cooperate with them. In fact, we need to make sure no one gets any of the terrorist's guns."

They spread out and put a foot on an AK-47 here or stood by a couple of AK-47s there. They identified where they thought all the terrorist weapons were. They also laid their weapons down, not wanting to appear to be the bad guys.

As expected, the SWAT team and police soon arrived. The Thorntons remained calm and followed orders to lie down on the ground. The police started asking questions, and when one officer was overly rough and aggressive, a lady yelled at him, "Hey! They saved a lot of lives tonight and they didn't do one thing wrong. Are you mad at them because they got here before you? Why don't you show them more respect?!"

Around the woman, all the moviegoers who could began to applaud and cheer. Some called out, "Thank you, hunters!" Others called out, "They are heroes!" Some held up both hands with a 2 and an A.

The sergeant glared at the woman until another officer who had just arrived, said, "Sergeant, she's right and all these people know it. Stand down; they're not a threat."

The sergeant backed away, grumbling a bit, and Ralph said to the second officer, "Thank you, sir."

As it turned out, twelve moviegoers had been killed and twenty-seven were injured, including Emerson. But hundreds more were unharmed. Eleven terrorists were dead, all of them killed by the Thorntons. The media started arriving on the scene and everyone they interviewed credited "the hunters" with saving their lives.

The Thorntons knew they wouldn't get to hunt coyotes tonight, but they realized they did get a lot of action shooting at some "varmints." The boys always told their hunting stories to their moms, who would just roll their eyes and shake their heads. But that night they just wanted to hug their moms and tell them they were glad to be home.

33 Take 'Em Out At The Ballgame

Nancy Kosmuch loved to play softball and she had a lot of talent. She preferred playing center field and she had a rocket for an arm, even out-throwing many men. She was excellent at hitting the ball into the holes when she was at bat and she could outrun everyone on the team. In high school and college she played fast pitch, but now that she was on a city league team she played slow pitch.

The team she played on, "Poke It Out," was a co-ed team and per the league rules there had to be at least as many women on the field as men at any given time. Some of the team members were married and both spouses played; others on the team were single. Nancy had been married but was divorced—no kids—so she identified with the singles, which was fine. This was Nancy's first year on this particular team but most of this group had played together for a few years and they got along very well.

She competed a little with Don, one of the single guys who was also an outfielder. She could run faster than he could but he had a better arm. If there weren't enough players Don slid over to Left; but if they had plenty, he stayed in Center and she played Short Rover. Some slow pitch teams turned the Rover into a fourth fielder and spaced them evenly, but Poke It Out liked to use their Rover as sort of a deep Short Stop and Nancy was good at it because of her speed. She slid over between first and second for lefties, but being a deep infielder gave her plenty of action and the team had done well with that strategy.

On Friday afternoon, her friend, Winona called, "Are you going to the game?"

Nancy replied, "Why wouldn't I?"

Winona said, "Oh, some of the team were concerned about the terrorist activity this week in the Phoenix area and decided maybe they shouldn't go. The Barretts aren't going and neither are Jemma and Monique."

Nancy said, "Well, if we are going to be missing three women then you and I have to be there so we can have enough. Besides, what's the chance that terrorists would end up at our ball game? We don't have enough people at our games to be a decent target."

Winona said, "Yeah, I guess you're right. OK. I'll see you there."

In spite of Nancy's belief that the chance was extremely remote that they would have terrorist activity tonight, she still put her Smith and Wesson .380 in her bag with her gear. She usually carried the gun in her purse and had done so for four years since she turned twenty-one, which was the minimum age for carrying a concealed weapon in Arizona.

Her dad and mom had carried weapons for a long time and had often taken her out shooting and hunting. Nancy learned to love guns. On her twenty-first birthday she and her parents went shopping for her present and spent the day at the gun shop. After much deliberation, she chose the Smith & Wesson Bodyguard Crimson Trace. She liked the Crimson Trace's laser sight, and after many shooting trips with her parents she had become quite proficient at holding the laser steady on a target while quickly shooting a close cluster of shots. The model she chose happened to have a green laser, in spite of the name.

With the terrorist activity this week in the Phoenix metropolitan area everyone was being very cautious. After three attacks on Monday and none on Tuesday, everyone thought it was over. But then on Wednesday there were seven more attacks. In each instance the shooting was over by the time law enforcement arrived, with armed citizens saving many lives. The terrorists' mortality was very high. Apparently, one man had gotten away from the attack at a church in Scottsdale and a few other terrorists were recovering from wounds in valley hospitals, heavily guarded by law enforcement.

Nothing happened on Thursday but some suspected that Friday might be another target day. Nancy still felt like a neighborhood softball game wouldn't draw enough of a crowd for terrorists to get much of an impact, so she wasn't too worried. But having been taught to be cautious she put her extra magazine, fully loaded, into her bag along with her gun.

She drove to the ballpark and found their field. The park was the typical layout with four diamonds arranged like a four-leaf clover, with the home plates in the center and bleachers between the fields. You could draw a perfect plus sign between them all.

The parking was mostly on the east side, with some parking spots around the outside of each field. The people who parked beyond the outfield fence always ran the risk of some slugger hitting a ball over the fence and breaking a car window, but that rarely happened.

Aaron, one of the guys on their team, had purchased a bright red Jeep that had a couple of cracks in the windshield but he didn't have coverage on his insurance plan to fix pre-existing damage. He always parked beyond the outfield fence hoping a ball would shatter his window and he could use his property damage coverage to replace it. Nancy wasn't sure that's really how insurance worked but that was Aaron's story and nobody really challenged him. At the end of each game they would always apologize to Aaron that they hadn't hit a ball through his window. Aaron took the teasing in stride.

When Nancy arrived it was 7:15 and their game didn't start until 8:00. She sat on the back row of the stands to watch the current game and wait for her teammates to come. The teams that were playing were called "Rounding Third" and "Safe at Home." Nancy had played on Rounding Third the previous year. She really liked Tyler Drew, the first baseman, whom everyone just called Drew. He was friendly but she could never get him to pay much attention to her or ask her out, in spite of her many attempts to flirt with him. He was an Emergency Medical Technician, or EMT, and he drove an ambulance. He was muscular, which Nancy liked, and he could really hit the ball. He was easygoing and kind of quiet, and his somewhat shy personality seemed to be his reason for overlooking Nancy.

At about 7:25 Drew got up to bat. Someone hollered from the Rounding Third dugout, "Over the fence, Drew!" As Nancy looked out at the fence, she noticed Aaron's red Jeep pull up behind it in left Center. He hadn't even gotten out of his car yet when Drew smacked a perfect pitch. The ball took off like a rocket and was one of those low fly balls that just seemed to keep rising as it went, and it carried and carried and carried.

Sure enough, the ball cleared the fence and banged right into Aaron's windshield with a loud pop. From the bleachers Nancy couldn't tell if it had broken the window, but Aaron jumped from the Jeep and started hollering and laughing and doing a happy dance. No one paid attention to Drew jogging around the bases because everyone was watching Aaron and laughing at his antics.

Just as Drew crossed home plate they heard gunfire. Nancy looked to her left and saw three guys with AK-47s, standing in the gravel walkway that led to the parking area. They were firing randomly at the bleachers. They were in kind of a V shape, with the point of the V near the middle of the softball complex and the other two gunmen spread out back toward the parking lot and closer to the bleachers. The guy in the position at the point of the V was already behind and past her.

Nancy quickly reached for her bag which was sitting next to her on the bench and unzipped it. She pulled out the Bodyguard and the extra magazine. She shoved the extra mag into her back pocket. The Bodyguard held seven rounds, with six in the mag and one in the chamber, and she immediately wondered if she would need both magazines.

Nancy quickly turned around and sat on the bench she'd just had her feet on, using the higher back bench to steady her arms. The terrorist closest to her was only about twenty or twenty-five feet away and she was slightly above him. There was not a bleacher behind him so it was a clear field of fire. Nancy pressed the button and turned on the green laser. The terrorist was looking to Nancy's right at the third-base dugout on the next field over, firing at the people trying to scramble out of the dugout. She put the laser on the back of the man's head and fired, then re-aimed and fired again. As he started to fall she was going to take a third shot but realized she didn't need to. The terrorist fell into the gravel of the walkway between the softball diamonds. There were now people running everywhere and she was glad that she had chosen to not shoot again.

There was so much commotion that she couldn't really tell what was happening, but she saw two armed men in the bleachers on the field across from her who already had the second terrorist going down.

As Nancy ran down off the bleachers she looked for the third man and saw him going toward the snack bar. When he didn't stop there she realized that he was heading for the children's playground on the other side of the building between two other fields. The area had a sandbox, some swings, a slide, and monkey bars. Nancy had played there many times as a kid while her parents played softball. In fact, one year she fell off the slide and broke her arm. She hoped that arm wouldn't fail her tonight as she tried to stop a madman.

She quickly aimed and fired two shots at the man as he started around the corner of the snack bar building. She wasn't really trying to hit him but she hoped her shots would cause him to stop and look at her or maybe challenge her. She was a young, single woman and had people who loved her and would miss her if she were killed, but she couldn't bear the thought of a gunman shooting at little children who were playing on the playground.

As she shot at the terrorist she was running toward the building. Her shots smacked into it, spraying bits of brick and bullet fragments around and causing the terrorist to turn and look at her just before he stepped behind the building.

The building was a snack bar at one end and a maintenance and storage area at the other end. When they built the back half of the building, they turned the cinder blocks sideways to allow the holes in the block to make a sturdy fence but provide ventilation for the lawn equipment. It made an enclosure that had perfect handholds and footholds up the back wall and halfway around the sides, and as kids, she and her friends had climbed up that wall and onto the roof of the snack bar many times. Eventually, their parents or some other grown-up would yell at them to get down before they broke their necks, and they would climb down—until the next time they came to play.

As Nancy ran, she popped out her first magazine and put it sideways into her mouth. She pulled the second magazine out of her back pocket and jammed it in the grip of the Bodyguard. She wanted a full mag for this encounter with the terrorist.

When she got to the side of the building, Nancy paused only long enough to stow the nearly spent mag in her pocket and shove her gun, safety on, into the back of her waistband. Then she went right up the cinder block wall.

She got to the top and climbed onto the roof. Drawing her weapon as she went, she quickly and quietly ran over the top hoping to surprise the terrorist below her. She feared he would start shooting at the children on the playground before she could get to him. As it turned out, the terrorist had stopped and was standing there waiting for her, somewhat away from the building. He was looking toward both corners, not knowing which side she would come from. As she came to the peak of the roof she was already pointing the Bodyguard in his direction, holding it with both hands in a proper defensive stance. By approaching from above, it gave her a split second advantage before the terrorist saw her.

Nancy pointed the laser toward him and aimed as best as she could, but she felt like she needed to fire quickly. She pulled off two shots before the terrorist started shooting. She emptied all seven rounds at him. Some of her shots hit home and the terrorist staggered back and started to go down. However, he had an automatic rifle and he was firing at her too. His shots climbed the building as he raised his weapon to point at her, and as he went down two bullets hit Nancy, one in her left thigh and the other in her left shoulder.

She tried to be tough and climb down the holes in the cinder block wall on the north side of the building, but the pain and the loss of blood from two wounds caused her to be dizzy. About halfway down the wall she blacked out. She fell and landed hard on the gravel.

She was only out for a few minutes, and when she came to, she was looking into the face of Drew. He was kneeling by her, checking her wounds. He said, "Sorry Nance, but I've got to cut off your pant leg at least. He had a knife that looked like a Leatherman or something. Drew made a ragged cut in the fabric across the top of her thigh, carefully going all the way around her leg. He then pulled the pant leg down over her foot.

The bullet had ripped into her thigh about half-way up. There was quite a bit of blood but no exit wound. Drew said, "Good thing it's on the outside of the thigh or it might have hit your femoral artery. It must have gotten hung up in your bone because there's no exit."

A woman was standing on Nancy's other side and Drew looked up at her. "Can you do first aid?"

The woman said "Yes."

Drew said, "Put pressure on this wound." The woman stepped over, knelt down, and put the heel of her hand on Nancy's thigh.

Nancy was grimacing at the pain but managed to say, "Do others need your help more than me?"

Drew said, "No, there are plenty of people here doing first aid, and thanks to you and a few others, there weren't that many people who were shot."

Nancy heard sirens coming from a distance.

Drew said, "I've got to look at that shoulder. Sorry Nancy, but I'm going to have to cut part of your shirt off."

Nancy said, "You can't just work around it?"

"No, but I'll cut as little as I can. Trust me, as an EMT I've seen a lot more of other women than what I'll be seeing of you."

"I know, but not every other woman has had a crush on you for two years." It was a really dumb thing to say, she knew, but it just came out. It must have been the shock from being shot.

Drew looked into her eyes and said, "Well then, I'd better make sure to save your life because the feeling's mutual."

She looked into his eyes and he into hers and nothing more was said at the moment, although Nancy thought she heard a repressed chuckle from the woman at her hip.

He pulled out his knife again and slit the top of Nancy's sleeve open like you would use a letter opener on an envelope. He cut from the collar to the end of the short sleeve and laid the fabric down across her chest. Next to her bra strap there was a hole going into her shoulder under the collar bone and a bigger hole coming out the top of her shoulder above the shoulder blade.

Drew said, "Not much blood and probably no broken bones thanks to the angle. Looks like he threaded the needle with that shot. I think your thigh is the more serious wound and they'll have to remove that bullet. You'll be out for the rest of the season."

She realized that she was still gripping the Bodyguard. Her hand was lying still on the ground and everyone was kneeling or stepping around it. They were so worried about her wounds that they hadn't paid attention to the gun. She mentioned it and Drew carefully put his hands around her hand and the gun and asked her if he could take it. She looked into his eyes as his hands touched hers. She released the gun and he took control of it, checking to see if there was a cocked hammer or if it was a double-action model. Seeing that it was double action, and pushing the safety up into place, he put it in his waistband. He knew he would likely talk to a police officer about the gun in a few minutes.

By now, the fire trucks and police had arrived and someone called for a gurney to come over. They all lifted Nancy up onto it, with the woman still applying pressure to the thigh wound. An EMT put some gauze on the injury and took over for the woman. The woman went into the restroom to wash Nancy's blood off her hands.

Nancy tried to thank them all but the initial shock was wearing off and the pain was getting worse.

She winced and then looked into Drew's eyes. "Thanks, Drew."

As they wheeled her away he said, "I'll get your bag and I'll come see you tomorrow. They may need your gun for evidence, but I'll let you know. Besides," and he smiled warmly, "we need to continue our conversation."

34 The Mall

"Come on, Tucker! Let's go! We're all waiting on you!"

"Just about finished!" Tucker said in exasperation. He and Harley were playing League of Legends and backing out of the game meant that your "team" out there in cyberspace would be missing you in the middle of a battle. Backing out could hurt your reputation among your allies, even though everyone knew you had to log out at times, usually on demand of your parents. However, legitimate gamers were independent enough that they didn't have parents who ordered them off of their computer, so no one wanted to admit that they were being told to stop a game.

Tobie and Tucker Shaw were sister and brother. She was twenty-one and he was seventeen. Their cousins, Sophie and Harley Crawford, were visiting their Arizona cousins from California. Sophie was nineteen and Harley was sixteen. Tobie and Sophie, being the older sisters, got along well, but of course they had to boss their younger brothers around, at least a little. Tucker and Harley didn't care too much that the girls did that, although they made a show of being exasperated. They enjoyed their sisters and got to spend time hanging out with them and their girlfriends at times; which wasn't a bad thing for teenage boys.

The four were excited about spending the weekend together while their parents talked about their grandpa's trust and estate planning. Grandpa had died several months ago after a long happy life and an extended illness so there was not much sorrow or mourning like there was when Grandma died unexpectedly a few years earlier. Now their parents were discussing all the ins and outs of grandpa's trust as they figured out what to do with the assets and investments. That gave the youngsters a chance to just be together, which they loved doing. That Friday night they were going to the mall. They also had plans to go out in the desert on Saturday morning with their parents to do some shooting, and Saturday evening they had plans for a movie. Their relationship was close and they got along well with each other, unlike some other siblings.

As they were getting ready to go to the mall, Sophie watched Tobie put her CZ 9mm pistol into the holster inside her front waistband. Tobie had grown up around guns and she and her parents had talked about concealed carry many times. Not long after Tobie turned twenty-one a few months ago, her mom and dad took her, with Tucker in tow, and bought her a weapon. She quickly took the concealed carry course and got her permit. She liked having it so she could carry her gun when their family went to Utah to visit relatives, which they often did.

Her CZ 9mm P-07 was imported from Czechoslovakia and when they were shopping for guns, she fell in love with it. It was a compact model, designed for concealed carry and was light and accurate. Tobie had gone out with her dad many times to practice drawing the weapon from her waistband to shoot. It held fifteen rounds in the magazine and she liked the de-cocking mechanism, which meant that she could chamber a round and then release it from being cocked. It made the first trigger pull a long, double-action trigger pull, and she felt that it was safer than a gun that just had a safety.

"Why are you taking a gun?" Sophie asked, wide-eyed and a little concerned.

Tobie looked at Sophie and wondered how much of a discussion she wanted to have right then. "Well, just so you know, Sophie, I always carry my gun wherever I go. I know in California they don't like citizens carrying guns but here in Arizona we do. I feel much safer when I have it, especially this week with all the terrorist activity. Would you really want to go anywhere unarmed—a helpless victim?"

"I guess not, but I'm just not around guns much. I'm excited to go shooting tomorrow but guns scare me."

Tobie rolled her eyes just like a teenager, and said, "I can see that your dad getting a job in California has caused you to grow up in a culture where guns are perceived as bad. They aren't bad. More people are killed by alcohol-related incidents than guns, and way more are killed by drugs."

"Well, I agree that drinking and drugs are bad."

"Yeah, but just because guns are misused doesn't put them in the same category as drinking and drugs. They are a tool, just like any other tool. Using them properly is safe. Using them improperly causes accidental death or injury. They are kind of like a seatbelt; when you need one and aren't using it, that's when you realize how important it is."

Tobie continued, "Wasn't there some lady in California a few years ago who survived a mountain lion attack while she was mountain biking. I remember seeing a video about that and they interviewed her afterward. Her face was all scarred. The lion was dragging her by the head into the bushes while her friend was pulling in the opposite direction on her legs. Some other bikers came along and had to throw rocks at the lion to finally get it to leave, and even then it was stalking them in the bushes while they waited for an ambulance. That would have been way different if one or all of them had been armed. I don't understand why people don't want to allow others to carry guns for protection."

Wanting to end the discussion, Sophie said, "Well, I can see the need for it this week for sure. But I thought the malls don't allow guns."

Tobie replied, "Only some of them. We'll drive past one mall to go to the Five Star Mall. They are glad I'm armed. Besides, if terrorists were going to attack a mall, do you think a 'No Weapons' sign would keep them out?"

"I guess not."

Tobie showed Sophie the gun, careful to aim it away from her. She showed her the decocking lever and how it can be pushed to decock the gun, making it safe to carry. Then Tobie tucked the gun into the front of her waistband. When Tobie was finished, she faced Sophie and said, "There. No one can see my gun and it's easy to draw if I need it."

Sophie inspected Tobie with approval, then smiled and said, "Well, it does help that you are grown up enough to stick out in the right places so your shirt hangs down in *front* of your waistline. My dad sticks out right *at* his waistline, so I don't think he could hide a gun there."

Tobie laughed and punched Sophie lovingly on the arm.

When they finally got the boys away from their League of Legends game, they headed out the door. As they were leaving, Tobie's mom said, "Take care of your brother!" like she always said when they went somewhere together.

As they walked through the laundry room toward the garage, Tobie hollered back, just like *she* always did, "OK, Mom. I promise!" It was one of their little rituals.

They got to the mall just about 6:30. The boys wanted to go to the computer game store and the girls wanted to look at clothes. They agreed to meet at the food court at 7:30.

Tobie and Sophie worked their way through a couple of stores, looking at clothes, shoes, and jewelry. As they walked into Rags & Bags, a high-end apparel and handbag store, they said "Hi" to the thirty-something clerk at the counter near the door and headed to the back of the store to look at a cute handbag Tobie had seen there before. As they walked past the racks of clothes, Tobie quietly said to Sophie, "Did you notice her shirt?"

"Nothing more than that it was black and had a V neck," replied Sophie.

"Her T-shirt has a Walther logo on it."

"Walther?"

"Yeah, Walther. They make really good guns. My dad has a Walther .45. I'd bet that clerk is carrying a weapon or her husband or boyfriend carries."

Nothing more was said about the clerk because they had reached the area where Tobie had seen the handbag and the conversation turned to fashion.

*   *   *

Deanna Wonderling had worked at Rags & Bags for about a year. She loved it. She enjoyed the nice clothes and nice bags and especially the employee discount. She was always well-dressed.

Her husband Steve was a computer programmer and worked from home but his income was up and down and they didn't have insurance. By her working full time at Rags & Bags they had insurance and he could stay home to watch the kids while he worked, and often while she worked too. It turned out to be very good for their family in spite of the hours required working retail. The one downside was the employee discount if you call that a downside. Steve teased Deanna about spending more of her paycheck on clothes and bags than on guns.

The Wonderlings were gun nuts. They went shooting together every chance they got. They owned many guns of all calibers, styles, shapes, and sizes. They both loved to hunt, fish and camp and at least twice a month when Deanna had a day or two off Steve would stop working and they would go camping or hunting with the kids. Sometimes they would leave the kids with one of the sets of grandparents and go on their own. Arizona was good for hunting because in the summer you could go to the mountains only a few hours away and in the winter you could go to the desert. For gun nuts, year-round hunting and shooting were good things.

Deanna always carried her concealed weapon in a Flash Bang holster that hung from her bra under her shirt. She carried a pink Diamondback .380 micro-compact because it was small and easy to carry in the Flash Bang. She owned other pistols that she carried concealed at times but she usually carried her Diamondback. With the terrorist activity going on this week she was glad to have the gun, although she doubted she would need to use it. There were many malls around the Phoenix area so why would terrorists come here, if they were even going to do that?

Deanna said "Hi" to two young women as they entered the store. She started to ask if they needed help finding something but her hands were full of some tangled hangers at the time and the girls seemed to know where they were going.

She watched them go to the rear of the store, and as she turned back around she was surprised to see a man standing on the other side of the counter, an AK-47 in his hands. He looked like he was Middle-Eastern. He started to say something but before he could get the words out of his mouth Deanna had already started to react. She dropped the hangers and

212

pulled the bottom hem of her shirt up with her left hand and pulled her Diamondback out of the Flash Bang holster under her shirt. The grip was powder pink and the slide was cream-colored. It looked like a toy but was much more dangerous.

She pointed the gun at the terrorist, for that was surely who he was, and he said with a strong accent, "Ha! Silly woman. I'm not afraid of a woman with a pink toy."

Deanna said, "Maybe you should be," as she pulled the trigger three times, putting all three shots into the terrorist's chest. He didn't even have a chance to raise his rifle. He fell back with a stunned look on his face and landed hard on the floor just as Deanna heard other gunfire throughout the mall.

The two young women came running to the front of the store. One of them said, "Are you OK?"

Deanna said, "Yes, but it sounds like the mall is under attack."

Deanna holstered her Diamondback, stepped around the counter, and picked up the AK-47. Tobie said, "Do you know how to shoot an AK?"

Deanna said, "Yes, I own one and I've shot it many times."

Tobie said, "I'm Tobie and this is Sophie. Are you sure you want to carry his gun and not your own?" Tobie was concerned about shooting an unfamiliar weapon.

Deanna said, "Let's take it in case we need it. I'm Deanna."

They both looked at Sophie whose eyes were wide; she looked terrified.

Tobie said, "Do you want to stay here or come with us?"

Sophie didn't speak but stepped up and put her hand on top of Tobie's left arm, as if to say, "I'm scared but I want to come."

Tobie said, "OK, but you can't hold my arm because I'll need it to shoot. Let's go."

During that brief conversation they continued to hear gunfire throughout the mall along with screams and yelling.

The three young women stepped out in front of Rags & Bags and looked both directions. About four stores down on the right they saw a terrorist come out of one store with his AK-47 and turn with his back toward them as he started into another store.

Deanna quickly threw the AK to her shoulder, pointed it at the man, and pulled the trigger. It turned out to be a machine gun and not a semi-automatic. She had fired machine guns before so she was only slightly surprised as several shots smacked into the windows above and around the terrorist and rained glass down on him. He jumped, turned around, and started swinging his gun into a firing position. Evidently, he hadn't expected to be shot at.

"*Welcome to Arizona!*" Deanna said as she sent another burst of automatic gunfire at him. That time she aimed and the terrorist crumpled onto the smooth tile floor.

As the three young women walked quickly toward the inert terrorist a young man peeked his head around the corner of the store. Deanna recognized him but didn't know his name. He worked in the athletic shoe store that the terrorist had started to go into.

The young man said, "Hey, thanks! I would have been a goner."

He saw the AK that Deanna was holding and he reached down to pick up the one on the floor in front of him. He asked, "Can I carry this one. I have guns at home but I don't have one with me."

Deanna glanced quickly at his name tag as she said, "Do you know how to shoot an AK, Justin?"

The young man said, "No, but I've shot ARs before."

Deanna said, "Pretty much the same, but it doesn't say Safe and Fire by the Safety button. And these seem to be automatic."

They heard more shots echoing in the huge mall. Sophie looked at her watch and said, "It's 7:30. The boys were going to the food court."

Tobie had a sudden realization, "I promised mom I would watch out for Tucker!" She turned and started running toward the food court, the others following her. They continued to hear shots in a distant part of the mall, but mostly they heard screams and crying from those who had been injured in the initial stages of the attack.

As they came around a ninety-degree corner to see a full view of the food court they froze in their tracks. The area was filled with people, some sitting in their chairs at the tables but most sitting on the floor amongst the tables. They were surrounded by three or four men with AK-47s.

One of the terrorists, an apparent leader of some kind, was positioned in front of Mike's Pizza Kitchen with three people standing in front of him. Two of the people were Tucker and Harley.

Just as Tobie and the others turned the corner, the man called loudly to the captive shoppers, "Who is a Christian?" As he did so, he waved a big knife in the air.

Tobie realized Tucker was wearing a T-shirt from youth camp that said, "Jesus Loves Me." She also knew Tucker was fearless and would proudly admit that he was a Christian.

As the terrorist took a step forward, Tucker boldly and loudly yelled, "I am a Christian!"

The man raised the knife as if preparing to swing it toward Tucker but Tobie jumped out from where she had been standing unnoticed and yelled, "WAIT!" Tobie still had not drawn her 9mm as she started walking quickly toward the terrorist.

The man paused and turned his head toward the sound, intrigued by this young woman who was daring enough to approach him in spite of his large knife. The crowd of shoppers was dead silent as she walked past them

"I'm a Christian too," Tobie said loudly as she drew near to the terrorist. As the man turned to face her she quickly drew the CZ from her waistband, aimed, and pulled the trigger four times. She was scared and she didn't group the shots very well but at least she managed to get two of them to hit home. They struck the terrorist right in the middle of his chest. The other two shots rang out as they hit the stainless-steel equipment in Mikes Pizza Kitchen. The terrorist sank to the floor.

By the time she pulled the trigger the fourth time the terrorist closest to her on the left realized what was happening and started shooting at Tobie. She had surprised everyone so much with her bold entry onto the scene that he was the first one to react, and he didn't even aim. Nonetheless, his burst of machine-gun fire caught Tobie with several shots. She fell toward the crowd of sitting shoppers just as Tucker ran to try to catch her.

Justin and Deanna had used Tobie's distraction to scoot around the edge of the food court toward the other terrorists. They concentrated on keeping low while all eyes were on Tobie and the man who had just shot her. They were now past him when Deanna deliberately aimed high from behind. She was afraid of hitting innocent people in her attempt to take him out. She hoped no one would jump up as she let loose with a short burst of fire. She caught the man in the shoulder, spinning him around toward her before the next shots hit his neck and head. The terrorist collapsed to the floor.

Justin rose, took a stable stance, and flung a burst of fire toward the two other terrorists. The terrorists had been focused on the other action and had not seen Justin and Deanna turn the corner. They started raising

215

their rifles but the shoe salesman's barrage of lead dispatched them before they could fire a shot.

It was over that quickly; the threat was gone but the damage had been done.

Blood was pouring from several wounds in Tobie's torso and one in her arm. Just before Tucker reached her she fell into the lap of a woman who was sitting there on the floor.

It was Cindy Clevenger.

*   *   *

When Cindy brought her boys past the food court Curtis asked if they could get pizza, his favorite food. They had a good dinner before coming to the mall and they already had an ice cream cone but Curtis loved pizza and asked for it any chance he got. As they got their pizza and made their way to the closest empty table, Cindy balancing the tray, pushing the baby one-handed in the stroller, and guiding Curtis, the shooting started. The terrorists fired at some people and yelled at others to sit down. She had her hands full of food and little boys and she thought about the Walther but didn't have a free hand to attempt to find it. She quickly sat on the floor and pulled Curtis to the side and behind her, pushing both boys under the table, the pizza forgotten. She wrapped her other hand around Carlton while she attempted to work the diaper bag free of the stroller handle.

She wasn't exactly sure what she would do, whether anyone else would be there to shoot with her. She knew that she was no match for four terrorists but she was determined to defend her sons or die in the attempt.

As she sat there she noticed a young man in a shirt that said, "Jesus Loves Me." He and two others had not dropped to the floor.

A terrorist yelled and raised his knife toward the boy when Cindy got hold of the Walther. Then a young woman came forward and started shooting and then others with rifles joined in, and by the time Cindy had her weapon part way out of the diaper bag it was all over and she slid it back in the bag.

Cindy noticed that the brave young woman had been hit. As the noise from the shooting echoed and died down in the mall, the girl, now covered in blood, sagged onto Cindy's lap and Cindy guessed that the girl only had moments to live. The boy skidded to the floor on his knees

216

next to them and cradled the girl's head in his arms. Cindy noticed how limp the body felt on her as the girl's vital organs bled out. Cindy just sat there, holding the dying girl, not knowing what to do or say. She didn't even know her name.

The boy cried softly, "No, Tobie, no." The young woman looked over at him and said, "I love you, Tuck. Tell mom and dad I'm sorry." She let go of her gun and it dropped to the floor. She reached for him and weakly clenched the front of his shirt in her right hand. Tears streamed down his cheeks as he lovingly brushed some hair from his sister's face. He whispered back, "I love you too, Tobie. Please hang on."

Tobie then turned to Cindy, a complete stranger, and looked into her eyes. The young woman winced and softly gasped with pain as she quietly and haltingly said, "I . . . promised . . . Mom," and then she was gone. Her eyes closed peacefully as if she was asleep and she lay still.

The last word spoken in her young life was the name of the mother who gave her that life. Cindy knew that the girl's mother would receive heartbreaking news in a just few minutes.

Tears were streaming down Cindy's face as Tucker quietly whispered, "No, no, no." Cindy realized two other teenagers were now kneeling nearby, touching any part of Tobie that they could reach; both were weeping. Cindy heard Curtis softly crying behind her. She pulled him close, careful not to disrupt the family of this courageous young woman who had just given her life for her brother. As Cindy held her son the thought registered in her mind, *Greater love hath no man than this, that a man lay down his life for his friends.* The death of this young teenager reminded Cindy of an Only Begotten elder brother who gave *his* life for all of his siblings.

Cindy's clothes, her Walther, and even her phone were covered with blood from being beneath Tobie as her life drained away. For some reason the sight was not scary or horrific to her. The words came into her mind from a patriotic song she had heard, *Courage of the fallen and their blood devoutly shed.* She realized that the word "devout" or "devotion" seemed to fit exactly with how Tobie had given her life for her brother and the others. It was actually a very reverent moment, as terrible as it was. She almost sensed that Jesus was there to take this amazing girl into his loving arms and welcome her home.

Cindy just sat there, a lifeless body on her lap, her son in her arms. She didn't want to move—didn't want to disturb a very sacred moment. She glanced back and saw that a nice woman was crouched under the table by Carlton, speaking softly to him to calm his crying. Cindy had a surge of love for all those offering relief around them.

Police and firefighters were arriving and starting to help with the injured.

Cindy noticed that the other teenage girl who had knelt close by had picked up Tobie's pistol. Cindy looked at her and said, "Can you keep that safe? It's probably ready to fire another shot."

The girl replied, "I already pushed the button to decock it like Tobie showed me. I guess that's right." Just then a police officer reached them and Cindy said, "That pistol was what this girl shot the terrorist with."

The officer said, "Can I have it?"

The teenager handed the gun to the officer, pointing it right at his chest. He gingerly took the weapon and turned it so it was not aimed at any of them. He examined it, popped out the magazine, and worked the slide to eject the shell, which he put into his pocket. He put the gun into his waistband.

The woman who was with Carlton told Cindy that she could stay and help. After Cindy handed Curtis over to her, Cindy gently worked herself out from under Tobie. Just then a family that she knew from Church came rushing over. After checking to make sure that none of the blood on Cindy belonged to her, they offered to take the boys home with them. Cindy knew Ryan and Lindsay Davidson very well and she was completely comfortable with allowing her boys to go with them. She lovingly said goodbye to Curtis and Carlton, telling them to go with the Davidsons and reassuring them that she would come get them as soon as she could. She wanted to hug her boys or even touch them but she was covered with blood. She retrieved her car keys, wallet, and the Walther from the diaper bag and handed the bag to Lindsay. Cindy slid the Walther into her front waistband. Her loose blouse covered the pistol completely. Ryan Davidson told her to just ring the doorbell any time she was ready, even if it was in the middle of the night or tomorrow morning. Lindsay asked about any food allergies, to make sure there wasn't anything they shouldn't feed the boys, but Cindy told them there were none.

With the boys safely cared for, Cindy thanked the kind woman and then felt compelled to be with the three teenagers. She had seen the other boy tearfully make a phone call; apparently to parents. The girl had wrapped her arms around Tucker from behind, as Tucker would not surrender his hold on his sister. Cindy knelt down by the other boy, putting her arm around his shoulders; feeling his body shake as he cried. Less than fifteen minutes later two sets of parents arrived. Cindy stepped back as the adults surrounded their children. Paramedics allowed them time with the lifeless body of their daughter before they put her on a gurney.

Cindy had tried to clean some of the blood off of her with napkins from one of the tables but hadn't been very successful. She sat quietly and watched the grieving family. One man held a woman in one arm and Tucker in the other. The mother was sobbing uncontrollably and the father wept with his eyes closed, tears streaming down his face. Tucker had his head buried in his father's shoulder. The other teenagers stood close by in the embrace of their parents. It was obvious that they were family members.

Cindy waited until the group regained a bit of their composure. She was embarrassed for how she looked when she approached and said, "Your daughter was very brave. When she . . . collapsed she fell on me where I was sitting on the floor. She only had two concerns. She told her brother that she loved him and she said she had kept her promise to her mom."

Tobie's mother struggled to speak. "Every time they leave the house I tell her to take care of Tucker and she always promises to do that. She is . . . was . . . such a good daughter and a good big sister. Is that her blood on you? I'm so sorry."

Cindy looked down at herself before she said, "Yes, it's her blood and you don't need to apologize. Your daughter made the ultimate sacrifice in fulfilling her promise to you, and I believe there's a great reward in heaven for her because of that. I was honored to be with her at the end. It was actually very spiritual; I could almost feel that Jesus was there to receive her to Him."

Tobie's father spoke, "Tobie and I have talked many times about the responsibility of carrying a concealed weapon and the sacrifice that may come with it, much like a mother protecting her young. Tobie told me that she was willing to make that sacrifice. I wonder if she ever thought that it would be for her own brother."

Just then someone came and asked the family if they wanted to go with the ambulance.

They thanked Cindy and she watched them walk away. She suddenly realized that she was exhausted. She wondered if this was how Alan felt after such an experience. She took that moment to pray for him and for the family that had just lost a beloved daughter.

35 Indecision and Frustration

Alan and Sheriff Concepcion and their teams were standing on the dam getting call after call about the Friday night terrorist attacks in the Phoenix area. Most of the team kept an eye on the dam and the surrounding area, while Alan and the sheriff discussed with their dispatchers and others the events going on in the valley.

They kept their teams updated on what had been going on and what they knew so far. There had been an attack at a movie theater in Phoenix, another at a sports complex in Chandler, and a shooting at the Five Star Mall in Mesa. In each of the three situations, armed citizens stopped the terrorists and minimized the losses, although there were a number of civilian casualties and injuries.

Alan's phone rang and it was Victor. Alan walked away across the dam to a private place as they talked.

"Alan, I know you've heard of all the things going on in Phoenix by now. It's been a mess. Through it all, I have continued to think about our conversation earlier. When was it, this morning? It seems like it was days ago after all that has happened today. Anyway, I still feel strongly that you are where you need to be. I don't know if you have wondered about coming back, but you need to stay there. Do not come back."

Alan replied, "Victor, I appreciate you telling me because it has been very frustrating. We can't find any sign of terrorist activity and some of the team are very critical about my decision to stay here. They think that I led us on a wild goose chase all in vain. We just can't find anything that leads to confidence in the tip we received."

"Well, don't give up. Stay there. You and I both know that the tip is reliable. And I would have never thought I would be the one telling you that."

"Thank you, Sir. Yes, I know. We will stay here." They ended the call.

Alan turned back to the others and called them all together. It took them a few minutes to gather from their positions across the dam, and when they were close enough he spoke loudly for all to hear.

"Ladies and gentlemen, I keep wondering if we need to go back to Phoenix and I'm sure many of you have had those same thoughts. I assure you, this has not been an easy decision for me but the tip we received was from a very confidential yet very credible source. I am not at liberty to discuss it but Victor Pilchick and I have had a thorough discussion and we both agree that it is reliable. Even though there is a lot going on back in the valley we are committed to staying here. We need to keep up our surveillance, but if we find nothing I think some of us will go to Globe for the night and come back in the morning."

The nods Alan got seemed somewhat reluctant as he dismissed the teams and walked again across the dam to be by himself. He called his house but there was no answer. He called Cindy's cell and it went straight to voice mail as if the phone was turned off. That seemed odd, but he knew there could be several possible reasons for that. He left her a message, telling her that they were still at the dam but had yet to find anything. He also told her Victor was still in full support of the mission, so that was a relief, and that he would try to call later.

After two and a half hours at the dam they had to admit that there was nothing there. Alan was puzzled and had been growing more frustrated as time went on. He had full confidence in the source of the tip, so there was no mistake on that front. Maybe he had misunderstood something or he had done something wrong. Maybe the timing was wrong or something had changed. There was still the possibility that something could happen there in the next few hours.

Alan called the team together and they consulted, standing there under the utility lights on the top of the dam, trying to decide what to do. As they had been trained by Victor, their boss, they were free to share their feedback and thoughts. Some of the group felt like they were on a wild goose chase and it was a waste of time and resources to be there. Some were clearly angry and felt that a bad decision had been made, especially when it was clear that they could be of use in the valley. Others suggested that maybe something *was* going to happen but didn't because they had shown up to investigate. They all agreed that it was still possible that something could happen but they disagreed on how long to wait.

The final decision was to leave four people on watch at the dam while the others went back to Globe. At daybreak, they would trade off or decide on another course of action. They felt that since they had received a reliable tip it wouldn't make sense to give up too soon. Four volunteers stepped forward to take the first shift, two from Alan's team and two sheriff's deputies.

As Alan drove back toward Globe just after 9:00 p.m. he felt discouraged and dejected. He was supposed to be leading this team and instead he seemed to be wasting their time. He kept wondering if somewhere along the way he had missed a key fact or a prompting from the Lord. He just didn't know what to do! He felt humiliated. Maybe he failed or maybe whatever was going to happen just hadn't happened yet. Even though he trusted in the Lord, he felt a familiar frustration with the Lord's timing.

36 Planning For Contingencies

Unbeknownst to the law enforcement personnel on the dam, they were being watched from high on the mountainside to the north. From that vantage point, a sniper in a ghillie suit had watched them through his own night-vision binoculars. He was an Afghani named Rasekh who had fought with the American troops in Afghanistan. He had learned American warfare and had then defected to the radical Islamic movement due to severe pressure and influence of his cousin. He spoke both Dari, the primary language of Afghanistan, and also Arabic and English.

Many months earlier, after a very intense firefight in Afghanistan in which the American personnel had to quickly abandon an area they had originally held, Rasekh had gone and retrieved the equipment left by the US forces. He had found a sniper who had been killed in the firefight and there were several pieces of high-quality equipment, including the ghillie suit, binoculars, a Swarovski 25-power spotting scope, and a sniper rifle with ammo. The rifle was a Lapua .338 Magnum, a very powerful and effective long-range weapon. It had a twelve-power scope and was covered with camouflage paint and tape.

After Rasekh had defected to the radical Islamic movement in Afghanistan, he had received funds from the movement. They had also provided him with connections that helped him make his way, gun and all, around the world to Mexico and across Arizona's weakly-secured southern border to the Phoenix area. Once he was in the U.S. it didn't take long to find contacts that were part of the anti-American movement and join their forces. He eventually ended up on Al-Musawi's team. In fact, hardly anyone besides Al-Musawi himself even knew of Rasekh. He and a few others were on a second team that was assigned to the Roosevelt Dam operation. Al-Musawi had not even told his first team that there was a second team. Doing so reduced the amount of chatter about it that could be picked up by counter-intelligence surveillance.

Rasekh's ghillie suit looked exactly like a bush . . . until the bush moved and you realized there was something else going on. In the suit, Rasekh had remained on the mountainside all day and all evening above Roosevelt Dam, undetected by the agents and deputies at the dam. Several of them looked his way with their binoculars but had not seen him, thanks to the ghillie suit.

Rasekh had arrived in the area on Thursday, driving in from the north and stopping on the side of a tiny dirt road a few miles off the highway. He had hiked through the night across the mountain until he was north of the dam before daybreak on Friday. He was about 400 yards from the dam, and with his sniper rifle he could have easily taken out any of the people who had been sent as the advance team or those of Alan's team when they arrived. However, shooting the Americans now was not the plan.

When law enforcement arrived, Rasekh immediately called Al-Musawi on his cell phone and told Al-Musawi to wait. "The party has not started yet," Rasekh said, which was pre-determined code, spoken in English so as not to arouse suspicion from any monitoring of the airwaves. He and Al-Musawi had devised this code months ago during the planning stages of this operation. They hoped that it would fit with the other kinds of cell phone calls which could be floating around in the airwaves near Roosevelt Lake.

While Alan and his team were at the dam, Rasekh waited patiently and watched. After the majority of the team drove away he quietly called Al-Musawi again. "There was a party on the beach earlier with lots of family members. Everyone has gone home now. Only four campers left to spend the night. I'll see you at breakfast on Saturday."

On the north edge of Globe, Al-Musawi had received both calls. He knew that the code words, "family members" and "campers" referred to law enforcement personnel. Al-Musawi and one other man on his team were standing near a small abandoned convenience store having a smoke, watching vehicles go by on the road. They had a big truck, an eighteen-wheeler, which now sat behind the convenience store.

Al-Musawi, his left forearm wrapped in a bandage, had seen Alan and Sheriff Concepcion's men head north about three hours earlier. Now he was watching for them to return to Globe. The phone call from Rasekh gave him the assurance that they were, indeed, on their way. They had discussed the possibility of law enforcement being in the area so this was no surprise to them. They had planned for several different contingencies and this was merely one of them. They were confident that things were going according to plan and that this time they had outsmarted the Americans.

Before long, Al-Musawi saw the black Tahoe and Suburban and the Sheriff's vehicles go past on their way into town. He had been standing slightly behind the corner of the building and he had not been seen by the law enforcement personnel as they passed. He was confident in his plan and his team.

When the law enforcement vehicles went past, Al-Musawi looked over at a beat-up Nissan sitting in front of the eighteen-wheeler and waved with his arm from north to south. The car started, the lights came on, and it sped off toward the south in pursuit of the law enforcement vehicles. The driver smiled excitedly as he sped off, revving the engine and eliciting a string of loud, harsh language from a grinning Al-Musawi. This was another part of the plan and the driver had already been instructed to find and take any opportunity to remove the law enforcement personnel from the picture. The driver knew where the sheriff's office was and he hoped they would stop there to talk before going to their next destination. He had a very loud and very deadly gift for them.

Al-Musawi and his driver turned and walked to the eighteen-wheeler, looking to see that no one was around. Behind the convenience store there was nothing but an open dirt field bordered by a wall of mesquite trees, since this was a flat area near a river bottom. This was desert and everything was dry, but the mesquite trees were thick due to past rain and occasional water in the small river bottom.

The swinging doors on the truck were slightly ajar to let in air. Al-Musawi stepped to the truck, and using his right hand, pulled one of the doors open about four feet. His left arm still hurt, but he had to show no pain, no fear, and no doubt at this time. Al-Musawi was truly an inspiring leader and this was precisely the time he needed to inspire his men, and himself.

As the door swung slightly open he smiled at what he saw. The truck was full of men—his men. They were all whispering quietly, each looking comfortable and happy, awaiting instructions to carry out whatever plans Al-Musawi had for them.

One man said in Arabic, "Is it time?" Al-Musawi replied in Arabic, "Almost. We were going to go earlier and take care of things this evening, but the FBI showed up. However, our plan has contingencies built in and we are still a step ahead of the Americans. We will sleep here in our truck. Our moment will arrive in the morning. By then the FBI will be out of the picture and we will wage holy war in a remote location with no one to stop us. The result will bring great destruction to one of America's largest cities. All of America will know that we are superior to them and they will learn to fear us."

37 Around the Globe

When Sheriff Concepcion and Alan reached Globe at the US Highway 60 and AZ Highway 188 junction they talked on the radio and decided they needed to eat. Alan's team hadn't eaten since Phoenix that morning except the quick emergency rations they kept in their tactical outfits, and it was almost 10:00 p.m. They turned right and drove three miles west to the small town of Miami to a mom and pop diner on US 60 called Mattie's. As they went in through the front doors Sheriff Concepcion said, "This is one of our favorite places. Open 24 hours too."

As they ate, the driver of the car that had been with Al-Musawi was searching Globe for the sheriff and the FBI vehicles. His name was Jassim and by the time he reached the junction in Globe the law enforcement vehicles had turned west toward Miami and he did not see them. He turned east and drove to the sheriff's office which was four and a half miles from the junction. Not finding them there, he waited near the office for a while and watched. When no one arrived he drove around the building looking for some sign of them. When that failed he expanded his search. There were several restaurants and hotels on the main highway that snaked through town but he saw nothing. He drove around the nearby side streets, growing more and more annoyed as he searched in vain.

Jassim drove into downtown Globe, the old part of town, searching for hotels or restaurants that were open. At each one, he drove through the parking lot, looking for the black Suburban and Tahoe. At first he was merely annoyed and anxious but now he was getting angry. He was also nervous about reporting to Al-Musawi that he had failed.

The thought came to Jassim several times that when he did find them he would die in a bomb blast but he pushed that out of his mind. His allegiance and devotion to Allah were more important than his own life and he had taken a personal vow months earlier that he was willing to die for the cause of overthrowing capitalism and the infidels' abominable way of life. He reached with one hand and felt the bomb that was wrapped around his body. He would not fail!

Besides, he hated the FBI. When he was in the training and indoctrination process in his home country they talked often of the FBI. Although he had only learned a few words of English, one of them was "F B I." His leaders talked often of the role the agency played in fighting against them. Jassim and his companions were dedicated to Allah and overthrowing the infidels, and their leaders taught them that the FBI was the greatest threat to their movement.

They didn't realize how wrong they were. While the FBI was a huge threat, an even greater one was the collective group of millions of Americans who were armed and who believed that the Islamic extremists were one of the greatest dangers to America. The FBI was perhaps the greatest *organized* threat but there were many Americans who would and could fight against Islamic extremism.

*   *   *

It took hours to deal with the confusion and clean-up at the mall, and Cindy Clevenger was in the middle of it. Law enforcement secured all the weapons and took statements from everyone, sorting out the entire situation for their reports. Cindy gave her statement to a female police officer but did not tell her she was armed, and the officer didn't ask. Firefighters and medical personnel tended to the wounded and those who had been killed. As more and more of the people left, the mall got quieter. Law enforcement teams remained, taking photos, measuring, analyzing, looking at evidence and gathering all the information they could.

As Cindy drove home around 10:30 she thought about all of it. She realized that Tobie's father was right. That urge to protect the life of someone else was much like the instinct of a mother defending the life of her child, or even animal mothers who guard their young. She suspected that military personnel and police officers must have that same feeling, maybe more so, knowing that by protecting the country or the society from evil, they are protecting their own loved ones as well.

As she continued to think, her thoughts returned to the feelings she had had earlier that week. It finally came to her that her mood of helplessness came from feeling like a victim. Unarmed. Helpless. Weak. She realized that even though Tobie had died, she died a hero instead of a helpless victim.

Cindy decided right there, at the corner of Gilbert Road and Baseline Road, that she was going to carry a concealed weapon for the rest of her life, and she suddenly no longer felt weak. It was a liberating feeling. She had a new urge to be a protector; no, not just a mere urge, it was a sudden deep inner commitment. She knew in her heart that if she were called on she would use a gun to protect not just her children, but any of God's children who were threatened by evil.

She thought about buying a gun the next morning, but she wanted to wait for Alan to help her choose the right one. She decided that for their anniversary she could give Alan the ring and he could help her buy a gun. On second thought, maybe they would decide she should just carry the Walther. This week it had become her trusted friend and it gave her a sense of security. Having watched a young girl who wielded a gun die in her arms, Cindy knew the Walther was not absolute security. However, she knew that with a gun in her possession she would no longer be a helpless victim.

As she thought about Alan she realized she couldn't call him. He had taught her that when he was on assignment any kind of interruption could disrupt something crucial and even cost lives. It was one of the downsides of being married to an FBI agent; she had to wait until he called or came home, and only then could they talk. Cindy knew that if something was extremely urgent, like one of the kids being critically injured, Cindy could call a special after-hours number at the FBI building and an operator could relay the message to Alan. She had never had to do that and she realized that now was not a dire emergency. Besides, her cell phone was covered with blood, now caked and mostly dried around the edges, but still sticky in other places. It wouldn't work anyway.

*　　*　　*

After a futile and aggravating search through downtown Globe, Jassim began working his way back toward the west, driving along the main highway and looking for restaurants and hotels on nearby side streets. Finally, he had worked his way back to the junction that headed toward Roosevelt Dam. He saw a blue sign that indicated the direction to a hospital and decided to turn south toward that. Just after he turned he caught a glimpse of a black vehicle in his rearview mirror. He lurched to a stop in the middle of the street, whipped his head around, and saw two black vehicles going east on the highway where he had just been driving.

He flipped a quick U-turn back to the intersection and saw a sheriff's vehicle follow the black vehicles through a green light, heading east. As Jassim reached the intersection he had a red light and he was going to turn right. He realized that now was not the time to roll through a turn instead of stopping completely. He carefully made the turn but grew more anxious as he watched the sheriff's vehicle drawing farther away on the road ahead of him. Jassim knew that he couldn't speed past the sheriff's vehicle to catch up to the FBI. He still had to be patient.

As the sheriff's vehicle approached another intersection a red light stopped it. Rather than stop right behind the sheriff's vehicle Jassim pulled into a cheap little road-side motel and pulled behind a couple of parked cars. He could still see the sheriff's vehicle and the traffic light. He waited until the light turned green and then carefully crept back onto the highway a block or two behind the sheriff's vehicle.

Jassim followed the sheriff at a safe distance as they worked their way through town. Jassim was relieved that the sheriff's vehicle turned into the sheriff's office and Jassim didn't have to follow him anymore, but now he had lost the FBI again. However, after a brief search for a few blocks, Jassim found both FBI vehicles parked at a hotel. Unfortunately, the vehicles were not close to each other. One was parked near the entry and the other was parked some distance away across the

228

parking lot. He didn't know why they separated until he noticed that the second vehicle had a dog and they were parked by an area of dirt and dry grass. One of the men was standing by the vehicle as the dog walked around in the dirt and relieved itself.

With the vehicles spaced too far apart Jassim's bomb would not be effective. He had to take out all of the FBI team, not just part of them. He stopped on the far edge of the parking lot and sat with the engine idling. After a few minutes some of the FBI personnel came out of the hotel and started unloading gear from both vehicles. They took their bags and left the vehicles where they were. The canine handler took the dog and joined the others in the hotel.

Jassim had no choice but to wait. He backed his car within the stripes of a parking space so as not to attract attention and turned off the engine. It was after 11:00 p.m.

As part of the training he received in his homeland he had learned to sleep sitting up in short spurts of fifteen or twenty minutes. That's what he did now, sleeping for a few minutes, then looking over at the cars, then sleeping again. It was also a very light sleep and noises woke him easily. Any time people came and left the parking lot through the night or a dog barked in the neighborhood up on the hill to the south or a car drove by, he noticed. That was one reason Al-Musawi had selected Jassim for this role. He was good at this—watching and waiting for something to happen and staying alert the entire time, all the while with a bomb strapped to his body.

SATURDAY

38 The Men in the Truck

Sitting among other terrorists in the back of an eighteen-wheeler before the break of day on a Saturday morning, Teymour Javadi liked what he saw. Someone had turned on the lights lining the inside top of the fifty-three-foot box trailer, so there was enough light to see inside the truck, which had been idling for a while. At the front of the cargo compartment was a huge pile of explosives and the equipment to detonate it, along with rappelling gear—ropes, carabineers, and figure eights. Teymour was told that they had enough explosives to destroy a huge building and kill many people. There was also food and water. There were more than eighty men who were seated in the remainder of the trailer, tightly packed, but pleasantly chatting with each other as if they were at a coffee shop. Some of the men were holding AK-47s.

Teymour had grown up in Pennsylvania in a community of Muslim refugees. He was fourth-generation American, a full citizen, and spoke nothing other than English, save for a few words. He had left home when he reached college age and ended up at Cal State Fullerton where he met and was indoctrinated into radical Islamist ideology by a friend in his fraternity. He had finally started learning some of the language of his great grandfather's homeland, although Teymour still knew only a few words of Farsi.

Next to him was the friend he had met at the university, Armeen Soomekh, who was from a Muslim family who immigrated to America sixteen years earlier when Armeen was seven years old. Armeen's parents never spoke a word of English to him and he spoke Farsi and Arabic and had exposure to several other Middle Eastern languages. He went to public schools in Peoria, Arizona on Phoenix's west side and he learned to speak fluent English. After high school he went to California with his girlfriend who had grown up there but who had lived in Peoria for the last two years of high school. Armeen eventually started school at Cal State Fullerton, and because of things he had read online, became interested in radical Islamic causes.

When Teymour met Armeen they became fast friends. Within a year Teymour and Armeen were fully indoctrinated into a radical Islamist group and they followed another friend back to the Phoenix area. Their reason for moving was to join a terrorist cell in Phoenix headed by an extremely radical Islamist named Mansoor Fatik Al-Musawi. Armeen never told his parents he was back in Arizona, although he was living only a few miles from them. They thought Armeen was still at Cal State Fullerton and when they communicated by phone or text or email he gave all indications that school in California was going well.

Teymour and Armeen both had a growing hatred of Americans and the evil infidels that populated the United States. Both young men could hardly wait to be trained in terrorist techniques. Their teacher, Al-Musawi, was calculating and cold in the development of his team, continually stirring their emotions and frustration, keeping them angry and yet still in check. Eventually Teymour and Armeen took a vow together to give their lives for Allah in a suicide bomb attack. They made the vow on January 20 and Al-Musawi promised that he had a mission for them soon that would kill thousands, maybe tens of thousands of infidels.

The location of Al-Musawi's training ground was in the heart of the industrial sector on the southwest side of Phoenix. The area was comprised of miles and miles of buildings that were actively used for all kinds of things. There were furniture manufacturing and recycling warehouses. There were warehouses that recycled aluminum cans, made wooden pallets, and applied chrome to auto parts to re-sell around the world. There were oil product distributors, machine shops, paint shops, and storage warehouse after storage warehouse after storage warehouse. There was a company that manufactured custom parts for motorcycles; there was a warehouse that manufactured complex industrial motors the size of a motor home, and many, many other similar businesses. The railroad ran through the middle of that industrial area and some of the businesses relied on rail transportation for the shipping of their products, both inbound and outbound. That area of town was a constant hum of activity, with people, raw materials, equipment, and machinery moving around and between buildings. There were also thousands of employees coming and going, and delivery vehicles arriving and departing at all hours of the day and night.

Among all this was a business called MC Produce. MC employed hundreds of people and ran their operation non-stop. They had a company cafeteria where they fed their employees at all hours of the day.

MC Produce worked with both fresh and frozen produce; receiving and repackaging tons of produce, shipping their product all around Arizona and the rest of the western U.S. They had so many men and women, trucks and service vehicles moving about, that it wasn't difficult for Al Musawi to run his clandestine operation out of a little-used part of the warehouse. Most of the employees of MC had no idea that a terrorist cell was operating in another part of their building, although a few select key people did know what was going on.

In fact, even the team of Al-Musawi's personnel who had met with him in the park on the previous Sunday didn't know that there was a sizeable terrorist cell in the MC Produce warehouse. They didn't even know such an operation or cell existed. In the corollary, the men at the MC location didn't know about any other terror cell operations being conducted by Al-Musawi. He gave each group only the information they needed about their part of his plans.

Al-Musawi never allowed himself to be seen entering or exiting the building. When he came and went he was always inside of a truck, semi-trailer, or rail car. The corner of the building that contained his operation was not easily entered, and any wandering employees of MC's normal operations were politely turned away by a receptionist. However, that corner of the building was used for housing and training. Their own security team was diligent at keeping their part of MC Produce unnoticed by anyone outside of their terrorist operation.

Pursuant to current plans, some of the men, once vetted and admitted to the training, would never leave the building until it was time to

232

commit a terrorist attack. It wasn't difficult for a produce operation with an employee cafeteria to provide food and support to a hundred men who were learning the techniques of how to make and use suicide bombs; how to handle, load, and clean weapons; how to rappel down the face of a cliff or a building; and a host of other things that terrorists might learn how to do.

It also wasn't difficult for Al-Musawi's team to load an eighteen-wheeler with explosives, equipment, and well-fed terrorist recruits and send them off to do their violent acts undetected by law enforcement. Teymour and Armeen had arrived at the MC warehouse a few weeks prior, where they had studied, trained, and taken their suicide vows; waiting for their opportunity to give themselves to Allah and the cause of destroying infidels.

Their glorious moment had finally arrived and now they were sitting in the eighteen-wheeler, ready and willing, filled with a mixture of fear and excitement.

The truck pulled out of the dirt lot behind the mesquite trees and started moving on the highway. Al-Musawi stood, steadying himself with one hand on the wall. Every man fell silent and listened while their leader explained the mission. Part of what Al-Musawi said was a severe stretch of the truth, only a hope really, but much of what he said was absolutely true. Now desperate, since his planned attacks this week had failed miserably, with only minor parts of the attacks being minimally successful, Al-Musawi's rage was not manufactured. In fact, he was fuming because the other half of his terrorist cell had by now been almost entirely wiped out by armed citizens. Al-Musawi had been up late the previous night in Globe talking to his contacts in Phoenix, who relayed to him in code the results of the failed attacks on the ball field, the movie theater, and the shopping mall. He hadn't slept well and even now was using sheer force of will and expert acting to hide his frustration and anger, but also redirecting it to motivate the men in the truck to carry out their part of the plan.

As Armeen translated for Teymour, Al-Musawi finally told them that there was another part of his terrorist cell that they didn't know about. He described the attacks in Phoenix all week but he lied to make it sound like the terrorists had been very successful.

Al-Musawi told the men that the culmination of this week's attacks was going to be carried out by them, and it would be a massive flood in the Phoenix area. They would start by destroying Roosevelt Dam. That would trigger a flood that would also destroy Horse Mesa Dam, which contained Apache Lake just below Roosevelt Lake. The water from Roosevelt Lake and Apache Lake would combine and rush downstream, overwhelming and washing out Mormon Flat Dam which held back Canyon Lake. With the water from three lakes, Stuart Mountain Dam, which held back Saguaro Lake, would also fail. The combined water would be almost 700 billion gallons of water, or about 2.5 trillion liters.

The water from the lakes would flood into Mesa, Tempe, Phoenix, Laveen, Avondale, Goodyear, Buckeye, and other cities and towns along the south side of the Phoenix Metropolitan Area. It would take out the industrial area on the southwest side of Phoenix, including the MC Produce warehouse, thereby obliterating all evidence of their terrorist activity. West of Phoenix, it would engulf the Palo Verde Nuclear Power Plant which would cut power to millions of people in Arizona and California and possibly trigger a nuclear disaster. Along the way it would join the Gila River, which was usually a mere trickle if there was any water in it at all. Once the flood began, there would be bridges, roads, buildings, airports, parks, businesses, schools, and homes that would be swept away or covered with water. Water levels would reach twenty to forty feet in some places and even higher in others.

The flood would flow through Arizona, engulfing small towns along the way, and then reach the Colorado River where it met the Gila River at Yuma, Arizona. Yuma would also be consumed, including the Yuma Proving Ground, an infidel military base, and then eventually the water would flow the few miles south of Yuma into the Gulf of Mexico. Many thousands and perhaps millions of people would die and millions more would have their lives completely disrupted. The aftereffects would cause chaos, cold, disease and misery to the infidel capitalists. It would do trillions of dollars in damage and make the bombing of the World Trade Centers look like a children's game.

All of this was heard by Armeen in Arabic and translated to Teymour in English. There were many exaggerations and lies to make the story better and more catastrophic, but telling the truth was not Al-Musawi's goal. The more he talked, the more excited the suicide bombers became, and that's exactly what he wanted.

The truck continued to roll along the highway as the men sat in the back. Al-Musawi let them rage and gloat and then he calmed them back down for further discussion.

Al-Musawi continued in Arabic, "We will use two methods to destroy the dams I have spoken about. For the past year we have been carefully stealing C-4, RDX, ANFO, and dynamite from industrial sites across South and Central America, and also from some local sites in Arizona, California, New Mexico, and other states. Dynamite, you all know, is in sticks. RDX and C-4 are plastic explosives, developed to be like modeling clay that can be shaped and molded to fit a desired application. ANFO is usually in granular form transported in bags. The explosives from south of us were flown into Arizona by contacts we have with drug cartels which bring drugs from the south into Arizona constantly. All of the explosives have been stockpiled and stored in a remote location. The RDX, ANFO, and dynamite will come to us this morning in an airplane which we are stealing from a nearby airport. It may be used to demolish Horse Mesa Dam at Apache Lake or it may be used to help with the demolition of Roosevelt Dam. We have contingencies built into this plan if needed.

"Secondly, we have arranged to have the C-4 already here with us." Al-Musawi grinned and motioned with his bandaged arm at the stash of equipment at the front of the trailer. The cheer from the men echoed loudly in the confined space of the truck.

"We will use the C-4 to blast a hole in Roosevelt Dam which will compromise the structural integrity of the dam causing it to fail completely. We will be using highly sophisticated explosive techniques called 'shaped charges.'

"It would take many hours to go through eighty to one hundred feet of concrete by using large, heavy boring equipment the size of a big truck. However, by using shaped charges and working quickly we can do the job in two to three hours. Shaped charges are used to pierce armored tanks and also to drill deep into the earth to open holes for oil wells. They are also used for demolishing buildings."

Al-Musawi pointed at one of the men and said, "Vahid was trained by U.S. coalition forces and U.S. government contractors in Iraq, Kuwait, and Afghanistan. He understands modern explosive techniques and the processes used to extract oil from deep in the earth. He has since joined our side and today will guide the rest of us in destroying Roosevelt Dam using shaped charges."

Vahid rose and began to speak in Arabic, with Armeen still translating for Teymour. "A shaped charge is a cone of copper or aluminum. Today we are using aluminum because that works better on concrete than copper. Each unit is about the size of an ice cream cone and will be packed on the outside with C-4. When the C-4 is detonated by a blasting cap the force of the explosion literally turns the metal cone inside out, sending what's called a "jet" of hard metal out the open end of the cone. The aluminum does not melt; it remains as a hard, solid piece of metal. The jet of metal is about as long as a man's foot and travels at a speed of about 22,000 miles per hour. The jet of metal will plunge four to six feet into the concrete, doing significant damage. Each cone must be held in just the right position at just the right distance from the concrete for maximum effect.

"I have spent the last year analyzing and testing C-4, making precision aluminum cones, preparing all of the equipment we will use, and planning all the details of how to destroy Roosevelt Dam. We drove all of our equipment across the U.S. border in a truck, far out in the desert away from the main roads. We were able to escape detection because we teamed up with Coyotes, the people that are paid to transport people or goods across the U.S./Mexico border. They are experts at exploiting the holes in the border, which is not very secure due to the Americans' political conflict. Stupid infidels!"

Vahid paused while the men cheered, filling the inside of the truck with sound.

"If we used conventional demolition methods it would take a tremendous amount of explosives to blow up a structure the size of Roosevelt Dam and it would take many hours to place the explosives in just the right spots. However, we have devised a way to accomplish the same thing in a fraction of the time. By detonating three shaped charges at the same time, spaced evenly apart in a triangular configuration, the resulting hole will be about two meters deep. Then, with the proper placement of additional shaped charges we can widen and then deepen the hole in the dam. We also have detonating cord, which is another explosive that is like a small rope slightly larger than a shoe lace. It can be easily looped around a piece of the reinforcing steel rods, called rebar, and when that piece of detonating cord goes off it cuts the rebar off just like a slip knot of string would cut through a soft stick of butter. By methodically and quickly working to widen and deepen the hole in Roosevelt Dam and also by clipping the twisted rebar out of our way it will take less than three hours to reach a point where the intense pressure from the water behind the dam will finally burst through the hole. Then, the cracks caused by the explosions will also widen and the entire dam will fail.

"Roosevelt Dam is almost 200 feet thick at its base, and about twenty feet thick at the top. About halfway down it is 80 to 100 feet thick. We tested this concept in a remote location in Iraq on a dam that was also 100 feet thick at the half-way point. We used shaped charges in succession as I have described and we successfully destroyed the dam. Each methodical but successive explosion removed more concrete from the same hole, causing the hole to become wider but also deeper in the same place. In Iraq, it took fourteen explosions of three shaped charges each to break far enough through the dam to trigger structural failure. As the concrete became weakened and cracks formed in the dam the pressure from the water behind the dam broke through and the entire dam failed. By our calculations, the final rupture occurred when the bombs had broken through to about twenty feet of remaining concrete."

Al-Musawi laid a hand on Vahid's shoulder, signaling to the man that Al-Musawi wanted to continue the narrative. Al-Musawi took over and his voice was strong and piercing. "This is where each of you will get the opportunity to complete your vow to Allah. Three of you at a time, accompanied by Vahid, will rappel down the face of Roosevelt Dam, holding your shaped charges at just the right position as instructed by him. Vahid will then swing away across the dam and detonate the explosives you are holding. Your suicide vow to Allah will be kept and you will proceed to your eternal reward. Then three more of you will descend to the same spot and fulfill your vow. The process will continue and the hole will get deeper and wider and begin to form cracks in the dam. Eventually the dam will fail and we will be victorious over the infidels!

Another cheer went up from the men in the trailer.

Al-Musawi continued. "People might say that we can't blow up a dam like this. Those same people said that we couldn't blow up the twin towers at the World Trade Center in New York, but we did!" Another cheer from the men.

"After adjusting for contingencies based on events yesterday we have timed our efforts and resources for today. If Roosevelt Dam breaks according to our calculations, the airplane with the RDX and dynamite will destroy Horse Mesa Dam at Apache Lake at about the same time Roosevelt Dam fails. If our work on Roosevelt Dam takes longer, we will fly the plane past Horse Mesa Dam and use it to finalize the destruction of Roosevelt Dam. Either way, Roosevelt Dam and Horse Mesa Dam will both fail. The combined flood will destroy Phoenix, one of the ten largest cities in the United States!

"Those of you with guns will take care of any law enforcement that comes to the dam. We have already slaughtered the FBI agents who were at the dam yesterday. This is a remote location and any other police or FBI will have to come from Phoenix and will not reach us before we complete our objective. Furthermore, we have four rocket-propelled grenade launchers that we obtained in Syria. If anyone comes in a plane or helicopter to try to stop us we will blow them out of the sky!"

Al-Musawi paused again, his face in a maniacal grin. The cheer that went up from his men nearly deafened them all as it echoed repeatedly inside the truck.

"We have all made a vow to Allah. We will all carry out that vow this day. None of us will leave Roosevelt Dam alive. We will fight to the end or we will be carried down with the water as it rushes through. I have also taken a vow and will carry it out today along with you!"

Al-Musawi stopped speaking. The men cheered raucously. Armeen finished translating the speech to Teymour in English as the noise died down, and Al-Musawi started explaining details to specific members of his team regarding what they would do when they reached the dam. By the time he finished discussing goals, timing, logistics, and assignments, they had arrived at the dam.

*　　*　　*

The truck full of suicide bombers reached Roosevelt Dam just before sunrise, although it was already light enough to see sufficiently. It was a crisp morning with the temperature near forty degrees Fahrenheit.

On the south side of the road that skirted the end of the dam was a cliff about 100 feet high. The road had been widened there many years earlier when the dam had been built. To the west of the widened spot in the road, the Apache Trail, State Highway 88, went back to two narrow lanes and jogged south and east around the mountain and angled gradually down the mountainside. After about 200 yards of going south the road doubled back at the end of Alchesay Canyon and turned back toward the northwest and ran down to where it drew close to the edge of the Salt River, which quickly became the upper end of Apache Lake.

In the mouth of Alchesay Canyon, between the ends of the V made by the road, was a small rest area with restrooms, a few picnic tables and an observation area where visitors could see Roosevelt Dam. They could read displays about the history of the dam and its construction and reconstruction and could see pictures of the original dam and then look up at the dam itself less than a mile away from the observation area.

Right about the break of dawn, the eighteen-wheeler pulled up next to the south end of the Dam where the road widened. In the growing light the two FBI agents and two sheriff's deputies who had stayed at the dam overnight took notice of the truck. One of the sheriff's deputies was on the road near the widened area where the truck stopped and he started walking toward it. The other deputy and two FBI agents were on the top of the dam, watching.

Al-Musawi, having been in contact with Rasekh, the sniper who was watching the events unfold, had planned this moment carefully and had coached his team on what to do. The man who was riding in the passenger seat in the cab of the truck was dressed in American looking clothing and was assigned to open the door of the trailer to let Al-Musawi and the gunmen with their AK-47s out of the back.

As the truck stopped, the driver pretended to be looking at the dashboard of the truck and was fiddled with the driving mechanism as if something was wrong. At the same time, the passenger got out and went to the trailer. As he did so he paid attention to where the sheriff's deputy was approaching. He opened one side of the large swinging doors and pointed to the driver's side of the truck. Several gunmen had been instructed on what to do at this point and they quickly jumped out and came around on the driver's side with their AK-47s ready to fire.

As the sheriff's deputy came toward the truck, suddenly three gunmen appeared from the back of the truck, mowing him down before he even raised his weapon. Meanwhile, several other gunmen went to the wall overlooking the south end of the dam. As the shots were fired killing the first deputy, the other law enforcement personnel started running toward the metal ladder that would take them to the road. The terrorists were at a distinct advantage, being twenty feet higher than the top of the dam and standing behind a three-foot concrete wall at the edge of the highway. A gun battle ensued that left only one American law enforcement officer alive on the top of the dam.

Special Agent Quinn LeTourneau had worked on Alan Clevenger's team for a few years. LeTourneau was a seasoned agent and when the shooting started and he realized they were out-gunned and in a no-win situation he quickly deduced that the best thing he could do was to alert Alan. He dove behind a metal vent coming up out of the top of the dam. It didn't provide much cover and wouldn't shield him for long but he only needed a few moments. He pulled out his cell phone and dialed Alan's number with the press of one speed-dial icon. Then he set the phone down behind him so a stray bullet would not strike it, and Special Agent LeTourneau started firing at the gunmen along the wall not far away above him. The other three who had guarded the dam with him during the night were already down. Still behind the metal vent, and with his phone call connected with Alan, he fought for his life. He only survived a few more seconds, but his quick thinking at the end of his life told his boss that the terrorists were attacking Roosevelt Dam.

39 Stolen

Sam Park looked toward the east just before sunrise on Saturday morning. He loved the way the early light of day made the morning glow with a soft pinkish-purple light. It was a crisp February morning with a few clouds in the sky which were now pink and reflected a rosy hue over the desert, businesses, and nearby houses that surrounded the Casa Grande airport.

The town of Casa Grande, about an hour south of Phoenix, had a population of about 50,000 and was growing rapidly, but it still had a small-town feel and a small airport. Most locals pronounced it as "Casa Grand," in an Anglicized pronunciation, with both words pronounced with the same "a" sound as "Master," and "Grand" pronounced without the "e" on the end. Very few used the correct Spanish pronunciation with a soft "aah" sound on the "a" letters and a rolled "r" to start "Grande" and finish with an "ey" sound. Some Spanish speakers still cringed as they heard the Anglicized pronunciation, but they had mostly learned to tolerate it. The town was named for the Casa Grande Indian ruins in the nearby town of Coolidge. Back in the late 1800s when the railroad first came through, Casa Grande was at the end of the rails and became the largest town in the area. The town picked up the name of the ruins even though the actual site of the ruins was about fifteen miles away. Although it had 50,000 people, Casa Grande still felt like a small town because the rapid growth had only occurred in the past few years.

The pink, pre-dawn sky reminded Sam of an elk hunt, high in the mountains of Wyoming years ago when he was a big game guide for one season. He and a hunter, John Wiggington, had gotten up very early on a chilly morning in early October, saddled their horses, and rode out of camp and up to the top of the mountain. They crested just before sunrise and the sun shining on the wispy clouds turned the sky pink. About 100 yards below them was a snowy basin filled with a herd of elk, feeding on the bunch grass by scraping the snow away with their hooves. Sam and his companion were hunting deer so the elk were safe, but as the animals trotted off through the pink-tinged snow, heads held high and blowing steam into the air with their noses, Sam and John just sat in their saddles, in awe at the beauty of God's handiwork.

Sam's thoughts left Wyoming and returned to Arizona. He always parked on the north side of his shop and had to walk west around the corner of the building to get to his front door. As he had pulled into his parking space he had noticed Donna's red Toyota Camry in her regular spot and he wondered why she was here on a Saturday morning at the crack of dawn. She was his office manager and bookkeeper and she was worth more than he paid her, although he paid her very well. She must have had to finish some project or maybe she forgot something yesterday and had come to get it. She had four kids and they kept her and her husband busy running to soccer, music lessons, swim team and all the other things kids did these days. Donna's husband, Ted, owned and operated a Gelato shop in the busy part of town, which did a booming business. Sam had visited the Gelato store many times and loved to order stracciatella, with its creamy-smooth texture and rich vanilla flavor, laced with wisps of dark chocolate.

Sam had grown up in Arizona, the son of Korean immigrants. He knew that one of the Japanese-American relocation camps had been established in Casa Grande back during World War II, but he tried not to dwell on the past even though he knew it was there. Sam was now the proud owner of Park's aircraft maintenance shop. His shop had developed a reputation for impeccable work in maintaining and repairing private aircraft, and pilots flew in from all over the U.S. to have their planes worked on at Park's. He had been in business for 12 years and had two repair crews. He actually could have retired already, and because

241

business was good he had the money to do so, but he loved his job and couldn't stand the thought of retiring and having nothing to do.

Sam's wife, Audra, had plenty of time with their grandkids and she didn't mind him being out of the house and down the road not far from their home. They had a nice, comfortable life and she knew that if he retired he would just be bored and in her way all the time. As long as he was healthy and able he would keep working. Besides, when he thought of all the trouble and expense it took to be an FAA-certified mechanic, he couldn't stand the thought of wasting one little bit of that by retiring too early. When Audra had a hankering to travel he could easily take a couple of weeks off to accompany her; a trip every year or two seemed to keep her happy and that kept Sam happy.

Sam had been a maintenance mechanic in the air force during the Vietnam War and had some hair-raising experiences at the time, even as a mechanic. Now that he owned his own shop, he didn't do the physically demanding work as often. He had a pilot's license and he had also obtained his IA certification, or Inspection Authorization, and also his A&P certification, or his Airframe and Powerplant certification. He was certified to do about any repair on an aircraft. However, his mechanics did most of the repair work while he did the supervising and also the work of running the business: procuring parts, dealing with inventory, doing the mountains of paperwork that were required, etc. Donna was invaluable in helping with the administrative work.

Two of his guys, Colton and Reggie, were extremely good and were certified with their A&P by the FAA. They were both working toward their own Inspection Authorization. Sam had discussed his desire for them to take over the business in a few years and they had already taken care of the legal documents for that plan to happen at some point.

As Sam reached for his doorknob he took one last look at the breaking day, relishing the serenity of the beautiful pink sunrise. Suddenly the stillness was shattered by several gunshots coming from the vicinity of a nearby hangar.

Casa Grande Municipal Airport had several private airplane hangars scattered across an industrial area, with aluminum buildings located all around the small airport. Each private hangar had aircraft access to the runway by way of a paved taxiway. There was also a main terminal building, complete with a café, and a few other buildings located there. Sam's shop was about a hundred and fifty yards south of the main terminal.

The front of Sam's shop faced west and had a concrete pad in front of the door, with a few parking spaces for customers and employees designated with white stripes of paint. The two large repair bays of Park's had wide roll-up doors on both sides of the building. The north, the groundside, was sometimes used for moving planes, but most of the time they pulled the planes in on the south, the airside. On the airside, Park's shared a ramp and taxiway with the neighboring hangar. The taxiway allowed aircraft to drive in or be towed in from the main runway. Since it was Saturday, there would be no mechanics in the shop and the service doors would all be closed.

The shots seemed to come from the hangar next to Park's, but right at his front door Sam couldn't see the hangar. He stepped to the edge of the building and carefully peeked around the corner. He could see a Beechcraft King Air 250 sitting in front of the hangar, idling as it warmed up in preparation for a flight. There were several people standing near it and two people lying on the ground. Sam knew that aircraft. It was a twin turboprop and he had worked on it a few times. It sat in the hangar next to his shop at least one day every week. The fuselage of the plane was white on the top half and royal blue on the bottom; a fine-looking airplane in the sky and on the ground. Over the past few months Sam had become friends with Edgardo, the pilot who flew the Twin Beech, and also with its lone passenger Brock Waldron.

Brock's company, a real estate development firm based out of Carlsbad, California, had been shuttling Brock in and out of Casa Grande each week for the past couple of years. The King Air would fly in with Brock on Monday morning and then leave for other flights throughout the week. Then the plane would come back into Casa Grande on Friday and Brock and the pilot, Edgardo, would fly out on Saturday morning so they could be home with their families for the weekend. Brock always had work demands or social events until late Friday which prevented them from leaving until Saturday morning.

The Beechcraft King Air 250 was a fine aircraft with a list price for the new models starting at just over $6 million and used models starting around $4 million. This one was a 2016 model and had all the upgrades, so it was worth over $4.5 million. It was a very comfortable aircraft with a range of about 1,700 miles and a cruising speed over 300 miles per hour. It was a turboprop plane with twin engines and was considered near the top of the line when it came to private aircraft that were not in the private jet class. Private jets ranged from a list price of a few million to well over $30 million. The King Air was basically in the same class as the lower end of the private jets, and those two types of aircraft were comparable in many of their features and characteristics. However, the Twin Beech was able to take off and land on a shorter runway compared to a jet so it was usually easier to get in and out of smaller airports. Also, jets were less efficient and usually more expensive to maintain than a turboprop.

When Sam drove to work he always approached his shop from the north. He hadn't seen anyone nor could he be seen by anyone at the hangar next door, even though the buildings were only forty yards apart. As Sam peeked around the southwest corner he had a clear line of sight to the other hangar and the King Air sitting on the concrete pad in front of it. Sam could see Edgardo lying on the ground along with a man dressed in black. Brock held a pistol in his hand as he faced three more black-clad men who were also armed. There was a minivan parked off to the side of the plane with all of its doors open. Based on all that had happened that week Sam immediately knew they were terrorists.

Just as Sam looked, one of the terrorists fired three shots into Brock and he collapsed onto the concrete. The terrorist's pistol had a suppressor, so there was little sound. Sam deduced that Brock and Edgardo had been confronted by the terrorists and that one or both of them had drawn a pistol and fired at the men, taking down one of the four and breaking the morning stillness. That caused the terrorists to draw their suppressed weapons and Sam had looked just in time to see his friend gunned down. That was troubling enough but what Sam saw next was even more concerning. There were cases of explosives stacked on the concrete next to the plane with a couple of AK-47s leaning against the pile.

Sam had a close buddy, Darryl, who was in Demolition while they were in Vietnam. Darryl had exposed Sam to enough talk about explosives that Sam knew a fair bit about them. From the markings he could see on the cases he believed they contained several kinds of explosives, including dynamite and some more sophisticated varieties, such as RDX, ANFO, and C-4.

It was not easy to acquire that much firepower but somehow this team of terrorists had fifteen or twenty cases of it. Just west of the airport was a mine, complete with a large round open pit. Sam had flown over it many times when he was test flying aircraft he had worked on. He wondered if they got the explosives from there although he thought the

244

mine was no longer in operation. Perhaps there were old explosives still stored there. There were also several other mines no more than a couple hours' drive from Casa Grande; in San Miguel, Superior, Globe, and Miami. There were government construction sites around too, like those being used to build bridges and highways. Somehow the terrorists had obtained a sizeable cache of explosives. If they had old ANFO, RDX or C-4, a formula variation of RDX, that was not a problem because those were more stable explosives, but if they had old dynamite, it could easily explode just by being dropped. Dynamite could be handled relatively safely when it was newly manufactured, but it got more unstable with age. The military preferred RDX or C-4 over dynamite because a bullet fired from a gun wouldn't detonate those other explosives. However, RDX, ANFO, and C-4 could be set off by what was called a "sympathetic detonation" if dynamite was detonated in any manner, including a gunshot, and both types of explosives were in close proximity.

Sam knew better than to confront the terrorists or to even be seen by them so he quickly stepped back behind the corner of his building and hurried through the door. He was carrying a .40 caliber Kahr Arms TP semi-auto, but one man with a pistol against a team of terrorists was suicide, as Brock's death had shown. However, he had a semi-automatic .300 Blackout in a locker in his shop and he knew he needed to get it as quickly as possible.

Sam had shot many guns over the years, including AR-15s, and as technology changed he changed with it. Suppressors to reduce the noise from gunfire were becoming more popular and were seen as being much safer in protecting the hearing of gun owners. The laws had also changed to make suppressors legal. When he was young, Sam hadn't used ear protection when he worked on aircraft or fired guns. However, he was now dealing with the consequences, one of them being that he had a difficult time hearing his wife, Audra, when she spoke, unless they were standing next to each other. Also, she was always telling him to turn down the volume on the TV or the radio. Therefore, when noise suppressors for guns came into greater popularity, Sam was very interested in taking advantage of that technology to preserve what hearing he still had. He was also much more careful to make sure he and his mechanics used hearing protection.

As Sam was shopping for suppressors he talked to one of his friends, an engineer who cared more than other people about the technical and physical aspects of things, and they discussed muzzle blast in great detail. Sam's friend explained that when a gun fires there are two loud noises, but they happen at almost the same instant so they sound like one boom. There is the explosion that makes the bullet fire and there is the small sonic boom that occurs when the bullet quickly breaks the sound barrier as it leaves the muzzle of the gun. Some ammunition does not break the sound barrier when it is fired, called subsonic ammo, and in that case, there is actually only one boom, but the sound is basically the same as with other ammo.

With a suppressor and subsonic ammo the .300 Blackout made very little noise. In fact, all Sam could hear when he fired was the click of the slide as a new shell was levered into the chamber. With the speed of sound being about 1,125 feet per second and the .300 Blackout shooting at about 1,000 feet per second the sound barrier was not broken. The bullet was a very heavy .30 caliber slug so the effective range was only about 100 yards—not very impressive for a high-powered rifle. When the rifle was sighted in at 100 yards with sub-sonic ammo, the bullet would be twelve inches low at 150 yards and thirty-four inches low at 200 yards. The effect of making no noise was what Sam wanted and that made up for the limited range.

Sam ran through the building and toward the back of the shop where his locker was. Donna had heard the gunshots too and had cautiously looked out the window. She hollered as he ran past, "I'm already calling 911. Do you need my help or just want me to stay out of the way?"

As Sam ran toward his locker he hollered loudly back toward Donna, "Just make sure everyone knows there is going to be at least one good guy with a gun, and please don't shoot me!"

He spun the padlock on his locker and dialed in the combination. Due to his excitement, he evidently misdialed one of the numbers because the lock didn't open. He mentally chastised himself and spun the dial several times and then dialed the numbers again. He was anxious and in a hurry. He had to catch those terrorists before they got away, and he hoped law enforcement would get there soon.

Again the lock didn't open. This time he said to himself, "Come on Sammy Boy. Get it right!" He spun the lock again to reset the numbers. He was losing precious time.

Finally, on the third try Sam forced himself to slow down and was more careful and the lock opened. He quickly pulled out his Blackout and grabbed two loaded thirty-round magazines lying in the bottom of the locker. Sam jammed one of the magazines into a pants pocket and worked the other into the bottom of the rifle. As he approached the door and passed Donna he heard her giving their address to someone on the phone. Donna and her husband both loved guns so she was untroubled by his rifle at work. Sam pounded the bottom of the magazine with the palm of his hand to make sure it seated well into the receiver of the rifle. He levered in a round and then stepped quietly back outside.

He planned to step cautiously out from behind the corner, remaining close in case he needed to jump back for cover. However, he saw that the King Air was already accelerating away from where it had been parked and the propellers were buzzing loudly as they cut the air. The Twin Beech was rapidly taxiing toward the runway, picking up speed every second. The door of the plane was still in the process of being closed. The cases of explosives were no longer on the ground and the terrorist who had been shot was gone as well. Only Brock's and Edgardo's bodies were still lying on the concrete. The minivan, most likely stolen or rented, was still sitting where it had been parked, with all the doors open.

Sam was angry at himself. The errors with the combination lock had perhaps cost him the chance to stop the terrorists right then. He hoped it wouldn't cost the lives of any good people—or himself.

Sam knew Donna was calling 911 right at that moment to alert authorities. However, he knew they would take a few minutes to get there and that would be too late. Once the plane got into the air he figured it would be harder to find and then stop. He had wanted to shoot at the terrorists but that window of opportunity had passed. He knew that to stop the plane he could put a bullet into the dynamite and that would likely do the job very well but he didn't want the plane to explode while it was still close to the other hangars. He also didn't know exactly where the dynamite had been placed inside the plane. He knew that once the plane got out onto the runway the surrounding buildings would be farther from the King Air and would be fairly safe. He hoped he could get some shots off to stop the plane before it took off. He could also take out a pilot or an engine and whatever worked would be just fine with him.

The plane would have to go west to the end of the taxiway by the buildings and then turn northeast and go along the taxi-way that ran parallel to the runway. It would have to get to the northeast end of the runway and turn back to the southwest for takeoff.

Sam turned and started running north, dodging between several hangars. He was trying to get to the northeast end of the runway before the plane did. The Casa Grande airport had a runway that was 5,200 feet long, just shy of one mile. The breeze in Arizona usually blew from west to east, as it was doing that morning, but it was blowing at a brisk pace which meant that an aircraft would need to take off from the northeast end of the runway traveling southwest into the wind and then continue southwest or west as it gained altitude and airspeed.

Sam wasn't as young as he used to be. In fact, there was more gray in his hair than black, but he worked out in his own weight room and he did lots of running all around Casa Grande and out in the desert, so he was in pretty good shape. As he ran, he tried to figure out what had happened. Probably Edgardo had the jet out of the hangar and was preparing it before Brock got there. Then the terrorists arrived and shot Edgardo with their suppressed pistols and started moving explosives out of the van toward the jet. Then Brock arrived and started shooting with his unsuppressed pistol and those were the shots that Sam heard. At least that could be one explanation.

Sam felt so bad that Brock and Edgardo would not be having an enjoyable weekend with their families, and instead, their loved ones would have to deal with the loss of their husbands and fathers. Sam figured the terrorists were trying to steal the plane without anyone knowing, which was why they were using suppressors. The noise from Brock's weapon had alerted Sam and Donna to the situation; otherwise, the plane may have flown away without anyone knowing. Brock had died a hero for having raised awareness, and the fact that law enforcement was now aware was a very fortunate thing to stop a subversive terrorist plot.

Sam was approaching the main terminal building for the airport. His location was about one-third of the way from the northeast end of the runway. He was trying to stay ahead of the plane before it took off so he ran straight north toward the runway itself. He had been watching the plane through gaps between the buildings and had seen it ahead of him and to his left. As he passed the terminal building and broke out into the open at the edge of the taxi-way he saw that the plane was just coming, about forty or fifty yards away from the building.

Sam stopped and fired five shots at the plane as it quickly taxied past. He was hoping to hit the pilot, an engine, or the explosives— anything to get the terrorists' attention. His Blackout made no noise, so the sound of the impact of bullets striking the plane was what he hoped for. He could also punch some holes in the windows or fuselage but that would actually *not* prevent the terrorists from being able to fly at high altitude under cabin pressure. However, he didn't think they were planning that. He figured they were going for some target in the Phoenix area, which meant they didn't have to fly too high anyway. He thought he heard a couple of the shots hit the plane but the King Air did not stop or slow down. He saw the terrorists looking out the window at him as they passed and it looked like they were animatedly talking to each other. *One goal accomplished.*

Sam realized that if he hit the dynamite when the plane was close to him the explosion could kill or injure him. He had learned in Vietnam that sometimes people or a fine aircraft had to be sacrificed for the greater good. It was painful but it was a reality of life. He was willing to make that sacrifice of either the King Air or himself.

Sam fired three more shots at an angle as the plane sped away from him. This time he was shooting at the right engine. With one engine out it wouldn't be able to take off. One working engine would be enough to maintain flight if an aircraft lost an engine while it was already in the air but one engine did not generate enough power for liftoff. Shooting at the engine was painful for Sam because he had just worked on that engine a couple of months ago. But he had to stop that plane!

He was also trying to pay attention to what was on the other side of the plane because his bullets would have to stop somewhere. Beyond the northeast end of the runway was a four-lane paved road running north and south and then a golf course, so he wasn't too worried, although he knew there would be golfers as the day grew lighter with the sunrise. In fact, Sam realized that the sun had come up off to the southeast and he saw the gleam of the sunlight on the sides of the buildings and occasionally on the beautiful blue King Air as it passed areas where the low angle of the sun shone between buildings.

Sam watched the plane as it reached the end of the runway, turned north, and then southwest to line itself up for takeoff. Then the plane stopped moving.

Sam ran across the runway to put himself on the side where that right engine would pass as the King Air took off. Then he slowed to a walk so he could catch his breath while continuing to get closer to the plane. He wanted to hit it before it picked up speed. He was also hoping that the terrorists would realize he was there and take more time to analyze the situation before taking off.

Sam was about 300 yards from the end of the runway and the plane just sat there as Sam walked toward it. Maybe one of his shots had done some damage in the cockpit and they were trying to figure out if they could take off. Maybe he had hit the right engine and an indicator was showing that there was a problem. Maybe they were just trying to figure out how to take off past Sam. At 300 yards they were still out of range so Sam decided not to shoot yet.

He thought about his magazine; he had about twenty rounds remaining. Enough. He didn't need to change magazines yet. On second thought, with a shell in his chamber, he popped out the first mag, put it in his jacket pocket, inserted the second mag, and slapped it into the receiver. Now he had thirty-one rounds to work with. Better to have as many as possible. He thought about the gun control fanatics who thought a thirty-round magazine was "high capacity." Thirty rounds was actually normal capacity and sometimes you did need thirty rounds. High capacity magazines were more like those that held sixty rounds or more.

Suddenly the door of the plane opened and one of the terrorists climbed down the steps. He had a rifle in his hand but from this distance Sam couldn't tell what it was. He figured it was a fully automatic AK-47. That's what the terrorists had been using all week in their attacks around Phoenix. The optic on Sam's Blackout was a Vortex Prism Spitfire 3x, so he had three-power magnification. That wasn't designed to magnify things to make them look close; it was designed for slight enlargement in order to better sight onto your target. If Sam had a nine power scope he could see more details about the terrorist and his weapon but that wasn't necessary right now. He just needed to see where his bullet was going to hit. He was still limited by the one-hundred-yard effective range of the Blackout so he wasn't going to start shooting yet.

Sam slowed his pace as he walked down the far north edge of the runway, right where the pavement met the dirt. He wanted to be breathing normally when the shooting started. The plane was aimed southwest but hadn't accelerated yet; the pilot must have been waiting for Sam and the terrorist to get closer or to start shooting.

As Sam walked, the thoughts he had were of anger and frustration at the anti-gun crowd in the U.S. Here he was, carrying a semi-automatic weapon up against someone who was carrying a fully automatic. The odds were clearly in his enemy's favor. As he walked toward the showdown Sam pondered on the misunderstanding of the gun haters. They thought, or at least argued, that the Second Amendment was only about hunting. They were completely wrong. The Second Amendment was only about the people being able to keep the government in check. If you allow a powerful entity to have automatic weapons, machine guns, but you only allow the citizens to have semi-automatic weapons then you have severely limited the ability of the civilian population to protect themselves. If your opponent has superior weapons you must use superior strategy or superior numbers but it would be better to not have inferior weapons in the first place.

Sam's thoughts were interrupted when he saw the terrorist move his gun to a shooting position. Sam swung the Blackout up to his shoulder although he knew he wasn't in range to be fully accurate. They were about 175 yards apart. It was kind of hard to tell because the runway was so flat and open and there wasn't much to use as a reference point from which to judge the distance.

As Sam kept walking, he decided to be the first one to start shooting. He thought about lying down to fire at the terrorist so he would be a smaller target and so that he could aim better but he still felt the need to be closer to the plane so it wouldn't be going so fast when it passed him.

Sam stopped abruptly, aimed about twelve inches high, and fired three shots at the terrorist. He loved the quietness of the Blackout as he fired. *Click. Click. Click.* The terrorist wouldn't really even know Sam was shooting until he was hit or heard bullets zinging past him. He also guessed the distance to be about 150 yards and his Blackout had been sighted in with the optics at 100 yards, so he figured twelve inches high was about right. The terrorist answered back with a short burst of machine gun fire. Sam heard bullets zinging over his head. He kept trying to decide when to lie down to shoot but he didn't feel it was the right time yet.

Sam strode toward the terrorist for about another ten seconds before pulling up and firing six more rounds. The terrorist kept coming and answered back with another burst of shots. This time they were closer and one even ricocheted off the pavement near Sam's feet.

Sam heard sirens approaching as law enforcement or perhaps medical personnel raced across Casa Grande toward the small airport. Before they got to him they would likely go to his shop where Donna had called from. He wondered if the terrorists inside the plane could hear the sirens.

Sam and the terrorist continued to close the distance between them. Sam guessed they were about 125 yards apart now. He would have to hold about six to eight inches high. He dropped to one knee to start getting into a prone shooting position when suddenly the terrorist started running toward him, firing the machine gun. Sam started firing back but some of the shots from the terrorist struck him. He didn't know where he was hit but he felt faint and he realized he couldn't move his left leg anymore. His arm was weak and he tried to raise his gun but it felt too heavy and he lowered it toward the ground. He stood still and wavered a bit as he looked at the terrorist, who had stopped shooting but was still running toward him. Sam teetered there on one knee on the side of the runway just as the sun peeked over the tall trees southeast of the Casa Grande airport.

The two engines on the plane accelerated and the propellers began to buzz loudly as they built up speed. The plane started forward, slowly at first, then rapidly moving to gain speed sufficient for takeoff. Evidently they were not going to wait for the terrorist on the tarmac. Maybe they were worried about more law enforcement coming. Maybe they had only been worried about Sam, and now that he was going down they felt safe to leave. Maybe they needed to be at some specific place at a specific time. At any rate, the terrorist that was approaching Sam would be on his own.

Sam Park started to pass out. His remaining thoughts were that he had tried. He didn't know if he did his best, but it was over now. He should have laid down sooner to be less of a target. He was angry at himself for his misjudgment and he was also angry at the gun haters that limited his ability to defend himself and his country. He thought about Audra being alone. He thought about Colton and Reggie taking over the shop.

Sam knelt there motionless. He looked up at the oncoming terrorist and then at the plane and then slowly toppled over to his left, landing on his side with his right hand still holding his rifle. The gun lay across his body with the barrel leaning gently against the asphalt. He lay on his left side at the edge of the runway, his legs slightly twisted; his head flopped over to the side at an angle.

The terrorist had by now reached Sam and walked up to his inert body. He raised his machine gun and pointed it at Sam's head. Sam's eyes were open; staring straight ahead. He had stopped breathing and his blood was trickling across the pavement and onto the dirt. The terrorist paused for a moment and then lowered his gun. There was no need to fire again. His enemy was dead.

The plane rushed forward and the terrorist turned to look at it, its wheels rolling rapidly on the asphalt. He raised his rifle over his head with one hand and pumped it up and down in victory and celebration.

40 Have a Blast at Breakfast

At about 6:00 Saturday morning before it was even starting to get light Jassim watched as two FBI agents came out of the hotel with their bags. One was the dog handler, who took care of the dog's needs in the dirt lot before joining the other agent at the vehicle. They put their bags inside the vehicles and waited with the doors open as the others came out of the hotel.

Jassim quickly looked at the bomb and checked the wires. The detonator button was nearby. He merely had to flip one switch, push one button, and the bomb would do its job. If both vehicles drew near each other with all the agents inside he would drive close and push the button. He would then have succeeded and won an eternal reward.

Jassim started the car and continued to watch and wait. He was across the parking lot and didn't think he had been seen by the FBI agents, although they had probably seen his car.

Finally, all of the agents came out of the hotel and loaded into the SUV's. The Suburban, the one with the dog, started to pull toward the Tahoe, which sat near to the building. Jassim put his car into gear and prepared to launch across the parking lot toward the two cars.

Suddenly the Suburban stopped and someone jumped out to pull something out of a bag in the back. As that happened the Tahoe backed out of its parking spot and made its way onto the road, heading west. The two vehicles remained too far apart. Jassim was so anxious he could hardly control himself but he would have to wait for another opportunity.

The three vehicles, the black Tahoe, the black Suburban, and the worn-out Nissan, proceeded west back toward the junction that would take them to Roosevelt Lake. There was very little traffic that early in the morning and Jassim followed at a distance, not trying to gain ground. He hoped they would end up stopping at the same red light or something but they remained too far apart.

As they got to the junction the two black vehicles went on past it and kept driving west. In just a few blocks the Tahoe turned south onto a side street and into the parking lot of a restaurant. It parked a couple of spots away from an old pickup but the Suburban passed them both and parked in the very last spot at the corner of the restaurant, next to a small wash. The wash allowed rainwater to flow through the town, not that it rained much. It was currently dry as a bone. Jassim was beginning to think that it was standard FBI procedure to not park their vehicles next to each other.

This was not a well-developed area of town and between the road and the restaurant were two empty dirt lots separated by a small road with no curbs. If anyone had been watching from the restaurant last night they would have seen Jassim drive by this location twice in his search for the agents.

Knowing exactly where they were, Jassim continued driving down the side street and circled back, hopefully giving them enough time to get into the restaurant before he approached. He turned off his lights as he pulled into the parking lot and backed into a space about one hundred feet from the front of the diner. It was still dark at 6:15 in the morning but there were a couple of old street lights casting dim circles of light here and there. However, the sky was starting to grow light in the east as the day approached.

Jassim hoped they would all sit at the same table and then perhaps he could drive into the front of the building and detonate the bomb. He would perform his glorious act for Al-Musawi and especially for Allah.

He was pleased to find that the FBI agents did just that. The waiter seated them in two booths near the front corner of the restaurant; Jassim could see them clearly through the windows. There were, as he had hoped, a couple of empty parking spaces directly in front of where they were sitting. Again, he could hardly contain his excitement. He started softly chanting Muslim prayers to himself as he prepared to launch forward into the restaurant. He sat and waited for a few moments, preparing, thinking, planning, and chanting. Through the window he could see that one of the agents got up and left the table. Jassim figured that the agent was going to the restroom, but waiting a few more minutes would not matter. He waited patiently, knowing that he did not need to be in a hurry now.

Jassim realized his position was perfect. He could easily drive right between the Suburban and the old pickup and just as he reached the front of the diner where the FBI agents were he could detonate the bomb. It would kill the entire team of agents as well as destroy one or both of their cars and probably the police dog.

Jassim's focus was on the agents and not on what was around him as he sat with his back to the vacant lot. But in fact, the lot was not completely vacant. Sitting in the lot a short distance away from Jassim's car, but unnoticed by him, was a tractor-trailer rig, softly idling. It had been idling all night while its occupants had slept in the sleeper cab. However, at the moment, there in the early morning, they were sitting in the cab of the truck, wide awake.

Two twenty-foot flatbed trailers were hooked to the truck's power unit. The trailers were completely full of hay bales, stacked high and tied down. The truck was sitting parallel to front wall of the restaurant. The driver had only to turn his head to the left to see the front of the diner. The driver's name was Lloyd and he and his wife, Beatrice, had been sitting there talking. They were wearing coats, with the heater going and the windows down. They liked the fresh, crisp February air, but it had been a cold night so they had to have the heater running, blowing onto their feet and the floorboards of the truck.

Lloyd said, "I knew Aaron would be late."

Beatrice replied, "Oh Lloyd, give him a break. He's a newlywed. We were late for a lot of things when we were newlyweds."

"I know, but we've got to get two loads of hay up the mountain today. It's an all-day job and Aaron is going to put us behind schedule."

"Don't be such a worrywart," she said as she patted his rough, calloused hand and then left her hand resting on top of his. Lloyd had been a rancher for many years and driving a load of hay was just another part of the hard work he was used to. She had learned over the course of their forty-two years of marriage that he tended to worry too much about the younger ranch hands not having the work ethic that he had.

Lloyd and Beatrice sat in silence for a few minutes, each caught up in their own thoughts, when a black Tahoe pulled into the parking lot followed by a black suburban. What appeared to be law enforcement agents of some kind climbed out of the vehicles.

After they went into the restaurant a small, beat-up car pulled into the parking lot a few moments later. The car stopped at the far edge of the diner's parking lot near the vacant lot. It had already turned off its lights. It backed up into a parking spot.

The small car was facing the diner and was positioned in front and slightly to the left of the big rig. The car was sitting under a street light, illuminating the interior of the car.

From his vantage point high in the cab of the big rig Lloyd could easily see down into the car. He quietly motioned to Beatrice and she rose up out of her seat, leaning slightly across the cab so she could also see what Lloyd was looking at.

The driver of the small car appeared to have some kind of contraption on his upper body, and they could see by the light of the streetlight that it was covered with wires.

Lloyd whispered, "That looks odd."

Beatrice whispered, "Oh, my heavens. It looks like a bomb. This must be another one of those terrorist attacks that have been happening this week. Who would have thought it would happen here!"

The law enforcement personnel, if that's who they were, had settled into their booths near the front windows.

The engine of the small car was running, and since it was an old car, it made a soft but audible knocking noise as it idled.

As Lloyd and Beatrice watched, the driver of the small car looked down at the contraption as if he were checking to make sure it was all in place.

Suddenly Beatrice realized that Lloyd had reached back behind his seat and pulled his Ruger Mini-14 from a pouch they had previously built into the front of the mattress on the sleeper section of the big rig. He quietly told her, "Watch your head," as he swung the gun through the cab and out the window. In doing so he levered in a round from the twenty-shot magazine.

The Ruger Mini-14 was called the "Ranch Rifle" and the caliber was 5.56 NATO; the same caliber as many military rifles carried throughout the world by U.S. troops. It was light but high-powered enough to easily shoot a coyote or deer, or enemy combatant, at a distance of up to 200 yards. The Mini-14 was also semi-automatic and could fire rapidly, as fast as the shooter could pull the trigger repeatedly. It was designed to be a rancher's companion whenever a handy but powerful gun was needed; it was rugged and effective. Lloyd didn't have a scope on it but he had been shooting with open sights for many years and did just fine.

Lloyd put the barrel of the Mini-14 out his open window. He started firing at the driver just as the car began to accelerate straight at the diner. Several rounds slammed into the car even before it had gone more than a few feet. From the sound of the engine the driver had the gas pedal jammed to the floor, but the car didn't have enough power to spin its tires as it accelerated. However, it did pick up speed quickly.

Inside the diner Alan's team heard the shots. They quickly looked out the windows and one of them pointed toward a car that was rapidly moving toward them. They noticed that shots were being fired by someone in the cab of a big rig, with a rifle sticking out the driver's window.

As Jassim held the pedal to the floor he heard bullets hitting his car. He felt a searing pain in his left leg but he kept his right foot jammed hard against the gas pedal. He was no longer chanting softly but was now shouting his prayers to Allah, trying to give himself courage and endurance.

Another pain, this time in his left shoulder, caused him to cry out and jerk the wheel slightly to the left. He fought to keep the car on target to shoot through the gap between the vehicles but he was losing control of his arms. He couldn't detonate the bomb yet because he was too far from the front of the diner, although he had the detonator in his left hand.

Lloyd kept firing. He had twenty rounds and he planned to fire until he heard a click on an empty chamber. He realized that the closer the car got to the diner the more dangerous his angle of fire and one of his bullets could strike someone in the diner. However, he was high in the cab of the truck, shooting down toward the small car, and that reduced the risk. He knew that lives depended on him stopping this suicide bomber. He also realized that he and Beatrice could be killed if the bomb went off too close to the truck.

Alan and his team leaped across the room to get away from the front of the restaurant. Employees of the diner and other customers started jumping away from the windows also. It was chaos.

Jassim felt more pain in his body and neck. He tried to flip the lever and jam his left thumb down on the detonator but his hand was not working. Another burst of pain in the back of his head and everything went black. As he slumped into the steering wheel the motion of his last effort in life both turned the steering wheel of the car to the left and also pushed on the detonator of the bomb. The car jerked to the left, passing behind the white Dodge pickup some distance from the front wall of the restaurant and several parking spaces away from the Tahoe. Just as the car passed the pickup, the bomb exploded, the blast flipping the pickup toward the Tahoe. The pickup turned upside down, then rocked over and its bottom frame and wheels bumped against the Tahoe, before rocking back down and landing on its top with a crunch on the worn pavement of the parking lot.

The explosion chewed a crater in the asphalt and blew the windows out of the entire front of the diner and many of the cars in the parking lot, scattering glass and gravel across everything. The bulletproof windows of the armored Suburban and Tahoe remained intact, although the car alarms went off. A huge cloud of dust filled the early morning air.

The left side of the diner, near the entrance and away from the booths where the FBI agents were sitting, took most of the blast. The entry doors and booths were shoved back toward the counter and blown to pieces as they smashed against the cash register and knocked over the sign that said, "Welcome! Please wait to be seated."

On the opposite side of Jassim's car from the white Dodge pickup was a small SUV that belonged to one of the employees of the diner. It was parked away from the restaurant, but due to Jassim's car turning hard to the left; the SUV was right next to the bomb when it went off. The blast sent the car flying through the air in pieces, and most of it landed on another car.

No one inside the diner remained standing. All were knocked to the ground by the concussion, but fortunately, because of the warning they had from the shots and the quick efforts to get away from the oncoming car, they were all still alive.

The blast threw pieces of Jassim's car backward toward the semi, and the back half of the gas tank and the rear bumper flew across the parking lot and skidded to a jumbled, fiery stop in front of the tractor. The left rear tire rolled toward the trailers, fully engulfed in flames.

Lloyd handed the Mini-14 to Beatrice and jumped down out of the cab as fast as his sixty-five-year-old legs could move. He grabbed a fire extinguisher from inside a panel on the side of the sleeper and started spraying the burning tire with the white chemical. He couldn't afford to have his rig catch fire. The hay itself was worth over $10,000 and the truck and trailers were worth $150,000.

As the FBI agents started getting back to their feet, their first concern was the well-being of each other and the other people in the diner. A waitress had been cut very badly by flying glass, her shoulder blade laid open to the bone. Two other employees were already giving her first aid.

Others in the diner had less severe cuts but nearly everyone was injured in some way; only the cook was unscathed as he was in the back of the restaurant at the time. He quickly called 911 for help. Alan had crashed into the side of a table as he was fleeing the front of the diner; he had a wicked-looking scrape and bruise across his left elbow. Ezzie had a big bump on her eyebrow where she crashed into someone else's head as they dove for cover. Brian, the dog handler, ran outside to check on Scout.

People were calling out to each other, trying to help where needed. Beatrice, no longer holding the rifle, got out of the truck and ran toward the restaurant to see if she could help anyone as Lloyd walked around using his fire extinguisher to quench burning chunks of car parts scattered around the parking lot. They heard sirens approaching.

Alan walked outside and approached the man who had come from the truck. He stuck out his hand and said, "Hi. Alan Clevenger, FBI. Thanks for the good shooting. How did you know what was happening?"

The man shook Alan's hand and said, "Lloyd Haught. We were sitting there waiting for my ranch hand to show up when we saw you pull into the parking lot. Then we saw the other fellow drive in acting kinda cagey . . . lights off . . . kept his motor running. With all that has gone on this week it didn't take long to put two and two together. I always carry my Mini-14 and I'm sure glad I had it this morning. I just didn't expect something like this in a tiny town out here in a remote area."

Alan said, "Yes, it's odd. Thanks. We would like to get an official statement from you or at least get your contact information for a statement later."

Lloyd replied, "Well, if my newly-wed ranch hand doesn't show up soon I'll certainly have time now, but if he comes I really have to get going. I'll wait around as long as I can but here's my card in case I need to leave."

Alan said, "Thanks!" and handed Lloyd his own business card. As Alan walked toward the Suburban he looked at the man's card. It said, "Pleasant Valley Polled Herefords" and showed Lloyd's contact information. Alan put the card in his pocket. As he arrived at the Suburban, his team was inspecting the damage to both of their vehicles.

Medical personnel had arrived and were treating the injuries. Fortunately, none of the FBI agents had serious injuries. Some Steri-Strips, small bandages, and cold packs here and there were enough. The injured waitress was being transported to the nearby hospital. One of the paramedics insisted on cleaning and bandaging the scrape on Alan's elbow. Alan thought it was unnecessary but it kept the air off the scrape so it didn't smart as much.

They saw that the Tahoe had sustained some damage to the passenger side but both doors still worked. They found no damage to the Suburban, but Scout was a bit jittery. However, he was a seasoned veteran and was probably more excited than scared. Brian let him out to sniff around a bit.

Sheriff Concepcion arrived and they filled him in on what had happened. They all agreed that the quick thinking of the old rancher, and the fact that he had a gun, had saved their lives and prevented serious injury to nearly everyone there.

They talked for a few minutes, trying to evaluate what to do next. By now it was just after 7:00 and the sky was relatively light, although the sun would not officially rise until around 7:20.

Alan's phone rang. He could see it was from Quinn, one of his agents who had volunteered to stay at Roosevelt Dam to watch through the night. He punched the button to talk to Quinn and his blood ran cold. All he could hear was a barrage of gunfire from automatic weapons. He said, "Quinn?!" and then he yelled into the phone, "QUINN!"

41 Not Finished Yet

As the Beechcraft King Air was rushing past him on the Casa Grande runway Sam Park jerked his rifle up—even as he lay on the asphalt—and rapidly fired five rounds into the body of the celebrating terrorist who was standing not ten feet away. *Click. Click. Click. Click. Click.*

The man fell back toward Sam, toppled by the weight of the gun held over his head. Sam fired two more rounds into the terrorist's head as the man landed hard on the asphalt just a couple of feet from Sam. Maybe seven shots were overkill, literally, but Sam wasn't finished fighting and they had made him mad.

With a superhuman effort Sam sat up, swiveled around, and fired at the right engine of the twin turboprop as it flashed past and continued to accelerate up the runway away from him. The plane was trying to get up to about 100 to 120 miles per hour to take off and Sam's bullets were going about 900 miles per hour, so he had the speed advantage. He didn't know if he was hitting anything but he aimed as accurately as he could and fired and fired until his gun made a final *click* on an empty chamber. He was glad he had been using a thirty-round magazine or he would have run out of shots much sooner. *Stupid gun haters!*

Sam dropped out his empty magazine and jammed in his first one, levered in a live round, and pointed the muzzle toward the terrorist. He soon saw that the man was very dead.

As the adrenalin in his system faded Sam glanced down at his wounds. He had been hit in the side and his left knee was mangled and bleeding profusely. He flipped the Blackout on Safe with his right thumb and laid the gun down on the asphalt. He put the heel of his right hand inside his thigh near his groin to put pressure on the main artery. He knew he had already lost a lot of blood and might not make it unless he could get medical help quickly. If he passed out his hand would relax and he could bleed to death before very long.

Sam looked toward the King Air and saw that it had cleared the end of the runway and was flying very low. It was trailing smoke from the right engine along with making an odd sound. As an airplane mechanic Sam had listened to a lot of engines, and for once in his life he liked the wrong sound of one. He could also see that the plane was flying very slowly for an aircraft of that type, probably just fast enough to stay in the air. One or more of his shots must have hit something important. Also, judging by the black smoke, he realized that he had, at the very least, hit an oil line and the leaking oil was burning. The King Air began to laboriously gain altitude as it turned into the breeze which was still blowing west to east.

Sam heard a vehicle coming toward him. He turned and saw a pickup rushing up to him across the runway. The truck screeched to a halt next to him and a familiar figure jumped out.

"Norman?" Sam said, weakly.

"Sam are you alive?! I thought you was dead. I watched it all through my binoculars over there by one of the sheds. I thought he killed you."

Sam leaned heavily on his left hand, trying to keep his right hand on his thigh. "No, I wasn't dead . . . exactly. When I was a kid my four brothers and I used to play a game of possum. We perfected the skill of holding our eyes wide open and motionless and also breathing shallow without moving our chests. I never knew I'd call on that talent in the real world. But it was really hard to hold still when he was pointing that gun at my head. I was afraid he was going to shoot."

Sam winced and continued, "If I don't get some help quick I may not make it. If I let go of this pressure point my knee will start pouring blood again and I can't afford to lose any more."

Norman knelt down and put the heel of his right hand on Sam's thigh, taking over for him. He looked at Sam's mangled knee and grimaced.

As Sam slowly lowered himself back to the ground he pulled out his cell phone. He said to Norman, "I have to make a very important phone call and then I don't know how long I'll be conscious."

Sam punched a speed dial icon and the phone started ringing. After a pause he spoke quickly, "Flash, this is Sam in Casa Grande. We've got some terrorists who have stolen a Beechcraft King Air. They have loaded several crates of explosives onto the plane and from the markings I could see it's dynamite and some other stuff, maybe RDX or C-4."

Sam's good friend from Vietnam was Arnold Briscoe and he had remained in the military after Vietnam. Brisco went by the call sign of Flash. Sam fixed the planes and Flash flew them, often bringing them back in need of patching and further repair. They worked together on many missions and Flash had many close calls while fighting. Briscoe was eight years younger than Sam, and although Sam was about ready to retire Briscoe still had several years of his career left.

Briscoe got his call sign one day when he was a young second lieutenant in training at flight school in Big Springs Texas. It was on the 4th of July and he had some fireworks. As he shot off some bottle rockets one caught some dry grass on fire and they had to call in the fire trucks to contain the blaze. Someone started calling Briscoe "Flash" after that and the rest of the guys joined in, sticking him with the name for the rest of his career.

Flash was now Brigadier General Arnold Briscoe and was the commanding officer at Luke Air Force Base on the far west side of the Phoenix Metropolitan area.

Sam spoke again to Briscoe, "Of course I'm sure it's explosives. Have I ever told you wrong? . . . OK, when I told you to bet on the Yankees against the D-Backs in 2001 . . . . Just that one time."

Another pause.

This time Sam yelled into the phone, although his voice was weak. "Flash, stop and listen! I don't have much time here. You'd better scramble some of your jets over here as fast as you can. Tell them to take down a Blue King Air 250 filled with explosives. I shot a few slugs into the right engine and its trailing black smoke. It barely cleared the runway."

Sam paused to grimace at the pain that was now washing over him. "Flash. . . there was some return fire and I've been hit. It may be bad but I can't really tell. If I don't make it just know that I was always proud to be your mechanic. You were a great pilot and we had some good times back in the day."

As Sam paused to listen he suddenly lost consciousness and dropped the phone, settling weakly onto the asphalt. Briscoe's voice could be heard through the open line but Norman couldn't tell what he said. Finally the sound from the phone stopped.

Norman picked up the phone and saw that the call had disconnected. He said out loud to Sam, even though Sam was unconscious, "I'm gonna call an ambulance for you. I hope they don't take too long gettin' here."

Norman adjusted his position so he could be fairly comfortable on the hard ground as he kept his hand on Sam's thigh. He called for an ambulance, explaining that they were out on the northeast end of the runway. His final words were, "Please hurry!"

When Norman finished his call, the phone still in his hand, he looked up into the sky and spoke out loud again, "Dear God. You know I ain't much for prayin' for which I'm truly sorry but this time I ain't prayin' for myself. I always felt selfish prayin' for myself 'cause I'm nobody special. I'm just a janitor here at a small-town airport and hardly nobody knows me. They just pass by and don't even say hello . . . but some do . . . like Sam . . . and like Margaret in the café . . . . I'm sure if Jesus saw me cleanin' floors he wouldn't treat me like I'm just part of the building. Jesus would care about my name and he would look into my eyes and say 'Hi, Norman,' and he would stop to talk to me . . . . Anyways, Sam here is in real trouble. Please, God, keep him alive until the ambulance comes and until they can get him to the hospital. Sam was always nice to me when lots of other people wasn't. And he was just doin' his best against some terrorists, fightin' to keep people safe. Please help him. In Jesus' name, amen."

Norman bowed his head and was quiet. He heard an approaching siren and looked up. An ambulance was coming across and up the runway. He sat and held Sam's thigh, looking over his shoulder to where he had last seen the plane. It wasn't in the same spot anymore but it was easy to follow because of the trail of greasy, black smoke streaming out behind it.

As the ambulance approached, the siren stopped wailing and the sound died out. Norman lifted Sam's phone again, punched a few buttons and waited. The call went straight to voicemail, so Norman left a message: "Mr. Flash. I don't know who you are but I'm here with Sam. My name's Norman. He got shot in the leg and the side and he has passed out but the ambulance is almost here and I hope Sam'll be OK. I just called to tell you that the plane is trailin' a lot of smoke and they are still flyin' west of Casa Grande, goin' into the wind to gain altitude. Whoever you are sendin', tell 'em to look for the smoke."

42 Luke

After Sam dropped the phone Brigadier General Arnold Briscoe dialed his contact at CONR, the Continental U.S. region of NORAD, the North American Aerospace Defense Command. NORAD was established in the late 1950s as a multinational defense organization to coordinate air defense for all of North America. Briscoe spoke to his contact and explained what he knew and CONR procedures took over from there. CONR alerted the Luke AFB Command Post, then alerted the 161st Air National Guard Refueling Wing at Sky Harbor Airport in Phoenix, and finally alerted AWACS command in Tinker AFB in Oklahoma. There were established protocols for each organization and their personnel rapidly and efficiently implemented their procedures.

At Luke Air Force Base a loud Klaxon horn sounded, alerting all base personnel to an emergency. The horn was followed by a set of instructions to scramble two F-16s to launch and prepare two more F-16s for runway standby. The instructions were followed by: "This is no drill. Repeat: THIS IS NO DRILL!"

Immediately all affected base personnel dropped what they were doing and started running. They had practiced this as a drill countless times and their goal was to get two birds in the air within eight minutes.

Briscoe himself was already headed for the base but wouldn't arrive for about twenty minutes. He had been off-base, preparing for a golfing outing with some friends. They would have to play as a threesome today.

Immediately the call went to strategic air command around the Phoenix area and a signal was sent out to ground all non-military planes. As had happened on Wednesday when the plane was temporarily stolen at Gateway airport, authorities grounded all commercial and general aircraft. Sky Harbor and all other airports in the entire state were stopping all arriving and departing flights, and all aircraft already in the air would land as quickly as possible somewhere in Arizona or would be re-routed to other airports in surrounding states. The Phoenix area was experiencing its second no-fly zone in four days.

Gen. Briscoe personally knew General Corliss Pearsall, the Wing Commander at the Air National Guard post at Sky Harbor Airport. Although CONR protocols had engaged the needed resources, Briscoe wanted to talk about it with his friend. The 161st Air National Guard Refueling Wing was in charge of refueling military aircraft all around the Arizona area wherever needed, and they were fiercely proud of their stellar reputation. They called themselves the Copperheads and they were actually one of the busiest wings of refuelers in the nation because of the remote locations they had to cover, all out of Phoenix. When Gen. Pearsall confirmed that there would soon be a tanker in the air he told Gen. Briscoe, "We don't know where it will be needed but we will surely find out. We'll just perform a circling pattern over the Phoenix area until more intel becomes available."

Due to the threat level decided earlier that week the Copperheads already had a KC-135 Stratotanker ready and full of fuel. They were already going through the final preparations for takeoff. They couldn't do it in eight minutes like the F-16s at Luke, but the Copperheads would have it in the air within fifteen minutes. Once in the air and with a full load of fuel the plane could fly at over 500 miles per hour with a range of over 1,000 miles.

Gen. Briscoe's next call was to Tinker Air Force Base in Oklahoma. Briscoe was good friends with General Dawson Zickert, the base commander. Tinker supported the AWACS E-3 Sentry radar planes, the big jets with the rotodome on top. That rotodome was actually a radar apparatus that could detect aircraft up to 400 miles away. They tried to keep an AWACS E-3 Sentry in the air at all times, and they would already know about the stolen plane in Casa Grande because of the alert that had gone out. They would be headed that way. Briscoe's personnel at Luke already knew the info he wanted but as he was still driving into Luke he wanted to know for himself.

Gen. Zickert took Briscoe's call personally and informed him that the nearest AWACS happened to be just south of the Grand Canyon when the call went out and it was already headed toward the Phoenix area. The distance from its current position to Phoenix was only about 200 miles so it was already investigating and identifying all aircraft in the Phoenix area by the time Briscoe called. The E-3, a modified Boeing 707, flew at about 360 miles per hour and had a range of about 5,000 nautical miles. It was very capable of providing full support to this situation and was already doing so. It had a flight crew of five pilots and a mission crew of twenty technicians with different skill sets to accomplish the mission objectives needed. Some of the airmen on the AWACS were radio and communications experts, some were radar technicians, some were analysts, the makeup and the total number of the crew could change depending on their specific mission.

After Gen. Briscoe finished his call to Tinker AFB he finally retrieved Norman's voice mail. He called Command Post at Luke AFB to relay the message from Norman to the control tower and the pilots.

Gen. Briscoe was glad they had prepared the base in advance. On Monday when the first bombs were set off and the train was damaged, he had sent an email to his contacts at Homeland Security and CONR, mentioning the possibility of needing to increase the alert level. Under normal conditions they did not arm the jets at Luke AFB with missiles. That level of weaponry was normally unnecessary. However, under well-established protocols, if the alert level in an area increased to a certain point, they could and would change the configuration of their jets to meet the alert level.

In response to Gen. Briscoe's email, Homeland Security and CONR said that they would consider the request and asked Briscoe to keep them posted of any developments. Looming in everyone's mind were the airliner attacks on the World Trade Center in 2001 and the possibility of that kind of situation re-occurring. Should the Air Force intercept a plane that was about to be used as a weapon, they could possibly take down such a plane and save lives and property if they were properly armed.

After the various attacks occurred on Wednesday, including the near stolen Airbus at Gateway Airport, Briscoe had contacted Homeland Security and CONR again. Since a second set of attacks had occurred, one of them involving a commercial airliner, the decision was made to increase the threat level. That decision on Wednesday had authorized Briscoe to increase the weaponry at Luke AFB accordingly and also increase the fuel capacity of the fighter jets.

Now, three days later, it appeared that the more advanced weapons may be needed. Gen. Briscoe was glad for the decision but was not pleased it had escalated to that point. Much like comments from the armed citizens he had been reading about this week, Briscoe stayed prepared for defense but always hoped it wouldn't be required because that meant people were likely in grave danger.

As the ground crews prepared the fighter jets, updates kept coming back to Briscoe by text message. Major McCasland and Lieutenant Andrus were flying today. McCasland was a well-seasoned pilot and had been at Luke for several years. First Lieutenant Andrus was relatively new to Luke but was an excellent pilot. McCasland was older, almost to the age of moving from being a flight lead to a position with more administrative responsibility, while Andrus was only a few years out of flight school.

This week they had kept four F-16s postured on alert and completely ready for immediate take-off. If there were multiple threats they would send out all four jets, but with only one plane to deal with two were enough. Besides, if another incident were suddenly called in they had to have two other jets ready. Ground crews were already preparing two more jets in case more than four jets were needed.

The F-16s were also equipped with extra fuel tanks mounted below the wings which the Air Force personnel called "bags." With the high speeds they would be flying and the possibility of having to make air to air fighting maneuvers, they would burn up fuel more quickly than normal. The bags allowed them to take off at higher speeds and move more quickly to a needed position and then still have plenty of fuel for combat maneuvers. Once a spare fuel tank was empty, it would be dropped off of the plane in a safe place so as to not injure anyone below. The empty tank would be tracked down and picked up later.

With his Air Force personnel all working at top speed and functioning like the well-oiled machine that they were, the jets and pilots were ready quickly. Gen. Briscoe was pleased. They were prepared. They had planned well. They would do their duty.

However, Arnold Briscoe had a nagging concern that worried him. He wondered if his old friend, Sam Park, was going to make it.

                                    *   *   *

Major Robert McCasland was on assignment at the base that Saturday morning and hurried to respond to the call of an incident in Casa Grande. However, as he ran to the F-16 that was being prepped for him he was thinking about the morning's events regarding his wingman. Flight crews were composed of two F-16s flying together and the pilots were usually a seasoned senior pilot, usually a major or a captain, and a more junior wingman, usually a lieutenant. The two airmen always flew together and McCasland's wingman was always Captain Lontell Franklin. But Franklin had gotten sick the night before after they had dinner at the base mess hall.

Their chief cook had been trained at a first-class culinary school before he joined the Air Force and he could prepare food that was as good as you'd get in any fine restaurant. On Friday nights the cook often served green chili chicken enchiladas, which were excellent and almost spicy enough to melt your fork. You also felt it a day later when your digestive tract had processed the chilies. The cook always said that good chili should burn twice, both coming and going. Most of those on the base who ate the enchiladas had to smother them with sour cream to dial back the heat. However, they were delicious, and those who weren't able to handle the heat still wouldn't miss the flavor, so sour cream was always in high demand on those Friday nights. Personnel who normally didn't eat on-base somehow found an excuse to do so on Green Chile Friday, as they came to call it.

After eating the green chili chicken enchiladas on Friday night, both Captain Franklin and Captain Jordan Beezer had come down with very severe food poisoning symptoms and were completely unable to fly. In fact, both were hospitalized. McCasland thought it was odd that only those two had gotten sick when they had all eaten the green chili but he wasn't able to think much more about it because there was a lot to do as he and Andrus were going over pre-flight equipment checks and instructions before they could take off. He was so focused on the quickly-called mission that he had to think hard to remember First Lieutenant Andrus's call sign: Smoke.

All pilots were given a call sign by their fellow airmen. There was always some story behind the name, and the names were given to each other during flight training where they spent many stressful hours

                                        268

together and needed ways to let off steam. They also developed tremendous camaraderie during flight school because of the need to work so closely together and trust each other with their lives, and usually, the call signs were terms of endearment to a certain degree, which helped them bond as a team.

McCasland's call sign was "Burp." He frequently told funny stories about his family's huge dog, Burt, who was his best friend and protector as McCasland grew up in Tennessee. One time as they were in the mess hall and McCasland was telling another crazy story about Burt, McCasland belched unexpectedly just as he said the word "Burt" and the dog's name came out as a burp. Everyone got laughing so hard that eventually they were all in tears and some were rolling on the floor. They continued to laugh off and on into the evening as they teased McCasland about his dog, "Burp." The event earned McCasland his call sign.

Captain Lontell Franklin's call sign was "Pig Pen." He was an Air Force Brat but spent most of his younger years in Idaho because his dad had been stationed at Mountain Home Air Force Base, near Boise, while Franklin was young. Lontell was a cowboy and had even worked on a ranch there in Idaho when he was a teenager. After his dad retired, Franklin's father, a full Colonel, bought an Idaho ranch of his own. His son, Lontell, loved to spend time on his dad's ranch every chance he got. He had told all of his flight school classmates that he proposed to his wife as they went on a walk down to the pigpen on his dad's ranch. She accepted his proposal, but the story earned him his call sign. He was short and stocky and people had learned to never make fun of his size or his love for being a cowboy. One time during flight school one of the other airmen, who was a big guy and tended to be a bully, kept calling Franklin "Little Cowboy" or "Little Piggy" or "Piggy Boy," and after several warnings to knock it off Franklin ran out of patience. He lit into the bigger man and after three punches the bully was on the floor, dazed and wondering what happened, with the smaller Franklin towering over him as he lay there. Everyone, including the commanding officer, agreed that the bully got what was coming to him, and no serious harm was done. After that, everyone made sure to use the terms "Pig Pen" and "Cowboy" with the proper amount of respect when talking with Franklin.

McCasland and Franklin spent many hours together both on and off the base. Their wives had become very good friends and their kids played together often. When the two families were together and the pilots called each other Burp and Pig Pen their wives just rolled their eyes.

Another flight crew at Luke Air Force Base was Captain Jordan Beezer and his wingman First Lieutenant Taine Andrus. Beezer's call sign was "Boo" because he enjoyed catching people off-guard and scaring them just to see their reaction. He didn't do it too often or in a mean way, but he did it often enough that they noticed. He usually drew laughs or at least a good-natured scolding from his victims. One time when he was fifteen he had scared his Aunt Winona when she was eight and a half months pregnant and it caused her to faint and then go into labor. Mom and baby both turned out fine and healthy but it was still a family joke in the Beezer household even though he was now grown.

Lieutenant Andrus had earned his call sign, "Smoke," by his speed on the basketball court. During the times when the airmen exercised together many of them had started playing three-on-three basketball. Andrus was a very good player and was extremely fast. Many times he blew right past his opponents and one time as the defender stood there with a bewildered look as Andrus scored, another teammate said, "Wow, he smoked you man!" The defender said, "He always smokes me. In fact, he has smoked all of us. After we finish playing I have to call the fire department because the smoke is still curling off of his shoes. I think his *name* is Smoke." Andrus just stood there with a proud smile on his face.

Another flight crew on base consisted of two female pilots. Male and female pilots could fly together and often did, but it just ended up with the seniority and how things worked out for Luke AFB to have a crew made up of two women. Air force lingo kept the term wingman even if the second pilot was a woman. Nobody cared as long as the wingman, be they male or female, earned their keep by their reputation of being a good pilot. Flight performance meant everything to your worth in the Air Force.

Captain Gloria Puckett was from the Midwest and was an excellent pilot. She was pleasant and fun-loving and was tall and tough as nails. She played on a women's rugby team. She had played during high school and college and during that time had helped win a couple of championships. The call sign of "Scrum" was an easy fit.

First Lieutenant Nellie Boyd, Captain Puckett's wingman, was a Native American who grew up in a hogan out on the Navajo Reservation in northern Arizona. Boyd had a reputation for being completely fearless even to the point of being reckless at times. Someone called her a daredevil a few times and that nickname probably would have become her call sign until she told them once about something from her childhood. Her family had a herd of goats back on the reservation and Nellie's little sister named the most troublesome goat "DeeDee." As the others were discussing the call sign for Boyd one of them mentioned the goat and commented how Lieutenant Boyd caused the most gray hairs for their commanders and trainers, and the call sign ended up as DeeDee.

As they rushed to the plane, Burp as the flight commander and Smoke as the wingman, Smoke didn't say anything. Burp noticed it but figured it was battle jitters and shrugged it off. He would have preferred flying with his usual wingman but when one wingman was out and another flight lead was out it was not uncommon to pair the remaining two pilots to complete the flight team.

McCasland didn't even suspect that something very bad was happening and that it was all part of a sinister terrorist plot. All he knew was that something seemed odd about the whole green chili enchiladas thing.

43 Betrayed

It was early Saturday morning and Squadron Commander Beverly Wickstead was filled with anger. She was mostly angry with herself and her soon-to-be ex-husband. What added to her anger and frustration was that the personal issue which caused her tremendous emotional pain, had at the same time caused her to fail in doing her job. It was double the pain: personal pain and then the pain of realizing that if she had been attentive to her duty none of this would have progressed to the point of possible catastrophe. *She could have stopped it!*

The unthinkable had happened—and on her watch. And she had made it worse!

Lieutenant Taine Andrus had defected to radical Islamist ideology.

He had been influenced by his girlfriend and had slipped into radical Islamist sympathy and then total immersion, and no one had realized it until it was now perhaps too late. Andrus and Major McCasland were preparing to take off in their F-16s. If she didn't stop it in minutes McCasland would probably die and the stolen plane they were being sent to intercept would proceed toward its target, wherever that may be.

For this week of terrorist activity and heightened alert status they had two flights of fully armed F-16s ready. Out of Wickstead's flight of sixteen pilots, the wingman of the first flight and the flight lead of the second flight had both come down with a sudden illness. Wickstead should have been the one to reassign the flight, and in doing so she could have stopped the terrorist plot from unfolding. However, right at the moment she was needed most for her pilots and for national security, she was going through a personal crisis and was unavailable, and at the same time she was emotionally devastated. Her commanding officer, someone she didn't get along with, had to make a decision that she should have made and he didn't know the details that would have completely changed his choice. *She would have seen it in time, but she failed!* However, even as she realized the problem, her pilots were preparing to blast their way down the runway and one of them would die.

Commander Wickstead had started to become suspicious early Thursday morning. The terrorist attacks during the week had led to several discussions among the pilots and civilian staff in the base office about ISIS and the war against terrorism in the Middle East. In one discussion on Thursday, the subject came up about Bowe Bergdahl, the soldier who purported to be captured by ISIS and then was used in a prisoner swap for five high-level Taliban terrorists. As the news stories unfolded many military personnel claimed that Bergdahl was not captured but instead he deserted and converted to radical Islam, but tried to cover his story with the explanation of being "captured."

During the conversation among several people in the office, Major McCasland said, "I think he's an Islamist sympathizer and a traitor and should face a firing squad."

Just as he spoke, Lieutenant Andrus had walked up but remained outside the circle of people having the discussion. He heard Major McCasland's remark and suddenly grew red in the face, turned abruptly, and stormed off.

No one noticed Andrus' reaction except for Commander Wickstead and Susan Montpellier. Montpellier was a civilian secretary working for Wickstead at the base office at Luke. Wickstead looked at Montpellier and as their eyes met both had a furrowed brow and a puzzled look. Wickstead shook her head slightly and went on about her business. Yet the situation nagged at her all day; she couldn't seem to shake the feeling that something was amiss with Lt. Andrus.

Just before 5:00 p.m. on Thursday as they were getting ready to leave for the day, Wickstead went over to Montpellier's desk and quietly said, "Susan, would you do me a favor and take on a stealth assignment and find out more about Andrus' background." After she said it she just walked off without another word. Wickstead worked until 7:00 that night trying to stay focused on some critical but unrelated issues she was dealing with.

Friday afternoon about 4:00 Montpellier walked up and handed Wickstead a file regarding a training matter. As she did so Montpellier turned the file slightly sideways so that Wickstead could see that there were two files, with her finger separating them. As Montpellier handed Wickstead the files she looked her in the eye, and then with obvious intent and with a little exaggeration, removed her finger from between the files. Montpellier said quietly, "Sorry it took so long, Commander, but some of it was hard to come by. I had to pull some strings from . . . well, you don't need the whole story." Wickstead saw the pained look on Montpellier's face before she turned away.

Wickstead realized the importance of the files and turned and headed straight for her office. As she turned around the final corner to her office door she was completely surprised to see Rick sitting in a chair by her door. She was totally caught off guard!

Rick was her husband . . . but just barely. They had been married for seven years and had no children. They married later in life when she was thirty-eight and he had just turned forty and they had decided to not have any children. Now, looking back, Beverly had decided that was probably a good thing.

A year earlier Rick had gotten into online gaming and had very quickly become addicted to it. After a couple of months of trying to spend the amount of time he wanted to spend gaming versus keeping his job, he let go of the job and totally embraced gaming. One day he just walked into his boss and lied that he had some critical personal issues out of state that he had to deal with and he was moving, and he quit right then and there. He had been an up-and-coming financial advisor and had even earned awards for top performance and hitting sales goals, and then gave it all up for online gaming. At least the part about the "critical personal issues" was true.

He played whatever he could play, Call of Duty, Battlefield, League of Legends, Fortnite. The names changed over time but the result was the same with each. He spent hours and hours in their spare bedroom, sometimes not coming out for days, at least that Beverly saw. He ordered food online and had it delivered to their door. All the money he had wisely saved as a financial planner was being slowly eaten up by fast food consumed while he played. He had gained quite a bit of weight due to unhealthy food and zero physical activity. He rarely shaved but at least he did shower from time to time. He was so disgusting that she didn't even try to interact with him when she left for work or went to bed. She had tried that early on but he just ignored her and she gave up.

Beverly was transferred to Luke soon after Rick quit his job and she had been able to keep the problem a secret from her co-workers but lately she had grown tired of hoping and praying that he would change. They lived off-base so that made it easier to hide. They had no love life whatsoever; in fact, *they* had no life at all. She slept alone. She ate alone. She did everything alone when she was not at work. She did her job the best that she could but then she had to go home at the end of the day. She ate and read a little or watched TV, by herself of course, and then went to bed and cried herself to sleep. It had been like that every night for months.

They never argued; he never gave her an opportunity. If she found the door to his gaming room open and started talking to him about their marriage or their financial situation, or if she suggested an addiction recovery program, he just gently pushed her back out the door, closed it in her face, and locked it again. Sometimes she would quietly walk to his door and slowly and gently try the doorknob just to find that it was always locked. He had finally installed a lock with a key and he was the only one who had the key.

He gamed with his headphones on and music playing, so she never heard him; she only heard a constant repertoire of music coming from his room. Sometimes the only way she knew he was alive was because of the food containers in the trash just outside his door—placed there so she could take out the trash and he wouldn't be interrupted. He had bought a couch and had it delivered into the gaming room and he slept there, whenever he slept. She didn't even know when he slept.

Beverly had managed to keep the secret from being discovered by anyone at the base but she was very tired of it. When she pulled into her parking spot at the base she always had to redo her makeup to hide the fact that she had cried all the way to work. The security personnel who checked her credentials as she drove in each morning either didn't look closely at her or were very polite to act like nothing was wrong to see tears on her face.

She was ready to give up and had recently started researching online, considering doing her own divorce versus hiring a lawyer. She had access to legal help at the base but she wasn't sure she wanted to do that. She hoped she could do it on her own so no one would know. She was so embarrassed by it.

They were in love once! For six years they had a good marriage and did fun things together! Life was good! Then along came online gaming and it was as if Rick died. He was just gone from her life. One day she realized it really *was* like he had died and she was still in mourning, hoping it wasn't true and praying each night that she would wake up from a bad dream; that Rick would be there next to her and would talk to her and kiss her goodbye as they both went to work.

Unfortunately, the bad dream continued and she had finally given up any hope that he was coming back. In fact, maybe it was worse that he *hadn't* died because if he had, at some point she could just move on. Since he was still living and breathing in her house, she had to solve that problem before she could try to find a way to put her life back together. It tore her apart to realize she was thinking of him only as a problem that she had to get rid of. She was ready for a divorce.

When Beverly rounded the corner to her office on that late Friday afternoon with the files in her hand, the last thing she expected to see was Rick sitting by her door. He looked good. He had showered and shaved and had even gotten a haircut. One of the security officers from the base was nearby watching. Military protocol prohibited an unauthorized person like him to be unsupervised. The fact that he was her husband and was holding a bouquet of roses for a romantic surprise convinced security that he was OK, but they still had to accompany him. She knew he had been frisked for weapons.

When she saw him she almost dropped her handful of files. He stood and said, "Hi, Babe."

They were the first words her husband had spoken to her in perhaps three months. She stopped right there by the corner, and he walked up to her and gently put his free arm around her waist, giving her a soft kiss on the lips. He continued, "I thought we could go have dinner and catch a movie tonight."

She was dumbfounded, glued to the floor where she had stopped. *Had he actually kissed her?* It would go down as one of those moments in your life where you could recall every minute detail years later.

She managed to reply, "Sure."

She stepped into her office, placed both files on her desk, and turned back to Rick. "Is anything wrong?" She expected him to say he wanted a divorce.

"No, nothing wrong. I just decided we should spend the evening together." He stepped over and finally handed her the flowers, and said, "I'm sorry I've been AWOL."

Beverly was still in shock. Total shock! Deep in her heart, she had a new flicker of hope that something had clicked and he was back. Maybe somehow he had stopped gaming for a few minutes and realized that he was missing his real life, and real wife. Her hopes and her heart raced together as she turned away from her desk and switched off the light.

Rick took her hand in his, interlocking their fingers as they walked down the hall. She glanced over at the security guard, who was watching to make sure that the visitor was now supervised and was leaving the area accompanied by authorized personnel.

As they got outside Rick opened the passenger door of his car to let Beverly in. As he walked around the car to get in the driver's seat, she lifted the flowers and smelled them. She knew what she'd find. They were developed for looks and shelf life, and the fragrance was missing.

Why did she even make the effort to smell the roses? *She knew what the result would be!* She closed her eyes and wondered why she even held his hand. She was caught up in the rush of the moment . . . and a powerful burst of optimism. But deep down, so deep she didn't want to admit it was there, was the realization that she knew what the result would be. She fanned the spark of hope in an attempt to overpower the reality of what she feared.

Beverly and Rick spent the evening together, just the two of them. It was like it had been when they first started dating and their love was exciting and alive. At some point, she even turned off her cell phone.

First, they went to a restaurant. He told her to choose where she wanted to go and there was a local Mexican food place called Tona's Tacos that she had seen and wanted to try out. It was very good. Good enough that she decided it made up for not being on the base that night for Green Chile Friday. Then they went and caught the most recent Avengers movie since they both loved those. Rick had proposed to her on one knee in a park after they had seen a Saturday afternoon showing of an Avengers movie, with several people in the park watching and smiling as they realized what was happening.

Beverly and Rick talked the whole time as if their marriage had always been good. It was a wonderful evening and her hopes remained alive. When they got home she noticed that he glanced at his door as they started toward their bedroom. They were holding hands and she held the grip, not relaxing her fingers interlocked with his. They kept walking.

They started through the door into their bedroom and he paused and pulled back. Still holding her hand, he looked into her eyes.

"Give me just a second to check something."

"Rick, please don't." Her eyes were pleading as fervently as her voice.

He tried to let go of her hand but she tightened her grip and also maintained their eye contact. He reached with his free hand and stroked her cheek with the back of his fingers. She reluctantly relaxed her hand and he pulled his free.

"Just one minute."

He turned and started toward his room and at that moment she knew it was over. The beautiful, fragile bubble had burst. Just like that! She couldn't hope anymore. She leaned back against the door jamb and closed her eyes, tipping her head forward as if she were saying "Amen" to end a prayer: a painful, longing, frustrating prayer without a miraculous outcome. She stood there for a few moments, her head bowed, aching inside and hating roses with no fragrance.

She heard music start playing.

She finally stepped into her room and softly pulled the door closed behind her. It was as if he had stabbed her with a knife. The emotional pain was so intense that it was actually physical. She turned off the light and settled on the edge of the bed, totally defeated. After a few moments, still fully clothed, she lay down on her side and pulled her feet up. She closed her eyes and clutched her hands to her chest as if to grasp the knife that wasn't there but was causing intense pain and slowly killing her. She had already been crying, the tears silently trickling sideways across the side of her face onto the bed. Now she began to sob, quietly at first and then more loudly as her whole body shook.

The music continued from the other room.

44 Recovery and Warning

At 4:07 a.m. Beverly Wickstead awoke. At first she didn't know where she was. Then she realized she was on her bed fully dressed and still wearing her shoes. She couldn't believe she had actually been asleep because she had cried and tossed and turned and sobbed all night, wishing she could sleep to escape the pain. Evidently she had finally fallen asleep at some point.

She lay there slipping in and out of sleep, then waking to remember the ache and pain, and then a moment of sleep again. She didn't have the determination to get up and she remained on the bed, continuing to toss and turn like she had done most of the night.

She could still hear music from Rick's room. It was a bitter reminder of her defeat and her dashed hopes. She cried and turned over, wishing the pain would stop. She finally kicked off her shoes and again drifted off into fitful sleep.

At 6:52 she awoke again and looked at the clock. On a sudden impulse she got up and went to his room. In a last-ditch hope for possible recovery she tried his doorknob. Locked.

Beverly knocked on the door, softly at first, but with no answer. She knocked again, this time firmly and loudly. Still no answer. If he had answered, she didn't know if she would have hugged him or slugged him. She went back to her room and sat on the edge of the bed.

The hurt and frustration had now turned to fierce anger. Anger that Rick was so weak as to give in right at the moment she thought he had succeeded. Anger with the disgusting addiction in the first place. Anger that his fleeting moment of strength had also sucked her into its selfish mouth, only to spit them both out into loss and separation . . . again! *Why did she give in!* Of course, it was because she still loved him and after months of longing for him she had a burst of wonderful hope that he was really coming back.

She sighed in exasperation, still burning with anger. *They were so close!* No, actually *they* weren't close at all. She wished they were close but they weren't. He was another universe away. Literally.

Suddenly Beverly's mind woke enough that she remembered yesterday. The reality of what had happened flashed into her consciousness like a jet blast. *The file!*

She jumped off the bed and growled in frustration. There was still anger at Rick that he had tried but only ended up abandoning her more painfully than before. Now pressed on top of that was irritation with herself that she had abandoned her responsibility toward her squadron at such a critical time.

Beverly didn't even shower. She quickly slipped her feet back in her shoes, ran outside, and jumped into Rick's car. Her car was still at the base and Rick certainly wouldn't be needing to use his. It was a good thing he left a set of keys hanging above the washing machine. She sped the fifteen minutes to get to the base, hoping that if she got stopped she could explain to a police officer that it was an issue of national security. They probably heard that line all the time.

As she was driving she glanced at her phone and realized it was off. She grimaced to herself and turned it on as she sped down the road. She mentally calculated that it had been off for about twelve hours. At a red light she keyed in her security code to reach the main screen. She saw several texts from her commanding officer, Wing Commander Colonel Camden Siddoway. He had had to make flight assignments that she was supposed to make. She was going to hear about this! Maybe even a court-martial. She had completely shut herself off from her duty for twelve hours without notifying her commanding officer . . . all for a stupid, weak, jerk of a . . . . She didn't finish the sentence because she had arrived at the base. As she slowed to a stop at the security guard station she noticed that the sun was just about to come up.

Commander Wickstead showed her ID and was saluted through the gate by the security guards. She zoomed across the base to her building, ran in, and worked her way to her office.

As she did so, she read more detail in the texts from Siddoway. At first, he asked her where she was because two of her pilots had suddenly come down with an illness and she needed to make re-assignments among her flight crews. The language got more intense and more colorful with each message. Finally, he told her that he was making assignments in her absence and she was in serious jeopardy of her command. She winced at that last one but had just arrived at her desk and her focus changed to the material she needed to quickly review.

The files were lying where she had placed them hours earlier as the stars in her eyes had blinded her from reality. She pushed that painful thought aside and hurriedly turned the top file toward the left, face down, so she could examine the second file. There was the background on Andrus that she had asked Montpellier to research. He had grown up in Indiana and was top of his class in school and in flight school. His file looked very normal at first.

Scanning as fast as she could while still getting the main points, she came across a new person. Andrus had a girlfriend that he had been living with for about a year. Her name was Priyanka Qahtan. Montpellier had made screenshots of some of Priyanka's Facebook posts, showing her and Lieutenant Andrus together at different places and events, along with her comments about her new soul mate and how happy they were together. She was very beautiful and Andrus appeared to be head over heels in love with her. Commander Wickstead wondered if Priyanka Qahtan had been noticed on Andrus' social media posts and if someone at Langley had done a background check on her. That's what should have happened. Maybe that would come out as she got further into the file.

The next page was also a Facebook post but this time with an Imam at a mosque in California. Evidently, Priyanka had taken Andrus to meet the Imam just a couple of months earlier and they had spent the whole weekend with the Muslim leader. If he was a radical Islamist, the Imam would undoubtedly influence Andrus's thinking and especially if his adoring girlfriend was supporting and encouraging that.

As Wickstead turned the next page, there was a sticky tab with an arrow pointing to Priyanka's mother's maiden name: Al-Sabah. The message on the sticky tab said that the Al-Sabah family was very influential in Kuwait, similar to the Kennedy family or the Bush family in America. Still further was information on Priyanka's grandparents, both from Kuwait. Priyanka's maternal grandfather, Tareq Al-Sabah, was a top government official in that country with ties to the Muslim Brotherhood.

The next page was a bulletin from what looked like a source in the CIA. The date was from about a year prior and it showed some prisoners who had recently been transferred to the prison in Guantanamo Bay. Wickstead didn't know if it was classified or not, and she didn't know how Susan Montpellier got it, but she had. About halfway down the list was a name highlighted in yellow: Fayez Al-Sabah.

The next page showed a hand-sketched genealogy or family tree, starting with Tareq Al-Sabah. Two generations below him, on different branches were the names Fayez Al-Sabah and Priyanka Qahtan. First Lieutenant Taine Andrus' live-in girlfriend had a cousin who had been in Gitmo for just over a year!

Raahhh! Beverly growled softly to herself. As she started connecting the dots she decided that Andrus' beautiful little girlfriend had influenced him to start doubting and then hating the U.S. for what they had done to her cousin. The influence of a radical Imam would have added to the hatred. She was quite likely involved with the terror cell that was waging the attacks on the Phoenix area this past week and had probably been working hard on Andrus for months. If that were true, she could have poured on the charm and the physical passion and captured his heart. Then she turned his heart against the country to which he had sworn allegiance. Beverly thought that if her love for her waste of a husband could make her shirk her duty for twelve hours when she was committed to her country, it was possible that Taine Andrus' love for his beautiful terrorist girlfriend could cause him to defect and turn into an enemy of the U.S.

Beverly was interrupted by a loud Klaxon horn followed by an announcement over the PA system. It was an alert to all base personnel that they had increased the alert code and a squadron of jets was to take off ASAP.

Her thoughts raced. It would be her pilots who would be launching within minutes. She knew her squadron. With Franklin and Beezer out of commission, per Siddoway's texts, that would leave Andrus to be wingman to McCasland. If this was all part of the terrorist plot, which she was certain it was, that meant Andrus was going to do something soon. She had to stop them from taking off.

She picked up the file and ran out of her office. Siddoway's office was in the next building.

Lieutenant Colonel Wickstead had been at Luke AFB for almost a year. She had been an excellent pilot, had demonstrated superior leadership in her previous duties, and was assigned to be a Squadron Commander when she was moved to Luke. She had come in as a replacement for another Lt. Colonel, Kolby Oetjen, who had been highly respected. However, Colonel Oetjen was diagnosed with pancreatic cancer and had to retire early. Sadly, he had passed away only a month before. Wickstead was brought in as his replacement but had had a very difficult time actually replacing him. The other airmen were still struggling with the emotional loss of Colonel Oetjen's illness and retirement and had a hard time accepting Lt. Colonel Wickstead as their leader. Most airmen didn't care if their commanding officer was male or female, but on occasion, an airman was quietly resistant to a female officer and there could sometimes be some passive-aggressive behavior.

Lt. Colonel Wickstead's commanding officer, Colonel Camden Siddoway, was her biggest challenge. The personnel under her command had generally accepted her and any resistance was minimal, although there was still a little. Colonel Siddoway was a whole different story. Siddoway's opposition to her was open and notorious. Siddoway didn't try very hard to hide his feelings or keep others from noticing. They had never argued but he frequently rejected her ideas and treated her with disdain. So far she had been able to get most things done in spite of his lack of support. Some of the personnel under her command noticed the problem and demonstrated support for her, although they were careful not to speak against Colonel Siddoway. Insubordination in the military was absolutely taboo and their support for Wickstead was subtle and carefully designed to stay under the radar.

Wickstead had to tell someone about Andrus, and since her direct command was Siddoway, there was no way around him. She expected outright rejection but they couldn't afford that. Jets would be taking off in minutes with her two pilots at the controls. With the Andrus File in hand she reached Siddoway's office, out of breath. Seconds counted because once the jets were in the air, Andrus could attack McCasland at any time. She had to warn McCasland before it happened.

She didn't even knock on Siddoway's door. She opened it and rushed into his office.

"Colonel, we have a very serious problem, and I only have seconds to explain it to you."

Siddoway rose from his desk, a scowl on his face. "Wickstead, you disappear for twelve hours and then expect me to care about what you have to say?!"

"I know it's very unusual, sir, and I know I was derelict in my duty."

"Where have you been for twelve hours?!"

"I'm sorry, Sir. I expect to be held fully accountable. I was trying to save my marriage in a last-ditch, surprise opportunity . . . and to be honest with you, Sir, I failed." She held up the file and said, "But this is way more important than my failed marriage. Sir, Lieutenant Andrus . . ."

He cut her off. Evidently the failed marriage melted his heart a little. "Wickstead, a marriage is very important and don't you ever forget that."

"Yes Sir, but mine was dying and it finally died last night. Quite frankly, it was already too late to save. But Sir, we really need to get to the next issue before *that* gets too late." She pushed the file toward him and continued. "Speaking of love and marriage, Sir, were you ever so much in love that you would literally do anything for your sweetheart?"

The Colonel smiled a little and got a far-away look in his eyes as he said, "As a matter of fact, my wife and I were like that forty years ago. I was reminded of it just last week when we celebrated our anniversary."

"Sir, Lieutenant Andrus has fallen head over heels in love with a beautiful young woman who is a terrorist. She is in league with the terrorists who have been attacking Phoenix this week. I believe she got him to defect and that it was carefully orchestrated for him to be wingman this morning. That explains Franklin and Beezer both getting food poisoning from the green chili enchiladas when no one else who ate them did. We have to stop Andrus. If we don't warn McCasland, Andrus will catch him by surprise, shoot him down, and then carry out whatever plan the terrorists have."

Colonel Camden Siddoway just stared at her. She stared back.

"You expect me to believe that?"

Months of pent-up frustration dealing with Siddoway boiled over and she had no fear. She wasn't angry or loud but she was completely determined as she opened the file and started pointing out facts. "Here's the file. Look at the Facebook posts. Andrus is totally in love. Now, look at this family tree. She is a descendant of key people in the Muslim Brotherhood. Now, look at this list of prisoners in Gitmo. Her cousin!"

Siddoway took the file and thumbed through a few of the pages, reading them quickly. Wickstead had the feeling she had won. The last page Siddoway looked at was a Facebook post of a selfie with the two young lovers smiling. They were standing on a beach wearing matching tank tops with the sunset behind them. Siddoway stared at the picture, expressionless.

Then his countenance clouded again. In a firm, menacing tone, he said, "You are dismissed, Commander. And don't you dare come in here again and tell me some cockamamie story when you have such flimsy evidence. And you may face a court-martial for your disappearance yesterday."

Wickstead knew Siddoway believed her. The smile and far-away look had given him away, and the final stare at the young lovers convinced her. She thought of McCasland, one of their best pilots. She would not back down. Siddoway's belligerence was a power play even though he knew she was right. He just didn't want to admit it. He was in charge and she was the underling. The "he" and "she" of it was the problem. His pride would sacrifice one of their best pilots and increase the threat level to the U.S. because he didn't want to have to give in to a woman. She knew he was a good airman, deep down, but he wasn't thinking about doing what was right at the moment. He was blinded by his pride.

For some reason, she thought of the 300 Spartans fighting the Persians in the battle of Thermopylae in 480 B.C. She had seen the movie and read various accounts retelling the story. Someone involved in the situation said that there were so many Persian archers that their arrows would darken the sky. In cool defiance, one of the Greeks calmly replied, "Good; then we can fight in the shade."

Wickstead suddenly realized that part of the problem since coming to Luke was that she was intimidated by Siddoway and she always backed down. *It was time to fight in the shade.* She didn't even try to mince words; she was probably going to be court-martialed anyway.

"I'm sorry, sir, but you're completely wrong, and I know that *you know* you're wrong. You're not thinking about saving McCasland or protecting the U.S. from a domestic threat as you took an oath to do. You're only thinking about *my* gender and *your* pride. McCasland and Andrus are just taking off. The only way to warn McCasland is to call him from the control tower. I'm going there now but it will be harder for me to convince them because I'm only the Squadron Commander and the tower will want orders from the Wing Commander. I'm going with or without you but if you don't help me try you will regret it for the rest of your life."

She scooped up the Andrus file, turned, and ran from the room, heading for the parking lot. As she reached the door she grabbed the keys to the base vehicle assigned to their office, an SUV. The key always hung on a hook by the door. She was glad nobody else was using it right then.

She ran out the door, climbed in the car and started it up. As she reached to put it into reverse, Siddoway came bolting out the door. She backed up to the right and stopped so she could put it into drive. By then, the passenger door, which was now facing Siddoway, was easy for him to get to. She paused a moment while he opened the door and then lurched forward when he had taken a seat. He swore as he quickly closed the door and reached for his seat belt.

"Wickstead, I don't want to hear one more word about pride or gender."

"Yes, Sir!"

Lt. Colonel Wickstead drove as fast as she could toward the tower. She didn't see the jets and figured they were at the far end of the runway since she hadn't heard them take off yet. She felt like the drive to the tower took forever. As she drove she said, "I quickly read all your texts about the airmen and the assignments, but I still don't know why we are scrambling jets."

Siddoway replied, "Terrorists stole a private plane just at sunrise, a nice one . . . from the little airport in Casa Grande. It's full of explosives and is headed somewhere. All air traffic has been grounded. We've got an AWACS out there trying to find the plane and our Vipers have to shoot it down where it won't hurt anybody." Then he added, "I'm sorry about your marriage."

By then they had reached the control tower and Wickstead barreled right up to the door and screeched to a stop. As she jumped out, she said, "Thank you, sir. People heal from failed marriages all the time, right?" She didn't even sound very convincing to herself.

The control tower itself stood eighty-seven feet above the rest of the base, and the rotating radar dish on top extended another eighteen feet. It felt like it took forever for the elevator door to open, then another eternity for the elevator to rise eight floors and the doors to slowly slide open.

As they stepped out of the elevator the two jets took off into the morning sun. Wickstead swore this time. She was getting more concerned that they wouldn't be able to warn McCasland before Andrus took action.

They pounded loudly on the door of the control room. Staff Sargent Barry Elgar looked out through the window. It was unusual to see the wing commander and a squadron commander in the tower. SSgt. Elgar just stared at them, confused. Siddoway pounded again and Elgar snapped out of his little trance, realizing that the Colonel was demanding to be let in. The click of the security mechanism in the door signaled that Elgar had pressed a button allowing entrance. There were four personnel in the tower. Per protocol, they were to stay focused on their tasks and not stand and salute. Elgar, already standing, quickly offered a salute and returned to his station.

Siddoway said, "Sorry for the surprise, but we need to talk to those pilots. Wickstead needs a headset *now!*"

As they readied the equipment Wickstead was in full-adrenalin mode and was thinking clearly. She had already formulated a plan.

The mic clicked on and Wickstead spoke. "Major McCasland, this is Lt. Colonel Beverly Wickstead."

"Copy that."

"Major, your seventeen-year-old daughter, Krisanne, has been injured in a car accident on her way to a friend's house for breakfast. It's serious enough that I need to talk to you on a different channel immediately." She hoped he'd figure it out and that Andrus would take the bait. She didn't know what she'd do if McCasland didn't get it.

Lt. Colonel Wickstead clicked off the mic and said to the Staff Sargent, "Dial it down to channel four."

The Staff Sargent said, "You mean seventeen?"

"No, Krisanne is four years old. I know my pilots. I'm hoping Andrus goes to seventeen."

Sure enough, noise on channel four indicated someone was there. McCasland questioned, "Commander Wickstead?"

"I was hoping you'd figure out what I was trying to do. I have to talk fast while Andrus works his way from seventeen down to four. You are in grave danger. Lieutenant Andrus has defected to radical Islam and is going to try to shoot you down so that you cannot stop that stolen aircraft. You worry about Andrus. We'll send more Vipers to go after that stolen plane and to help you if needed. *This is no drill.* Do you understand?"

"Yes, Colonel. I'll do my best."

"Very good, Major."

"Copy. Out."

Lt. Colonel Wickstead looked over at Colonel Siddoway. He had a very serious look on his face. "Good thinking, Wickstead. May God help Major McCasland. I think we should stay here and listen to the transmissions. . . . And when we go back to my office let's talk about making that other issue go away without any serious consequences. I apologize for my behavior."

The other personnel looked at each other with puzzled expressions while Wickstead breathed a sigh of relief and said, "Thank you, sir."

45 Vipers Over the Valley

As they took off, McCasland was still thinking about the green chili situation and his assignment to Andrus. Nothing really seemed wrong on the surface but something just didn't feel right.

They flew low as they headed toward Casa Grande, staying just above the tallest structures on the outskirts of the city, the big power poles and the cell towers. The straight-line path from Luke AFB to Casa Grande went right through the west end of Phoenix and up over South Mountain, which was little more than a rough, rocky hill, although it was about ten miles long and three miles wide and had an elevation 1,600 feet higher than Phoenix. Flying over South Mountain required little more than an altitude increase of 2,000 feet, a simple task for an F-16.

They had no sooner started away from Luke when Colonel Wickstead came on the radio and curiously informed Major McCasland to change frequencies. Then she explained the plot for the now defected Andrus to shoot him down. The fact that she was able to do it so discreetly was intriguing to him but he had no doubt that it tipped off Andrus that they knew something was going on.

Because McCasland was a major and the senior officer he was the flight leader and he made the decisions. However, that also meant that the secondary officer could more easily drift back and fly slightly behind him, making him more vulnerable to an attack from the rear. That thought went through his mind as he flew.

McCasland was in the lead with Andrus just off his right wing, the standard formation when two jets were flying together. After they cleared South Mountain it was a straight shot across the flat valley floor to another small mountain on the north edge of Casa Grande, a distance of about forty miles. Because they were carrying "bags," the spare fuel tanks hanging below the wings of the jets, their top speed was around

500 miles per hour, which meant they would reach Casa Grande in just under five minutes. McCasland had no doubt that between South Mountain and Casa Grande Andrus would make his move.

They were watching their APG-630 radar to try to find the plane based on its altitude, airspeed, and approximate location. "Wonder how hard it will be to find that turboprop when we get over there," McCasland said to Andrus by radio, not expecting a substantive answer. "If it's still trailing smoke we may find it before the AWACS." Andrus did not answer at all, which was unusual, and further confirmed to McCasland that Andrus was now the enemy.

They were about a third of the way to Casa Grande when McCasland saw a faint trail of smoke out ahead of them above Casa Grande. His APG-630 indicated an aircraft in the same location. He radioed to Andrus, "There's the smoke, and my radar's got a target." It was barely above the city and the low mountains scattered around Casa Grande. It looked like the plane had turned toward the south a bit. After determining just that much information McCasland quickly changed his focus to Andrus and he realized there was no longer a jet beside him. Andrus had suddenly slowed to get behind him but McCasland was anticipating that move.

McCasland snapped his F-16 in a quick hard turn, down and to the left. He didn't have much room to work with because they were flying so low but that was the preferred defensive move in that situation. The sudden move saved his life as Andrus simultaneously fired a burst of bullets from the machine gun on his jet. Because McCasland was already turning, the bullets that would have struck the main fuselage only scattered across the tail of the jet; only a few of the bullets even connected. McCasland was also saved by the fact that because they were so close, Andrus had to use the machine gun instead of a guided missile.

McCasland was rapidly approaching the ground and quickly changed direction and started to climb and turn, attempting to curl back around to get behind Andrus. However, Andrus was a good pilot and stayed basically behind McCasland, trying to match his evasive maneuvers so Andrus could stay within firing range. At the same time, McCasland wanted to gain altitude. If there was going to be a dogfight between two F-16s, he wanted all the room he could get. At the moment, altitude was his friend. The valley floor was quickly being lost far below.

There was a saying that the F-16 had never lost a dogfight. It was a superior fighter jet, agile and quick, and it had a reputation of coming out on top. However, McCasland knew that there were many F-16s being used by different countries all around the world, and for sure one or more had lost a dogfight. Maybe the saying applied only to the US Airforce. In any case, today that was going to change. Either he or Andrus was going to get shot down sometime in the next few minutes, and McCasland was doing his absolute best to make sure it was Andrus that met his end today instead of him.

The F-16 was developed during the 1970s and was first released for operation in 1976. It was designed to be light, fast, and fly well in all kinds of weather. Its official nickname was the Fighting Falcon, but some in the Air Force thought it looked like a snake when it was coming directly at you, so it picked up the informal nickname of Viper.

McCasland was now above 18,000 feet and still climbing. However, he had been pulling to the left and had now come clear back around toward Phoenix again. That was not good because of the heavily populated city below. All other aircraft had already been grounded by the FAA alert.

McCasland pulled the stick back to the right but the plane didn't respond. It turned slowly to the right, but could not turn quickly, which was a critical move in a dogfight. He was going to be at a serious disadvantage! He tried it several more times, jerking back and forth from right to left so as to not be an easy target for Andrus even as he tested the functionality of his jet. He could turn sharply to the left and he could fly straight and fast, but any turns to the right would only be gradual. This was a serious problem. McCasland also wanted to get out over the open desert. He didn't want Andrus' plane to crash into the city when he shot it down. *He was trying to think positive.*

Andrus continued to trail him, although at enough of a distance that McCasland was staying out of the line of fire and away from radar lock.

McCasland spoke into his mic, "What are you doing, Smoke?"

Andrus didn't reply.

As McCasland continued to work his way toward the desert he switched his radio to a different frequency. He had recognized Staff Sergeant Barry Elgar's voice from the tower when they had taken off and knew Elgar always monitored several frequencies. Elgar and McCasland were very good friends. Elgar was known as "Big Bear" because he was a giant of a young man and had once had a run-in with a bear in Montana. He was on a bow hunting trip and a bear actually came into their camp. As the bear was digging in Elgar's brand new ice chest Elgar shot an arrow right into the ice chest instead of the bear. He was not in any danger and it turned out to be a humorous event, and since then everyone called him Big Bear. If he had been a pilot that would likely have been his call sign.

On a random frequency McCasland radioed, "Luke tower, this is HAVOC 52." He paused, waiting for his friend.

He repeated: "Luke tower, this is HAVOC 52. Come in."

"I read you loud and clear, Burp. You two are awfully quiet up there. What's happening?" Elgar was still accompanied by Colonel Siddoway and Colonel Wickstead.

"I've got a problem. Colonel Wickstead's warning was accurate. Andrus fired at me and did some damage to my Viper. He's hot on my tail. We are not at all in pursuit of the King Air full of explosives. I have had to take evasive action and the damage to my aircraft is preventing me from full functionality. I can't turn to the right very well. I am trying to get out over the desert because there's going to be a dogfight and I intend to blow him out of the sky. You'd better get more Vipers going immediately because right now that flying bomb of a King Air has no one going after it. In fact, when I did get a look at it, it was heading south. It's trailing smoke, so it's a broken bomb, but a bomb nonetheless."

"10-4. We're on it. We have an AWACS coming in range now to try to locate it, and we already have Scrum and DeeDee prepping for takeoff. Good luck, Major. Fly crooked and shoot straight."

"Roger that. Tell Uncle Sam I'm sorry about the loss of an expensive piece of hardware today and cross your fingers it isn't mine."

* * *

Before General Briscoe got to Luke Air Force Base his cell phone rang. It was SSgt. Elgar. "Sir, Major McCasland has confirmed the intel originally reported by Colonel Wickstead. He says Lieutenant Andrus has shot at his aircraft and done some damage to his Viper. McCasland can't turn very well. However, so far McCasland has evaded Andrus. Sounds like we're going to have an engagement between our own two jets. I'm sorry, Sir."

There was a pause and Elgar could hear only dead air. Then Briscoe said, "No need for apologies, Sargent. Scramble four jets even faster than the first. We still have to stop that stolen plane, and McCasland could use some help."

"Already underway, Sir. We've got Puckett and Boyd alerted and they are a couple of minutes away from takeoff. I'm not sure yet who's next in line, but we'll get them going ASAP."

"Very good, Sargent."

After SSgt. Elgar hung up and as Gen. Briscoe continued driving quickly to the base, he thought of his personnel. He was angry at Andrus. It was totally unexpected and he was disturbed that they didn't realize it sooner. Andrus was a very good pilot and showed great promise. *What a shame!*

McCasland was as good as they came. Briscoe had told anyone who would listen that McCasland had a sixth sense about flying and could do things with a plane that few pilots could do. If Briscoe had to choose anyone to evade their own pilot and turn the tables while flying a damaged jet, he would choose Major McCasland.

Puckett and Boyd were both excellent pilots. They were young and still learning but were doing very well and were eager to prove themselves. Boyd had a reputation for being completely fearless even to the point of being reckless at times. He was glad that Puckett was the lead in their flight.

As Briscoe continued to contemplate his personnel, he realized that there were countless times when individuals who were engaged as Air Force pilots were responsible for saving lives and protecting freedom, even if doing so meant having to take lives. Often the rising generation was influenced by the news media and Hollywood, and even politicians got it wrong many times trying to figure out who or what was good and who or what was evil. But most of the people in the U.S. military knew the side they were on was the good side and had come to grips with the reality of taking the lives of those who were evil as a means to protect the freedom of those who were good. Briscoe was reminded of the struggle for good over evil many times in movies and books such as Lord of the Rings, the Harry Potter series, Les Misérables, and many, many others. It was such a part of humanity that the theme repeated itself in the stories that humans told each other. He hoped today that good would prevail over evil.

As he pulled into his parking spot and jumped out of his car to hurry inside where he could listen in on the communications with Command Post, Briscoe reflected on how proud he was to be leading such great people as McCasland, Elgar, Puckett, and Boyd. America couldn't be in better hands. At the same time, Briscoe was a religious man, and he offered up a silent prayer for all the help God could give them. He hoped they were all in God's hands too.

Unfortunately, the radical Islamists had exactly the same belief.

*　　*　　*

Major Robert McCasland continued to work his way east over the Valley of the Sun, further and further away from the more densely populated areas. He was intensely focused because he knew he was in serious danger. He was flying a damaged F-16 with another fully functional F-16 right behind him trying to blow him out of the sky.

But what First Lieutenant Andrus didn't know was that Bob McCasland had prepared for this very moment in a way that Andrus probably hadn't thought of. In the past, McCasland and his flying partner, Captain Lontell Franklin, had spent many hours in the flight simulators and in their jets, practicing and practicing their flying technique under unusual situations.

They always tried to think of scenarios they might be in at any given time, and they even got creative about placing artificial limits on themselves to see what they could do. Sometimes they imagined they were shot in one arm or the other and had to fly using only their right hand or their left. Sometimes they put a bandage over one eye to learn to fly without the depth perception that comes from having the use of both eyes.

One time for a period of about a month they practiced pretend dogfights where they could only turn to the left or to the right. They both became fairly proficient at it. They never told anyone else about their strange hypothetical training situations.

McCasland flew east, continuing to get away from the city. If he needed to move to the right he would do a corkscrew to the left, but as he came upside down and back around he would linger longer into the part of the turn that would pull him to the left. He knew it looked clumsy and awkward, and he tried not to do anything repetitive so as to avoid any patterns and to keep Andrus from anticipating his next move. He could always tell a rookie in a dogfight because his maneuvers were textbook. The most successful combat pilots were the ones that relied on experience and instinct to be completely unpredictable.

As McCasland flew crookedly through the air ahead of Andrus he felt more confident as he realized he had spent many hours practicing for this very situation. It took intense mental ability to fly this way but so far it was working.

Over a period of a few minutes McCasland was able to work clear out over the rocky, rugged mountains east of the Phoenix area. He also continued to try to find a way to get behind Andrus but his wingman managed to stay on his tail, albeit not close enough or direct enough for a clean shot.

F-16s were equipped with two types of offensive weapons: missiles and bullets. They normally carried two sidewinder air-to-air missiles, or AAMs, and two to four AMRAAMs, a more advanced version of the sidewinder. The sidewinder was the preferred weapon of choice at a closer distance but the AMRAAM was more for medium range fighting, even when the enemy was not within sight. The guided missiles were very effective against an enemy aircraft because of the ability to chase down the target using sophisticated technology. It wasn't just heat-seeking technology either. The blast was triggered by the proximity of the missile to the target that had been designated during radar lock. If the missile got within a certain distance of the enemy jet, even if the jet suddenly turned, the weapon could detonate, thereby damaging or destroying the target. The missile didn't have to fly up the hot tailpipe behind the jet engine as some people used to think.

Against the King Air, a sidewinder would be a very powerful and destructive force and would detonate all the explosives on the plane. C-4 had been developed to detonate in response to a powerful shock wave, which is why a bullet fired from a rifle wouldn't be enough. It would take a blasting cap or an explosion from another device. Dynamite, on the other hand, could be easily detonated by a smaller shock wave, such as a bullet. Either way, a blast from a sidewinder in or near a plane filled with C-4 and dynamite would detonate everything and the plane would be obliterated in the explosion. The King Air would be a very easy target for a sidewinder. The private aircraft was much slower than an F-16 and certainly much slower than a sidewinder.

Against another fighter jet, the sidewinder missile was a very formidable and dangerous weapon. The F-16s flew at a top speed of just under Mach 2 or about 1,500 miles per hour. The sidewinder could fly at Mach 2.5 or just under 2,000 miles per hour. During a dogfight F-16s flew at only around 500 miles per hour. Needless to say, a difference of

1,000 miles per hour meant that a dogfighting jet could travel five miles in 3.6 seconds but a sidewinder could travel that same distance in just less than one second.

If McCasland made one wrong move and got into Andrus' radar path, and if Andrus could at that very instant press the button for radar lock, it would be very difficult for McCasland to avoid being destroyed. Outmaneuvering a missile was possible, although Hollywood made it look like it could be done all the time, but it was rare, and pilots didn't want to get into that situation in the first place.

As McCasland flew, twisting and turning over the city and the desert, he recalled a story about an incident that occurred during the development of the sidewinders back in the early 1950s. A test pilot named Wally Schirra launched a sidewinder from his plane and the missile doubled back and began chasing Schirra's own plane. Using some skillful flying, Schirra was able to maneuver his jet away from the sidewinder until the sidewinder ran out of fuel and fell harmlessly out of the sky. McCasland knew sidewinder technology had been drastically improved in the last sixty years and he knew out-maneuvering a sidewinder was much more difficult now. However, he reassured himself that F-16 technology had also improved over the years.

The other weapon built into the F-16 was a twenty-millimeter Vulcan machine gun, called a cannon. If a jet fired all of its missiles, it still had 500 rounds of ammunition for the cannon. It was a Gatling gun, named after the inventor, Richard Gatling, who in the 1800s designed a gun with six rotating barrels that could fire rapidly in succession. The F-16 cannon also used the configuration of six rotating barrels and could fire 100 rounds per second. The shells of the Vulcan were about the size of a large man's index finger and the bullets flew at a muzzle velocity of over 2,300 miles per hour. The F-16's cannon was designed to be shot in short bursts since the weapon was fast enough to shoot all 500 rounds in five seconds.

At one point McCasland decided to try to outsmart Andrus with some clever maneuvering. McCasland started from about 25,000 feet in elevation and went up and up and up, with Andrus trailing behind him at a distance. An F-16 would top out at about 50,000 feet, but at 42,000 feet McCasland whipped around to the left with a roll and a turn to try to get Andrus in front of him but Andrus quickly shot out to the side and also came around. For a split second McCasland was in front of Andrus and Andrus fired his gun. By the time the bullets reached McCasland he had already jerked to the left again and the bullets sailed off and fell to the floor of the Valley of Sun below them. Fortunately, the likelihood of anyone being injured by them was very remote.

Andrus remained behind him and was doing well at keeping up with McCasland but was not close enough or on target enough for McCasland to feel immediately threatened. McCasland knew that up close Andrus would have an easier time shooting at him but a more difficult time reacting to his maneuvers. At a further distance it would be easier for Andrus to respond to turns and maneuvers but it would be more difficult to get McCasland into his sights for either the missiles or the cannon.

McCasland did not feel desperate and was trying to egg Andrus on to help him feel like he was close. He didn't want Andrus giving up on pursuing him only to go after another target that couldn't defend itself or couldn't flee. At the same time, McCasland kept mentally reminding himself to not become complacent. One mistake and this dogfight would be over quickly and Andrus would fly off to other targets while McCasland smoldered on the valley floor.

On a couple of occasions Andrus pulled the trigger on the gun of his F-16 and sent a burst of fire toward McCasland. However, it did nothing more than send bullets harmlessly in his general direction which then rained down on the ground below.

As McCasland approached the dry, rocky mountains east of the Phoenix area he came up with a plan. He was originally supposed to be on a sightseeing cruise on Canyon Lake that morning with some friends who were involved with a birdwatching group. He could have been calmly and peacefully watching birds with binoculars but he ended up having to fly that day. Well, he hoped his plan would give them a show with a good outcome and that they'd forgive him for scaring the birds.

46 Let the Dam Break

With the four law enforcement guards out of the way Al-Musawi's team went into action as he called out instructions. Four of them were dressed in stolen police officer uniforms and were carrying AR-15s. Two went west on the highway to stop traffic from coming east up the road.

Two more went east through the narrow gap between the cliff and the thumb of rock to stop the cars coming west. The Apache Trail didn't get much traffic, especially at daybreak, so there really weren't many cars to worry about, although that would likely change as the sun came up and the day wore on.

Four more of Al-Musawi's men climbed up on the thumb of rock to keep any law enforcement personnel from coming up the road. They discovered that there was a place near the top where they could kneel down in a shallow trench in the rock, providing a natural protective wall for them to shoot from. Erosion and blowing dirt over the years had opened up a gap in the rock and left a layer of dirt and sand in the bottom of the trench. It was similar to a foxhole and was about four feet wide and ten or twelve feet long. This naturally occurring cavity in the rock and the resulting low wall in front of them would give them ample protection if they knelt or crouched. With enough ammo they would be able to hold off many law enforcement personnel for quite some time. One man carried a heavy duffel bag filled with fifty-round magazines, already loaded with ammo. The other three men carried the AK-47s for the four men to use.

The other men in the truck piled out and, with Al-Musawi and Vahid calling instructions, they unloaded the explosives and rappelling gear. Some climbed down the metal ladder and others began handing gear down to them. Al-Musawi kept yelling for them to hurry, and those on the dam were running back and forth along the top, carrying equipment and climbing gear. The shaped charges were packed loosely in boxes and looked like little conical contraptions with wires sticking out of the end. The wires were like long spindly legs and each cone resembled a miniature version of a three-legged water tower that one might see standing high in the air over a small town to provide water pressure to the inhabitants.

As the men were quickly getting the gear into place Al-Musawi noticed four crates of dynamite and heard Vahid yell at the men to carry those very carefully. Al-Musawi asked Vahid why they had dynamite and Vahid replied that the boxes had arrived at the MC Produce warehouse after the shipment of explosives had been sent with the group who was going to steal the plane. Since they had cleaned everything else out in preparation for the warehouse to be flooded, he brought them along in the truck. He figured they would find a good use for the dynamite somewhere, and he had already been thinking about strategic places where it could be quickly detonated as the dam started to collapse, to help the dam come apart.

Roosevelt Dam was shaped like an L, with the center of the L pushing toward the lake and the legs extending out toward the sides of the canyon. The middle of the L bore the greatest amount of pressure from the water of the lake. Vahid and Al-Musawi directed the men to carry the equipment and explosives to the middle of the dam, right at the deepest part of the L. They looked over both sides of the dam to make sure they were in the right place. As the top of the dam was only about twenty feet wide, they carefully piled the equipment on the dam in an organized fashion so that they could easily access the different things from either side of center.

While at the MC Produce warehouse the men were trained in rappelling techniques. Al-Musawi had directed them to construct a makeshift wall about sixteen feet high inside the twenty-eight-foot warehouse. They learned how to get into a rappelling harness, how to use a carabiner and a rescue figure eight, how to lean back over the edge in order to walk backward down the wall, and how to tie the correct knots for securing the ropes. They were also taught how to configure the rope around the extra tabs on the rescue figure eight to lock the rope in place. This prevented any sliding so that they could hang freely without having to use their hands to hold their position. That technique would now be used to help them sit at a designated spot on the rope and hold a shaped charge against the face of the dam. By the time the men had finished their training at the warehouse they were all very comfortable with the basics of rappelling.

Vahid directed them to lower three blue rappelling ropes over the downstream side of the dam and tie them securely to the poles on the upstream side. There were light poles built into the top of the dam about every forty or fifty feet on both sides of its over 700-foot length. They would use the poles on the upstream side to secure their rope, giving them ample room to link into the rope and go over the downstream side of the dam. Vahid pulled two more ropes from the pile, one red and one yellow. He and Al-Musawi had thought this through very thoroughly.

Vahid instructed one man to tie the red rope to the light pole just north of the three blue ropes and another man to secure the yellow rope twelve poles further north. The free end of the red rope was thrown over the side but the free end of the yellow rope was to be secured to Vahid's climbing gear. The blue ropes were 150 feet long, while the red rope was twice that length. Finally, Vahid directed one man to tie a 102-foot-long length of paracord to a pole on the downstream side of the dam and throw it over the side. It would designate the location where they would initiate the first blast. The blue ropes would allow all the suicide bombers to safely lower themselves 100 feet down the face of the dam. Vahid would be on the red rope, its extended length allowing him to help each man place his charge correctly and then pull himself up and out of the way of the explosions using the 400-foot yellow rope to do so.

When Vahid was ready he instructed three suicide bombers to rappel down to the end of the paracord; the middle man would be slightly higher, achieving the triangular configuration that would allow the explosives to be most effective. Clipped to each bomber's rappelling harness by a carabiner was a shaped charge with detonating wire coiled around and taped to the side of it. Vahid rappelled down with the men and when they were all in position he started giving detailed instructions.

With their ropes secured on the rescue figure eights so they wouldn't descend any further, the men listened to Vahid explain where they had to hold the shaped charges with the spindly wires touching the dam. Vahid used a thick Sharpie marker to make an X where each charge should go. The result was that all three shaped charges were about two feet from the concrete surface of the dam and about six feet from each other. Each man then carefully untaped the coiled wire from his cone and handed the end to Vahid. He tied them together and hooked the knot to his rappelling harness with a carabiner. He told the men he would let them know when he was ready.

Vahid pulled himself along the yellow rope until he was higher on the dam and a good way to the north of the location of the three bombers. He connected the wires to his detonating device and then yelled back at the three men to tell them he was ready. A chorus of "Allahu Akbar!" sounded and Vahid pushed the button. There was a terrific blast and a flash of light. Dust and smoke flew, and rubble tumbled down the face of the dam. The resulting holes were six feet deep and about the same distance across, joining each other into one crater. The three suicide bombers were disintegrated by the force of the blast. Three men at the top of the dam took care of the damaged ropes, cutting each one to sever it, allowing the remaining length of the ropes to lazily drop to the base of the dam. Even as they did so, more men had already tied off three new rappelling ropes and as soon as the first ropes dropped, the next set of bombers went over the side.

Vahid rappelled over and down to the small crater caused by the first explosion and met the next three bombers as they descended with three new shaped charges with their spindly wire legs. Vahid used his Sharpie marker and made three more marks for the men, positioning them slightly back from the edge of the crater. Again he strung the wires and pulled himself away on the yellow rope. He called out that he was ready, and the three fanatics shouted "Allahu Akbar!" and Vahid detonated the bombs. It took about four minutes between explosions.

The steady process continued three bombers at a time, although the going got slower as Vahid had to crawl into the growing crater and clip off rebar with the explosive cord he carried. He also had to take more time to determine the best locations to place the cones. On occasion, a large piece wouldn't come out cleanly and that would be the location of the next blast.

Al-Musawi was watching over the side of the dam, and after a few rounds he could no longer see the bombers as they crawled into the ever-widening and deepening crater in the face of Roosevelt Dam. As the crater got deeper into the dam Al-Musawi got more excited. His plan was working. He was anxious to reach that magic number of eighty feet into the dam, hoping that the remaining twenty feet would fail to hold back the water.

*   *   *

Before sunrise Ebenezer Hamilton and Ignacio Flores were driving near the east end of the Apache Trail, listening to music on their CD player. They had camped for the night in a canyon south of the Salt River and its series of lakes. They had varmint called right at shooting light in another canyon but hadn't gotten a single shot at anything. They were now headed to the foothills and mountains east of Roosevelt Lake to do more varmint calling.

As they drove they listened to John Denver singing about Rocky Mountains, country roads, feather beds, and sunshine. They were singing along and reminiscing about the old days when they were teenagers, listening to John Denver's top hits when they were first released on the radio. The men still enjoyed the folk singer's music even now that they were in their late fifties.

Ebenezer and Ignacio had become best friends in High School. One day in geography class the teacher was discussing the ebb and flow of

299

the tides when a quick-witted classmate referred to Ebenezer and Ignacio as Eb and Flo. The name stuck and they were Eb and Flo after that, even when they became adults. They lived close to each other and had jobs that allowed them to hunt and fish frequently. Their wives had no choice but to become best friends as well, and when Eb and Flo went camping Melissa Hamilton and Alexis Flores would spend time together. Their families would often join Eb and Flo on their adventures, and to their children and grandchildren they were Grandpa Eb and Grandpa Flo.

As Eb and Flo drove east on the Apache Trail just after daybreak on that Saturday morning in February they decided they would take advantage of the restroom facilities at the rest area in Alchesay Canyon.

As they came out of the restroom they heard a very loud explosion coming from the direction of Roosevelt Dam. They figured there was probably some construction going on and walked down the path to an area by the signs where they could see the dam. They were quite a distance from the structure and it was just after daybreak so they couldn't see perfectly what was happening, but they noticed what looked like some workers rappelling down the face of the dam. To their surprise, as they watched, the men stopped on their ropes and then there was a second large explosion. It looked like the construction workers were blown up in the blast. Eb and Flo stood there gawking and then started talking excitedly to each other trying to make sense of it.

Shortly after the second explosion three more workers rappelled down the face of the dam and then after a few minutes a third explosion occurred, seeming to blow up those workers also. Eb and Flo were confused and kept debating what was going on. They finally decided they needed to get closer; this looked very strange and couldn't possibly be what it seemed like. They ran to Flo's truck to go up the highway but they could see as they got near to the truck that there were a few cars stopped on the road just past the parking lot. The cars were stopped far enough away so that the people in the cars could not see the dam.

Eb and Flo had not gone far before they too were stopped in the short line of traffic, along with the few other cars that were out and about that morning. Flo pulled to the side of the road to get off the pavement and turned off the truck. As he jumped out he said, "Come on!" Eb climbed out of the truck but he was grumbling about the fact that Flo had parked too close to the brush at the side of the road and a small mesquite tree with its thorns was catching on his clothes and scratching his arms. Finally, Eb won the battle with the mesquite tree and ran to catch up with

Flo who was already running slowly along next to the line of cars. Both were huffing and puffing because of their age and because the road ran at a fairly steep grade uphill. As they ran they heard a fourth explosion.

When they got to the front of the line of cars, two police officers were standing in the road with military-style weapons. The guns looked like AR-15s but were probably M16s or something because they looked more like law enforcement or military firearms.

Eb said, "What's going on?"

One officer said, "Construction."

Flo said, "Can we go see?"

The officer held his gun across his body as if holding a barricade and said, "No one to pass! Construction!"

Eb and Flo just stood and stared. Then Flo grabbed Eb's arm and pulled him back along the line of cars heading toward their truck.

Eb said, "What's going on?"

"That's not a cop. And construction people carry a stop sign, not an M16." Flo answered.

Eb asked, "Are you sure?"

Flo replied, "Eb. Get a clue! These are terrorists. I'm getting my gun."

A fifth explosion split the air.

Flo continued, "Construction doesn't happen like this. After what's been going on this week I'm sure these are terrorists. They're trying to blow up Roosevelt Dam. I'm shooting first and asking questions later."

"Flo, come on! You don't just start shooting at police officers." Eb tried to reason with his friend.

Flo quickly raised the camper shell hatch and lowered the tailgate, grabbing his Rock River AR-15 .308 out of the back of the truck. "Eb, have you ever seen a police officer at a construction site with an AR-15 or an M16 or whatever that was? And his uniform was about two sizes too big. What cop wears a uniform that is oversized? And he wasn't wearing a Kevlar vest—when have you seen a cop these days without a bullet-proof vest? And he couldn't even talk right. How many words did he say? In fact, nobody who has graduated from any police academy in America would say 'no one to pass.' And the second one didn't even talk at all; they just kept looking at each other like they didn't know what to do. What the heck do you think is going on? Those aren't police officers and this isn't construction; this is a terrorist attack!"

301

By now Flo had his gun ready. He said, "Eb, am I going shooting alone or are you coming with me?"

A sixth explosion interrupted their conversation.

Eb finally said, "OK!" And then added, "Then you better have every magazine filled." Even as he said it he saw that Flo was jamming .308 shells into a thirty-round magazine.

As Eb grabbed his Bushmaster AR-15 .223, he said, "It's a good thing I stay busy reloading while you drive. It makes it faster for me to get ready." He picked up four mags of his own.

Flo turned around and started walking up the passenger side of the line of cars, brushing bushes away from his face with his free hand in places where they hung out close to the roadway. Fortunately, none of the other cars had pulled clear off the road as he had done. He had four thirty-round magazines tucked in various pockets of his pants. Eb was right behind him, similarly armed. Flo and Eb crouched as they hurried past the gaps between cars, hoping the "police officers" wouldn't see them. Several people in the cars gasped as they went by.

As they passed an SUV a man jumped out, saying, "I see it the way you guys are seeing it. I'll help where I can. My name's Bruce."

Explosion number seven split the air.

*   *   *

Alan and his team of FBI agents accompanied by several cars from Sheriff Concepcion's team sped as fast as they could toward Roosevelt Dam. They radioed ahead to the Sheriff's Department substation at Roosevelt. The secretary who answered, Erlinda, said the three deputies who were on site had already headed toward the dam as soon as they heard the gunfire. The sheriff's station in Roosevelt was not far from the dam and they had been gone for a while. She could not reach them on the radio although she had tried several times. Erlinda also told Alan and Sheriff Concepcion that there were explosions going off about every five or six minutes over by the dam but they didn't know the cause yet.

They drove as fast as they dared on the winding road from Globe to the dam, with the deputies in the lead; sirens wailing and lights flashing. Luckily there wasn't too much traffic so early in the morning. On a couple of straight stretches where the deputies knew the road their speeds topped well over 100 miles per hour. They had agreed to turn off the sirens when they got close enough so the noise would not alert the terrorists of their presence.

At one point along the way, Ezzie, who was sitting in the back seat on the passenger side, exclaimed, "Alan, you're bleeding!"

He reached up and touched his right temple. He had noticed that it hurt a little but hadn't paid much attention in the commotion to leave the diner and head toward Roosevelt Dam. When he drew his hand back, there was blood on his finger.

Ezzie leaned closer and said, "I think you have a piece of glass stuck in the side of your face. Hold still."

Ezzie turned to the back of the Suburban and rummaged through some of the bags. With a few one-handed tugs on a zipper she exposed a first aid kit and wrestled it from the bag. She placed it in her lap and pulled out some surgical gloves, quickly putting them on. With a pair of tweezers from the kit she carefully pulled a small shard of glass from the wound on the side of Alan's face. The task was not easy with all the turning and jerking from the Tahoe as they drove quickly on the winding highway.

Ezzie dug deeper into the first aid kit and then smiled, holding up a bright pink adhesive bandage. She cried out "Aha! Hello Kitty! Must have been one I was saving for my little Juanita."

Alan moaned and said, "You're not putting that thing on me!"

She silenced him with some rapid-fire Spanish. Then in English she added, "Oh hush! It will be fine and no one will care." As gently as she could in the speeding car she cleaned the wound with an alcohol wipe and then she squeezed out a small dab of antibacterial ointment onto the bright pink bandage and applied it to the side of Alan's head. He was just about to complain some more but right then they arrived at the junction near the dam and the bridge.

There were half a dozen cars backed up along the road. With their lights flashing, they started up the wrong side of the road toward the dam.

Suddenly Alan jumped on the radio, "Sheriff, wait! Stop immediately!!"

The lead cars quickly stopped. Alan came back on the radio, "We should go first. Our cars are armored."

The Sheriff's voice answered, "Good idea. Go!"

The Suburban and the Tahoe sped around to the left of the county cars, throwing gravel as their tires spun in the dirt on the left shoulder of the road.

As they passed the cars sitting in the right lane they heard an explosion even with their windows up. They came around the last corner and saw two Pinal County Sheriff's Office cars sitting on the edge of the road. The two vehicles were turned at an angle and full of holes. Immediately gunfire erupted and bullets started hitting the front windows of both of the federal vehicles. They jammed the cars into reverse and started backing up, but one of the sheriff's cars behind them was also struck by the gunfire and appeared to be incapacitated. They were stuck.

They debated jumping out, but it was obvious that the terrorists were shooting from a high vantage point. Exiting the vehicles would take careful strategic planning and they would be out in the open for a few seconds. Given the fact that the terrorists were shooting automatic weapons, even brief exposure was suicide.

They turned the cars sideways, the passenger side facing the terrorists, but the barrage of automatic gunfire was pounding them. Even with the armoring of the car, they were not completely safe because the windows would not last long. The bullet-proofing was designed to absorb a few moments of gunfire and give them a chance to escape, but in their current situation they could not escape and the barrage of bullets was unrelenting. They felt they would be relatively safe out of the Suburban and Tahoe on the driver's side, but they couldn't peek around the sides or the top to return fire without being at great risk.

While the terrorists continued the onslaught one of the sheriff's deputies managed to crouch low around his bumper and shoot the two terrorists standing in the roadway, but by then all the cars were immobile and no one could drive up the road. Sheriff Concepcion had been hit in the side by a bullet and was cut from flying glass but he sank to the floorboard of the patrol car and said over the radio that he'd be OK.

The law enforcement officers were in a serious bind and didn't have any way out as far as they could see. If they had air support or could lob a grenade up onto the rocks above them where the terrorists were, they could turn the tables, but neither of those options were available right then. They were pinned down and couldn't remain there for long; the danger was becoming more severe every minute.

Another powerful explosion boomed even above the noise of the gunfire.

47 The Pirate and the Queen

Jack Yeager owned and operated the Superstition Queen on Canyon Lake. It was a paddlewheel riverboat like you would see on the Mississippi River or would read about in a Mark Twain novel, but it wasn't really a steamboat. This one was modernized and modified and the 100-foot boat was powered by twin 225 horsepower diesel engines made by the John Deere company. The paddlewheel at the rear of the boat did not propel the boat but was there churning the water for nostalgic effect. Jack had owned and operated the Superstition Queen on Canyon Lake for nineteen years.

The Superstition Mountains were just south of Canyon Lake and the name "Superstition" was included in many business names on the east side of the Phoenix metropolitan area. The name came from the superstitions of local Native Americans who thought the mountain was haunted. The mystique surrounding the area grew with the accounts of an old German prospector named Jacob Waltz who reportedly discovered gold there in the 1860s, but after his death the mine was never found. The "Legend of the Lost Dutchman's Gold Mine" seemed to point even further back to the 1600s when Spanish explorers or Apache warriors or several others stashed or found or fought over hidden gold. Whatever the case, the legends and stories of the Superstition Mountain remained in the local culture, and Jack Yeager chose that name for his beautiful riverboat.

Business for the Superstition Queen had some ups and downs, but for the most part, Jack stayed busy year-round. One amenity on the boat was air conditioning, which was an absolute must in the summer when temperatures on the lake could reach 110 or sometimes even 115 degrees Fahrenheit.

While at work, he went by Captain Jack, which in recent years always led to the comment, "Captain Jack Sparrow." He didn't mind the fame that wasn't really his, and his customers loved the fun of sailing with a famous pirate. Captain Jack Yeager had tried to perfect his pirate accent and used it frequently when talking over the intercom to the passengers. He *loved* his job.

The main attraction on the Superstition Queen was an afternoon sightseeing cruise around Canyon Lake and up the channel toward Apache Lake. The channel ranged from about fifty to 100 yards wide and several miles long and had 200-foot-high sheer rock walls on both sides for much of the way. Many other boats went up and down the channel, fishing and water skiing, which added to the sights worth seeing. The river channel had a depth of about 100 feet, while Canyon Lake was twice that deep in the middle. The main part of the lake was about a mile across.

On a slow-moving riverboat it took about an hour to go up the channel and another hour to return. Captain Jack never took the Queen clear up to Horse Mesa Dam, which formed Apache Lake upstream from Canyon Lake, because the channel became too narrow to turn the Queen back around.

The two-hour round-trip gave ample time for Captain Jack to point out the rock formations, petrified tree trunks in the side of the canyon walls, and different animals and birds. Captain Jack especially liked to point out the desert bighorn sheep that climbed along the cliffs in the canyon feeding on the sparse vegetation that grew out of the cracks in the rocks and in pockets of gravel up along the rugged mountains on both sides of the canyon.

The second main attraction on the Queen was a twilight dinner cruise, complete with a full course menu. The twilight cruise was not designed for sightseeing but was more of a romantic dinner and party atmosphere. Passengers could gaze at the stars and the moon while they visited and lounged on the boat or they could dance to the music that was played over the Queen's sound system.

The mountains around Saguaro, Canyon, and Apache Lakes were formed from lava flows ages ago that had cooled and then eroded into rugged cliffs, peaks, and canyons. The bare stone of the cliffs was mostly reddish-brown with some yellowish colors. There were many caves and openings caused by bubbles or erosion of softer stone over the years. In some places soil had built up and there were sparse desert trees, bushes, and cacti growing. In other places it was just bare rock, with an occasional bush or cactus precariously clinging to the side or top of a cliff. Where occasional rainwater would run the sand was coarse and bleached white by the sun.

One interesting attraction of Canyon Lake was a rock formation on the northeast edge of the main body of the lake. Visitors could see where a landslide sometime in the past had occurred, causing the rock face to break away from the main cliff and tumble down right to the water's edge. Based on the colors of the surrounding rocks the rock slide appeared to have happened within the last five or ten years. However, it was actually documented as having occurred in 1935.

The Superstition Queen dinner cruise was ridden mostly by couples or small groups who would make reservations and come for the evening, mingling with others just as if they had gone to a restaurant. However, sometimes larger groups rode the Queen, making up sometimes half or more of the 200 passengers that the boat could accommodate. Some businesses reserved the Queen for their company parties, and other groups reserved it for weddings, family parties, and celebrations of different kinds.

On that Saturday morning in February Captain Jack was pleased to have a birdwatching group on board. They made it an annual event to ride the Queen early in the morning, spending most of the day going around the lake and up the channel using binoculars and spotting scopes to view the different birds they could see up and down the canyon. They especially enjoyed seeing bald eagles that nested at nearby rivers and would occasionally come hunting fish in Canyon Lake.

The plan of the birdwatchers was to gather and board the boat before sunrise so as to be on the water just as it started getting light. However, on that morning three of the key leaders of the organization who were carpooling together had had a flat tire down the road a few miles. The owner of the disabled vehicle insisted that his passengers go on ahead in another car while he changed the tire but he made them promise to not leave him behind. By the time he arrived at the Queen the sun had been up for a while. No one was too worried about his being late because breakfast was being served: breakfast burritos with pico de gallo, biscuits and gravy, sausage, juice, fruit, and all the items and treats that would go with a fun breakfast.

Once the latecomer arrived they launched quickly and Captain Jack's voice came over the loudspeaker, "Avast, ye landlubbers. Welcome to the Superstition Queen and Aaaahrrr-izona's Canyon Lake. I'm glad you're here for a haaaahrrrrrrty breakfast. I'll be needin a few more slaves . . . I mean deckhands . . . so in case ye don't eat enough or don't have a good time today, you'll get the great pleasure of joinin' my crew on a permanent basis. Last year when we had your group out here, we ended up with a few extra crew members and a few more caaaaahrrrrrrrs left to rust in the paaaaaarking lot." Judging by the smiles and sometimes laughter from around the boat the passengers loved it!

The plan for the morning was to go up and down the channel several times to give plenty of opportunity to look for the different birds that could be seen on the cliffs and at the water's edge.

As they moved gently across the main body of the lake and reached the middle, the morning sun was lighting up the rugged mountains west of the lake while the mountains on the east side of the lake were still partially covered in shadow. Suddenly a fighter jet blasted past them, literally right over their heads. It had come very low from the west, right over the top of Mormon Flat Dam which creates Canyon Lake. Anyone with a good arm could have probably thrown a baseball high enough to hit the jet as it blew past them just overhead. The jet was going so fast that the sound came a split second after the jet had already thundered over their heads, shattering the morning stillness with jet blast.

A second jet was following some distance behind the first and it also blew over their heads with a roar. Both jets shot out to the east, rising above the rugged reddish-brown cliffs and mountains near Canyon Lake. The jets then turned south and zoomed over Tortilla Flat, the tiny clapboard tourist spot at the southeast edge of the lake. The people on the Superstition Queen watched in awe as the first jet banked, twisted, turned, and suddenly shot up into the sky, executing a jagged, clumsy corkscrew motion as it rose into the air. The second jet remained behind and tried to copy the maneuvers of the leading jet but the second jet was flying much more smoothly.

Captain Jack picked up the intercom mic and interspersed with a little pirate talk said, "Well, mateys, looks like we've got a bit of a show this mornin'. As you all know, our good friend and bird lover, Bob McCasland, who flies F-16s out of Luke Aaaaaahrrrrr Force Base, couldn't be here this mornin' because he had to work. Well, it looks like Major Bob brought work home, or maybe more accurately he brought work to the Queen. Give him a wave if he comes back over."

By this time, the first jet had banked, inverted, and was flying upside down as it turned and started back toward the lake a second time, heading back toward the riverboat. The second jet continued to play follow the leader at a distance. Every eye on the Queen was glued to this spectacular airshow except for Captain Jack's. He had to occasionally look away in order to steer the boat. The two jets maneuvered off to the south end of the lake and then started turning as if they would be coming back around.

Suddenly another airplane entered the scene. A small, but nice-looking blue and white private plane flew across the main body of the lake. The early morning sun glistened on its sleek fuselage. It wasn't too far above the top of Mormon Flat Dam and was flying almost as low as the Air Force jets. It crossed the lake and then barely cleared the cliffs as it flew on past and headed further east. There was heavy black smoke trailing behind its right engine and it made a whining sound that didn't sound normal.

This spontaneous airshow was full of variety.

As the first jet came back to the lake from the south it flipped upright and roared across the lake in front of the Queen, flying right into the mouth of the canyon itself. It was flying so close to the surface of the lake that the jet blast was blowing a rooster tail of water up behind it. The sight was spectacular as the spray blew into the air behind the screaming jet. The trail of the rooster tail followed behind the jet as it skimmed the water at a few hundred miles per hour. The spectators couldn't tell how fast the jet was going; they just knew it was fast.

Captain Jack thought to himself, *Darn it, Bob, you're scaring the birds! And I don't know what you are doing flying up the channel, because you're going to get yourself killed!*

While the first jet went into the canyon the second jet rose a bit and stayed above the canyon, not playing follow the leader anymore. The first jet had disappeared from the view of the people on the Superstition Queen as it went into the canyon but the second jet was still visible above the cliffs for a few more seconds.

Suddenly, they heard a hissing noise and a missile detached itself from under the wing of the second jet, screaming off into the canyon and trailing white smoke as its burst of speed out-distanced the aircraft from where it had just launched.

Captain Jack picked up the mic and spoke to his passengers. This time he forgot all about a pirate accent: "Uh . . . maybe that wasn't just for show. I have a feeling something more serious is going on here, folks. I don't think they would be shooting expensive missiles if it were just play. If our friend, Bob McCasland, is involved then I would say he needs our thoughts and prayers."

As McCasland got to Canyon Lake he saw the Superstition Queen right in the middle of it. He continued to twist and turn and jockey his jet around in the sky, attempting to keep Andrus from gaining any advantage while trying to position himself for the execution of his plan. He managed to work his way around so as to fly right into the mouth of the canyon and go up the channel. He had been up this canyon on a boat many times and knew the turns and configuration of the path the river took through it.

Just before McCasland entered the canyon the stolen King Air laboriously flew low over the lake in front of him but McCasland couldn't get a shot at it because he was still maneuvering his Viper. He chastised himself because if he had realized the stolen plane was coming he would have arranged to divert at the last second to shoot it down. To do so would likely have gotten him shot down by Andrus but the sacrifice would likely have been worth it because the stolen plane threatened hundreds or thousands of lives, and shooting down that plane was the mission given to him by his commanding officer.

Not far into the canyon there was a sharp turn to the right and then an equally sharp turn back to the left, followed by a fairly straight stretch for about 200 yards. Because of his jet's damaged tail, however, he knew he couldn't make that right turn; but that was part of his plan.

As he entered the canyon and approached that right turn he saw the small hill in the bend of the lake channel. It had a beach, some picnic tables, and a Forest Service restroom on it. It had been developed for campers and picnickers.

Instead of turning to the right, McCasland flew straight ahead and rose up over the hill. The rooster tail of spray behind him suddenly died as he lifted away from the water. There was a tent on the beach and a guy was standing at the shore, fishing. As McCasland blasted over the top of the hill he wondered if there was anyone still inside the tent who just got the surprise of their life as a screaming fighter jet flew just a few feet above them.

Pilots trained for these moments and spent countless hours in the simulator and in the jets themselves practicing maneuvers over and over. The goal was to do them so many times that they became reflex and didn't require a thought process. At high speed and in closed-in areas like a canyon everything happened in split seconds and there was no margin for error.

As McCasland guided his F-16 up over the hill, the maneuver put him back up out of the channel and at approximately the same elevation as Andrus who was still flying slightly above the canyon. Suddenly a growl from a speaker in McCasland's flight helmet warned him that Andrus had just obtained radar lock. This was the riskiest part of his plan but it was what he had anticipated. McCasland knew that Andrus could see the twists and turns in the canyon ahead and before McCasland dropped back down near the water level on the other side of the hill he had made himself an easy target.

Andrus did just what McCasland hoped he would do, immediately getting radar lock and firing his air-to-air missile, or AMRAAM, just as McCasland rose above the hill. That gave McCasland a very short distance of straight flight, and he hoped he was far enough ahead of Andrus that he could outmaneuver the AMRAAM as it came speeding toward him. The missile was flying faster than the jet and it was programmed to detonate when it got within so many feet of the F-16. McCasland had only a few seconds for his next maneuver.

Just at the end of the straight stretch in the canyon the main channel turned slightly to the right, but there was a small, short canyon that came into the main channel from the left, forming a V point in the cliff. At the last second and with the missile now upon him, McCasland jerked up and to the left of the V made by the junction of the two canyons.

The missile was almost close enough to detonate but it took a few seconds for its radar and programming to change its course to follow McCasland's abrupt turn. It didn't change course as quickly as McCasland had, and instead smacked right into the point of the V shape of the rocky cliff and exploded in a ball of flame. It blew pieces of the cliff sky high. A cloud of dust rolled outward into the air and pieces of rubble flew up and fell into the water below, but by then McCasland was gone.

As he came shooting out of the canyon to the left, curling up sharply and coming around back over the main channel of the lake, he saw exactly what he wanted to see. There was Andrus dead ahead in the near distance. McCasland had expected Andrus to be looking for pieces of the jet as it exploded and smashed into the cliffs. He also expected Andrus to follow the main channel of the canyon as it turned slightly to the right.

With McCasland partially hidden by the flame and dust from the missile explosion, he had come up and around from the left and was now flying behind the other jet.

Andrus was caught by surprise but was still a seasoned pilot, and had obviously noticed McCasland's odd flight patterns. He jerked to the right, taking him back toward the south end of the lake. McCasland corkscrewed, inverted, and turned to follow. What he couldn't do down close to the water and next to the towering cliffs he could now do with room to move. He stayed right behind Andrus.

*   *   *

All eyes on the Superstition Queen, including Captain Jack's, were now watching this wonderful, and yet terrible, airshow taking place right in front of them. Two U.S. planes were chasing each other in an apparent fight to the death and the spectators couldn't tell who was the good guy and who was the bad guy. Actually, it could have been women flying for all they knew; maybe it wasn't Bob McCasland at all.

Captain Jack had stopped the motors and the steamboat was drifting lazily on the smooth blue lake. The reflection of the sky in the water was serene and peaceful but what was happening in the sky above them was incredibly loud, extremely fast, and very violent.

The people on the Queen had heard the missile blast in the canyon and many of them gasped and started praying, while others were just hoping for good to prevail. Listening hard to determine the location of the jets, someone shouted "There!" pointing into the sky as the planes came into view and screamed off to the south. Then the jets turned and came back in the direction of the Queen.

After flying south for a few seconds, Andrus turned hard right again, this time taking him back toward the lake. McCasland corkscrewed and followed Andrus closely, still upside down. McCasland worried that Andrus would shoot at the Queen as a distraction, thereby continuing the terrorism and slaughtering more civilians.

The hours and hours of practicing these strange moves paid off. As Andrus zoomed toward the lake he crossed McCasland's target point and the major was ready. Still upside down, McCasland pulled the trigger on his control stick to fire his twenty-millimeter Gatling cannon.

The throaty *BRRRRRRRRRRP* from the cannon which was built into the side of the plane was a welcome sound to McCasland as he fired. He had 500 rounds to work with and he fired about eighty rounds in less than a second. The twenty-millimeter bullets raced toward Andrus' F-16 as it approached the south edge of Canyon Lake. McCasland was careful to follow through with his aim, keeping his jet pointed right at Andrus' jet as the shots were firing and even after they cleared the end of the Gatling gun barrels.

The HEI, or High-Explosive Incendiary bullets, were designed to burst into flame on impact and generate intense heat, sometimes even 1,000 degrees. The bullets fired by McCasland caught Andrus' jet just before it reached the south edge of the lake. The bullets pierced the fuselage of the jet, igniting and burning and fusing any metal they contacted. They tore into the main body of the jet triggering fire throughout the cockpit and the engine and igniting the fuel. The intense heat killed Andrus quickly and at the same time, the controls and computers of the plane were destroyed, making it impossible to control even if Andrus had survived. Andrus didn't get the opportunity to fire at the Superstition Queen.

No longer able to maintain controlled flight, the F-16 started a slow, fiery spin toward the lake, still going 650 miles per hour. The jet spiraled down and splattered right into the 1935 rockslide on the northeast edge of the lake, scattering burning fuel and pieces of hot metal across the mountainside and into the water. The old attraction would now be a new attraction of a different kind.

The people on the Queen watched, mesmerized, as the plane plowed into the mountainside not 200 yards away from them. Some of them had pulled out their smartphones and caught it all on video, which would be posted on social media, going viral within minutes.

The second jet flipped right-side-up and roared over their heads and sailed above the cliffs. It turned left in a tight circle just above Mormon Flat Dam and flew straight over the top of the Queen again. It wagged its wings at the boat as it flew overhead and then sped off upriver toward Roosevelt Lake.

Captain Jack suddenly let out a huge sigh. He realized that at some point he had begun to hold his breath but when the jet wagged its wings instead of firing at the Queen, he was confident that Bob McCasland was the victor.

Captain Jack was overcome with relief as he fell back into his captain's chair and picked up the mic. He switched back to a gravely pirate voice to ease the tension. "Well ya lily-livered landlubbers. It

313

appears that our friend, Major Bob McCasland, came out the victor. I'm sure we will hear something on the news later but we sure got a display from the Aaaahrrrrr Force this mornin'. We didn't get to watch little birds but we had a show from three big metal birds that was pure pirate treasure. What a great day on Canyon Lake aboard the Superstition Queen in beautiful Aaahrrr-izona!"

Little did they know that the bird that got away was the most dangerous of the three.

*   *   *

Burp breathed a sigh of relief as Smoke's Viper lost control and crashed into the mountainside. He swooped out over the lake and wagged his wings at the Superstition Queen, then headed toward Roosevelt Lake, hoping to get there before the shooting was over. He had heard Scrum and DeeDee on the radio and knew they were very capable of doing what needed to be done but he wanted a piece of the action.

Suddenly his fuel indicator sounded and he looked down at a red flashing light on his control panel. Dang! He wouldn't have enough fuel to get to Roosevelt and then back. He didn't want to crash a nineteen-million-dollar aircraft because he was stupid enough to run out of fuel. He was disappointed but he flipped on his mic and asked for the location of the refueling tanker. The reply he got assured him it was nearby, back toward the city. He turned slowly to the right and headed toward the tanker.

McCasland smiled to himself and shook his head but there was a mix of pain. He was relieved to be going safely home. At the same time he was sad that Andrus had defected and become a traitor to his country. McCasland was also sorry to have killed a former friend and destroyed an expensive jet that had been paid for by the American taxpayers. At the same time, McCasland had the exhilaration of a successful dogfight in a marvelous aircraft. The life of a fighter pilot could be somewhat boring at times but could also be very exciting, and today had proven an emotional roller coaster.

McCasland looked up ahead and got a visual on the air tanker. As he started to maneuver into position to be refueled he smiled again. The Luke pilots loved those Copperheads. Without them the Vipers would be limited in their range and effectiveness. McCasland acknowledged to himself that the heroes in support roles never got all the credit and glory they deserved.

48 Teenagers Pitch In

Early Saturday morning Landon and Brandon Morgan were driving from their home near Punkin Center, Arizona, a few miles north of Roosevelt Lake. They worked at the PJ Ranch where their parents, Patrick and Jessica, had started raising horses—and sons—years before. Of course, with the last name of Morgan, Patrick couldn't help but feel the need to raise Morgan horses. In fact, Patrick Morgan was a descendant of Justin Morgan, the founder of the fine breed of horses that began back in the late 1800s.

Landon and Brandon were twins and had just turned eighteen. Their hard work and many days in the sun had given both of them rich suntans and bleach-blond hair. They were young and muscular and anywhere they went they turned female heads of all ages. They had many horses on their ranch, but one in particular had a ruddy brown coat and white main, like the boys. They named him Sandon and their mom called all three of them triplets.

Landon and Brandon were headed to their Aunt Faye's Marina and RV Park down at Apache Lake. She had called Jessica on the landline Friday morning and said that she was almost out of propane. Jessica sent the boys up to Rye on Friday afternoon and they filled all the five-gallon tanks of propane they could fit in the back of the pickup, and then had planned to deliver them early Saturday morning. It was a routine they had done many times and Aunt Faye always rewarded them with some homemade cinnamon rolls.

As Landon and Brandon started across Roosevelt Lake Bridge on Saturday morning just about daybreak they heard a heavy explosion but couldn't tell where the sound was coming from. They wondered if there was construction somewhere nearby.

When they came off the bridge and turned west on Apache Trail they hadn't gone far before they had to stop behind two cars that were sitting in the lane ahead of them. Landon, who always drove, leaned out his window and could see that there was a police officer in the road ahead of them stopping traffic.

Another explosion split the air.

The boys sat and waited. Construction delays usually didn't last long. However, they soon noticed four or five guys on top of the thumb of rock on the north edge of the highway. They had AK-47s, which the boys recognized because they owned one and had shot it many times. They continued to sit in their truck, not yet knowing what to do but certainly not comfortable with the situation. As of yet, the terrorists were not shooting at any of the stopped cars so the boys were unsure if they should just wait, or turn around, or what. They figured if they jumped out and tried to run, the guys on top of the rock would just gun them down, so since they weren't being shot at currently they would try to lay low and just wait.

Brandon texted their mom and dad. There was so much noise from the explosions that he wasn't sure they could carry on a conversation. Besides, he figured that his mom would go crazy with worry to hear explosions near her boys. Brandon told his parents that there was some kind of terrorist activity at the dam, but they couldn't tell yet what was going on. Landon told him to add that they were both fine, knowing their mom would worry.

After about two minutes they heard sirens and saw two sheriff's department cars come racing up the eastbound lane of the highway. Landon and Brandon were worried about what would happen and then their fears were realized as the terrorists with their guns stood up on the rock and filled the cars full of holes. The people in the cars ahead of them were screaming and crying. The Morgan twins were scared but remained in their truck.

After about five more minutes they heard another huge explosion. They wondered what it was. Maybe the terrorists were doing something to the road or the dam. They couldn't see any activity on the bridge behind them. Every four or five minutes they heard another explosion.

After about ten more minutes they saw more flashing lights. They could see other law enforcement cars coming up the road. They both grimaced and said, "Oh, no!" since they knew what had happened to the previous cars. However, the cars that came up the road were black, a Suburban and a Tahoe, and when the terrorists started shooting, the cars were still functional.

"Bulletproof!" They both exclaimed together, and the black cars maneuvered a bit and then stopped.

However, the gunfire didn't stop. The terrorists kept shooting at the law enforcement vehicles, although the shots had slowed a bit. It seemed like the terrorists intended to just keep them there with enough fire going to ensure that those behind the cars couldn't return fire. The law enforcement personnel managed to shoot the two terrorists standing in the road but that didn't change the fact that they were still in a really bad spot.

Finally, Brandon said, "I have an idea. Let's throw a propane tank up there. If we can get it up on top of the rock with the gas turned on, maybe that will start a fire or maybe blow up or it might at least give our guys something to work with."

Landon replied "Great idea, but let's throw more than one. I'll be seen if I get out on this side. You climb out your side and quietly open the tailgate. Do you think you can get four tanks out? I'll holler if they see you. And I'll slide out your door when we're ready to run."

Brandon didn't reply but quietly opened the passenger door of the Tacoma. He stayed down behind the truck, snuck around to the back, and quietly and slowly opened the tailgate. He was exposed when he reached up to grab the tanks but it was only for a moment each time and he stayed low and remained undetected. The terrorists were totally focused on the law enforcement personnel and their vehicles. Before long Brandon had four propane tanks sitting by the passenger side rear tire.

By that time Landon had slid across the seat and also climbed quietly out of the truck. They both grabbed a tank in each hand. The five-gallon tanks were slightly larger than a basketball and weighed about twenty pounds each. The two boys had been bucking hay and working hard on a ranch for years, and twenty pounds in each hand wasn't much to them.

They would be exposed once they left the side of the truck but they grabbed the tanks and stayed down as much as they could as they ran along on the outside of the two cars ahead of them. Once they reached the base of the thumb of rock they wouldn't be in the line of fire from the terrorists but they would be exposed for about twenty or thirty feet before that point. They rested down behind the front of another car, and fortunately the driver was busy watching the highway or maybe praying because he didn't notice them.

They said "one . . . two . . . three" and took off. They had gone about ten feet when the terrorists saw the movement. By the time the terrorists could react and start firing, the shots ended up behind the running boys and soon the teenagers were safe under the overhang of the rock.

The thumb of rock was about fifty feet at its highest point but the face of the rock sloped a little since it was originally part of the mountain before the road was cut through next to it. The groove in the rock where the terrorists were crouching was only about eighteen to twenty feet up, but still back away from the edge. The bottom of the thumb of rock was straight up and down for about ten feet and the boys were completely protected as long as they stayed close to the rock.

Brandon said, "Just like throwing bales of hay into the loft back home." Landon knew exactly what he meant.

When they worked in their barn they had to stack the hay high in the loft. Together they would stand on the ground floor and grab a bale of hay, one on each side of the bale holding the bailing twine with both hands. They would swing the bale away from the loft, out and up in a full, circular arc, and then throw it above and behind them into the loft. It was almost like when two cousins would hold another cousin by the arms and legs and throw him headfirst into the pond at a family reunion. However, instead of letting go and launching their cousin out into the pond, Brandon and Landon continued the swing and launched the bale of hay high over their heads into the loft. When the bale landed flat on the boards of the loft above and behind them, it would be upside down and flipped end for end from its original position when they started their swing. The loft of the barn was ten feet high and a bale of hay weighed eighty to one hundred pounds, so it was no small feat. However, they were young and strong and they used the momentum of the swinging bale to launch it high into the loft. They had done it so many times that they had perfected their technique and they could usually get the bales neatly stacked right on top of each other, two bales high and six to eight bales wide, side by side and lined up almost perfectly.

At the base of the thumb of rock, they each grabbed one side of the propane tank, one hand on the handle and one hand on the bottom of the tank. Brandon said, "Hold your breath," and he opened the valve on the propane tank. They swung it out away from the cliff, once . . . twice . . . and then threw on the third time, just like in the hay barn, releasing first with the upper hand and pushing all the way through in a smooth motion with the lower hand. They had thrown hundreds of bales of hay that way and this time with a propane tank it was automatic and as smooth as if they had practiced with propane tanks many times. The tank, with gas hissing out of the wide-open valve, only weighed twenty pounds and it sailed an easy twenty-five feet into the air.

As the tank sailed up over the edge of the rock, one of the terrorists saw motion, whirled and started firing. The muzzle from his automatic AK-47 shot out a blast of flame about six to twelve inches with each shot. The tank sailed past the terrorist, barely missing him, and fell to the rock behind him, the flame from his muzzle blast igniting the propane gas.

A spout of flame came shooting about a foot out of the valve on the top of the tank as it clattered around and then came to rest among the terrorists. They jumped back, just in time to have a second hissing propane tank come arching up into the midst of them. The second tank rolled past the first and also ignited, coming to a stop with its spout of flame spurting at the duffle bag of ammo, which was half empty by now. The terrorists had stopped shooting at the FBI and were totally focused on the flames and danger literally at their feet. They were shouting at each other in their own language.

A third tank sailed up into the melee, bounced a couple of times, and settled next to the second tank, its gas igniting and spewing flame directly against the first tank.

About that time, Alan's team realized what was happening.

The fourth tank came floating up through the air and landed amidst the rest of the commotion. That tank did not ignite immediately but was filling the air with the rotten-egg smell of propane.

There was total chaos on the thumb of rock. The ammo that had a foot of flame heating it up started popping and exploding. The tank that had a flame right against it exploded. The fourth tank finally ignited and the invisible cloud of propane around it burst into a small mushroom cloud of flame with the sound of a soft but deep poof. Metal and gravel and flame were flying in all directions as they were blown from the point of each explosion.

The terrorists were screaming and jumping around, and at that moment Alan's team and the sheriff's deputies, who had watched it all from behind the vehicles, opened up with their rifles. The terrorists were jumping around in the middle of flame and explosions, totally focused on the propane tanks, and were quickly cut down by gunfire from the law enforcement officers. One or two propane tanks were still spouting flame and they lasted longer than the terrorists. All four terrorists were killed in a matter of seconds.

One of the agents hollered over, "Great thinking, guys!" and all the FBI and Sheriff's deputies turned and ran up the road toward the gap in the mountain, cautiously covering each other and following their usual assault protocol.

Landon and Brandon stood at the foot of the rock, laughing and giving each other high fives. Landon pulled out his phone and called his Mom, this time getting a good signal. "Mom, we're OK. We won't get to Aunt Faye's yet, but we'll be there in a while. We'll call you from there to explain. Don't worry about us." He hung up quickly before his mom could hear another explosion.

49 Let the Earth Shake

As they got to the second to last car in the line of vehicles stopped on Highway 88, Flo turned around to Eb and Bruce and said, "We can't put these cars and their passengers in the line of fire so let's jump out in front of the first car. If the terrorists shoot at us their angle of fire will be off to the side of the road in front of the car, rather than near the passengers."

Eb and Flo kept watching the "police officers" to see if they could see them, but they were preoccupied with things going on back up the road and toward the dam. The two friends crouched and paused briefly behind the first car in line, but just before they stepped out they heard what sounded like a battle from around the corner of the mountain by the thumb of rock. There was a lot of gunfire which continued in sporadic bursts for what seemed like forever. Then there were several explosions and then more shooting.

As they listened to the barrage from around the corner of the mountain, the fake police officers were talking rapidly with each other and then they turned and ran toward the gunfire. Either they were supposed to help out or they forgot to stay at their post.

Another explosion was heard from the area of the dam. It was the eighth one but by now everyone had actually lost count.

With Eb and Flo walking cautiously in front of Bruce the three men stepped out from behind the first car and went up the road past where the phony police officers had been. As they warily came around the corner of the mountain they saw an eighteen-wheeler parked near the wall above the end of the dam with several terrorists crouched behind the truck looking toward the east where the shooting had come from.

Eb and Flo's guns were already positioned to fire, and with the terrorists' attention elsewhere they were able to take them by surprise. The two friends opened fire and several of the terrorists collapsed, while another ran around the end of the truck to hide on the other side.

One more terrorist returned fire but the shots from his automatic weapon were just flung in their general direction. Eb and Flo both aimed, fired, and the man promptly dropped beside his companions.

About that time several FBI agents and sheriff's deputies came through the cut in the mountain, walking on the road with their guns ready. Eb yelled to them, "Watch out! There's one more behind the front of the truck." Just then, gunfire came from near the front of the semi. Dust burst up around the feet of the deputies but that was as close as it got. The law enforcement officers were quick to fire back and the man by the truck was soon silenced.

Bruce picked up the M-16 rifle and ammo from one of the phony police officers they had first encountered. He wasn't about to remain unarmed.

Flo hollered out, "They are trying to blow a hole in the front of the dam by rappelling down with suicide bombers!"

Before any more could be said they heard a shot, with a sound unlike the other shots they had been hearing, and Bruce yelled in surprise. As he stood there while Flo called out about the suicide bombers, suddenly the M-16 jerked out of his hand as they heard the report of a rifle. The M-16 had been shot in a near miss that almost killed Bruce but hit his weapon instead.

They looked around to see where the shot had come from, all with their weapons ready, but they didn't see anyone. Suddenly another shot rang out and one of the sheriff's deputies jerked around and swore. He grabbed his right arm and gritted his teeth against the pain.

Someone yelled, "Sniper! Everyone get down!" Several of them jumped behind the eighteen-wheeler and the others ran to get down behind the wall at the side of the road. From the safety of the cover they had found, the deputy who had been hit looked at his arm. Another deputy asked how bad it was. "Just nicked me. It'll bleed some but I'm okay." Just then another shot smacked into the wall right by one of the men.

The ninth explosion blasted on the face of the dam.

Eb said, "We've got to stop those blasts on the dam!"

Alan shouted commands to his team, directing some of them to begin firing toward the mountainside where they thought the sniper was. He directed the ones behind the truck to get in a position above the dam and start firing at the terrorists on top of it.

As the barrage of gunfire was hurled toward the mountainside on the north of the dam, a tenth explosion split the air. That blast was not as delayed as those previously, so evidently, the terrorists were trying to speed up their process and were sending bombers partway down the dam before the previous bombs were detonated.

Eb and Flo stayed and helped shoot at the mountainside and they had a completely clear field of fire. There was a lot of lead being thrown at that location across the canyon 400 or 500 yards away.

From his firing position, Eb glanced toward the dam and noticed that he could see through a gap in the wall that was made for a person to walk through to get off the side of the highway. He had a good view of the men rappelling down the face of the structure. He tapped the forearm of the sheriff's deputy next to him and pointed toward the dam. The deputy smiled and he and Eb shifted their aim. Three suicide bombers were just above the growing hole in the dam and the deputy said, "Go." He and Eb began firing at the bombers that were at least 300 yards away.

Suddenly one of the bombers coming down a rope jerked and then lost his grip. He slid down the rope and then right off the end of it, free-falling to land hard at the base of the dam on the flat concrete area at the bottom. Eb and the deputy kept firing and eventually a second bomber also slid off the rope and then fell to the bottom. The third bomber was apparently hit and stopped moving, but he did not slide to the end of the rope. Perhaps he had quickly locked in on the rescue eight. None of the bombs of those three terrorists detonated, evidently due to the stability of the plastic explosives.

*   *   *

From across the face of the dam Vahid watched as the three terrorist bombers were shot down, two of them falling from their rappelling lines to the hard concrete below. Thinking quickly, he loosened his hold on the yellow rope and swung. He hoped to get inside the hole in the front of the dam in order to be out of the line of fire. As he tried to work his way as quickly as he could he heard bullets smacking into the dam all around him. He kept moving and finally reached the edge of the opening. Just as he swung inside, using the rough edges of concrete and a jutting piece of rebar for leverage, a bullet struck him in the lower leg.

By then his momentum carried him into the gap and he was safe from the shots of the men. As he crawled deeper into the crater, he looked down and saw blood soaking into his pants. His leg hurt but the wound didn't seem to be too bad. The crater in the dam was littered with strips of fabric from the clothing of the suicide bombers along with more gruesome evidence of their sacrifice. Vahid tied a few bits of cloth around his leg to staunch the bleeding as he thought about his predicament. He could remain safely there in the hole, although he probably couldn't get out. He didn't know what to do but he hoped Al-Musawi would come up with something that would allow him to get to safety. He realized that his survival was now all up to Al-Musawi.

Vahid looked around the hole and tried to judge the distance. It was about thirty feet across and fifty feet deep; not big enough yet to make the dam fail. If they couldn't get more bombers into the hole, which now seemed to be their predicament, they would have to rely on the plane full of explosives.

Vahid and Al-Musawi had discussed the airplane at great length, although not many of their team knew much about it. Vahid had been the one who convinced Al-Musawi that they might need the plane at Horse Mesa Dam or they might need it at Roosevelt Dam. The explosives needed for the shaped charges had to be consistent so they used all the C-4 for making the hole in Roosevelt Dam but the plane just needed all the explosives they could get. That's why the plane had RDS, ANFO, and dynamite, as well as a little bit of C-4 left over from what they needed for the cones. Regardless of where they needed the plane, Horse Mesa or Roosevelt, they just had to detonate the large amount of explosives right at the moment of impact. It would cause enough damage to destroy or weaken the dam, and the water pressure behind the dam could do the rest.

*   *   *

Mansoor Fatik Al-Musawi was in a panic. This final part of his plan, which had been going so well, was suddenly taking the path of failure like every other one of his plans this past week. He was furious and

323

anxious at the same time. He sent three more bombers over the face of the dam but he had now lost count. The dam had not failed and it looked like the infidels were gaining the upper hand. Shots were being fired at his sniper on the mountainside and now shots were being fired at him and the other men on the top of the dam.

As he took cover Al-Musawi pulled out his cell phone and dialed a number. He yelled into the phone a long string of words in Arabic. Among them was one word spoken in English but repeated over and over: "Roosevelt!" "Roosevelt!" "Roosevelt!"

Al-Musawi hung up the phone and sent another bomber quickly over the wall. By now they had completely lost their routine and it was nothing more than chaos. Some of the terrorists on the top of the dam had weapons and were firing back at the men that were shooting at them from the roadside above the dam. However, this time it was the good guys who were above the dam and behind the wall. Al-Musawi was screaming at his team, trying to motivate them to work more quickly.

*   *   *

Captain Gloria Puckett was flight commander on a quickly-called mission of two F-16s headed toward a plane full of explosives. She was accompanied by First Lieutenant Nellie Boyd. She and Boyd had become very close friends and they flew together almost all the time. Scrum was introverted, unassuming, and always in control; DeeDee was fiery, boisterous, and lived life to the fullest.

From what Puckett had learned of the Navajo culture, Boyd did not exactly fit the mold. Puckett thought that Navajos were quiet and reserved by nature when around other people, but she had also heard from past historic accounts that Navajo braves were known for being fierce warriors and fearless opponents against their enemies. Boyd must have inherited the fierce and fearless genes but not the quiet and reserved genes.

Boyd was also an excellent pilot and was willing to do about anything she could think of doing with a jet fighter. She had been chewed out many times by senior officers for taking foolish risks but Boyd always came away safe and with a huge grin on her face. She had never messed up so badly that she damaged a plane but she had come very close at times.

This mission was very urgent. General Briscoe had personally spoken to them on the radio as they raced across the valley toward a stolen plane packed with explosives and told them that they had to get to that plane in time. They had to find it and shoot it down before it could be used as a weapon of mass destruction. Briscoe had also told them that Lieutenant Andrus had defected to radical Islam and that he and Major McCasland were in a dog fight against each other somewhere in the same area as the stolen plane.

General Briscoe made it very clear that if Puckett and Boyd encountered McCasland and Andrus, they were to completely ignore them. Their first priority was to take down the King Air full of explosives. If they were available after that and if it was needed, then they could help McCasland engage Andrus.

Puckett and Boyd flew as fast as their jets could go, screaming low across the valley. The AWACS in the area had reported a few minutes earlier that it had identified what it believed to be the stolen plane and gave the plane's coordinates. The AWACS officer stated that the plane was apparently attempting to fly above the Salt River up to Roosevelt since that course had the lowest elevations. They had already been briefed on reports of shooting and explosions at Roosevelt Dam.

As Puckett and Boyd approached Canyon Lake they picked up the small aircraft on their radar just over Horse Mesa Dam, headed toward Roosevelt Dam. Just off to their left they also saw two Vipers, one chasing the other, but they couldn't tell who was who. As ordered, they kept their full attention on the target just out ahead of them.

Because they were flying over 1,000 miles per hour they closed the gap on the King Air very quickly. It wasn't long before they could see the smoke in the air and then they could see the plane ahead of them. By that time they were drawing close to Roosevelt Dam. They knew they only had seconds before it would be too late to fire.

*   *   *

The law enforcement officers behind the wall kept firing across the canyon in the direction of the sniper and the shots coming from the mountainside finally stopped. It was unknown if anyone had actually hit the shooter but they decided to keep their weapons ready and stay behind the wall.

On the other side of the semi-truck, law enforcement officers also stayed behind that section of the low wall beside the road above and on the south end of the dam. They kept firing at the terrorists giving them everything they had. They could see many men milling around in a cluster near the middle of the dam about 200 yards away but only some of them had weapons. The FBI Agents and sheriff's deputies kept firing at the terrorists hoping to either kill the bombers or detonate a bomb. If there were plastic explosives their bullets wouldn't trigger an explosion but if there were any less-stable explosives, such as dynamite, a bullet could cause a detonation which would then trigger the plastic explosives to go off.

The terrorists who had weapons kept firing, and there were enough of them still shooting that it seemed the deputies and FBI weren't gaining any advantage.

Suddenly an explosion erupted in the middle of the cluster of bombers. That set off a chain reaction and all the explosives on the top of the dam detonated. It turned out to be like one long explosion and it blew flame and flying pieces of the bomb across the dam and through the air, along with bits of rock, metal, concrete, and human body parts. It was a spectacular yet gruesome sight. The sound was deafening for several intense moments and then everything was quiet and still.

Alan Clevenger and the others stood and waited to see if any terrorists remained a threat. After a few moments with no sign of life, they moved over and climbed down the metal ladder and walked slowly across the dam, still on guard with their rifles in case any of the terrorists were hiding or waiting to take them by surprise. Finding no more threat Alan started giving commands, instructing some of their team to search for survivors and live bombs. He told some to look over the edge of the dam to see if they could see any sign of dam failure. He turned to Ezzie and somberly said, "Look for Quinn, would you?"

Alan turned to Evan and Bella, two of his team, and said, "We need to see if we can find any sign of Al-Musawi. You've seen his photo many times. Look for him or for any hands with tattoos."

As they moved around and started searching, Eb, Flo, and Bruce sat on top of the wall where they had been shooting at the mountainside. They didn't feel the need to be in among the law enforcement personnel. It looked like this terrorist attack had also failed for the most part, although there was significant damage and loss of life for some of their key people.

326

Puckett and Boyd knew they were racing against time. They were flying at maximum speed, having left Luke Air Force Base only minutes previously. They knew they had to get to that plane to stop the pilot from carrying out whatever plan he had in his twisted mind. They could see the plane ahead of them and beyond it they could see Roosevelt Lake. They couldn't see the dam yet because of a curve in the canyon and their angle of flight but they knew from the reports they had received that there was great chaos at the dam and they believed the plane was headed there.

As they flew side by side, Puckett in the lead, she was the first to get radar lock on the plane full of explosives. Using their cannon was not the best strategic move at that point. A missile was a sure kill and a much better choice since it would track the plane and then detonate, causing immediate destruction.

They had flown these drills many times and had discussed it about one minute ago. At that point, they didn't need to communicate by radio as to who would do what, and besides, there was no time to discuss it since they were almost within striking range. Boyd knew that Puckett would fire a missile and they both would be prepared for a follow up if needed.

Puckett could now see the dam ahead of her at a distance, and having already established radar lock she pushed the button to fire a missile. It hissed off the end of her right wing as a faint wisp of smoke began trailing out of its tail. With the F-16s flying at over 1,000 miles per hour, and with the sidewinder flying at 2,300 miles per hour, the missile quickly outdistanced the jets as it raced toward the slow-moving plane. However, by then the plane was almost to the dam.

She hoped the missile would get there in time.

* * *

The two terrorists in the Beechcraft Twin Turboprop King Air were desperately trying to reach Roosevelt Dam and were getting very close. The plane was only flying about 100 miles per hour and at that speed was barely remaining in the air. One of the terrorists was an experienced pilot and he knew that the engine mounted on the right wing of the plane was fading fast. They just had to stay in the air for a few more minutes.

Everything had gone wrong with that part of the operation. The initial plan was to steal the plane on Friday evening as the pilot brought it into Casa Grande, but at the last minute Al-Musawi called them and reported to them in code that law enforcement had unexpectedly showed up at Roosevelt Dam, so they would have to wait until morning. They had already planned for contingencies so they were not worried.

However, the next morning when they went to steal the plane they were caught by surprise when the pilot pulled a gun and fired several shots, killing one of their team before they could shoot the pilot. Then the other infidel associated with the plane came right at that time and they killed him too. However, the damage had been done. The shots fired by the pilot alerted another American in the next hangar over and that was actually the bigger issue. They wanted to sneak away but that failed. That was a major threat to the mission.

As they quickly sped down the taxiway to leave the hangar the terrorist who was closing the plane door saw the American step out of his building with a rifle of some kind. As they taxied toward the end of the runway the American came out from between the buildings and shot at them as they went past. Instead of sneaking away in a stolen plane full of explosives, someone probably reported them to law enforcement and they were also shot at. Their plan for a stealth attack with a large amount of explosives was foiled.

When they got to the end of the runway they saw that the infidel was walking toward them on the side of the runway. They couldn't afford for him to stop the plane or perhaps shoot their pilot, or worse, to shoot some of the dynamite and blow up the whole plane. As they sat at the end of the runway preparing to take off they debated what to do. Suddenly a warning indicator sounded, indicating that something was wrong with the right engine. The engine seemed to be working, but there was obviously a problem. After further debate they decided that one of their team would have to be left behind so as to shoot the man on the runway. The problem was, they couldn't wait any longer because they needed to be there at Horse Mesa Dam or Roosevelt Dam at precisely the time the rest of their team punched through the dam. The timing was critical and this infidel on the side of the runway with a rifle was jeopardizing the success of the mission.

They knew that the American on the runway wouldn't be shooting a fully automatic weapon so they were confident that their fighter would win in a gun battle. However, they couldn't afford to wait to see the outcome of the battle because they needed to take off soon. Also, if the shots had caused someone to call law enforcement, they couldn't afford to be there any longer and risk being stopped by police or a SWAT team.

Their fighter got off the plane, and the pilot and their explosives expert who remained on the plane watched their fighter walk toward the infidel. As they saw that he shot the infidel and the infidel went down, they were delighted but they had to get into the air. They sped down the runway and flashed past their fighter who was celebrating his victory in the shootout. They were relieved to become airborne but the pilot knew quickly that the plane was not flying well. The indicator kept going off and the plane just didn't have the power it needed. However, they were still flying and they hoped they could remain undetected.

As the pilot continued nursing the plane to the southwest to gain altitude and then swung around to head northeast toward the direction of Roosevelt Dam, the explosives expert busied himself with the explosives, hooking up wires and preparing the detonator. He finished rigging up the explosives and then strung a long wire to the front of the plane so he could sit next to the pilot. He wanted to watch out the front window and detonate the explosives right at the impact with the dam.

Suddenly the pilot cursed as he realized that they were the only plane in the air. He had turned off his transponder that emitted outgoing signals, called a "squawk," so they couldn't be tracked by Air Traffic Control by their squawk. However, he was listening to the radio and he heard the call grounding all air traffic. He had hoped other planes would take their time landing but that turned out to not be the case. That was a problem they hoped would not occur because now they would be more easily detected. Nonetheless, they had to continue and hope for the best.

They originally planned to fly directly to the dam but with engine problems they wouldn't be able to gain the altitude that would be needed to get over some of the mountains that they would come to. When they finally reached the mountains east of the Valley of the Sun they turned north and skirted along the west edge of the mountains instead of trying to go up and over the mountains. When they reached the Salt River they turned and followed the river's path up through the mountains. With that strategy they didn't have to clear any mountain passes but it was slower than a direct path to Roosevelt.

As they passed over Canyon Lake they saw two F-16s in a dogfight off to the south of them. Al-Musawi had told them earlier that an American Air Force pilot had defected to their side and would be providing them some cover as they flew toward the dam. However, instead of helping them it turned out that the Islamist pilot was caught up in a dog fight of his own. Something must have gone wrong.

The King Air went on past Canyon Lake and headed for Horse Mesa Dam.

Suddenly Al-Musawi called, frantic, yelling at them to bypass Horse Mesa Dam and go to Roosevelt Dam. They could hear a lot of gunfire in the background. Things must have gone terribly wrong at the dam.

The pilot sensed that the right engine was just about gone. However, they were nearing the middle of Apache Lake, and Roosevelt Dam was just a short distance away. At one hundred miles per hour, they were still approaching the dam quickly. They needed less than thirty seconds. They could now see the top of the dam in the distance.

Suddenly they saw the top of the dam erupt in a huge blast of flame and smoke. They suspected that many people died in the blast, perhaps including Al-Musawi, and it angered them. They both instinctively cried out in frustration.

If the dam was still intact but all of their explosives were now detonated, then it was up to them to use their plane full of explosives to destroy the dam.

They were now very close. The right engine was whining. The pilot seemed to be using the controls with intense focus as if to squeeze all the power out of the plane that he could get. They could see the entire dam now, including the large hole that had been blasted in the face of the dam. The pilot planned to fly the nose of the plane right into that hole.

The explosives expert had visually checked his detonating mechanism. He was ready. He was watching out the front window of the King Air. His thumb was poised to push the detonator button right as they smacked into the hole in the front of the dam. This was for Allah and for Al-Musawi. At 100 miles per hour they were covering about 100 yards every two seconds. They were about 300 yards or six seconds away from the dam and the terrorist sitting next to the pilot placed his thumb gently on the detonating button in preparation.

*   *   *

Because the shooting had stopped it was relatively quiet on the top of the dam, but the citizens and law enforcement personnel at the dam suddenly began to hear a loud whining sound coming from the west. They looked toward the sound and saw what appeared to be a private plane flying toward them up the middle of the canyon. It looked like it was headed straight for them. There was black smoke streaming out of one engine and it seemed to be barely staying in the air as it moved in their direction.

Alan yelled at everyone, "Get off the dam, quick!" and they all started running for whichever end of the dam was the closest to where they were at the moment.

The King Air was perhaps 200 yards away from the dam when the running people heard a hissing sound, and suddenly the plane burst into a spectacular fireball accompanied by a massive explosion. The boom was deafening and many of them winced and grabbed at their ears. The earth shook and the dam trembled but remained intact.

The shock caused by the massive blast detonated the explosives of the three bombers who were shot by Eb and the deputy. One explosion was on the face of the dam where the bomber still hung and two explosions were at the base of the dam. The shaped charges drove the jets of aluminum into the nearest object but the explosions had no serious consequence other than to blow the three bombers to bits.

Vahid, who had still been hiding in the crater that the terrorists had blown in the face of the dam, had a shaped charge in his backpack. He had put it in his backpack as a last-minute thought, and now it served to end his life. The shock from the exploding plane triggered the shaped charge to detonate. The aluminum jet punched into the side of the concrete crater but the explosion that created the jet was against Vahid's back and he was killed instantly, just like the bombers he had destroyed just minutes before as they created the hole in the dam.

The sleek, blue King Air was blown into millions of pieces which flew in all directions. Some were on fire, some sizzling, some large, some small; all of which gradually fell to the earth, landing in the river or at the base of the dam or in the brush along the mountainside or on the road along the side of the river. Some of the parts of the plane had been blown high in the air as it exploded and they were fluttering and falling back to earth.

The running men and women on the dam stopped and cheered when they saw that the plane didn't strike the dam. Just at that moment, two

Air Force jets blasted over them, one higher in the air but one diving right past the dam as if it were going to impact the water of the lake.

*   *   *

As Second Lieutenant Nellie Boyd flew toward the ball of flame which had previously been a stolen King Air full of explosives, she guided her jet so she would pass through the now-dispersing flame high and to the left of the main part of the explosion. However, at the last second she noticed a large piece of sheet metal floating downward. It had apparently been blown high in the air and was now directly ahead of her. It was large enough that she couldn't risk contact with it. However, there was so much other debris in the air that she had to find an opening in a split second. She saw a hole in the debris down and a bit to the right and she expertly guided her Viper into that small gap. Unfortunately, that took her right toward the dam and the lake surface beyond.

With all the commotion and blocked highways, the bridge beyond the dam was full of people, most of them by now out of their cars and watching all the commotion on the dam. They had heard the intermittent explosions, they heard the gunfire, they saw the explosion when the remaining suicide bombs were detonated on the top of the dam, and they saw the explosion on the other side of the dam as the plan was obliterated.

Then, to top it all off, an F-16 was headed toward them!

No, it was headed into the lake!

No, it went right under them—right under the bridge!

As the jet blasted beneath the bridge it turned and rocketed up into the air. The pilot inside was a fun-loving daredevil named Nellie Boyd and she couldn't resist adding some acrobatics by doing a tight corkscrew as she flew straight up above the lake, with dozens of awestruck people watching.

The jet blast from the F-16 skimming and launching upward right above the surface of the water caused a rooster tail of spray from the lake as high as the bridge was tall. There were screams of fright from some but there were oohs and ahhs of excitement from others. Still others were getting it all on video with their smartphones, and within minutes it would be on social media.

As the spray from the jet blast fell back into the lake, some water falling on the road surface of the bridge and on the cars and people who

332

were watching this terrible yet exciting airshow, one little boy turned to his father and said, "Wow! I'm glad the water soaked us because I got so excited I wet my pants!"

50 Aftermath

Rasekh, the sniper who was hidden in his ghillie suit on the mountainside north of the dam, had been hit. When the FBI and sheriff's deputies had all started shooting at the hillside where he was hiding he just hunkered down and waited, hoping they would miss. Unfortunately, one of the shots had hit him in the left side of his lower abdomen. The pain was intense but he held as still as he could so as not to create motion that would allow them to pinpoint his position. They continued to shoot but he was hit just the one time.

After a few minutes the shooting stopped but the damage had been done. Rasekh knew instinctively that from the severity of his injury and his location on the hillside he would not leave this place, or if he did he would not go far.

He was angry with himself. He was not a seasoned sniper, having had some training but no real experience, so when he started shooting at the Americans he missed. He had several chances but he misjudged the distance and the wind drift that affected the accuracy of the shots. With the wind blowing up the canyon and with the distance of the shots being about 400 yards, the bullets drifted a little off course. He didn't have a range finder to determine the distance accurately and an experienced sniper would know how to dial the knobs on the scope to adjust for the wind. He had tried to adjust the knobs but he ended up slightly off.

Out of the four shots he fired he killed no one. He was disappointed and mad, and now that he had been shot his anger turned to smoldering hatred. He already hated all Americans anyway, but with the frustrations of failure and now the sure end to his life, he vowed to not fail again.

He was also angry with the outcome of the morning. Unexpected people had ruined their plans and killed his teammates. Some ordinary citizens and the FBI had surprised their gunmen, and the Air Force had come in at the last possible moment to blow their plane out of the sky.

Rasekh muttered under his breath, cursing the Americans, mumbling about revenge, and planning what he would do in the next few minutes.

Rasekh remained still for a while, conserving his strength and waiting for a chance to shoot when he could do more damage and be assured of a kill, knowing it would probably be his last act of devotion to Allah and to the cause he fought for. He knew he was severely injured and his breathing came in painful gasps. He also waited because he wanted the Americans to drop their guard, thinking he had been killed. If they thought he was dead they would not worry about the threat from him on the hillside.

He was near a large boulder, nestled among the bushes on the mountainside and he painfully crawled over behind the rock, giving him cover from those who had shot at him before. He wished now that he had thought of using that boulder to begin with, but he had trusted in just the ghillie suit. Of course, he didn't expect to have a small army of armed men and women firing at him.

After lying behind the boulder for a few minutes he pulled off the hood of the ghillie suit which covered his head. He edged out on the east side of the boulder so he could see the top of the dam. He slowly raised the binoculars that had been hanging around his neck by a strap. He started looking at the Americans, trying to find the best target. If he was going to have one last chance, he wanted to find a leader or someone of influence. As he looked through the binoculars for several minutes, focusing on people on the dam and on the road, he finally identified the person who appeared to be giving orders.

Rasekh watched him for a while. The man he watched was not dressed like a sheriff or a police officer. He looked kind of young and inexperienced and was wearing plain clothes, but he was obviously in charge. He pointed and people went and did some task. Others came up to him and stood talking for a few moments and then they moved away to do something else. Of course, Rasekh could not hear their conversation, but after watching their behavior he was sure he had the right man. He also noticed that the man had a bright pink adhesive bandage on the right side of his head near his temple. It was so pink that it stood out against the pale skin of his face and his dark hair. Rasekh started planning how to put a .338 bullet traveling over 2,000 miles per hour right through the middle of that bandage.

*   *   *

As Eb and Flo sat on the low wall at the end of the dam they were completely captivated by the explosion of the small plane. It was terrible and horrific and exciting all at the same time. After the loud boom, when everyone ducked to avoid the heat and flying objects, Eb exclaimed, "Wow! That was even better than Tannerite."

Eb and Flo, like the rednecks that they were, had shot small piles of Tannerite with their rifles to make the Tannerite explode. Tannerite was quite powerful and the explosion was ear-splitting and very concussive. They had blown up rocks and tree stumps and various other objects just for fun. However, Tannerite was nothing like what they had just witnessed, which was an awesome demonstration of complete, massive, fiery, explosive power.

They watched as the FBI agents and sheriff's personnel started doing what first responders do after a terrorist attack—they started caring for the injured and those who had been killed, securing the area, trying to get traffic flowing again, doing an investigation, and marking evidence. The actual clean-up would come later.

Bruce, their companion for the shooting just minutes before, got up and went back to his car. "One near miss is enough for my whole lifetime," he said as he walked away, even though the road was still blocked and the cars were not moving yet.

Eb and Flo both checked their magazines to make sure they had a full thirty rounds each.

Suddenly Flo said, "I want to get up on that thumb of rock."

Eb replied, "Why? There's no need, and they are still doing some investigating up there. See? One of the FBI agents is up on top of there right now looking around."

Flo answered, "I know it doesn't make sense but I have the urge to get up there. Maybe we won't be in their way and they won't kick us off."

They got up from behind the wall where they had taken cover from the sniper and, carrying their guns, they walked along the road past the eighteen-wheeler and through the cut in the rock where the terrorists had climbed up on the thumb of rock. There was no one there at the bottom for the moment so they slung their ARs over their shoulders and climbed up.

When they reached the top of the rock two sheriff's deputies were crouched down looking at the terrorists and examining the unexploded ammo and the propane tanks. The terrorists, the rocks, and the little bit of grass and small bushes showed signs of being burned and jostled about.

The deputies looked up and one said, "Can we help you?"

Flo said, "We don't want to disturb any evidence but we wanted to get up on the top of this rock just to watch."

The other deputy said, "I'm not sure we want you still walking around with your guns."

The first deputy turned to the second and said, "They were just shooting terrorists to keep you from getting shot and you are worried about them?" The second deputy just shrugged and said, "OK, whatever."

The first deputy turned to Eb and Flo and said, "OK, but please stay as far as you can from this part of the rock so we can preserve the evidence."

Flo said "No problem. It looks like there's a little room over on that end." He pointed to the north edge of the rock that looked down on the dam and the canyon.

Eb and Flo stepped around the deputies and Flo found a semi-smooth chunk of rock to sit on. It was kind of a boulder, although it was part of the thumb of rock itself. Eb found a place where some smooth dirt had accumulated in a flat spot, and he crossed his legs and sat down too. They both looked down onto the chaos of the dam, which was now relatively quiet.

Flo pulled up his rifle and started looking through the scope at the hill where the sniper fire had come from. He said, "I wonder if we could see any sign of that sniper without going clear over there. Someone is going to have to cross the dam and climb that mountain. Maybe they could do that with the dog."

Eb replied, "I think that's a bomb dog and not a search dog, but maybe they train them to do that too. I don't know."

They continued to sit there just watching. From time to time they would use their rifle scope to look at something, but they never used their scope to look at a live person who wasn't an enemy or a threat. That would be unthinkable. Everyone in front of them who was alive was on their team.

Or so they thought.

* * *

Alan and his team, accompanied by the sheriff's deputies, searched through the mess that remained on the top of the dam. They called for engineers from Salt River Project to come inspect the dam but for all they could see it was holding just fine.

Erlinda, the secretary at the Roosevelt station had called for a helicopter and any rescue personnel in the area to hurry to the dam. Sheriff Concepcion was going to be OK. He was quickly airlifted to the hospital in Globe and then on to Scottsdale Memorial trauma center in the Phoenix Metropolitan area.

The two deputies who first arrived in their car at the scene had made the ultimate sacrifice, along with the two other deputies and the two FBI agents who were killed on the top of the dam before the others arrived. Alan and his team were sure that if they had not been in the armored vehicles, they would likely have all died or been seriously wounded.

For all the shooting that happened at the dam, having only a few injuries and a few deaths was actually a favorable turnout, although they all felt great sorrow for the first responders who were killed and their families.

The fact that there were armed citizens who effectively stepped up to help made all the difference. Eb and Flo shooting at the terrorists from the west while the terrorists were waiting to ambush Alan's team coming from the east saved their lives. Even more, perhaps, was the quick thinking of the two teenagers who came up with the brilliant idea of using the propane tanks to disrupt the terrorists on the thumb of rock.

As the law enforcement personnel searched along the top of the dam, one of the sheriff's deputies came over to Alan carrying something. He said, "Is this what you were looking for?" as he held out a forearm and hand that had been blown off of a body. The arm had been severed above the elbow and it was a bloody sight. Alan took the gruesome object and examined the palms and inside of the fingers of the hand. Sure enough, there were the tattoos that he had photos of in his files, identifying Mansoor Fatik Al-Musawi. Alan breathed a sigh of relief. He had felt all week that if they could get Al-Musawi that would probably be an indication of the end of the terrorism that was plaguing the Phoenix area. Alan realized it was possible that more terrorist attacks could happen but he had surmised from the beginning that Al-Musawi was the leader and if they took him out the others would become disorganized and give up.

As Alan was looking at the hand, he pulled out his phone to take some photos of it. Just then, Ezzie walked over to take a look, and just as she reached Alan he dropped his phone. He quickly bent over, trying to catch it before it hit the concrete. At that second, a shot split the air and Ezzie was knocked to the ground. She lay there writhing and moaning in pain. Everyone dropped to the ground behind any cover they could find.

*   *   *

Rasekh waited as long as he dared. He was getting weak from pain and from loss of blood. He stayed mostly behind the boulder but inched the gun past the east edge of it so he could shoot toward the dam. He carefully and slowly levered another round into the Lapua. He sighted toward the leader with the pink bandage, using the marks on the crosshairs to adjust for the distance and the wind. He had carefully thought through what went wrong with his prior shots that day and he was confident that his next shot would hit exactly where he wanted it to.

The leader with the pink bandage turned to talk to someone and Rasekh watched through the scope, waiting for him to be still. Another man in a uniform walked up, carrying something. Rasekh leaned slightly away from the scope of the rifle and carefully pulled up his binoculars. Suddenly he cursed to himself in his mother tongue. He switched to the 25-power spotting scope and through the increased magnification, he could see details that he couldn't see clearly through his rifle scope. The men were looking at the arm and hand of Al-Musawi. Rasekh could see the dark color that marked the tattoos on the inside of the fingers and the palms as the infidel leader held the hand up for inspection. Rasekh had talked to Al-Musawi many times and had even chided him about the tattoos, saying that they positively identified him. Al-Musawi had brushed off Rasekh's concerns.

Rasekh now wanted revenge more than ever. He loved Al-Musawi as a devoted follower loves a great leader. He lowered the spotting scope, gripped the stock of the Lapua, and put his eye to the scope. He adjusted for distance and wind and knew that his bullet would go through the back of the head of the infidel leader. He didn't care about the bandage now. He exhaled and slowly squeezed the trigger.

Just as he shot, the man suddenly leaned to the side for some reason and in the time Rasekh's shot traveled the 400 yards to where the leader was standing, the leader's head moved completely out of the path of the bullet. However, the shot struck another agent who was standing nearby and had accidentally ended up in the bullet's path. It appeared to be a

338

woman. The shot hit her high in the shoulder and spun her half-way around, knocking her to the concrete of the dam which was already littered with debris and blood from the prior explosions.

Everyone on the top of the dam dropped to the ground, most of them below objects which obscured Rasekh's view of them. The others on the road by the big rig started shooting at the mountainside again but this time Rasekh was behind the boulder and they could not hit him.

Rasekh was confident he could kill the leader if he had a chance. He continued to look through the scope, scanning for the leader. Suddenly he saw that bright pink bandage. Once he zeroed in on it, he could then see the other details of the leader, his ear and his eye and the hair on top of his head. The leader was sitting behind the sidewall of the dam, his body protected but the profile of his head exposed to full view. He was completely motionless, waiting to see if the sniper would shoot again.

If he only knew!

Rasekh would have his revenge. He worked the bolt to lever in another round.

Rasekh stilled himself mentally and put the crosshairs where they needed to be, using the extra marks on his scope to make the adjustments. He knew he was right this time; his last shot proved it. He could hear the barrage of gunfire from the other side of the dam and he could hear bullets smacking into the boulder and tearing into the brush around him. However, he knew he was completely safe because those shooting at him were directly across the canyon from him and the boulder was blocking their line of fire. The barrage of gunfire had absolutely no effect on him. He took a ragged breath, mentally blocking out the pain, and then let his breath out slowly. He was relaxed and calm and confident. He saw the pink bandage holding perfectly still. His aim was likewise perfectly still. He slowly squeezed the trigger of the Lapua.

*　　*　　*

Cindy Clevenger had slept well. The emotional roller coaster of the day before, which wore her out mentally, accompanied by the fact that her boys were at the Davidsons' house, allowed her to be completely relaxed throughout the night. She was sound asleep at about 8:00 Saturday morning when she suddenly awoke with a start.

Something was wrong with Alan! She had a terrible feeling that overwhelmed her.

She quickly slid out of bed and her knees hit the floor. She didn't even follow the usual wording, she just pleaded, "Heavenly Father, please bless Alan. He's in terrible trouble and only you can help him."

The feeling was overwhelming and dark. The emotional pain was so intense she began to cry. She didn't know if she was crying because of the pain or because of her worry about her beloved husband.

She continued her prayer, "Heavenly Father, please protect Alan, or help someone else protect him."

She knelt there, pressed against the bed. Her eyes were closed, her focus was intense. She thought of a loving God who she knew could accomplish all things if it was His will.

*   *   *

Eb and Flo had been sitting on the top of the thumb of rock for a few minutes. They weren't doing anything in particular other than watching the first responders doing their job. Some cars started moving through the cut in the cliff between the mountain and the thumb of rock. Some of the traffic on the bridge started moving also.

Eb asked if they should move their truck but Flo reminded him that when they stopped, Eb had to climb through a mesquite bush to get out of his door. Eb remembered the incident and started grumbling and looked down at the scratch of dried blood on his arm.

Flo smiled. *No, they didn't need to move the truck.*

Flo was looking through his scope at the hillside from where the sniper had fired and suddenly said in that quiet half-whisper that they used when one of them spotted a game animal when they were hunting, "Eb, look at the hill!"

Eb could see what Flo was referring to even before he got his scope up in front of his eye. There was a bright reflection of light on the mountainside. Apparently, some movement had caused the scope of a rifle or a pair of binoculars to rest in a position it had not been in before. The early morning sun was almost directly behind Eb and Flo as they looked toward the sniper. Their angle from the thumb of the rock was different from the angle of those down on the road and on the dam.

Just then a shot rang out and someone on the dam moaned in pain. They looked down and saw that all the people on the dam had dropped behind anything they could find which provided cover from the sniper.

340

The gunmen on the dam began firing toward the hillside, but the reflection coming from the vicinity of the sniper remained unmoving.

Eb and Flo threw their guns to their shoulders. Flo said, "How far?"

Eb said, "I'd say 500 yards. We have to hold about two to three feet high and an inch or two upwind."

They both started firing. They had sixty rounds to work with and without having to say anything about it they knew that's what the other was thinking. They put shot after shot toward the bright reflection that they could still see perfectly. They varied their aim slightly up and down a few inches each shot, and from side to side, trying to get just the right combination of distance and windage to stop the sniper once and for all.

*   *   *

As Rasekh kept his steady aim at the pink bandage and slowly squeezed the trigger of the Lapua, his rifle suddenly jerked slightly to the side and there was a searing pain in his face and a bright flash.

The bullet from one of Flo's shots had struck the Lapua right on the top of the bolt and below the scope a fraction of a second before the gun fired. The impact of the bullet moved the weapon just enough that as the .338 bullet traveled down the barrel, the aim was thrown off by a fraction of an inch of muzzle movement. However, with the target 400 yards away the bullet was off course by several inches near the target and it struck the concrete of the dam, failing to hit the pink bandage on the side of Alan Clevenger's head.

The angle of Flo's shot came from the top of the thumb of rock almost straight in front of Rasekh. When the bullet struck the Lapua it ricocheted upward, breaking into several pieces and also shredding the scope of the rifle. The bullet fragments and the pieces of the scope, which acted like shrapnel, tore into Rasekh's face and penetrated his veins and nerves, moving on into his brain.

After the bright flash, Rasekh, the sniper, felt no more pain and heard no more sound and felt no more sensation. He was no longer filled with revenge or with hatred for the American infidels. His grasp on the Lapua relaxed. The gun clattered against the boulder as it came to rest next to the body of the terrorist.

*   *   *

341

The last act of the terrorists in the Phoenix area ended like all the other acts of the terrorists that week. General failure. Yes, there were some minor successes on the part of the terrorists. Some people died. Some people were injured. Many people were in fear. However, the overall result was that the terrorists only accomplished a very small percentage of the damage and destruction, death and pain that they planned to achieve.

Again and again, armed citizens stepped up, were prepared, and took quick action. For the most part the first responders were only that— responders. They were prepared and diligent, heroic in their duties, but they were only responders. The armed citizens were the participants.

However, in the final incident at Roosevelt Dam, law enforcement participated in the fighting and they made the difference between success and failure. If they had not been there at that time, pursuant to the prompting Alan and Victor received, the terrorists would have overpowered the few armed citizens at the dam who would have died in vain. In that case, the shaped charges would have probably succeeded and the dam would likely have failed. The additional success was the U.S. Air Force and their quick response and effective attack on the damaged plane loaded with explosives, rendering it yet another broken bomb.

In nearly all of the cases throughout the week the shooting was effectively over before the first responders arrived. It was a great demonstration of the power of the Second Amendment and the power of everyday, law-abiding citizens being armed and ready to defend their country, just like the Minute Men from Revolutionary War days.

51 Official Visitors

Three F-16s cruised over the top of Casa Grande airport at 2:00 in the afternoon on Tuesday following the final terrorist event at Roosevelt Dam. By Tuesday, life had begun to return to normal in the areas that had not been attacked.

As the FBI had expected, once the leader of the terror cell, Mansoor Fatik Al-Musawi, had been killed the terrorist attacks stopped. It was also believed that all of the terrorists had either been killed or seriously wounded and the cell of radical Islamists had been obliterated. With the information provided by Lieutenant Colonel Beverly Wickstead, Priyanka Qahtan was tracked down and arrested. Also arrested was a civilian food server in the Luke Air Force Base cafeteria who also had ties to the Muslim Brotherhood.

As the jets cruised over the airport and then zoomed out over the city of Casa Grande, people in town noticed. The jets were flying slow enough and low enough that the flyover caught their attention. The jets leisurely flew out past Casa Grande to the southeast and circled back around in tight formation, cruised over the city again, and then landed at the airport. The first in line was a two-seater F-16 followed by two single-seater jets. They landed and then began leisurely taxiing back toward the main terminal building of the airport, which sat nearer the northeast end of the runway.

As they taxied, cars started arriving from across town as those who had seen the jets started calling and texting their friends and family to come to the airport. This was only four days after two F-16s were involved in a dog fight with each other over Canyon Lake and two other F-16s shot down a stolen plane full of explosives. Both of those events had been caught on video and had gone viral over social media. For three F-16s to fly over Casa Grande twice and then land at the airport was a major attraction and anyone who could, came as quickly as they were able.

Many businesses were located in buildings around the airport and when the people saw and heard the jets they quickly walked over to the airport control center. By the time the airmen climbed down the flip-out side steps of the F-16s and descended to the ground, there was a small crowd, with more coming every second.

As a group, the four airmen stood together near the two-seater jet as if they were waiting for something. They were dressed in their flight suits and had removed their helmets, holding them in one hand or the other. There were two men and two women. One of the men was carrying a duffle bag.

The crowd continued to gather in front of the main terminal building. As he was responsible to make sure everything followed proper order, the airport manager, Rodrigo Ornelas, walked out to talk to the four airmen. Margaret Schroeder, the chef in the café, had pulled any food off the stove that would burn and came out with the crowd. She kept looking around as if she were amazed by the gathering or was perhaps looking for someone. She noticed Norman, the janitor, come out of a corner of the building and she waved at him. He always took pride in his work, and the building, café and surrounding area were always in tip-top shape, and she told him often that she appreciated his good work.

Rodrigo returned to the crowd of people and walked over to Margaret. He leaned his head toward her and spoke quietly. He knew her well as they had worked at the airport together for years. Everyone continued to wait for something to happen, glancing at each other and sometimes asking if anyone knew what was going on.

Cars continued to arrive at the area by the terminal building. The parking lot filled up quickly and people parked wherever they could find a place. Finally, Donna Crandall, Sam Park's office manager, pulled up in the jumble of parked cars and got out of her red Toyota Camry. Another woman climbed out of the passenger side and then helped a small girl out of a car seat in the back. A young boy about six years old climbed out of the back seat on the other side and held Donna's hand as they walked around the car. The women and children moved quickly from the car toward the terminal building, went through the building, and came out the double doors onto the tarmac where the crowd was standing. They saw Norman and walked quickly over to him. The little boy gave him a hug and the woman handed the little girl to Norman.

Donna looked over at Rodrigo and gave a thumbs up. Rodrigo raised his hand so it could be seen above the heads of the crowd and with his index finger pointing into the air he swirled his hand around as if he were twirling a lasso. The four airmen approached the crowd, one obviously leading, with the other three a few steps behind.

When they reached the crowd they stopped, and one of the airmen spoke loudly for all to hear, "Is Norman Huber present?" Most of the crowd looked around at each other as if they didn't know who Norman Huber was. The little boy looked up at his dad and smiled importantly since *he* knew who Norman Huber was. Norman just stood there and didn't make a move or say anything. Finally, at some prodding from Donna, Norman stepped around some other people and timidly raised his hand, "I'm Norman."

The airman said, "Norman, would you come over here please?"

Norman cautiously walked toward him. The man reached out and shook Norman's hand and then turned toward the crowd and said loudly, "I am General Arnold Briscoe, commanding officer of the 56th Fighter

Wing at Luke Air Force Base in Phoenix. We happened to be *up* and about this afternoon and thought we'd come pay a visit." Some in the crowd chuckled at the pun and others smiled warmly.

Norman suddenly cut in. "Are you comin' to tell me Sam Park died?" He had a pained and worried look on his face. "I remember my grampa tellin' me about official visitors comin' to his house to tell him his older brother was killed in World War Two."

Gen. Briscoe paused and smiled. Then he replied, "No, Norman. We are here to tell you that Sam Park is alive and doing well. He almost lost his leg but it appears that won't happen and he should be just fine."

Norman said with obvious relief, "OK. Thanks. That's really good news."

Briscoe turned back to the crowd and continued speaking. "In fact, we are here on official business to honor a hero, but the hero we are honoring today is not Sam Park."

Briscoe motioned the other three pilots forward. "But first, let me introduce to you some other heroes. This is Major Robert McCasland. He is one of the Air Force's top pilots and will be receiving special honors for his expert flying of a damaged F-16 and for stopping a terrorist plot by shooting down an enemy of America. Many of you have seen parts of that event on social media."

He paused and the crowd clapped and cheered and whistled for twenty or thirty seconds while he waited.

Briscoe continued, motioning to the second pilot, a woman. "This is Captain Gloria Puckett and next to her is First Lieutenant Nellie Boyd. These two brave pilots stopped the jet that was stolen from this airport . . ." and Gen. Briscoe pointed with his index finger toward the ground and moved his hand slightly up and down a couple of times.

"While Major McCasland was involved in a dog fight over Canyon Lake, Puckett and Boyd raced to stop the stolen plane before it could crash into Roosevelt Dam in an attempt to break the dam and flood the Phoenix area. Captain Puckett fired the missile that stopped the plane, and as you all saw on social media, Lt. Boyd actually flew *under* Roosevelt Bridge." Gen. Briscoe had a smile on his face as he shook his head gently. He paused and the crowd cheered again. Lt. Boyd was grinning from ear to ear.

"Norman Huber is also a hero and we are here today to recognize him for his courageous acts. As most of you know by now, last Saturday morning there was an event here at the Casa Grande airport and Norman was involved in saving the life of another man that morning. For those who haven't heard the story, I'll relate a few details that I learned from Sam Park and others." Donna looked at Vanessa, Norman's wife, and then looked at the general and smiled.

Briscoe continued "A group of terrorists stole a private plane and filled it with explosives. Tragically, the two men associated with that plane were both killed. Sam Park, who runs a mechanic shop right over there . . ." and he pointed toward the south ". . . saw what was happening and took action with his rifle. While his office manager called 911 he ran out onto the runway and tried to stop the plane from taking off. He didn't know why it was being stolen or where it was headed but he knew that if he could stop the plane out here on the runway he could probably save lives and stop a terrorist plot. He also knew that if the plane blew up near him on the runway he would be killed.

"Unfortunately, one of the terrorists had a machine gun and shot Mr. Park several times. Sam was able to kill the man and even shoot and damage the plane but by then Sam had lost a lot of blood."

Gen. Briscoe patted Norman on the shoulder and turned Norman to face the crowd. He said, "That's when Norman Huber came on the scene. Norman arrived in the nick of time and helped Sam stay alive until emergency personnel could reach him. He put pressure on Sam's most serious wound and, using Sam's cell phone, he called me personally to report the direction the stolen jet was flying, giving us important information that helped us track down that aircraft. With one hand he saved the life of a friend and with the other hand he saved the lives of many others."

The crowd applauded and cheered.

"Not all heroes shoot a gun or fly a supersonic jet. Some heroes live quietly and help in gentle ways at just the right time, but their help is no less valuable than the others we more often hear about.

"At the end of flight school, every airman, and the term "airman" includes both men and women, are given a name in a special ceremony. The name they are given is their call sign, which is the name they use as they are flying. Way back when I first met Sam Park, I was given the call sign of Flash, and there's a story behind that name that I won't go into today."

Norman's face brightened and he looked intently at Gen. Briscoe as Norman suddenly realized this was the "Flash" that he had called that day.

Gen. Briscoe continued, "Major McCasland's call sign is Burp. Capt. Puckett's call sign is Scrum and Lt. Boyd's is DeeDee."

Maj. McCasland, who held the duffle bag, stepped closer and unzipped the bag but kept its contents a secret.

Gen. Briscoe continued. "A pilot's call sign is usually based on some event or story. Today we want to have a naming ceremony with all of you and give an honorary call sign to Norman Huber, to recognize him for his bravery and life-saving action last Saturday."

Briscoe turned slightly toward Norman and said, "Norman Huber, we give you the call sign of Dex, spelled D-E-X. That indicates that you are ambidextrous and that you used that skill to save lives."

Norman said, "Oh, like when you can use both hands at the same time."

Briscoe smiled, nodded his head, and said, "Yes, precisely."

At the general's motion Maj. McCasland pulled a flight jacket out of the duffle bag. He handed it to Capt. Puckett and she held it up for all to see. It was olive green and was made of Nomex fabric. It had Air Force insignia all over it, including the symbol of the 56th Fighter Wing. She turned the jacket around and showed the crowd the back. The word, "DEX" was embroidered near the top of the jacket in bright orange letters. The crowd applauded heartily.

Maj. McCasland pulled a pilot's helmet out of the bag and handed it to Lt. Boyd and she held it up. It was gray, and on the front near the top of the helmet it said in white letters, "DEX." The crowd cheered again.

Gen. Briscoe said loudly for all to hear, "Norman Huber, you are now known officially as an honorary pilot in the United States Air Force." The crowd was cheering and clapping as Capt. Puckett walked over and held up the flight jacket while Gen. Briscoe motioned for Norman to put it on. Lt. Boyd had come over with the flight helmet and Norman put that on too. Both fit perfectly. Gen. Briscoe turned Norman to face the crowd again and they continued to cheer as Norman beamed with excitement and pride from inside the flight jacket and helmet. Gen. Briscoe was not in any hurry and continued to let the crowd celebrate.

Finally the cheering died down and the general said, "I hope you noticed that was a standing ovation." Everyone laughed at the observation.

No one was more proud than Norman's family. Vanessa kept wiping tears of joy from her eyes as she smiled and laughed. Little Jeffrey ran to his father, hugged his leg, and stood next to him grinning with pride. Many in the crowd laughed or said, "Ahhh" at the cute little boy.

Gen. Briscoe continued, "Dex, every good pilot flies a plane. How would you like to go for a ride in an F-16?"

Norman said, "Really?!" His eyes were alive with excitement.

Gen. Briscoe said, "Really. Major McCasland will fly the jet and you can sit in the training seat. Just don't pull any levers or push any buttons." The crowd laughed and the general motioned for Norman to follow Maj. McCasland over to the two-seater. Then Gen Briscoe held out his hand to Jeffrey and they stood there as the boy's father walked toward an F-16 for a flight of a lifetime.

When they reached the jet Maj. McCasland talked with Norman briefly and helped him climb up the side steps into the rear seat of the cockpit. Then he climbed in too and closed the canopy. They sat there for a few minutes while Burp instructed Dex on what to do and what to expect. The jet engines started up and the hatch closed and after another minute or two the jet began moving slowly, heading toward the northeast end of the airport. Everyone in the crowd was watching.

The jet lined up on the runway and paused. Then the engines suddenly roared and the jet blasted down the runway and lifted off into the sky. As it gained altitude and moved away from the airport, Gen. Briscoe spoke again to the crowd, "We have a few minutes to wait while a new pilot has his first flight. So who would like to come see an F-16 up close?"

The crowd cheered as Capt. Puckett and Lt. Boyd waved the people over toward them and led the way to the other jets.

Gen. Briscoe worked his way against the flow of the crowd and led Jeffrey back to his mother. He, Vanessa Huber, and Donna talked pleasantly as the crowd milled around on the tarmac, and in the distance a two-seater F-16 flew a brand-new pilot out over the desert.

52 Reflection at the Rooste

It was March, and Alan and Cindy Clevenger, dressed in their boots and jeans and western shirts, were sitting across from each other at

Rustlers' Rooste Restaurant. The events of that horrible week of violence were a month in the past. They had left the boys with their grandparents for the weekend and were finally celebrating their anniversary. The restaurant turned out to be just what Cindy had hoped for, with a western atmosphere complete with sawdust on the floor and cowhides hung on the walls. It also had a commanding view of the Valley of the Sun, and the lights of Phoenix glimmered below.

As they were sitting there in a cozy corner Cindy talked with Alan about carrying his Walther for that week of terror. She had told him before that she had it in her hand that night at the mall but didn't know what she could actually do against so many terrorists. She did not tell him she continued to carry it all the time but she suspected he knew. Finally, that night at dinner she told him she had been carrying it and would like to buy one of her own.

Alan said, "I knew you still had it but I didn't want to push. I knew you'd bring it up when you were ready. There's no need to get another because I am giving mine to you. It is now your Walther to carry as you wish but let's go get you some training. And by the way, it is a dream come true when a man who carries a concealed weapon has his wife tell him she wants to carry. I'm very happy that you are taking that step in your life because I believe every law-abiding adult should be prepared both physically and mentally to use a gun in defense of themselves or others."

She said, "I am glad to have the Walther as mine and I *am* ready to bear that responsibility in my life. I learned a lot that week and did some real soul searching then and since."

Even with all the events of Cindy's trip to the mall on that awful Friday night in February, she had managed to keep the secret of having purchased a new wedding ring for Alan. She had told him all the other details and especially about the young girl dying in her arms but she never brought up the reason she was at the mall in the first place.

When Cindy pulled the ring out Alan was completely surprised. She read to him the G-man reference inscribed on the inside of the ring and he smiled. She asked for his hand and tried to work his wedding ring off his finger. She thought to herself, *Why is it so easy for someone to remove their own ring but so difficult to remove someone else's?* After some exertion Cindy gave up and Alan removed his ring with a smile.

"Well, that went well!" Cindy said with a slightly perturbed chuckle.

349

The tender moment not completely spoiled, Cindy then pushed the new ring onto Alan's finger. This time she persisted and the ring went almost all the way on. Alan held up his hand to look at it and nonchalantly worked it on completely as he admired it. She pretended not to notice and took his hand again across the table.

Cindy looked lovingly and deeply into his eyes and said, "I ordered this ring before the terror week started and I picked it up that Friday night at the mall. That's why I was there that night. I told you I was at the mall but I didn't tell you why. I have wondered if the events of that night would make me have bad feelings about this ring, but they haven't. In fact, they have given deeper meaning to this and to the love that it represents between us. We went through a lot that week, you and I . . . and our community and nation. It's made me realize even more how much I love you and how much I want to be with you forever."

Alan was touched by her explanation. "Thank you, my love. And I want to be with you forever, too. There are things I also haven't shared with you either. I didn't tell you that right at the end I was almost killed by a sniper—twice. His first shot missed me by less than an inch and hit Ezzie. I told you she was injured but I didn't tell you how. As she walked up to me to look at some evidence, I dropped my phone. I bent quickly to try to catch it before it hit the concrete and just then the sniper's bullet went right through the place where my head had been. It caught Ezzie high in the shoulder at an odd angle, just missing her Kevlar vest as it entered. As it came out the back of her shoulder it caught in her vest and the force of the bullet yanked her to the ground. The impact of the bullet did some damage to her but she will be fine. It was just very dramatic because of the way it spun her around and slammed her to the ground . . . and the fact that it was almost my head that caught the bullet. A second shot from the sniper also barely missed me because an armed citizen shot the sniper before he could shoot me.

"As we drove home that day I realized how closely I had come to not coming home alive. It made me realize how grateful I am for your courage when I am out on assignment. It also made me grateful for God's protection and all your prayers for me."

Tears filled Cindy's eyes as she said, "I woke from a sound sleep that morning with a terrible feeling that you were in serious danger. I prayed with all the intensity I could and after a few minutes the dark feeling went away. I'm also eternally grateful for a loving Father in

Heaven who brought you back home safely. I didn't realize how close I came to losing you."

"We have a lot to be thankful for."

"Yes, we do."

"Alan, do you think the terrorists will return?"

"That's a good question. When we were at the dam and after all the bombs went off and we found that part of Al-Musawi, one of the rookie sheriff's deputies said, 'We will be ready for them when they come back again!' I thought a lot about that and realized, in his inexperience, he was wrong. But I'm not faulting him; I would have said the same thing as a rookie.

"I believe the terrorists will not come to Arizona again. I think they learned a painful lesson here. They picked what they thought was an out-of-the-way big city, thinking it would be unsophisticated and an easy target. However, they made a serious mistake, because Arizona law favors citizens owning guns. It is perhaps one of the most armed places they could have gone. Maybe Texas or Utah would be comparable. No, I think the terrorists learned that if they do something like this again they'll have to do their homework. They'll choose Chicago or New York City; somewhere like that."

"Why?"

"Because those places mistakenly think guns are bad and that only military and law enforcement should have them, which leaves most of the weapons in the hands of the criminals. The states that don't trust the constitution make it difficult for their law-abiding citizens to defend themselves. They think it makes them more secure but it does just the opposite. It just puts a higher percentage of the guns in the hands of the criminals.

"Cindy, 94% of mass shootings happen in a gun-free zone, like a school or a mall or a government building. You'd think the anti-gun crowd would see that statistic and put two and two together. However, they don't think logically to begin with. If you make your entire state or city a gun-free zone, that really just serves to make your community less safe.

"And then the Liberals go one step further and they want to ban all weapons, or at least "just the assault rifles."

Alan let go of Cindy's hand and made quotes in the air with his fingers as he said, "just the assault rifles." Then he pulled his ballpoint pen from his shirt pocket.

"The liberals don't even realize that the term 'assault weapon' doesn't really mean anything. If I assault you with this pen it's an assault weapon. It's a meaningless term but they like it because it makes certain guns sound scary and supports their agenda. They think if they ban firearms or 'assault weapons' that America won't have to worry about those weapons anymore. How dumb can they be? Heroin has been banned for years. Crack cocaine has been banned for years. Methamphetamine has been banned for years. Since we banned illegal drugs why are there so many of them in our society? It's because banning something doesn't remove it from your world. It just makes it illegal in your world. If the liberals ban firearms the firearms won't go away. The firearms will still be here but they will be illegal, and then only law-breakers will have them. Why did the United States give up on prohibition? Because the problem was still there. It didn't go away. Banning something doesn't make it go away. The Liberals never want to accept that. Well actually, some of them realize that, but they want to make firearms illegal so the government can justify confiscating them from the people. I doubt that would ever happen. I think there would be a second Civil War first."

Alan paused and put his pen back in his shirt pocket. Then he took Cindy's hand again in his and continued speaking.

"Now back to the terrorists. Last month certainly showed that armed citizens can stop crime and save innocent lives. Law enforcement never fired a shot until the very last day at Roosevelt Dam and that was only because Victor and I followed a prompting from God and an airplane mechanic took heroic action at a small-town airport. And it's a good thing the FBI and the Air Force were there in the right place at the right time or the terrorists may have succeeded in destroying the dam.

"Every other event that week was stopped by armed citizens. I'm very proud of those people. They saved so many lives, including yours and mine, Curtis's, Carlton's. Thinking about the three of you at the mall that night scares me to death.

"I'm so glad for those brave people. Some lost their lives in doing so, like Tobie and the law enforcement officers on the dam. Others almost did, like that veteran in the Motor Vehicles office and the mechanic on the runway. They barely made it but they did make it. They are huge heroes and I'm glad they are still alive.

"If that week of jihad had happened in a gun-free state there would have been no heroes like these that we've had. There would have been many, many lives lost, and the heroes would have been people who helped the wounded in the aftermath or jumped in front of bullets to save someone else.

"The terrorists learned a painful lesson but I hope our country can learn an even more important one. Those who continue to distrust the Constitution will realize too late that they have brought the problem on themselves. Actually, some of them won't ever realize that because they will die in the onslaught."

Alan stopped talking and Cindy just held his hand and mulled his comments over in her mind. She was glad she married someone who loved and trusted the Constitution, who was willing to use his gun to fight to protect her, and who had helped her learn that she was willing to do the same for herself and her children.

Cindy let go of Alan's hand, smiled, and held up her hands in front of them both, with her left hand holding up two fingers and her right hand in a fist with her thumb along-side.

The Second Amendment.

The End

Coming next from Ron Lee Jones

Shattered Schemes

Someone has outed the Establishment.
The Establishment is not happy.
Things are going to get really ugly.

They are a rag-tag band of freedom fighters who call themselves Minute Men and Minute Maids. They include a grandma with a gun who's not afraid to use it, two teenagers who are protected by a medieval spell, three college students who have figured out how to expose the corrupt schemes of the Washington Establishment, and a group of former marines who are still willing to fight and die for their country. The freedom fighters have uncovered a secret that is so shocking it could force 90% of the Democrats and 30% of the Republicans out of Congress and into prison. However, the corrupt government officials know the freedom fighters have the information and are determined to do anything and everything to prevent its release. The freedom fighters must fight to stay alive so they can reveal the secret but they soon realize that this government scheme may be too tough to shatter.

1   Thwarted

FBI Special Agent William Moultier pulled up to the spindly barbed-wire gate and eased the Ford Explorer to a stop. It was almost noon but he was in no hurry.

A worn and weathered ranch house was about two hundred yards farther along the dirt road, surrounded by some cottonwoods, a dilapidated barn, a corral, and some parched pasture land. Above the house about a mile to the west was a small mountain with scrub brush and a few trees covering its rocky slopes. Nearer to the house were the foothills, with smooth contours and more dry grass and a few spindly bushes. Across the small valley to the east were more low hills. Scattered scrub oak and juniper splotched the hills, in places growing in thickets and in other places sparse and scraggly. A few gaunt cattle grazed here and there inside the fence. The overall look of the old ranch revealed neglect and disrepair.

Through the front windshield Moultier double-checked the house with his binoculars to make sure no one was around. He had no doubt he was being watched from inside but he didn't want anyone outside the house yet. There would be time for that later. This was not a surprise, pre-dawn raid by the FBI. They didn't care about the element of surprise this time but they did care about carrying out this operation according to plan.

Moultier spoke into the microphone clipped to his shoulder which was connected to a radio. "Moultier at the gate. Wait for my signal." Earpieces on several radios within a one-mile radius quietly transmitted the announcement to his personnel.

He looked at Special Agent Nick Dunevant who was riding shotgun in the Explorer. Moultier said what Dunevant already knew, "No need to hurry. We have plenty of time." Truth be told, Moultier was relishing the thoughts of what was soon to come and he was enjoying the moment. Dunevant smiled, evidently feeling the same.

Moultier turned off the black Explorer, climbed out, and pocketed the keys. He closed the door quietly, easing it slowly closed until it touched against the vehicle, and then pushing firmly until it clicked tightly into place. He knew they weren't sneaking into this situation, but he still didn't want the noise from the slam of a car door. He hated that sound on an assignment like this. Dunevant, having been trained by Moultier, also closed his door quietly in the same manner.

Moultier was mildly surprised when his cell phone rang, but he didn't recognize the number. His friends or family or anyone at an FBI office would show on his caller ID and he rarely got a call from anyone he didn't know. He touched the icon on the screen with his finger and slid it down to ignore the call.

Within seconds the phone rang again. He said softly to himself, "Same number." He slid the icon down again to dismiss the call.

Within seconds the phone rang yet again. This time he paused, his finger hovering above the icon. He waited until the third ring and slid the icon up to take the call.

"Yes." It was a statement; not a question.

The answer came from an electronically distorted male voice. "Moultier, get back in your vehicle and leave . . . and all your personnel too."

He was incredulous and somewhat amused, "Excuse me?"

"We know what you are doing. We have been waiting for you. You must leave."

"We?"

"Yes. There are more of us than you and your men, and the one woman. You need to leave or you will all die."

"This is a bad joke, Riggins."

"This isn't Riggins. Riggins doesn't know we are here."

"Why should a team from the FBI back down because of a weak threat from someone who won't identify himself?"

"We are not weak at all. We have you surrounded and outnumbered more than two to one."

"That's a lie."

"No, Moultier. The lie is that you came here on the pretense of executing an arrest warrant for Mr. Riggins but you and I both know that your real goal is an actual execution. You were instructed to shoot Riggins and plant evidence on him so you can pretend you were within the law. I know that you are personally happy to carry out that order."

"I don't know what you are talking about."

"Yes, you do. You know exactly what I'm talking about and you know I'm right."

Moultier swallowed and looked at the surrounding hillsides.

"It won't do any good for you to try to find us because you won't."

"We came here only to serve an arrest warrant. Nothing else."

"No, Senator McKee's orders to you were to set the house on fire, then kill old man Riggins when he came out, then put a gun in his hand and a gas grill lighter in his pocket and photograph all of it. You were to make sure the wife's body remained inside the burning house."

"That's as far from the truth as one could imagine and I don't know why you think Senator McKee is involved."

"Moultier, you know what's worse than a liar? A *stupid* liar. That's a liar who keeps lying even though he knows the person to whom he's lying knows he is lying."

The electronically distorted voice paused briefly. Then began again.

"I know that was complicated logic for you, Moultier, so I'll repeat it. A stupid liar is a liar who keeps lying even though he knows the person to whom he's lying knows he is lying.

"Senator McKee ordered the hit by law enforcement because Mr. Riggins spoke up in that town hall meeting last week about the highway project and exposed the senator for taking a nice fat bribe to make sure Stone Pine Construction got the bid."

"Wow, you're really stretching for facts now."

"There you go, lying stupid again, Moultier."

"I'm done with you." Moultier started to move the phone away from his ear.

The electronic voice was louder. "YOU'D BETTER WAIT!"

Moultier frowned and shook his head and then moved the phone to his ear again.

"Moultier, if you hang up and proceed with your assignment you will die, along with all seven of your personnel—Dunevant next to you and the other five men and one woman scattered around the property."

This time Moultier blinked in surprise.

"What evidence do I have that you are for real?"

"Well first of all, think about all that I just told you which is spot on, which would have been impossible to guess. Or if that doesn't convince you, you could just try me and all of your team *will die*. A third alternative, since we don't really want to take any lives unless absolutely necessary, would be for you and Dunevant to look at your faces in the side mirrors on each side of the Explorer."

Moultier paused, not wanting to go along with this humiliating game that was being played. *He was being played!* He didn't like any of the three options given to him.

"Go ahead, Moultier. Look!"

Moultier moved the phone away from his mouth and said to Dunevant, "Look at your face in the side mirror."

Dunevant replied in surprise, "Huh?"

Moultier's anger at the caller now boiled over at his assistant, "JUST DO IT!"

As Dunevant leaned down Moultier himself also leaned down. He looked at himself in the side mirror and saw in the middle of his forehead two small points of light from two laser sights originating from some distance away. The lights were bobbing ever so slightly on his forehead due to the distance between his forehead and the guns on which the laser sights were mounted. However, in spite of the slight motion the points of light remained near the center of his forehead. The sight terrified him.

Moultier straightened and looked over at Dunevant who also had a look of terror in his eyes as he stared at Moultier.

Moultier raised the phone to his ear.

"I told you I wasn't lying, Moultier. Corrupt government officials lie. I'm talking about people like you and Senator McKee. The establishment is a parasite on our system. The good people in America are fed up with the lying and the corruption, and the fact that your kind keeps cheating the American people and covering for each other. You are going to go back to your superiors and to Senator McKee and tell them that the people are onto them. We are sick and tired of you guys—and women too—lying to the American people for personal gain. It's most of the legislators, but not all of them, and a percentage of the bureaucrats like you—The Establishment. The corrupt legislators are not following their oath of office. They are only out for power, for money, and to be re-elected. You support them because they give you the opportunity to do the same—to keep your job and commit illegal acts for personal gain. Most of the people had you figured out long ago but you thought you were so smart that they didn't notice. You were wrong! The media helped support your self-deceit and they helped the uninformed voters believe your lies but the thinking Americans weren't fooled. You corrupt government officials think you are clever but you're not. The time has come. We are tired of your corrupt schemes, like the one you came here for today. We have you outsmarted and we insist that you start following the rule of law—follow your oath of office! If not, we will do more than just out you. We will stand up and destroy the establishment . . . and you will lose!"

Moultier had had enough and he shouted into the phone, "OH SHUT UP!"

A shot rang out from somewhere in front of them and a bullet crashed into the side mirror that Moultier had just looked in, shattering the glass as the bullet passed through the mirror and tumbled off into the dirt somewhere behind the Explorer.

Moultier jumped. His radio began to chatter with several men trying to talk to him at the same time.

The electronic voice was calm. "Moultier, *we* are in control here, even though you thought you were. But now you are getting too excited, and if you don't keep your cool you won't live to drive out of here. You are still alive because we allow you to stay alive. We could have killed you and every one of your team already if we had wanted to do that. In fact, that shot was intentionally made with an unsuppressed rifle but the rest of our arms are suppressed. You won't even know what hit you. Now tell your men to stand down."

Moultier stood there for a few moments as if trying to decide what to do, with some sporadic radio chatter still going. Then he leaned his head toward the mic on his shoulder and pressed the button with his thumb. "This is Moultier. Stand down. It's under control. I'll explain later."

The electronic voice said, "Good, Moultier! You said 'under control.' I'm glad you understand that the people are finally in charge again. By the way, did you notice that I haven't called you by your official title of Special Agent? That's because you don't *deserve* it. If you were doing your sworn duty you would deserve the title you have but when you go outside the law and cheat the system and the American people like you have been doing, then you are a disgrace to the title and it's offensive to call you by that designation. The same goes for the rest of the Establishment.

"Now, Moultier, I'm finished talking and it's time to end this . . . peacefully, as long as you cooperate. You need to get your sorry carcass out of here. Call off your team and leave. We will give you one minute to start moving. If you don't, we start shooting and none of you will survive."

Moultier cut in, stalling while he tried to think of something. "How did you know about this operation?"

"You think we're foolish enough to tell you?" The electronic voice paused. "Let's just say the people have figured out how to level the playing field against government corruption and the clandestine schemes of the establishment."

"We'll catch you for finding us out, and make you pay!"

"Thanks, Moultier. That statement just proves that you know you are wrong and we are right. . . . And I can tell by the grimace that I can see on your face right now that you just realized that was a stupid thing to say to me.

"Now get going. You've got sixty seconds before the fireworks begin. And don't try anything funny on the way out of here, because we have the entire area and the dirt road covered. Just clear out and get on the highway and go back to your field office and none of you will get hurt. And leave Mr. and Mrs. Riggins alone . . . forever!

"By the way. As you are leaving, just before you get to the highway, look off toward the east. You'll see a big pine tree out there surrounded by some bushes. We tied some yellow surveying tape around it so you can't miss it. You'll want to stop and get your guy, the one who hiked into here at midnight last night. He's handcuffed to a couple of trees by his hands and feet on the other side of that pine tree and if you don't pick him up on your way out he'll die. He's probably getting hungry and thirsty about now because he's been struggling for hours to try to free himself.

"Oh, and he wet himself too."

ACKNOWLEDGMENTS

The following have made invaluable contributions to help Broken Bombs come about:

Jan, my wife of over thirty-eight years. She has been patiently supporting, waiting, and praying for this book to happen for a long time. Thanks, my love!

Andrea Colvin, my editor for the vast majority of the text. She offered her support a few years ago and she has been extremely helpful. I'm not sure how this book could have been published without her involvement. She has also given me much patient encouragement along the way as I have gone through the emotional ups and downs of putting together a project like this.

Ty Moyers, retired Air Force Lieutenant Colonel, who gave many insights and explanations to help the "Air Force Chapters" make sense. Also Steve Chapman, who gave additional insights into the same chapters.

Preston Hon, my son-in-law, who has been my sounding board for much of my writing, and also one of my beta readers. He's a fellow gun lover, and I bounced many ideas off of him along the way about the storylines and also the types of guns and carry methods covered in Broken Bombs. Preston speaks Spanish, which has helped when I felt the need to include Spanish words. He's also a techie so I have relied on his abilities regarding many of the technical aspects of getting this book into publication. He created the 2 A graphic.

Jenessa Hon, my daughter, who has been a tremendous asset on the social media and administrative aspects of marketing this book.

Maury Jones ("Jonesy"), my oldest brother, who has been my best beta reader and who has given me many insights and pointed out critical issues that needed to be fixed. Jonesy has also given me tremendous moral support to help me through the process. He has many informative and entertaining articles about conservative thinking on his blog www.cowboycommonsense.com. He's also got some fun cowboy poetry on there too.

Susan Crane, another editor who helped with the beginning chapter of Shattered Schemes.

My other beta readers, some of them mentioned previously: Ty Moyers and his wife Valerie, my son-in-law Preston, my in-laws Lowell and Glenda Heaton, my brother-in-law Sean Heaton, my wife Jan Jones, my son Jaylan Jones, my Uncle Alan Turley, and fellow author Brock Booher. Thank you all.

Four gentlemen who graciously provided endorsements for the book (shown on the back cover):
- Clyde Helquist, Owner of Pistol Parlour in Mesa, Arizona (I hope to buy many guns from Pistol Parlour in the years to come);
- Bob Albert, Co-Owner of Right on Target Sporting Clays, also in Mesa (For a great day of shooting, Bob and his team guide you at shooting clay pigeons out on the range, with the targets flying and even "running" all directions and from all angles)
- Ike Devji, Managing Attorney with Pro Asset Protection (He helps many people, particularly professionals, with unique estate-planning situations)
- Dave Bacon, Attorney (currently in Mesa, Arizona, but knows everyone who has lived in Albany New York in the past)

Different people and sources along the way gave me help, information, and insights when needed. They are listed in no specific order: Taylor Anderson regarding Japanese language and culture; Steve Shumway regarding propane tanks; Cassie Prinke regarding helicopters (there was something about helicopters in the early version, but that section ended up being moved to a later book—I can hardly wait to get it finished and published!); Gwen Bjornson regarding the King Air and aviation in general; Zarinah and Aneesah Nadir regarding Muslims in America and Muslim culture; fellow author Marsha Ward for her insights and encouragement; fellow author Julie Bihn for her info and encouragement regarding self-publishing on Amazon; Vearle Jones on his insights regarding self-publishing and Create Space (now a part of

Amazon); Hickock 45 regarding guns and ammo (I watched many of his videos trying to better understand the aspects and functionality of different guns); my father-in-law Lowell Heaton, a civil engineer, regarding explosives and concrete dams; Brent Boyse regarding suppressed 300 blackouts; Nathan and Nixon LeSueur regarding hay and hay trucks; Noah Bacon for tips and pointers regarding marketing and name recognition; Aaron Murdock for listening to many insights about possible story lines; Matt Laws for insights on police procedures and weapons; and probably some others that I overlooked and I'm sorry if I overlooked you.

AUTHOR'S NOTES

As this book was in the very final editing stages in November 2019 (in the old vernacular, "as it was going to press"), the news reported that an ISIS website had recently posted new instructions to terrorists. Those who support the cause of the Islamic radicals were being encouraged to start forest fires in Europe and North America to cause ecological damage and property damage and disruption to infidels. This book is fiction, but the threat is very, very real. I almost took the time to add a chapter to Broken Bombs but could not do so due to time constraints. The chapter will be left to the imagination of my readers, but it likely would have been about a church youth group who were preparing to hike to Fossil Springs in northern Arizona on the Saturday morning about the time that the terrorists attacked Roosevelt Dam. The youth group saw three Islamic terrorists starting a fire in some brush on the western edge of the tiny town of Strawberry in the Tonto National Forest. The terrorists were going to fan their small blaze into a raging forest fire. As four of the leaders of the youth group confronted the terrorists, the terrorists started to pull guns, but the youth leaders drew their concealed weapons first and shot the terrorists. Then all the teenagers quickly put out the fire before it could get out of control. (So many stories, so little time.)

With my books I hope to help average citizens realize that carrying a concealed weapon can be done safely and responsibly. I want to show the soccer moms and the business people and the young people and the older people (that's the group I'm in) that there are many types of weapons and many ways to carry them safely. It's easy and it's a rational thing to do. It protects us, our families, our schools, our churches, our businesses, and all our society when law-abiding citizens responsibly carry concealed weapons. I encourage people to think it through, be prepared, be responsible, be well trained, and defend themselves and their loved ones if the occasion requires.

If books were to follow the rating system of movies, most of today's fiction intended for the adult audience would be rated R or worse. Many conservatives would not choose R-rated literature if given the choice. Unfortunately, there aren't enough choices. I respect and admire writers like Clive Cussler, Marsha Ward, and others who leave that kind of content out of their good books. My books are written for the purpose of giving conservatives another choice. I base my stories and themes on the traditional values that made America great and I intentionally write to an audience who doesn't need or want R-rated entertainment. My books are not G rated, because they are about guns and the age-old struggle of good versus evil and that mix almost always leads to violent encounters. My ambition also stems from the way I was raised. When my mom, Ethna Jones, would read a book and come to a part that was inappropriate due to foul language or adult content, she would skip over that part and then either use a felt-tipped marker and black out that part or she would just tear that page out of the book. She avoided that material and then protected her family from exposure to those parts of the book. In my books, I'm trying to do what my angel mother taught me and not even start with that kind of content to begin with.

In this book, I intentionally left out descriptions of the effects on the body when a person is shot. I included a few of those details but not many. I started to include all those gory details but felt that it made the book inappropriate and too graphic (R rated). One of the problems with Hollywood is that some movies and TV shows don't show the real effects of gunshot wounds and therefore some people don't realize the reality of the situation. In other situations movies *overemphasize* what happens from a gunshot. In the real world when someone is shot there is usually a significantly unpleasant mess, to put it mildly, but it doesn't throw the person across the room like Hollywood sometimes likes to show. Guns are to be respected and are both extremely useful and extremely dangerous, just like vehicles and many other good things in our society. It may help people to have greater respect for guns if someone takes the time to tell them the gory details. However, that would be in a different setting and those details were intentionally not included in this book.

Some places and some organizations in this book are purely fictional. Some are not fictional but I have tried to change names as much as I could to make them fictional. I tried to maintain the reality that all of this pretend story "happened" in places in and around the Phoenix area, many of which do exist. This is a work of fiction but there may be similarities with characters in the book because I drew many ideas from people and places I know. The characters Eb and Flo are loosely based on my relationship with my best friend in high school, Verl Washburn. As teenagers, Verl and I spent many, many hours hunting, fishing, camping, and driving around the deserts and mountains of the western United States. Verl always drove and we always listened to music, John Denver being high on our playlist.

I hope the gun manufacturers welcome my usage of their firearms in my book. I went to some length to spread the recognition around to as many guns and as many brands as I could reasonably manage. If you weren't included and want to be, feel free to contact me and I'll include your firearm(s) in an upcoming book. I must add that I thoroughly enjoyed going to many websites to learn about the different guns. I wish I could have bought one or more of every gun that I looked at. I've already got a couple more guns in mind for my next book.

The Air Force portion of the book was the most difficult. I was on a plane flying from Atlanta to Dallas, working on some of the early versions of one of the chapters involving the Air Force. The guy next to me kept looking at the screen of my laptop and I told him I was working on a novel and didn't mind if he read along. At one point he said, "You don't know much about the Air Force do you?" I laughed and heartily agreed and told him that's why I was struggling. He was retired Air Force and gave me further insights, and I told him I did have an Air Force consultant who would be helping me fix all the mistakes I was making. I acknowledge that I didn't get all the issues fixed. I hope I ended up more right than wrong. The errors are not the fault of the consultants and I take full responsibility. I apologize to those who have

364

been in the Air Force and have flown fighter jets. I know that many of you will say "That part's not right." I did take much literary license in two specific areas which I didn't realize until my Air Force consultants pointed it out, but by then I needed to leave it in. An extended dogfight between two fighter jets will only last a few minutes due to the limitation of fuel. Jets can't dogfight as long as I have McCasland and Andrus doing because the jets can't carry that much fuel. However, I needed to move the action from Casa Grande to Canyon Lake, so it turned out like the old westerns where the gunfighters would shoot about twenty shots from the same six-shooter without reloading. Also, radar lock isn't something you obtain right at the last minute. Apparently, you are bouncing radar off the other jet the entire time and probably get lock much sooner than my book or Hollywood portrays. I'm sure a real pilot could explain it way better than I just did. I must say that I was totally awed with the technology and science of the Air Force. Researching online and listening to a pilot on YouTube talking about all the systems that are built into a jet aircraft to deal with this issue or that problem or fight in that manner filled me with tremendous respect for our military.

I also love to tell stories and I hope this story has been captivating and entertaining for you to read, as much as it has been for me to write it. If you enjoyed reading this book please take a few moments to go onto Amazon and give it a good review and also recommend it to your friends. I have several other books started and that many more in my head. I hope to get them all published. Visit my Facebook page for updates: https://www.facebook.com/ronleejonesbooks/

ABOUT THE AUTHOR

 Ron Lee Jones is an Arizona native. He grew up in Mesa, a suburb of Phoenix, in a loving Christian home as the youngest of eight children. He learned at an early age to work hard and to love the outdoors, hunting, and fishing. When he was young his family worked for years on a dude ranch near Telluride, Colorado, and he spent many hours riding ponies and horses among the blue

spruce and aspen of the Colorado Rockies. Campfire programs and lots of other music has also been a big part of Ron's life. Ron has worked on other ranches in Utah and Wyoming and worked one season as a hunting guide in Wyoming. Ranching, horses, guns, hunting, music, and the outdoors are in his blood. Ron also believes the United States Constitution was divinely inspired and that adherence to the Constitution will provide the greatest degree of liberty and safety for Americans. Ron is an attorney with a law firm in the Phoenix area. He and his wife have five children and twelve grandchildren at last count.

Made in the USA
Columbia, SC
21 June 2020

11909986R00224